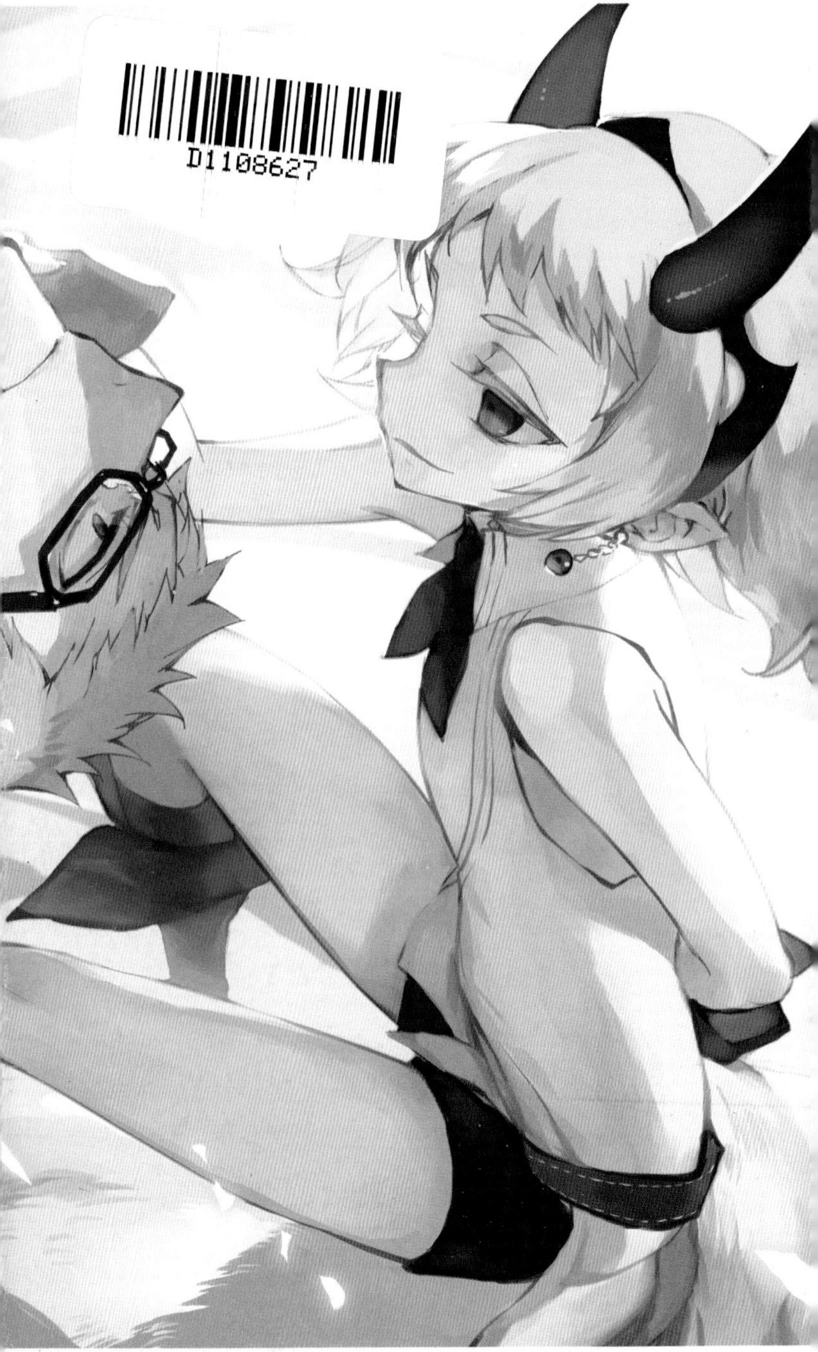

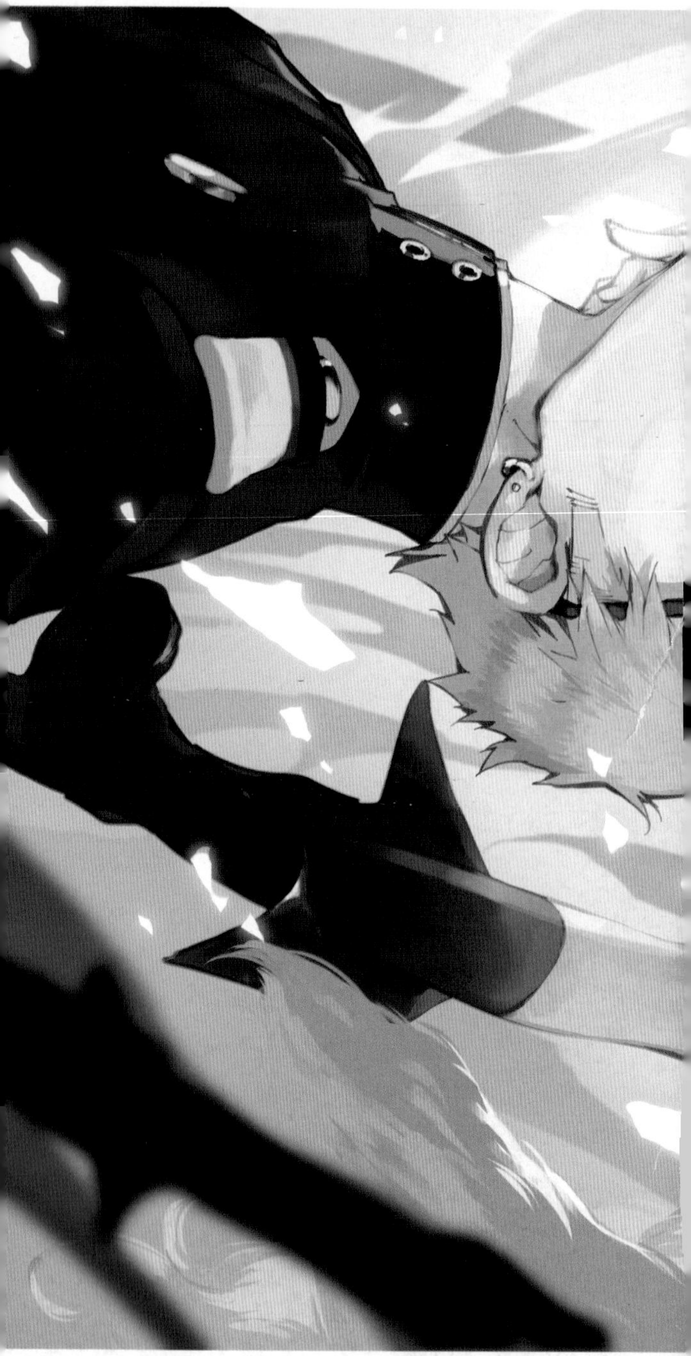

Seraph of the End
—VAMPIRE REIGN—

6

STORY BY **Takaya Kagami**
ART BY **Yamato Yamamoto**
STORYBOARDS BY **Daisuke Furuya**

CHARACTERS

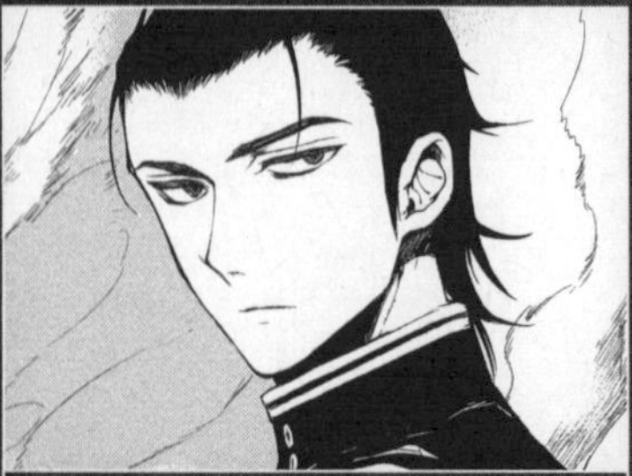

GUREN ICHINOSE

Lieutenant Colonel of the Moon Demon Company, a Vampire Extermination Unit. He recruited Yuichiro into the Japanese Imperial Demon Army.

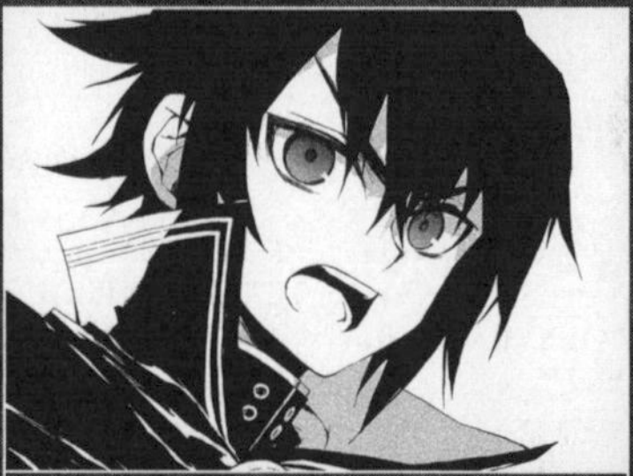

YUICHIRO HYAKUYA

A boy who escaped from the vampire capital, he has both great kindness and a great desire for revenge. Lone wolf.

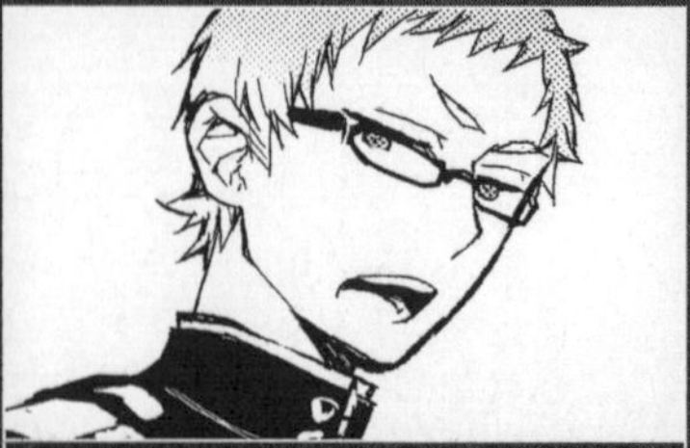

SHIHO KIMIZUKI

Yuichiro's friend.
Smart but abrasive.

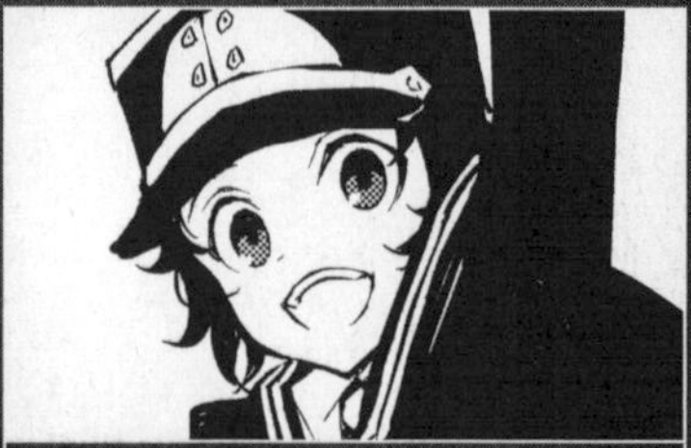

YOICHI SAOTOME

Yuichiro's friend.
His sister was killed by a vampire.

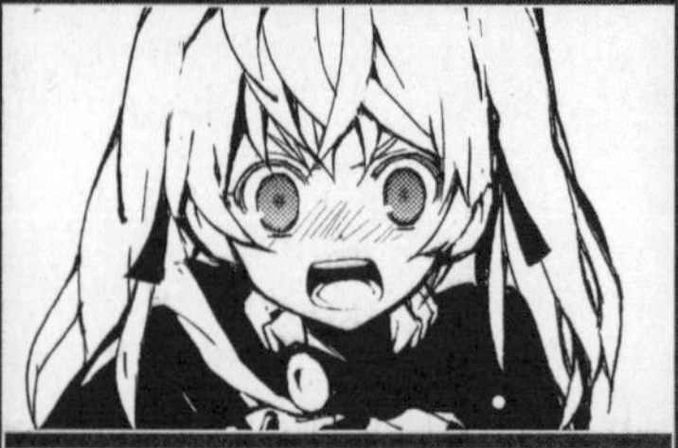

MITSUBA SANGU

An elite soldier who has been part of the Moon Demon Company since age 13. Bossy.

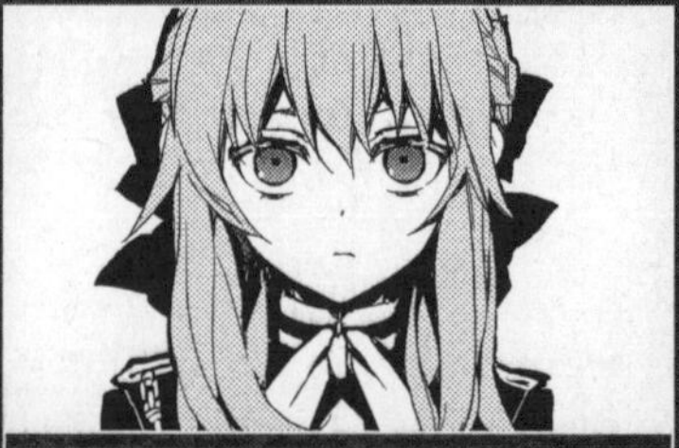

SHINOA HIRAGI

Guren's subordinate and Yuichiro's surveillance officer. Member of the illustrious Hiragi family.

STORY

A mysterious virus decimates the human population, and vampires claim dominion over the world. Yuichiro and his adopted family of orphans are kept as vampire fodder in an underground city until the day Mikaela, Yuichiro's best friend, plots an ill-fated escape for the orphans. Only Yuichiro survives and reaches the surface.

Four years later, Yuichiro enters into the Moon Demon Company, a Vampire Extermination Unit in the Japanese Imperial Demon Army, to enact his revenge. There he gains Asuramaru, a demon-possessed weapon capable of killing vampires.

Along with his squad mates Yoichi, Shinoa, Kimizuki and Mitsuba, Yuichiro deploys to Shinjuku with orders to thwart a vampire attack. But in the midst of a fierce skirmish, he sees Mikaela—and he's with the enemy vampires! Confused and lost, Yuichiro is overtaken by a mysterious power within and goes berserk.

Left with conflicting thoughts after the battle, Yuichiro is determined to train properly with his Cursed Gear. But that may be more dangerous than he expected...

Seraph of the End
VAMPIRE REIGN

MIKAELA HYAKUYA

Yuichiro's best friend. He was supposedly killed but has come back to life as a vampire.

FERID BATHORY

A Seventh Progenitor vampire, he killed Mikaela.

KRUL TEPES

Queen of the Vampires and a Third Progenitor.

Seraph of the End
—VAMPIRE REIGN—

6

CONTENTS

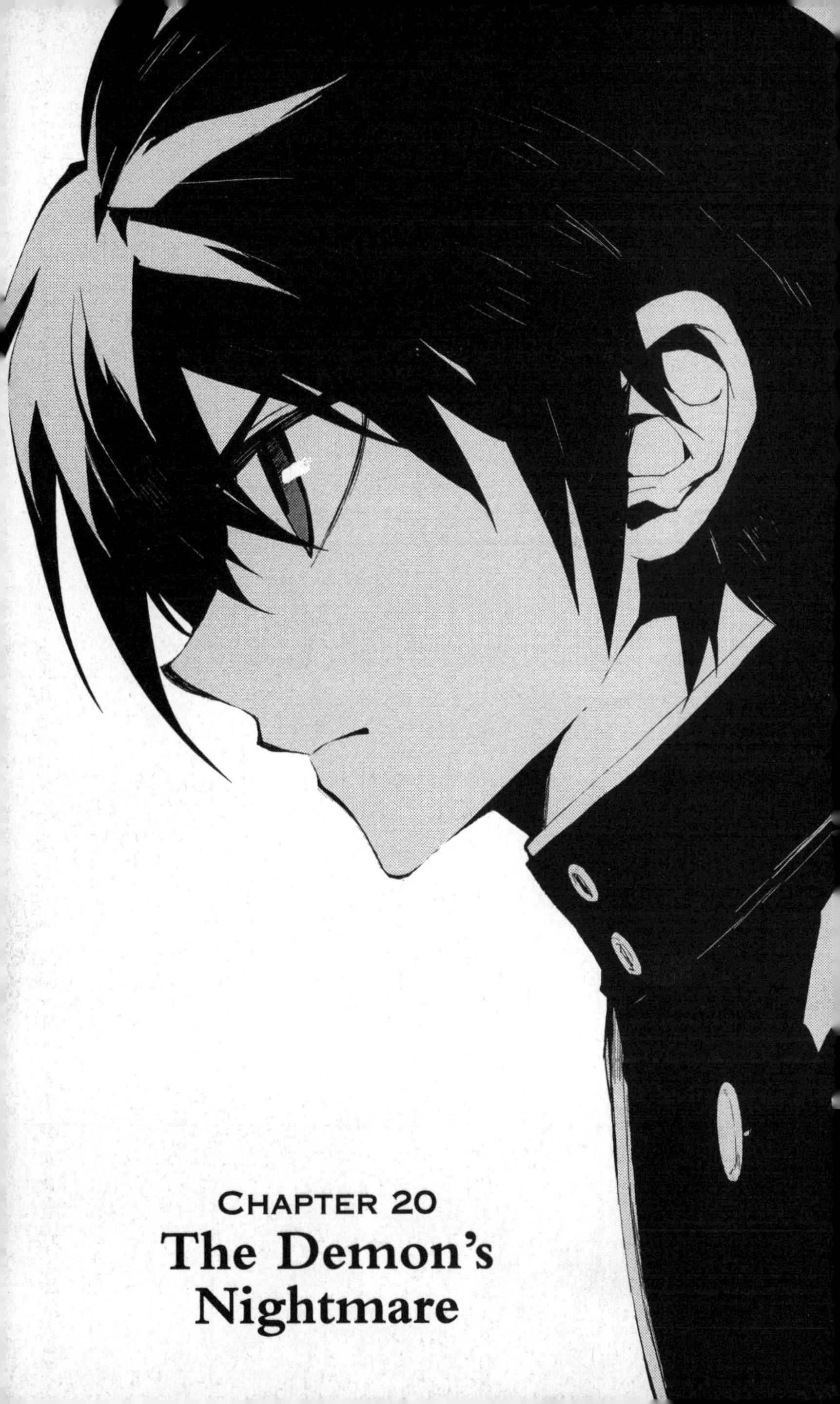

CHAPTER 20
The Demon's Nightmare

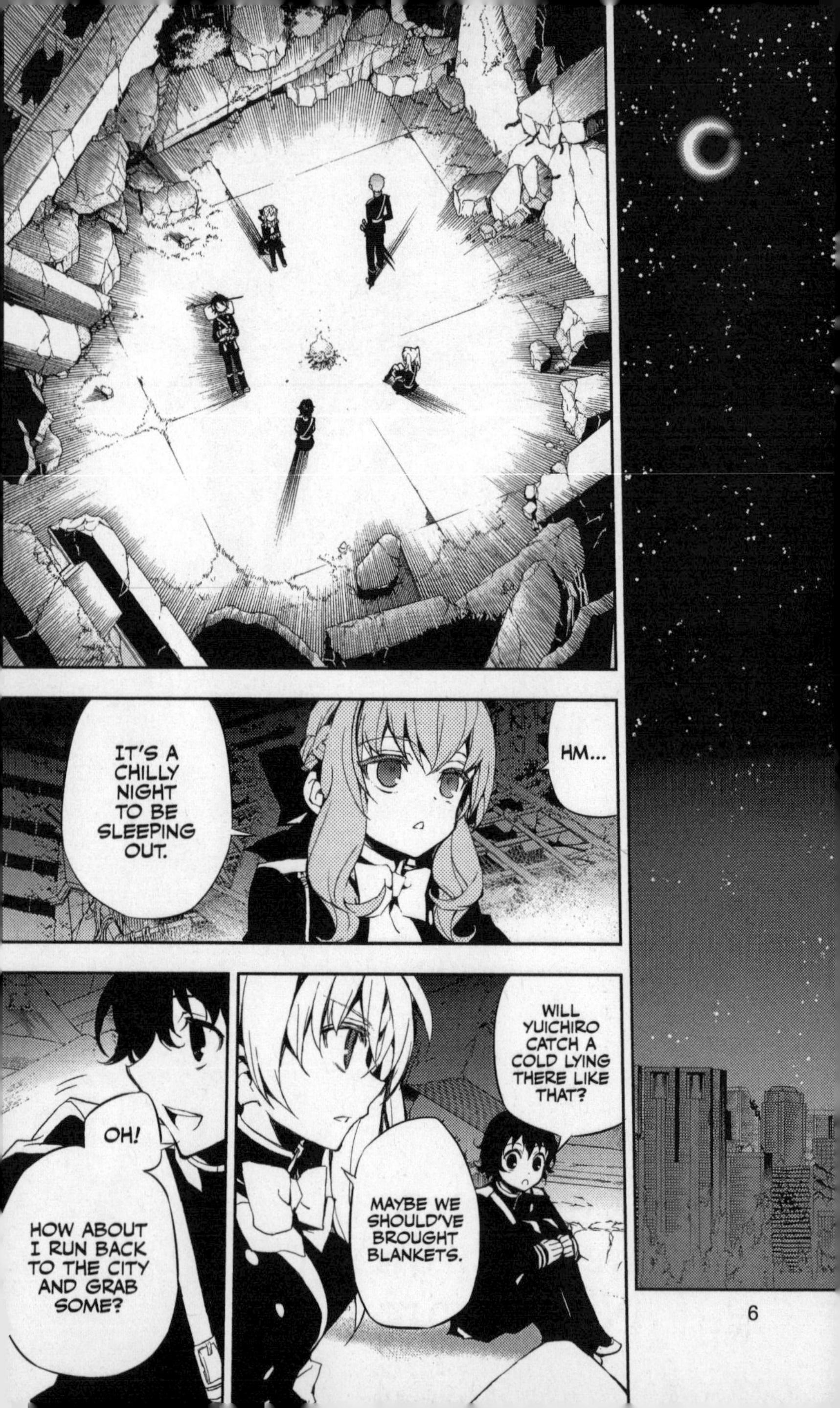
HM...
IT'S A CHILLY NIGHT TO BE SLEEPING OUT.
WILL YUICHIRO CATCH A COLD LYING THERE LIKE THAT?
MAYBE WE SHOULD'VE BROUGHT BLANKETS.
OH!
HOW ABOUT I RUN BACK TO THE CITY AND GRAB SOME?

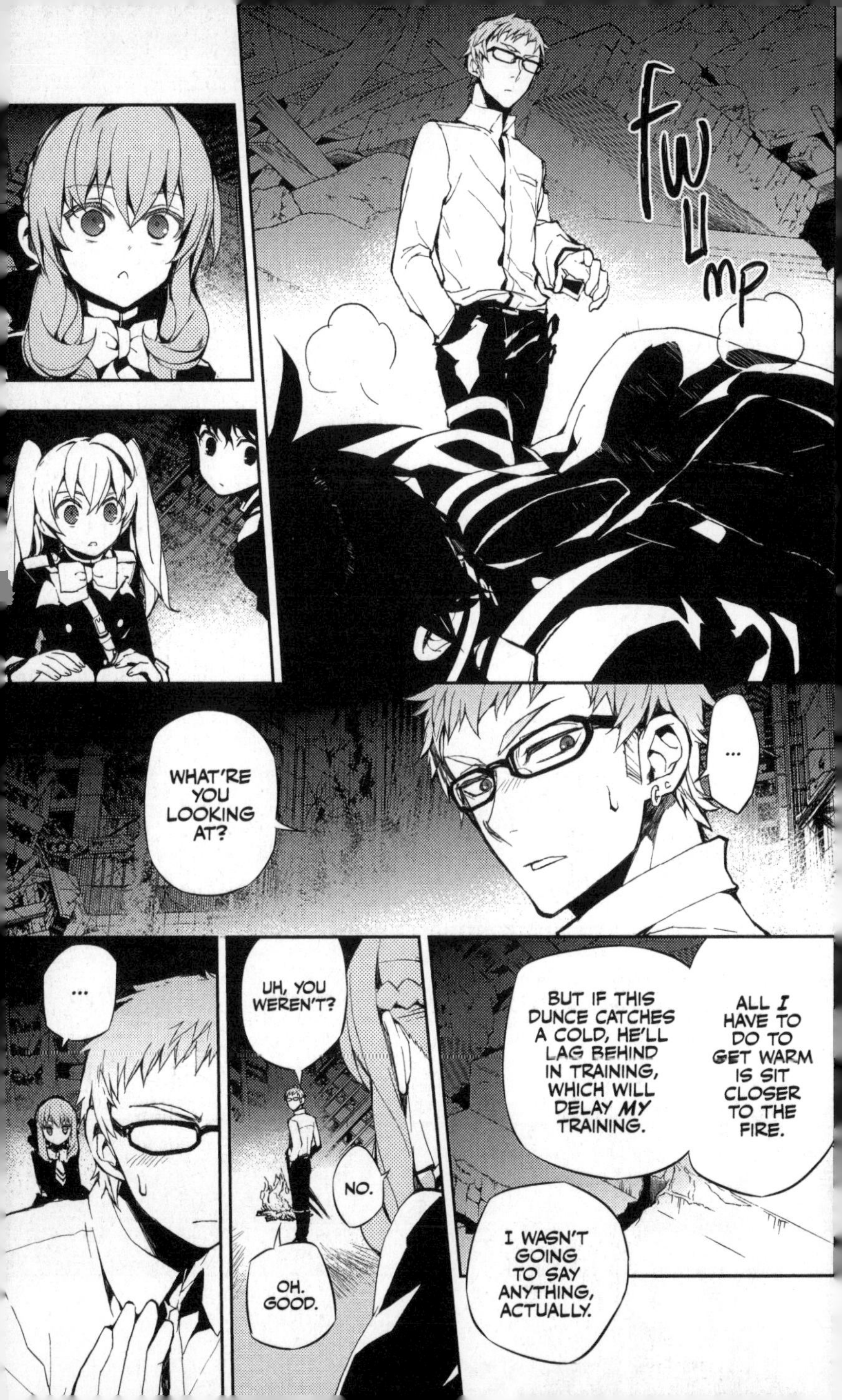
FWUMP
...
WHAT'RE YOU LOOKING AT?
ALL *I* HAVE TO DO TO GET WARM IS SIT CLOSER TO THE FIRE.
BUT IF THIS DUNCE CATCHES A COLD, HE'LL LAG BEHIND IN TRAINING, WHICH WILL DELAY *MY* TRAINING.
I WASN'T GOING TO SAY ANYTHING, ACTUALLY.
UH, YOU WEREN'T?
NO.
OH. GOOD.
...

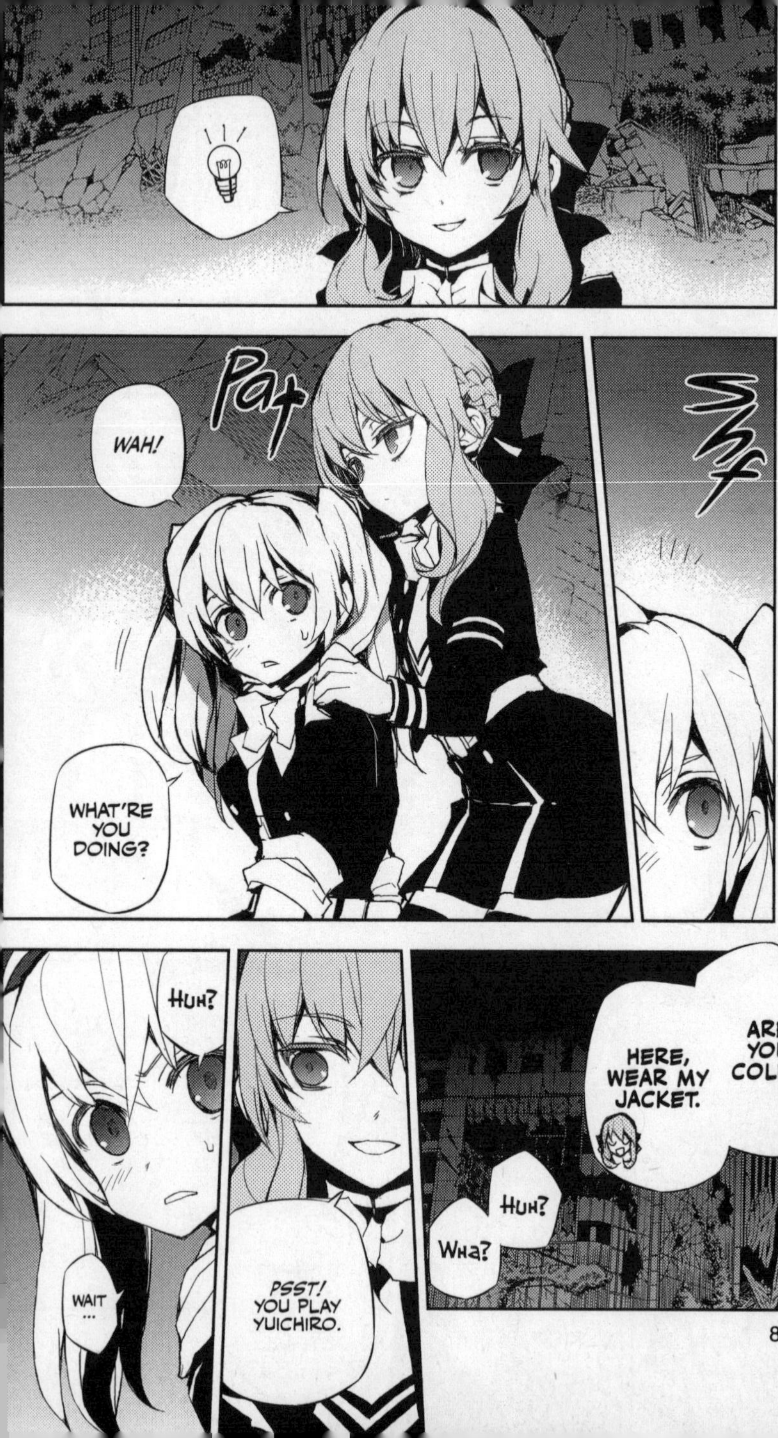
Snf
Pat
WAH!
WHAT'RE YOU DOING?
ARE YOU COLD?
HERE, WEAR MY JACKET.
HUH?
WHA?
PSST! YOU PLAY YUICHIRO.
HUH?
WAIT ...

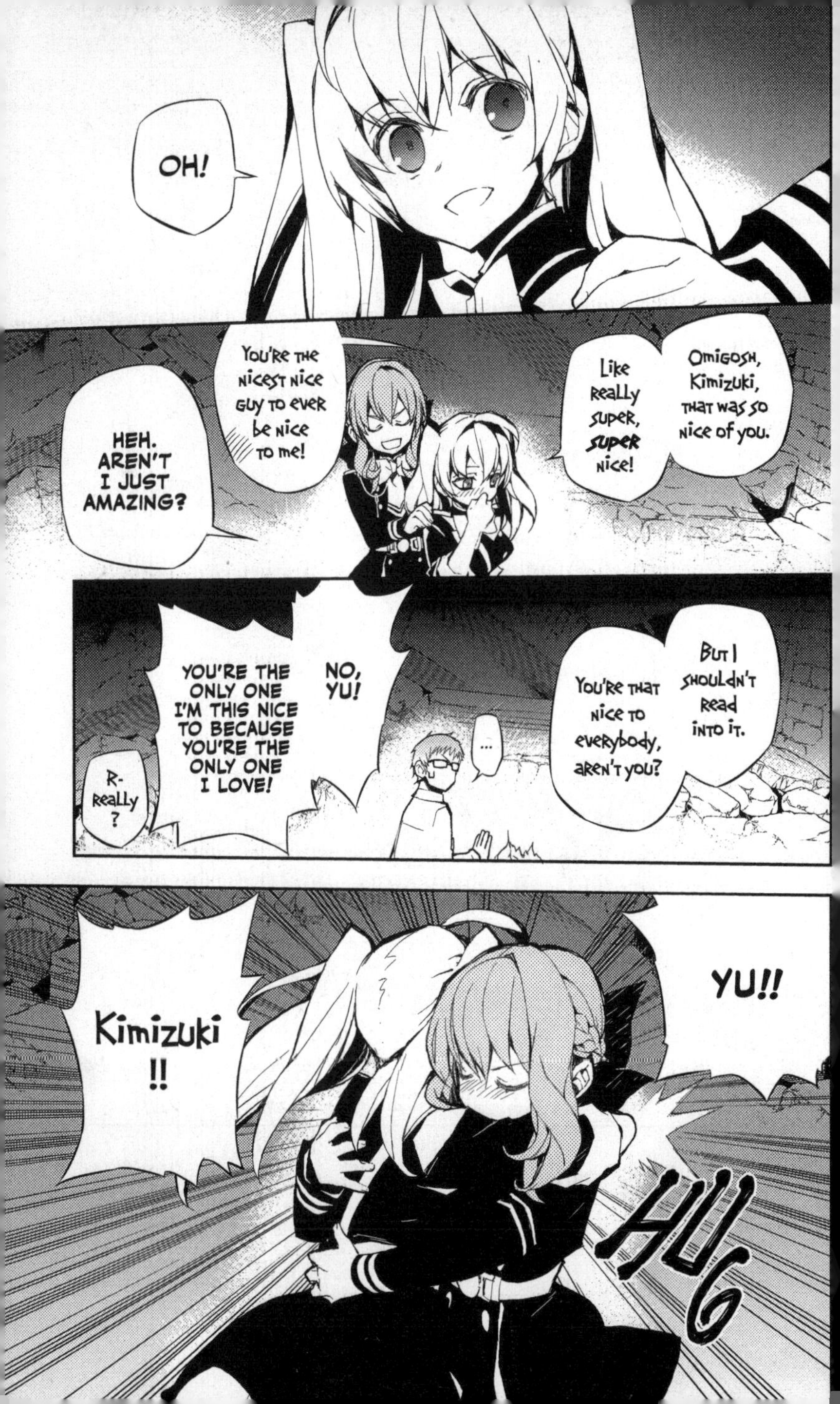
OH!
Omigosh, Kimizuki, that was so nice of you.
Like really super, super nice!
You're the nicest nice guy to ever be nice to me!
HEH. AREN'T I JUST AMAZING?
But I shouldn't read into it.
You're that nice to everybody, aren't you?
...
NO, YU!
YOU'RE THE ONLY ONE I'M THIS NICE TO BECAUSE YOU'RE THE ONLY ONE I LOVE!
R-really?
YU!!
Kimizuki !!
HUG

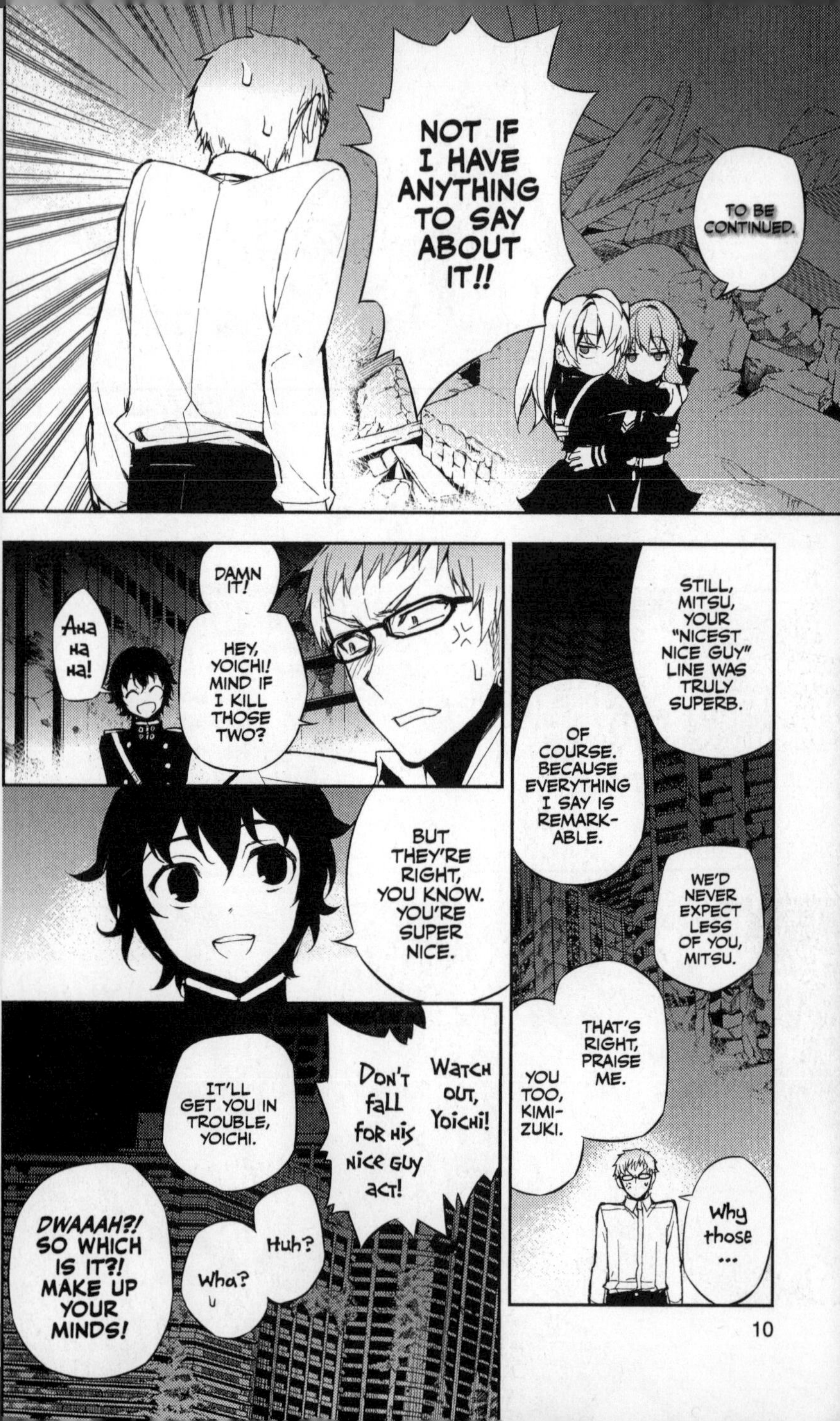
NOT IF I HAVE ANYTHING TO SAY ABOUT IT!!
TO BE CONTINUED.
STILL, MITSU, YOUR "NICEST NICE GUY" LINE WAS TRULY SUPERB.
OF COURSE. BECAUSE EVERYTHING I SAY IS REMARK-ABLE.
WE'D NEVER EXPECT LESS OF YOU, MITSU.
THAT'S RIGHT, PRAISE ME.
YOU TOO, KIMI-ZUKI.
Why those ...
DAMN IT!
HEY, YOICHI! MIND IF I KILL THOSE TWO?
Aha ha ha!
BUT THEY'RE RIGHT, YOU KNOW. YOU'RE SUPER NICE.
Watch out, Yoichi!
Don't fall for his nice guy act!
IT'LL GET YOU IN TROUBLE, YOICHI.
Huh?
Wha?
DWAAAH?! SO WHICH IS IT?! MAKE UP YOUR MINDS!

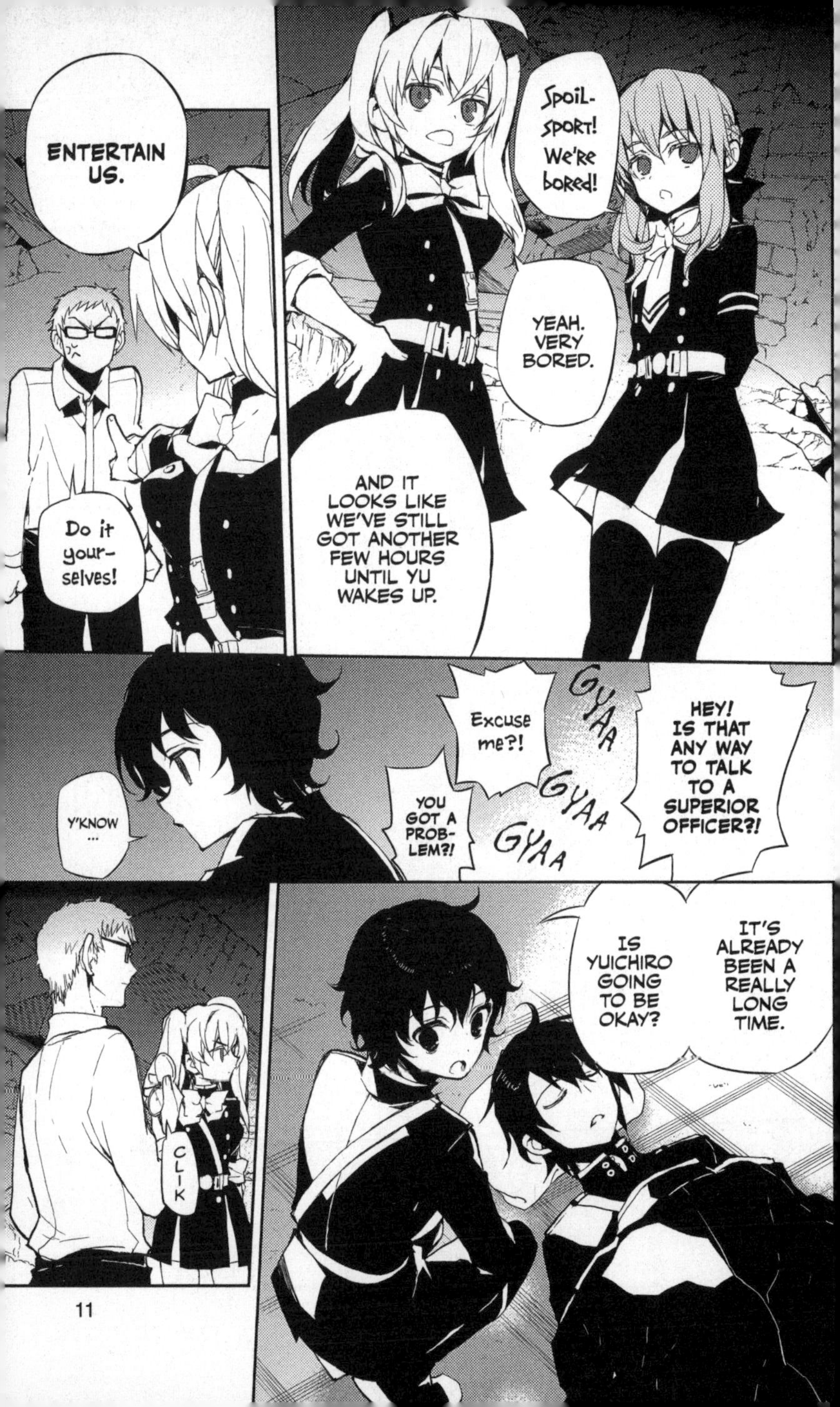
Spoil-sport! We're bored!
YEAH. VERY BORED.
AND IT LOOKS LIKE WE'VE STILL GOT ANOTHER FEW HOURS UNTIL YU WAKES UP.
ENTERTAIN US.
Do it your-selves!
HEY! IS THAT ANY WAY TO TALK TO A SUPERIOR OFFICER?!
Excuse me?!
GYAA
GYAA
GYAA
YOU GOT A PROB-LEM?!
Y'KNOW ...
IT'S ALREADY BEEN A REALLY LONG TIME.
IS YUICHIRO GOING TO BE OKAY?
CLIK

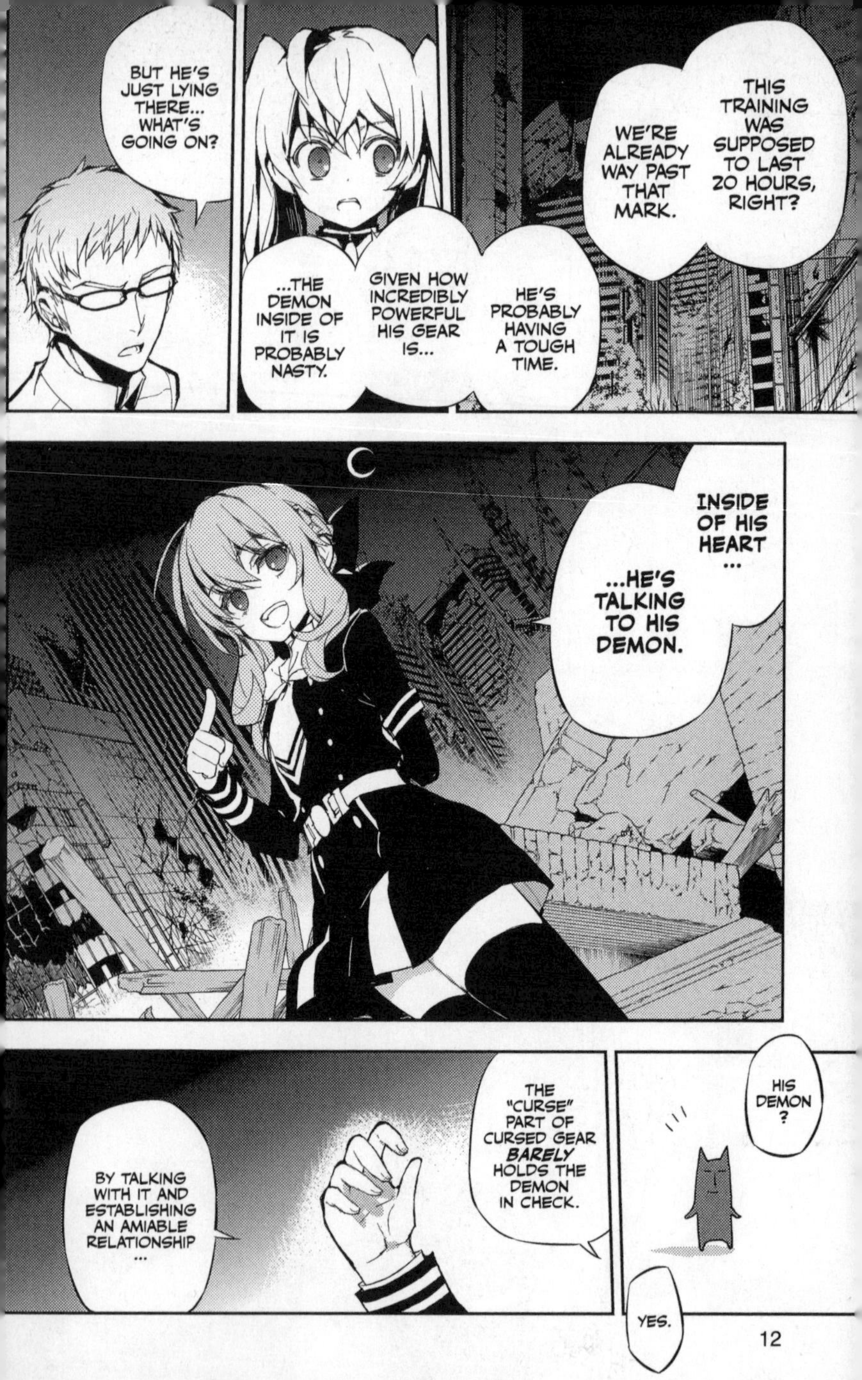
THIS TRAINING WAS SUPPOSED TO LAST 20 HOURS, RIGHT?
WE'RE ALREADY WAY PAST THAT MARK.
HE'S PROBABLY HAVING A TOUGH TIME.
GIVEN HOW INCREDIBLY POWERFUL HIS GEAR IS...
...THE DEMON INSIDE OF IT IS PROBABLY NASTY.
BUT HE'S JUST LYING THERE... WHAT'S GOING ON?
INSIDE OF HIS HEART...
...HE'S TALKING TO HIS DEMON.
HIS DEMON?
YES.
THE "CURSE" PART OF CURSED GEAR *BARELY* HOLDS THE DEMON IN CHECK.
BY TALKING WITH IT AND ESTABLISHING AN AMIABLE RELATIONSHIP...

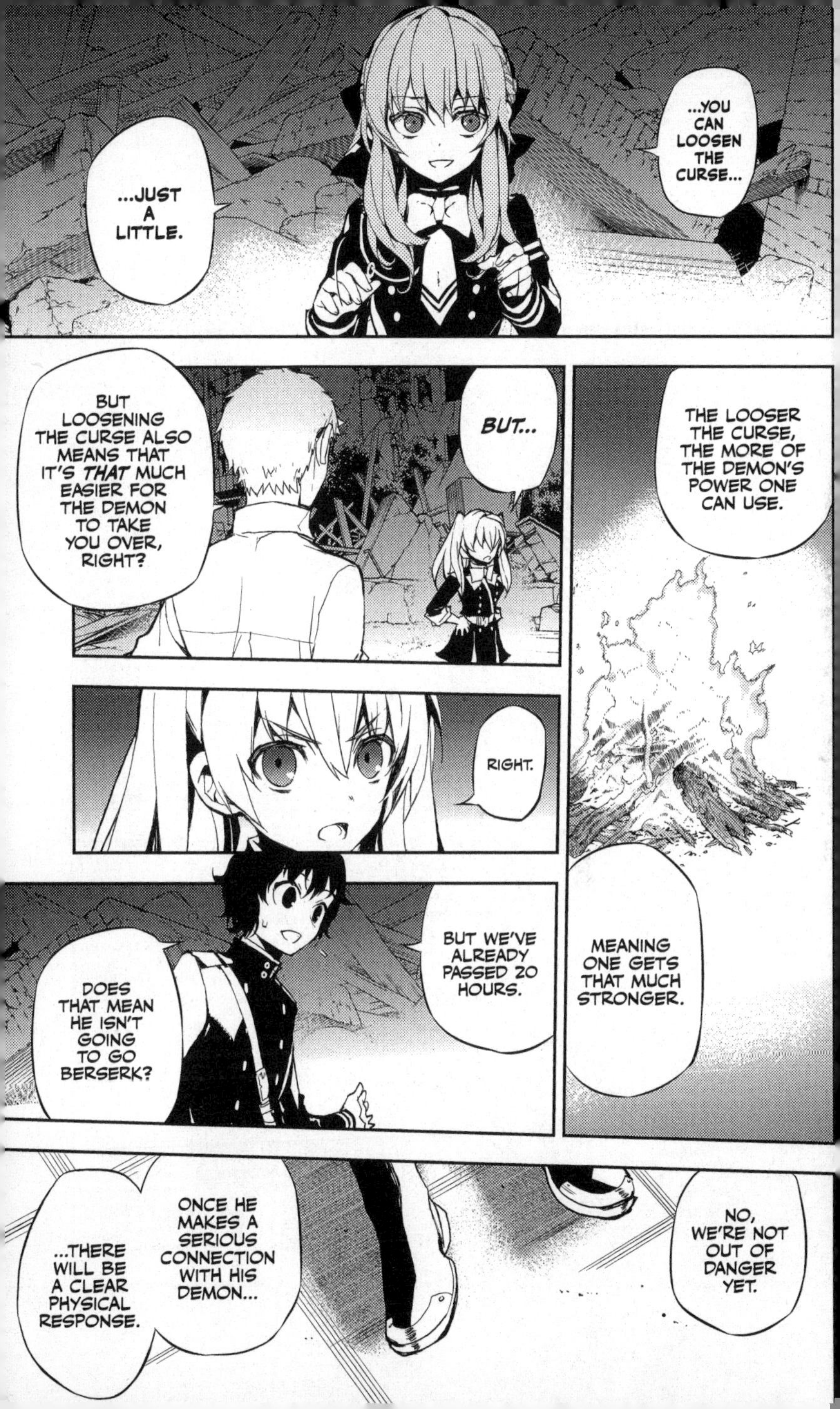
...YOU CAN LOOSEN THE CURSE...
...JUST A LITTLE.
THE LOOSER THE CURSE, THE MORE OF THE DEMON'S POWER ONE CAN USE.
MEANING ONE GETS THAT MUCH STRONGER.
BUT...
BUT LOOSENING THE CURSE ALSO MEANS THAT IT'S *THAT* MUCH EASIER FOR THE DEMON TO TAKE YOU OVER, RIGHT?
RIGHT.
BUT WE'VE ALREADY PASSED 20 HOURS.
DOES THAT MEAN HE ISN'T GOING TO GO BERSERK?
NO, WE'RE NOT OUT OF DANGER YET.
ONCE HE MAKES A SERIOUS CONNECTION WITH HIS DEMON...
...THERE WILL BE A CLEAR PHYSICAL RESPONSE.

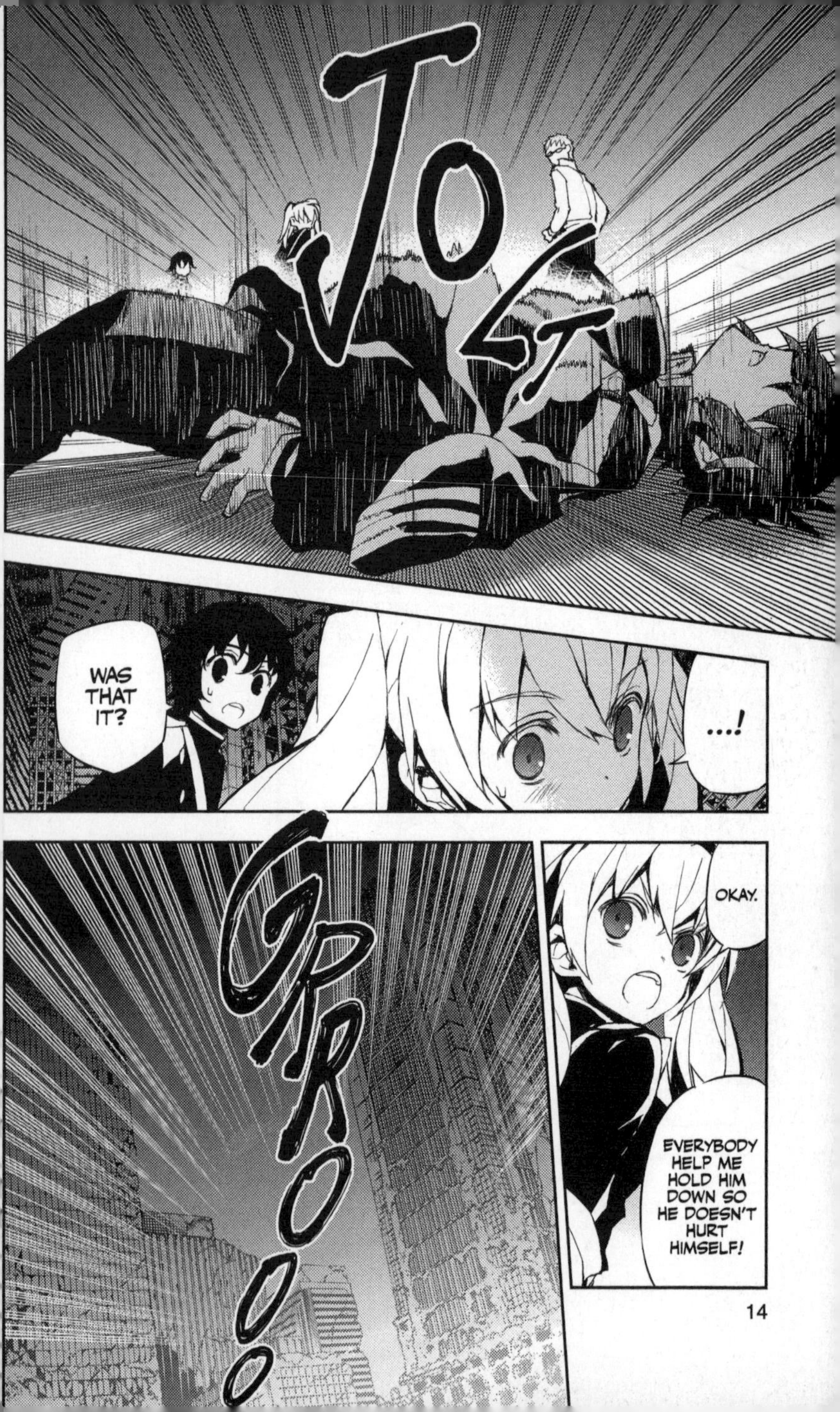
JOLT
...!
WAS THAT IT?
OKAY.
EVERYBODY HELP ME HOLD HIM DOWN SO HE DOESN'T HURT HIMSELF!
GRROOOOO

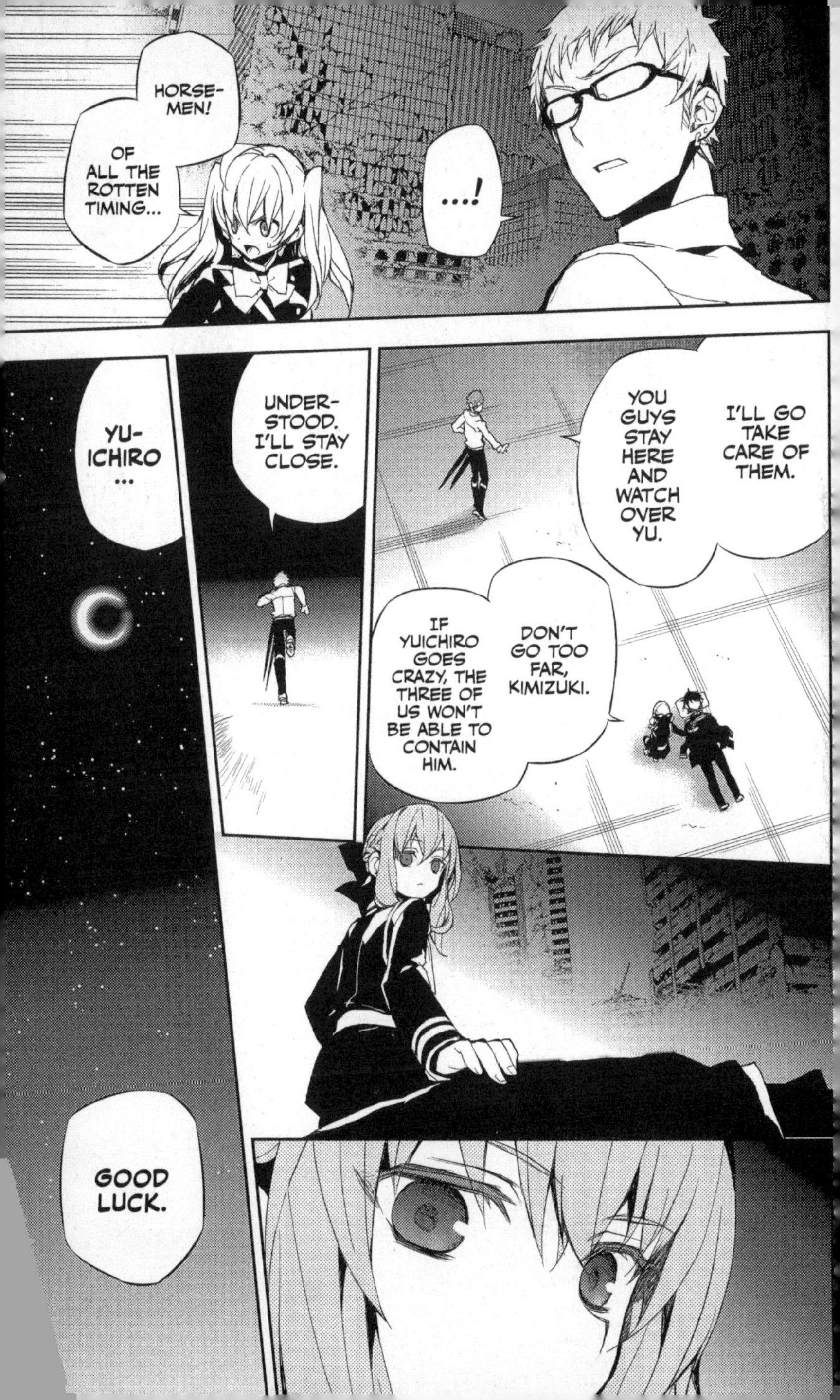
...!
HORSE-MEN!
OF ALL THE ROTTEN TIMING...
I'LL GO TAKE CARE OF THEM.
YOU GUYS STAY HERE AND WATCH OVER YU.
DON'T GO TOO FAR, KIMIZUKI.
IF YUICHIRO GOES CRAZY, THE THREE OF US WON'T BE ABLE TO CONTAIN HIM.
UNDER-STOOD. I'LL STAY CLOSE.
YU-ICHIRO...
GOOD LUCK.

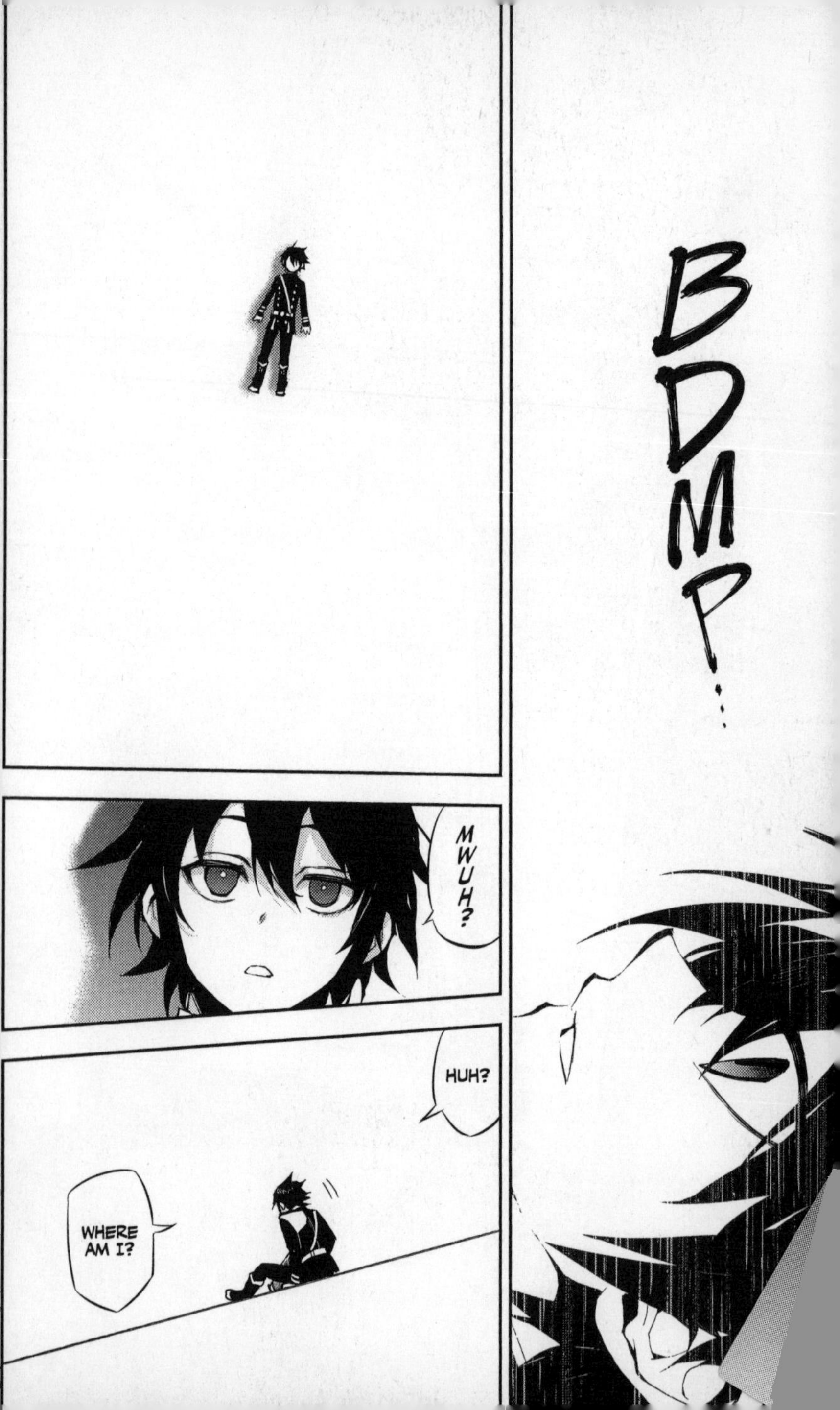
BDMP...
MWUH?
HUH?
WHERE AM I?

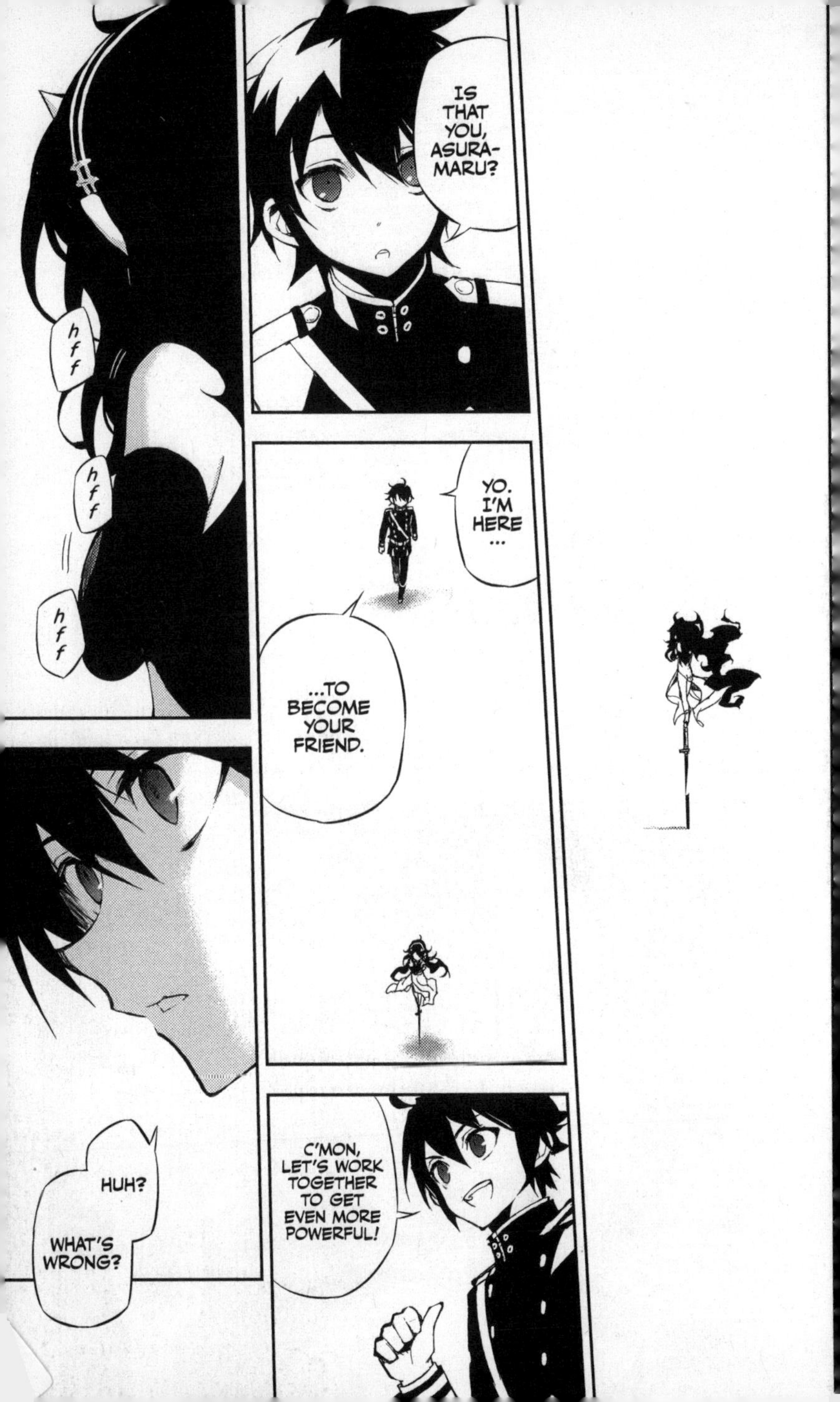
IS THAT YOU, ASURA-MARU?
YO. I'M HERE...
...TO BECOME YOUR FRIEND.
C'MON, LET'S WORK TOGETHER TO GET EVEN MORE POWERFUL!
hff
hff
hff
HUH?
WHAT'S WRONG?

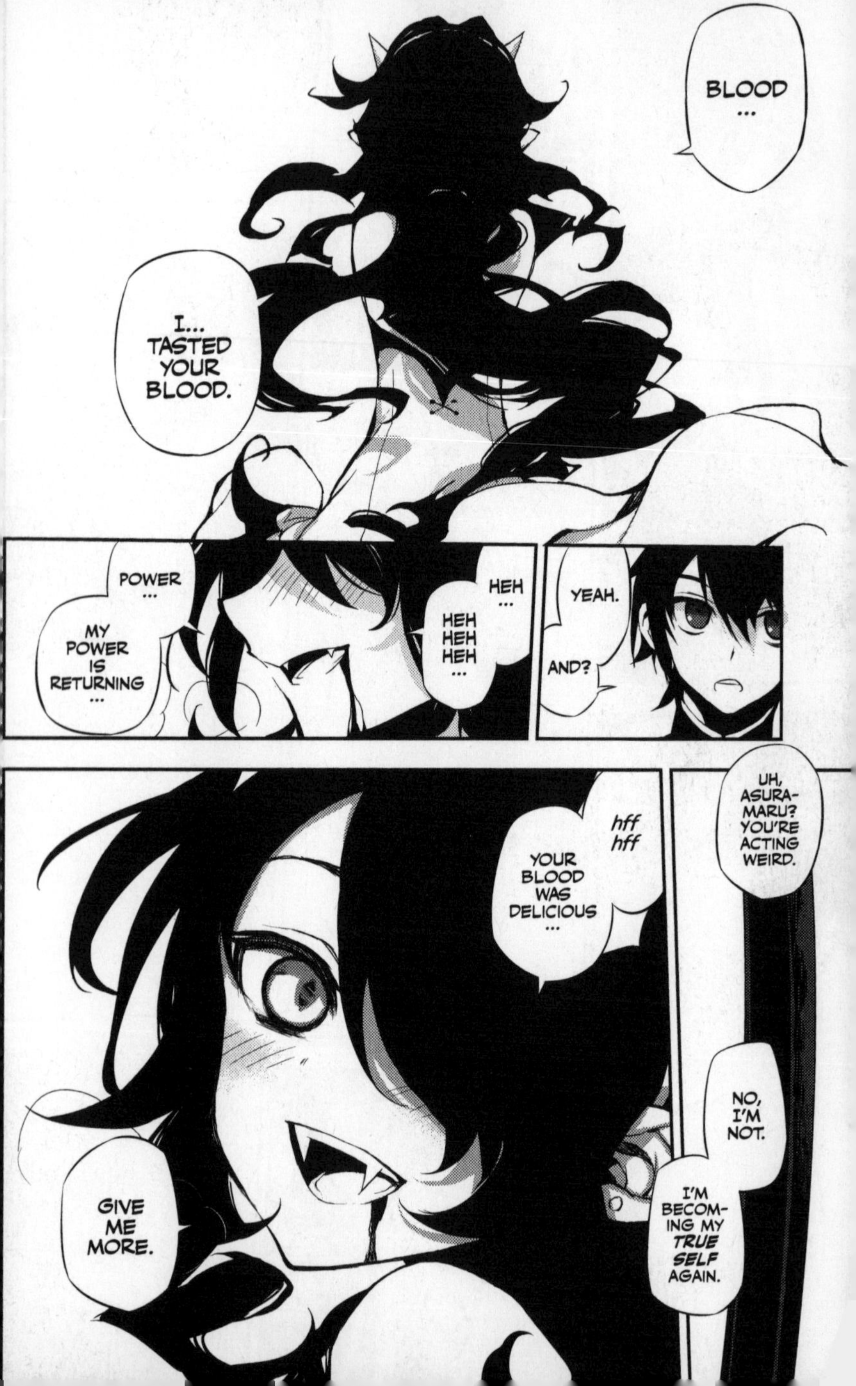

BLOOD...
I... TASTED YOUR BLOOD.
YEAH.
AND?
HEH...
HEH HEH HEH...
POWER...
MY POWER IS RETURNING...
UH, ASURA-MARU? YOU'RE ACTING WEIRD.
NO, I'M NOT.
I'M BECOMING MY *TRUE SELF* AGAIN.
hff hff
YOUR BLOOD WAS DELICIOUS...
GIVE ME MORE.

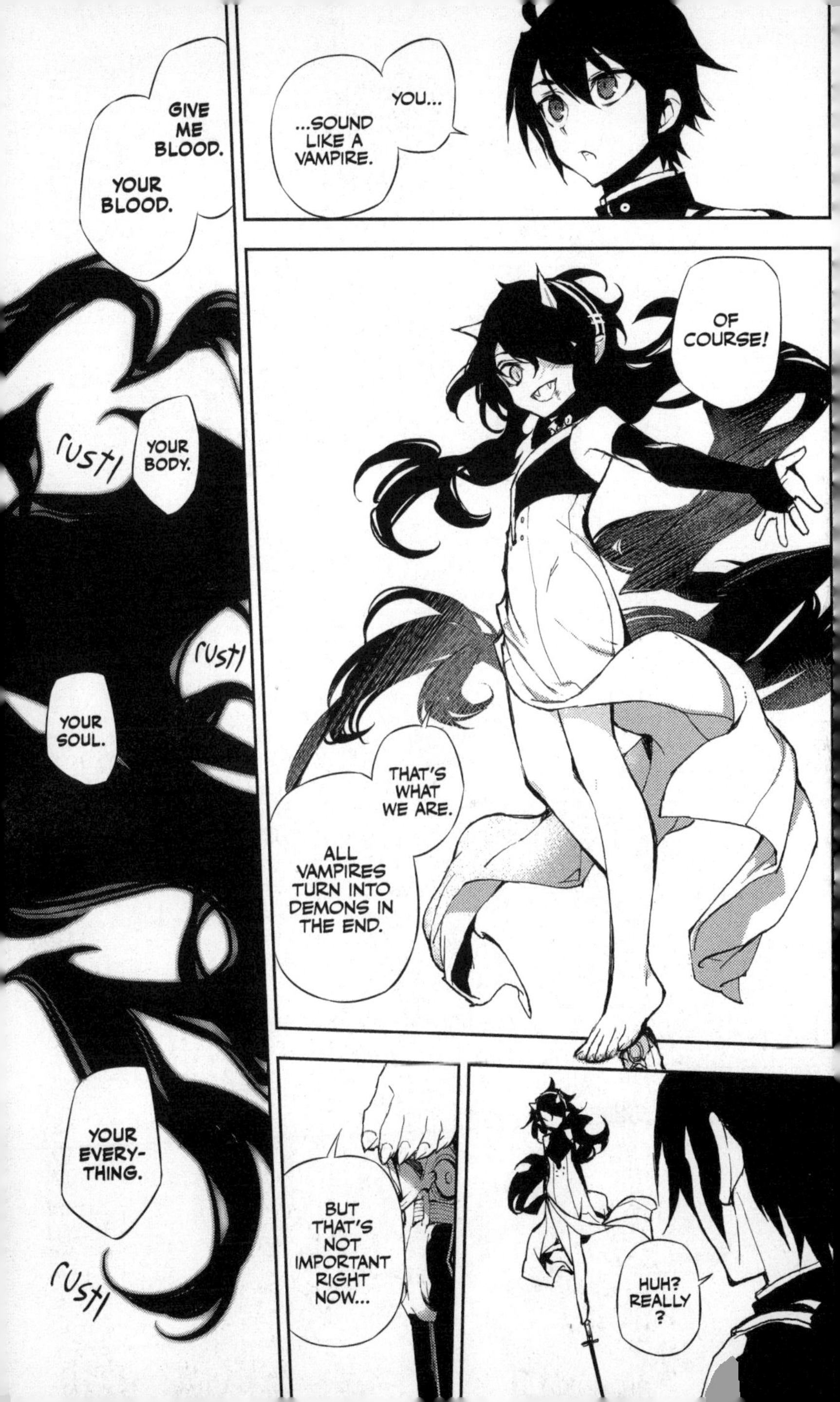
YOU...
...SOUND LIKE A VAMPIRE.
OF COURSE!
THAT'S WHAT WE ARE.
ALL VAMPIRES TURN INTO DEMONS IN THE END.
HUH? REALLY?
BUT THAT'S NOT IMPORTANT RIGHT NOW...
GIVE ME BLOOD.
YOUR BLOOD.
RUSTL
YOUR BODY.
RUSTL
YOUR SOUL.
YOUR EVERY-THING.
RUSTL

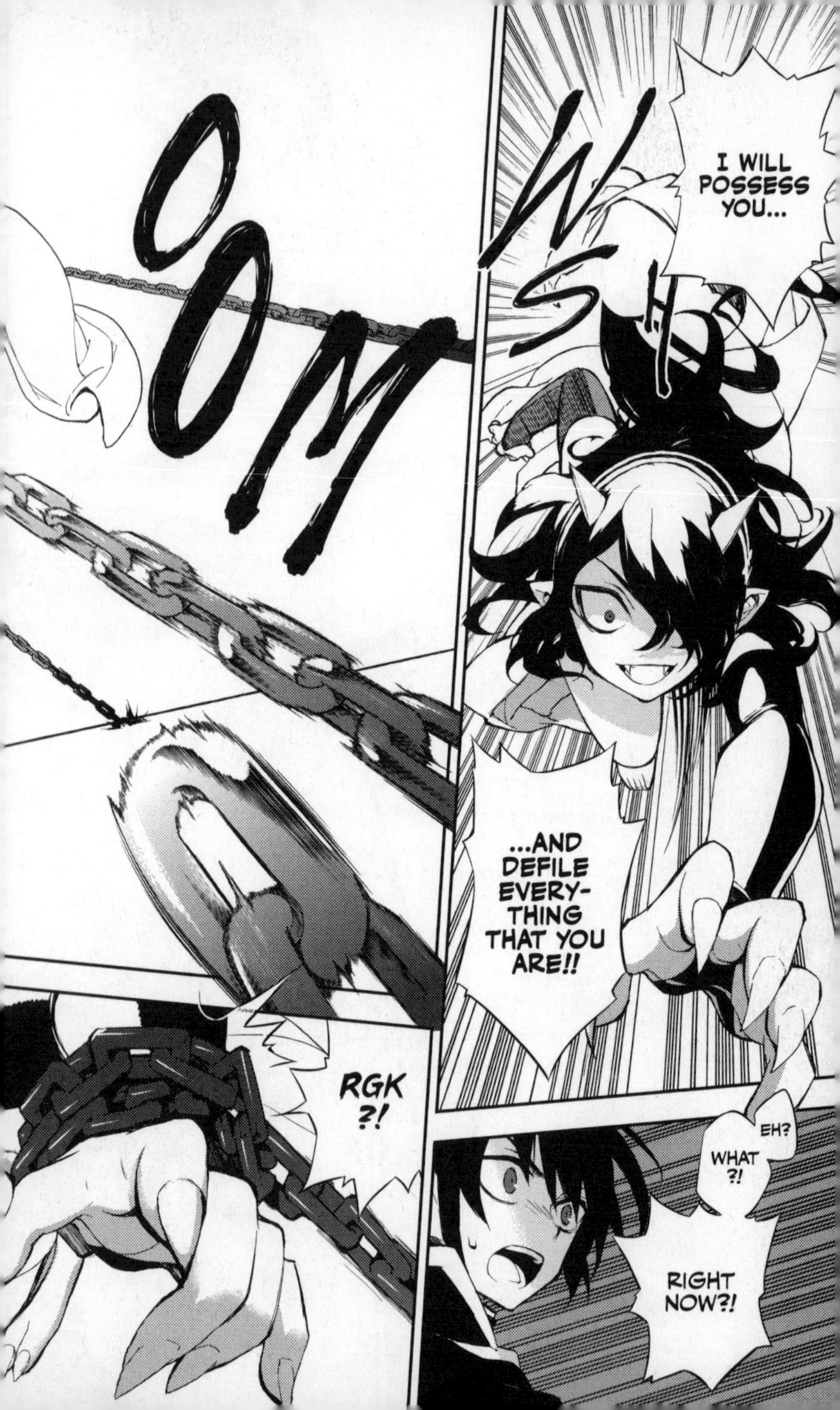
WSH
I WILL POSSESS YOU...
...AND DEFILE EVERY-THING THAT YOU ARE!!
EH?
WHAT ?!
RIGHT NOW?!
OOM
RGK ?!

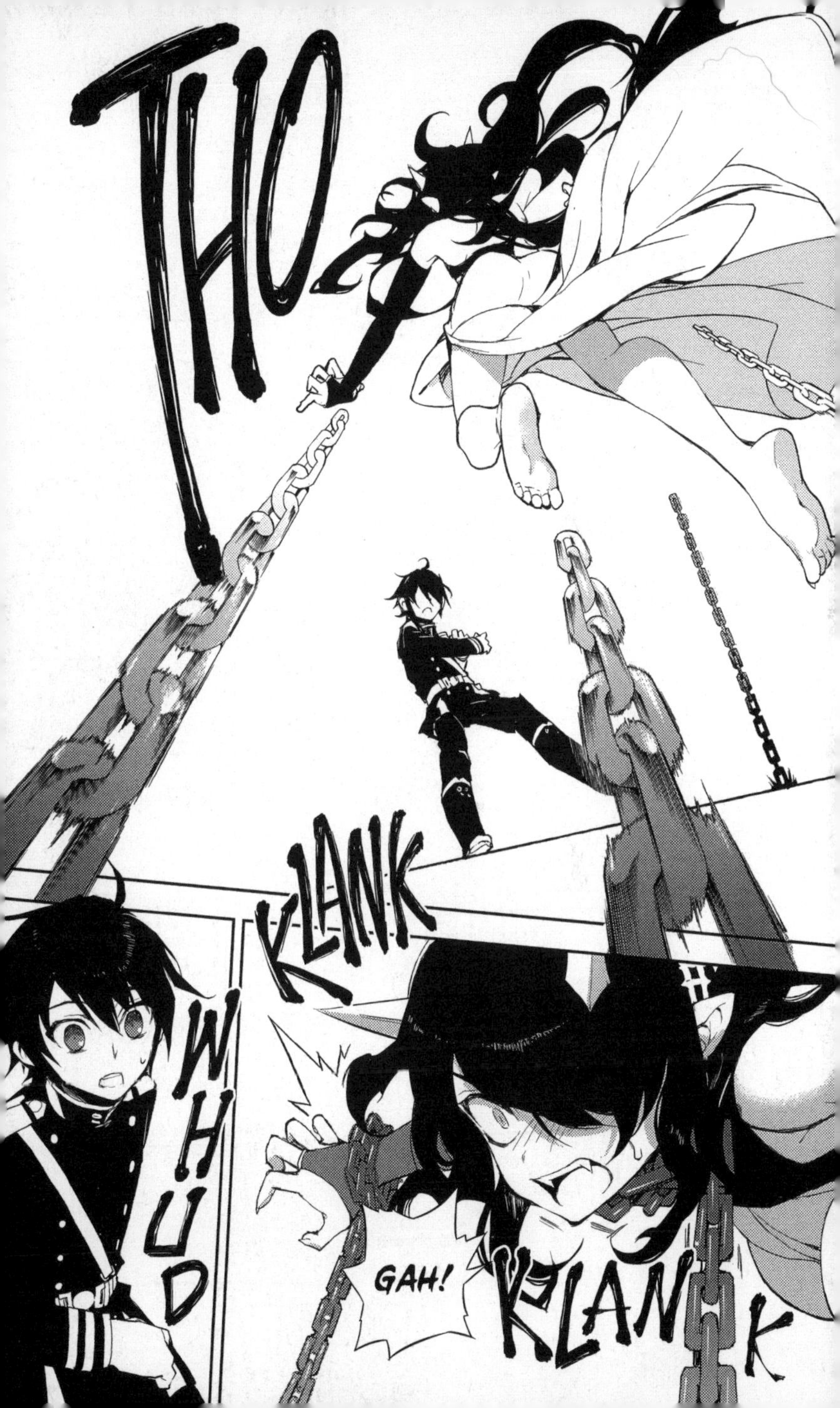
THO
KLANK
GAH!
KLANK
WHUD

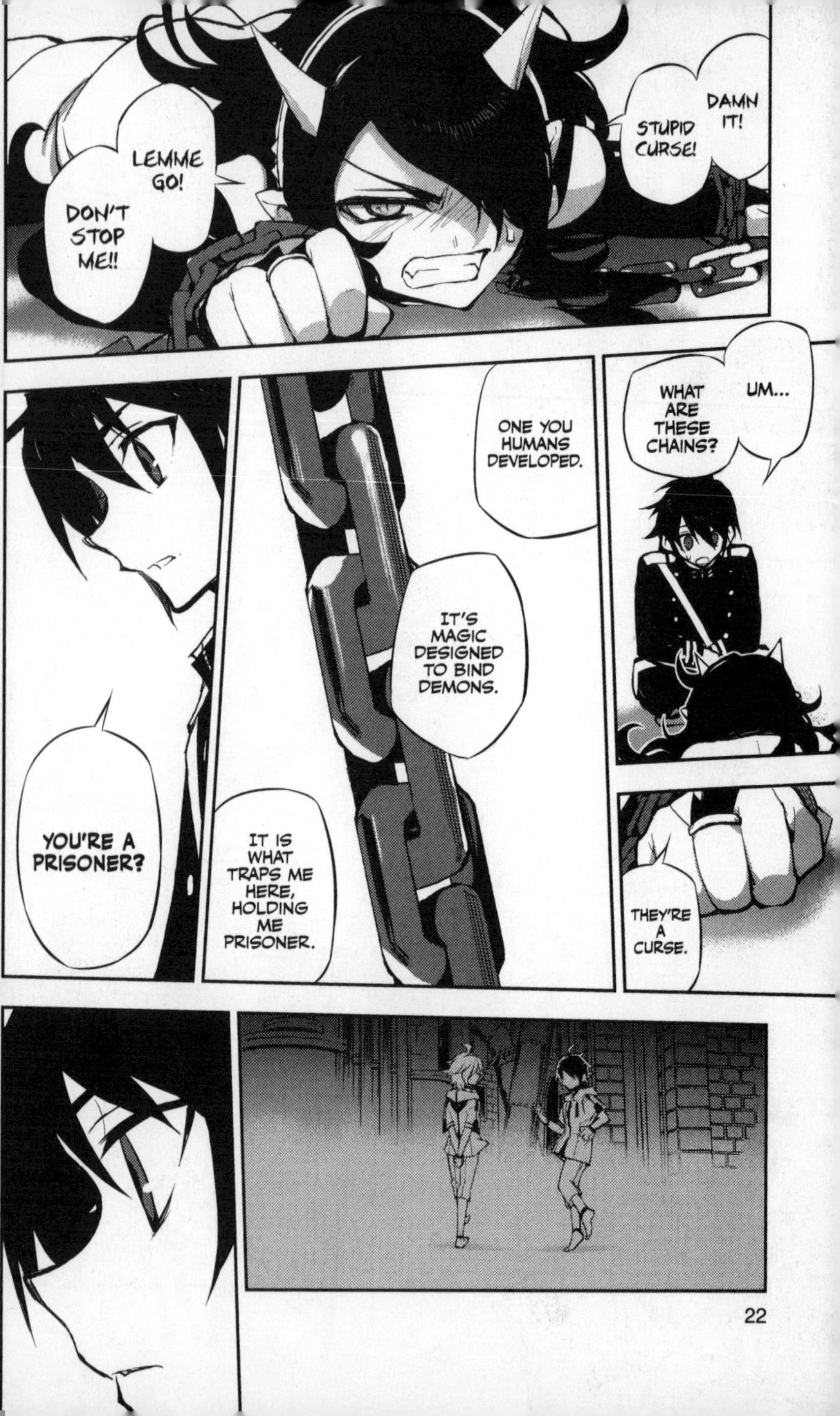
DAMN IT!
STUPID CURSE!
LEMME GO!
DON'T STOP ME!!
UM...
WHAT ARE THESE CHAINS?
THEY'RE A CURSE.
ONE YOU HUMANS DEVELOPED.
IT'S MAGIC DESIGNED TO BIND DEMONS.
IT IS WHAT TRAPS ME HERE, HOLDING ME PRISONER.
YOU'RE A PRISONER?

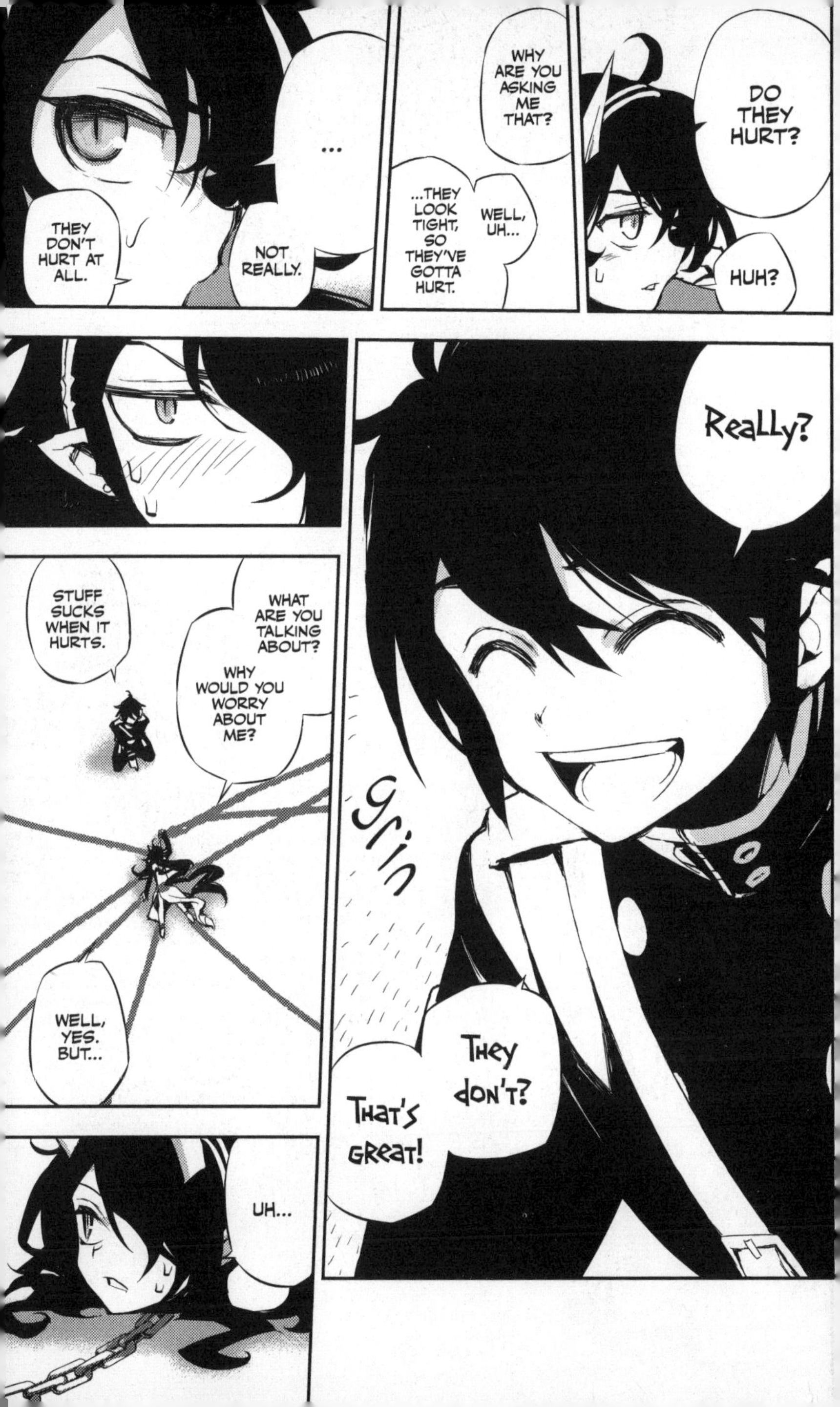
DO THEY HURT?
HUH?
WHY ARE YOU ASKING ME THAT?
WELL, UH...
...THEY LOOK TIGHT, SO THEY'VE GOTTA HURT.
...
NOT REALLY.
THEY DON'T HURT AT ALL.
Really?
grin
They don't?
That's great!
WHAT ARE YOU TALKING ABOUT?
WHY WOULD YOU WORRY ABOUT ME?
STUFF SUCKS WHEN IT HURTS.
WELL, YES. BUT...
UH...

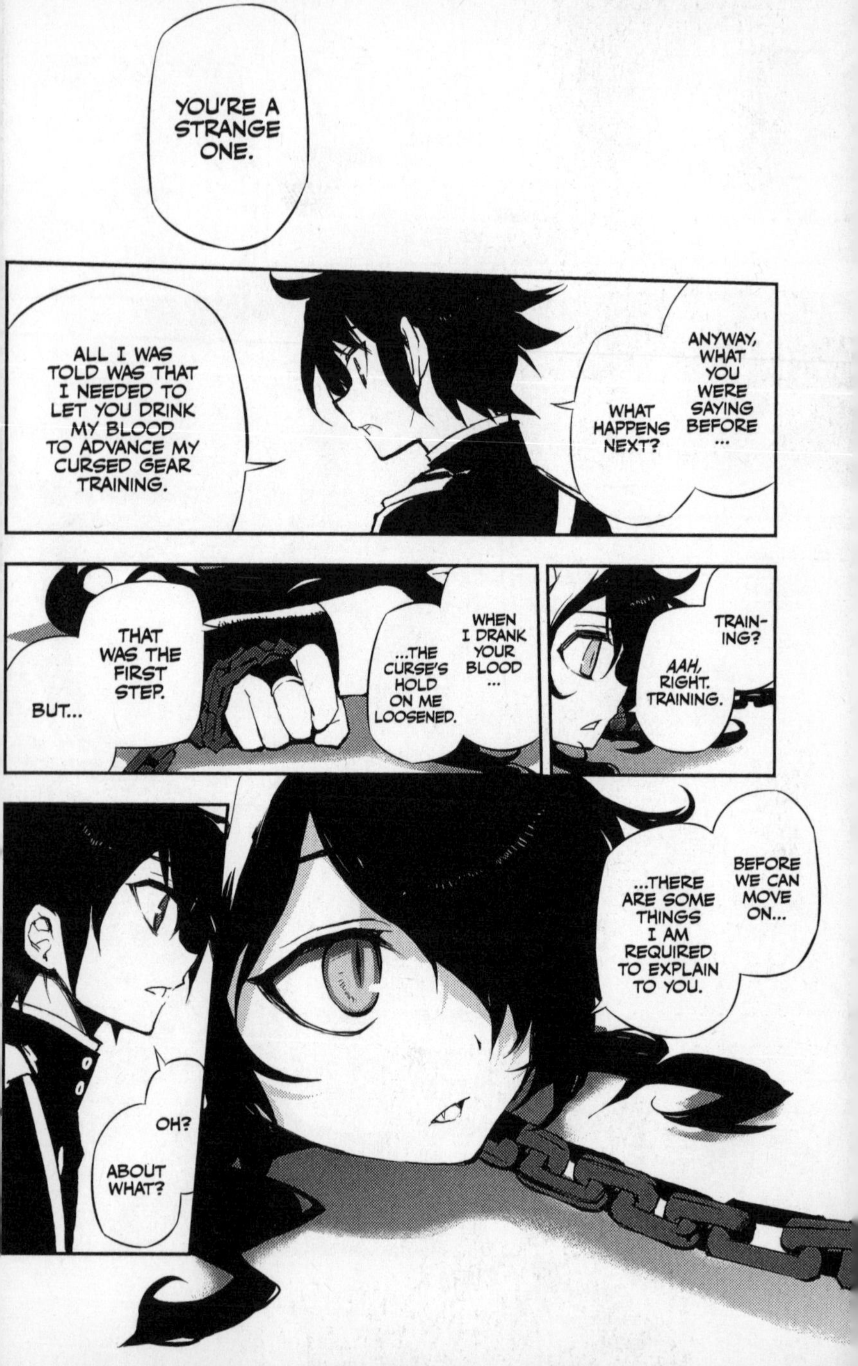
YOU'RE A STRANGE ONE.
ANYWAY, WHAT YOU WERE SAYING BEFORE...
WHAT HAPPENS NEXT?
ALL I WAS TOLD WAS THAT I NEEDED TO LET YOU DRINK MY BLOOD TO ADVANCE MY CURSED GEAR TRAINING.
TRAIN-ING?
AAH, RIGHT. TRAINING.
WHEN I DRANK YOUR BLOOD...
...THE CURSE'S HOLD ON ME LOOSENED.
THAT WAS THE FIRST STEP.
BUT...
BEFORE WE CAN MOVE ON...
...THERE ARE SOME THINGS I AM REQUIRED TO EXPLAIN TO YOU.
OH?
ABOUT WHAT?

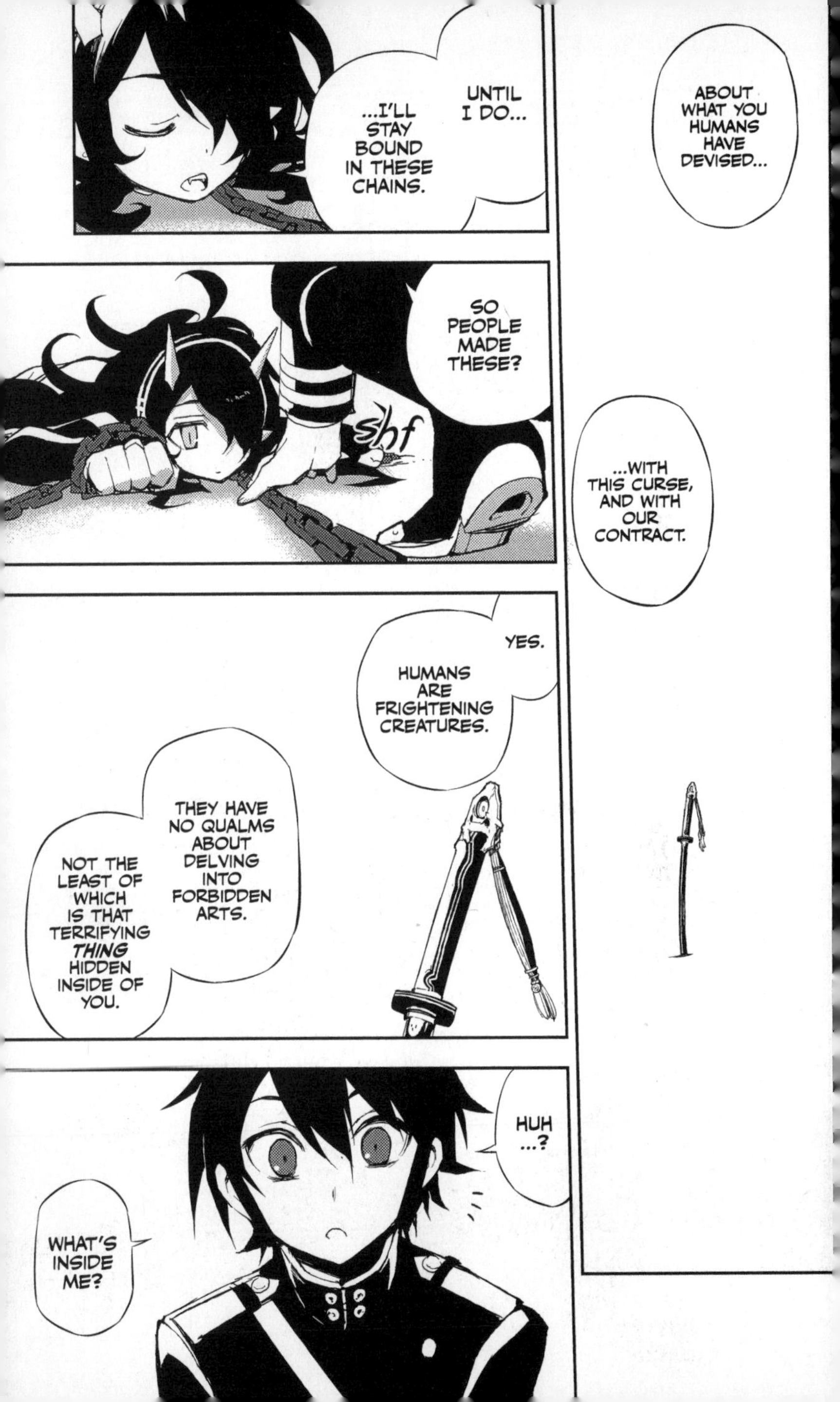
ABOUT WHAT YOU HUMANS HAVE DEVISED...
...WITH THIS CURSE, AND WITH OUR CONTRACT.
UNTIL I DO...
...I'LL STAY BOUND IN THESE CHAINS.
SO PEOPLE MADE THESE?
shf
YES.
HUMANS ARE FRIGHTENING CREATURES.
THEY HAVE NO QUALMS ABOUT DELVING INTO FORBIDDEN ARTS.
NOT THE LEAST OF WHICH IS THAT TERRIFYING *THING* HIDDEN INSIDE OF YOU.
HUH ...?
WHAT'S INSIDE ME?

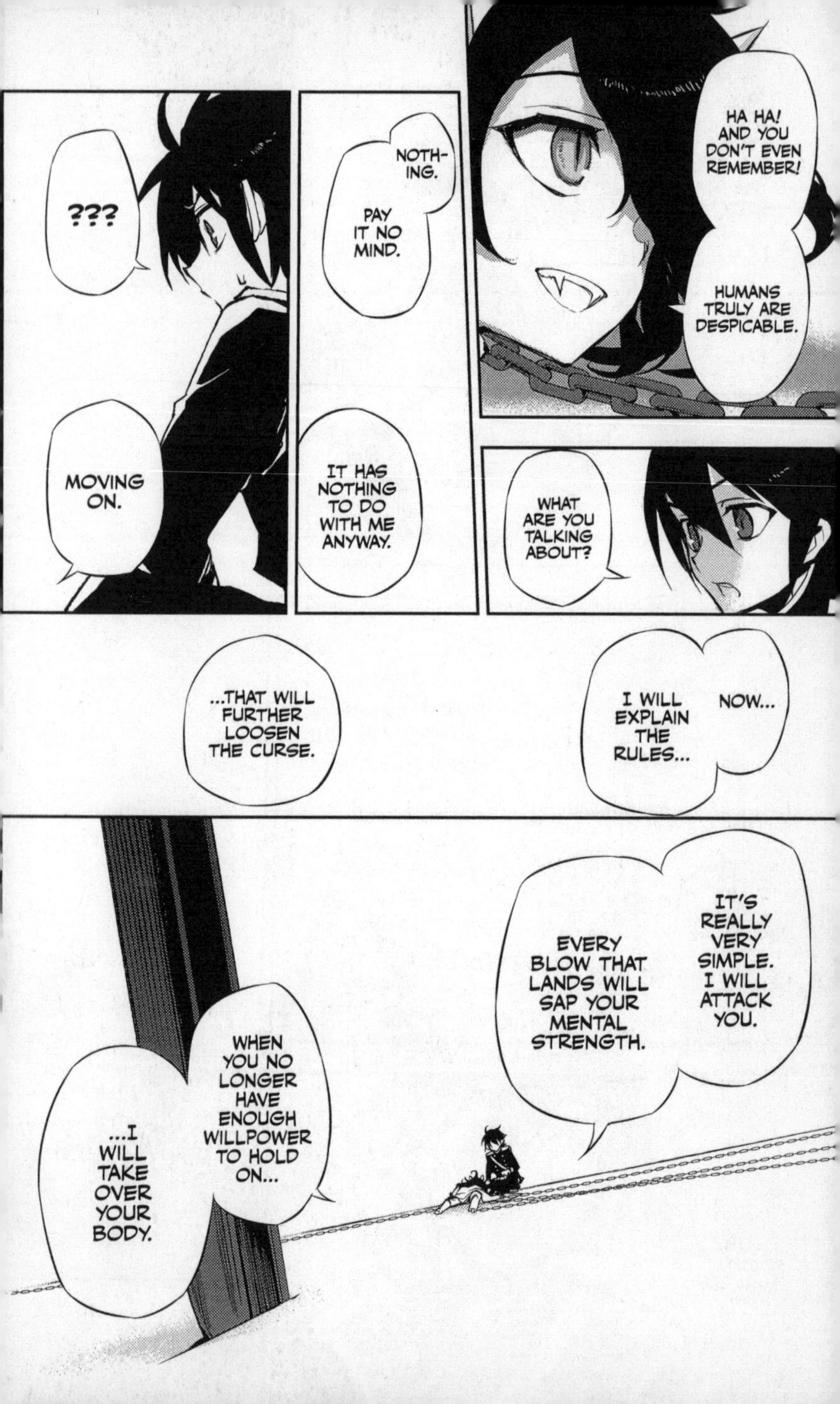
HA HA! AND YOU DON'T EVEN REMEMBER!
HUMANS TRULY ARE DESPICABLE.
WHAT ARE YOU TALKING ABOUT?
NOTHING.
PAY IT NO MIND.
IT HAS NOTHING TO DO WITH ME ANYWAY.
???
MOVING ON.
NOW...
I WILL EXPLAIN THE RULES...
...THAT WILL FURTHER LOOSEN THE CURSE.
IT'S REALLY VERY SIMPLE. I WILL ATTACK YOU.
EVERY BLOW THAT LANDS WILL SAP YOUR MENTAL STRENGTH.
WHEN YOU NO LONGER HAVE ENOUGH WILLPOWER TO HOLD ON...
...I WILL TAKE OVER YOUR BODY.

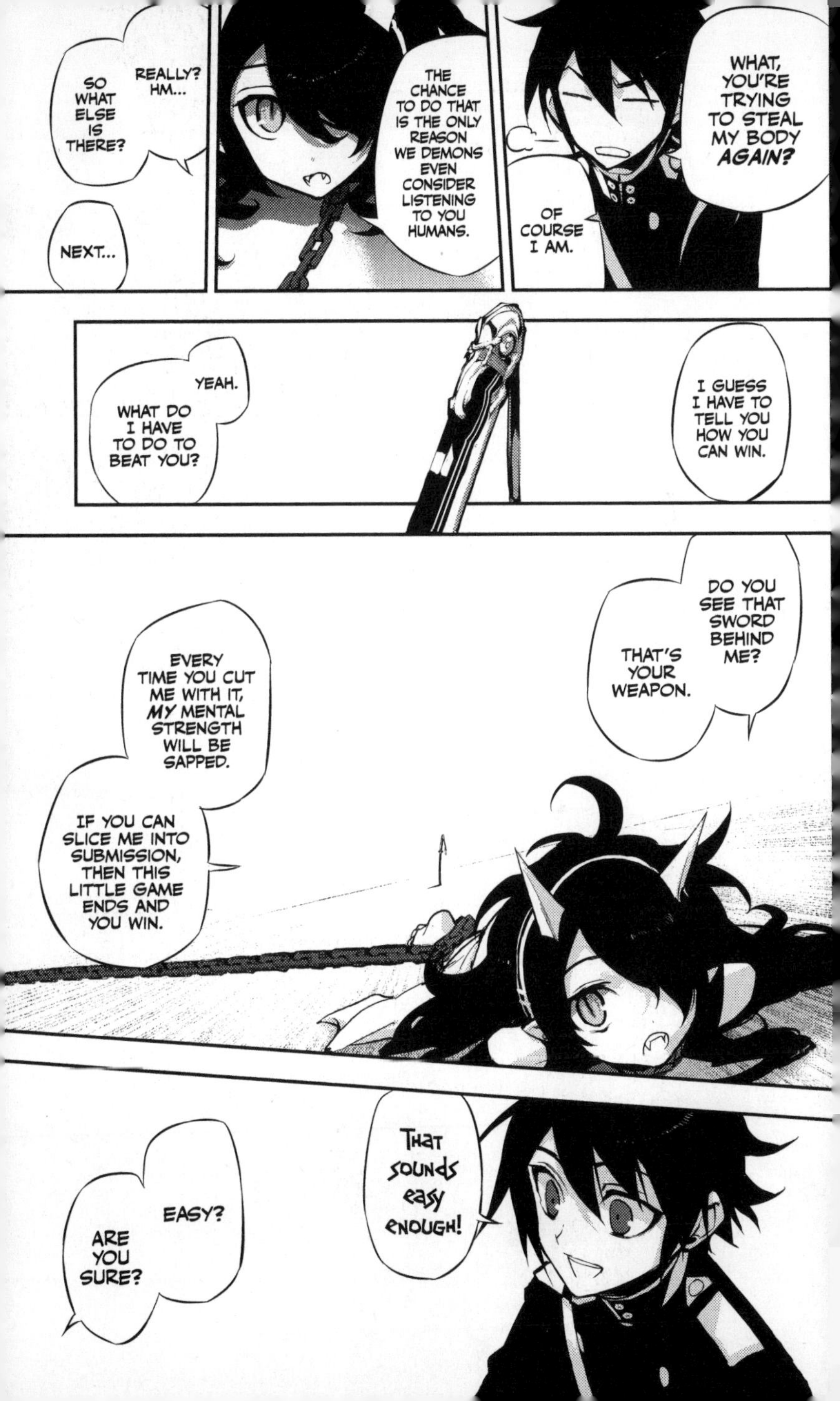
WHAT, YOU'RE TRYING TO STEAL MY BODY *AGAIN?*
OF COURSE I AM.
THE CHANCE TO DO THAT IS THE ONLY REASON WE DEMONS EVEN CONSIDER LISTENING TO YOU HUMANS.
REALLY? HM...
SO WHAT ELSE IS THERE?
NEXT...
I GUESS I HAVE TO TELL YOU HOW YOU CAN WIN.
YEAH.
WHAT DO I HAVE TO DO TO BEAT YOU?
DO YOU SEE THAT SWORD BEHIND ME?
THAT'S YOUR WEAPON.
EVERY TIME YOU CUT ME WITH IT, *MY* MENTAL STRENGTH WILL BE SAPPED.
IF YOU CAN SLICE ME INTO SUBMISSION, THEN THIS LITTLE GAME ENDS AND YOU WIN.
That sounds easy enough!
EASY?
ARE YOU SURE?

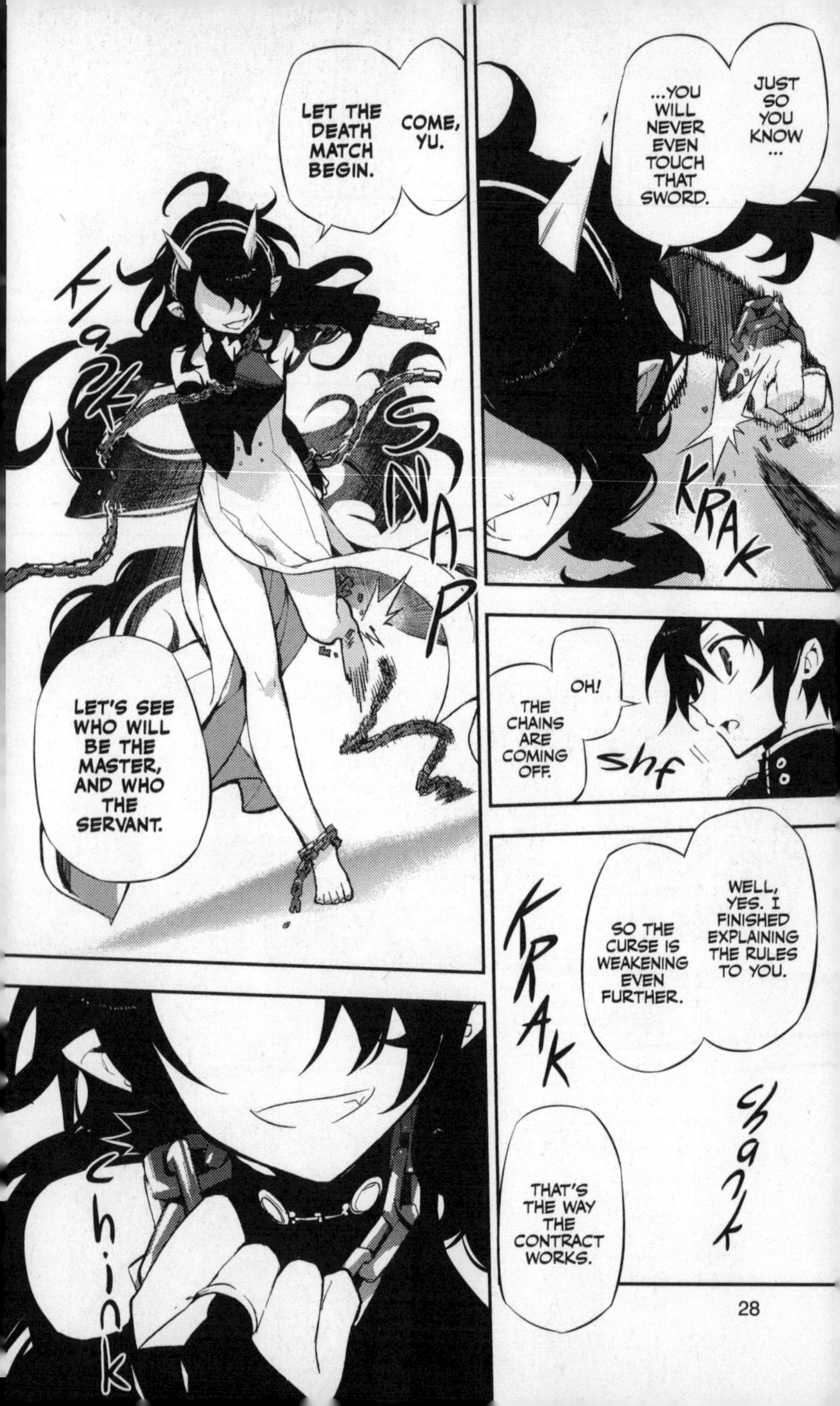

JUST SO YOU KNOW...
...YOU WILL NEVER EVEN TOUCH THAT SWORD.
KRAK
OH!
THE CHAINS ARE COMING OFF.
shf
COME, YU.
LET THE DEATH MATCH BEGIN.
klak
SNAP
LET'S SEE WHO WILL BE THE MASTER, AND WHO THE SERVANT.
KRAK
WELL, YES. I FINISHED EXPLAINING THE RULES TO YOU.
SO THE CURSE IS WEAKENING EVEN FURTHER.
chank
THAT'S THE WAY THE CONTRACT WORKS.
chink

...IS
MINE.

HWAAH...

THE
BONDS
ARE
LOOSEN-
ING...

LOOSEN-
ING...

I CAN
FEEL MY
SANITY
SLIPPING
AWAY...

BLOOD.

FLESH.

EVERY-
THING
THAT YOU
ARE...

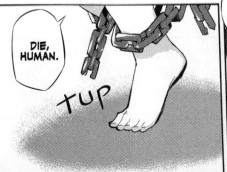

DIE,
HUMAN.

TUP

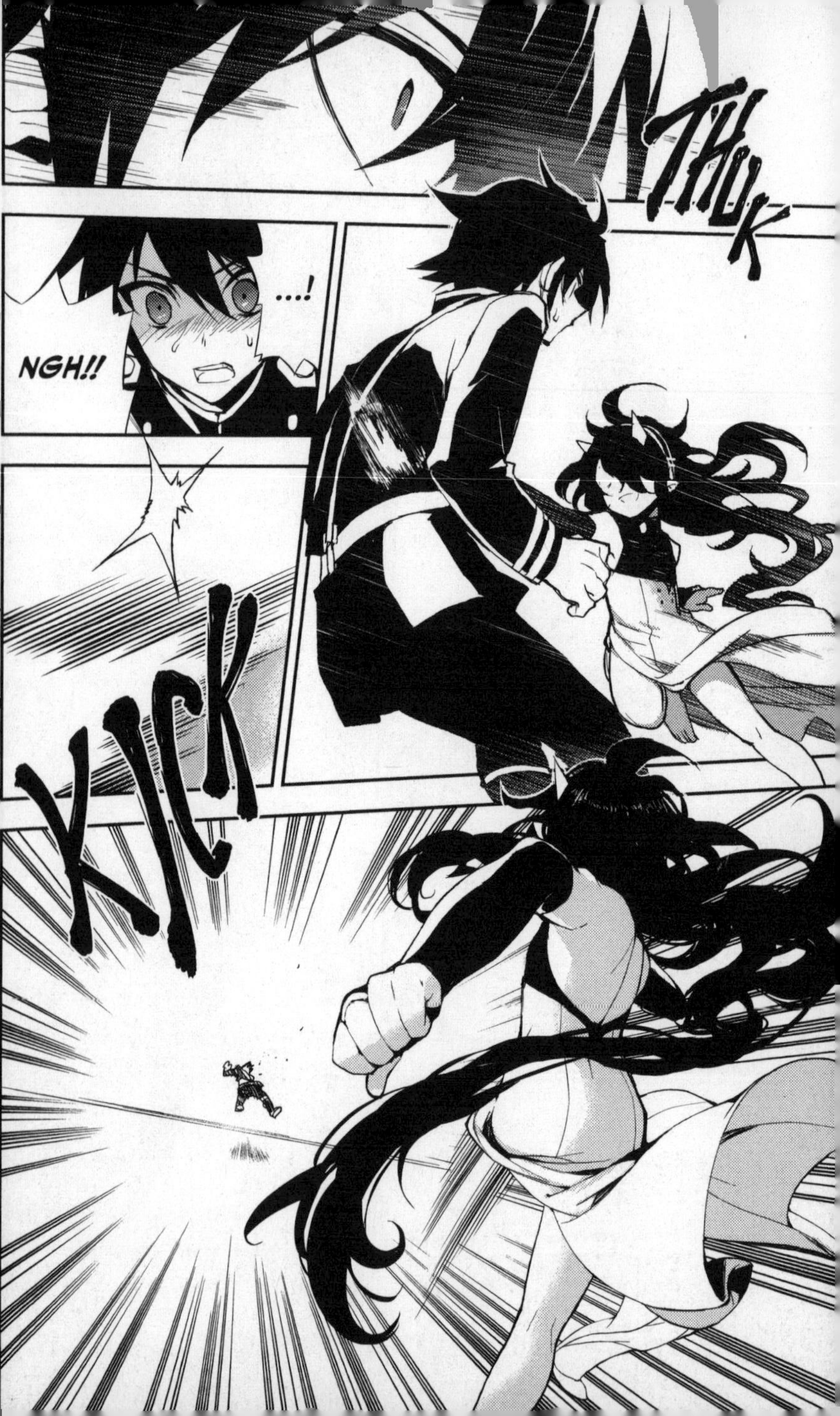

THUK
...!
NGH!!
KICK

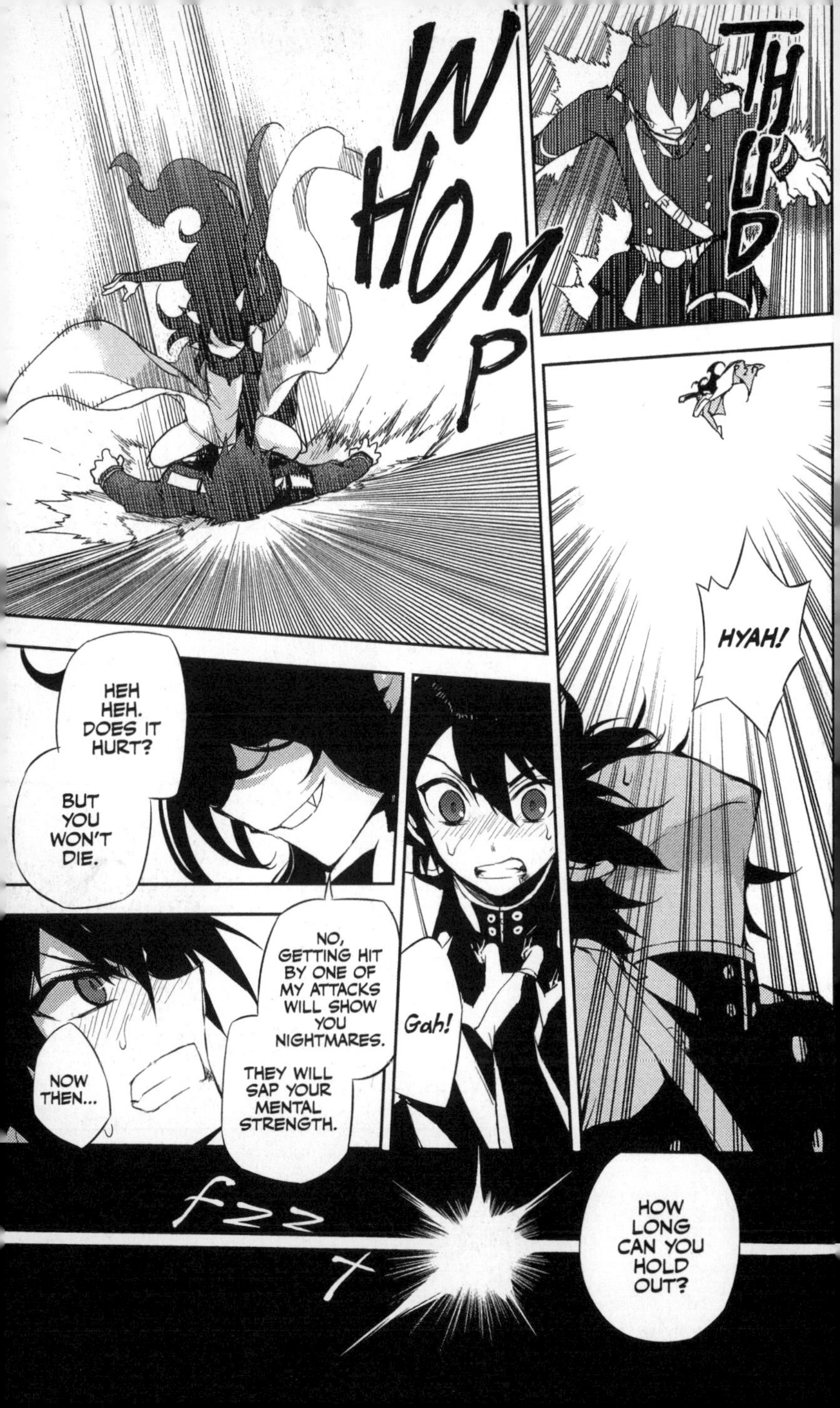
THUD
WHOMP
HYAH!
Gah!
HEH HEH. DOES IT HURT?
BUT YOU WON'T DIE.
NO, GETTING HIT BY ONE OF MY ATTACKS WILL SHOW YOU NIGHTMARES.
THEY WILL SAP YOUR MENTAL STRENGTH.
NOW THEN...
HOW LONG CAN YOU HOLD OUT?
fzzt

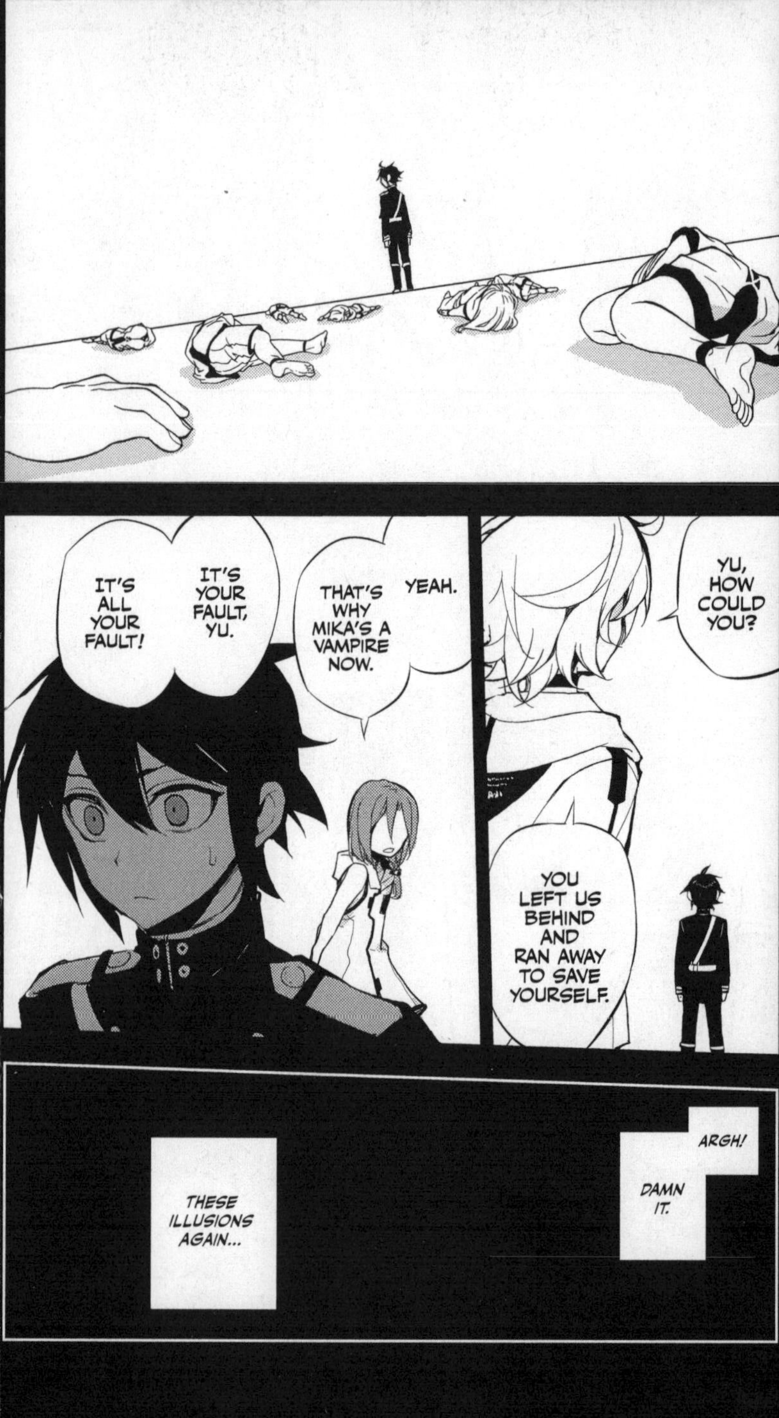

YU, HOW COULD YOU?
YOU LEFT US BEHIND AND RAN AWAY TO SAVE YOURSELF.
YEAH.
THAT'S WHY MIKA'S A VAMPIRE NOW.
IT'S YOUR FAULT, YU.
IT'S ALL YOUR FAULT!
ARGH!
DAMN IT.
THESE ILLUSIONS AGAIN...

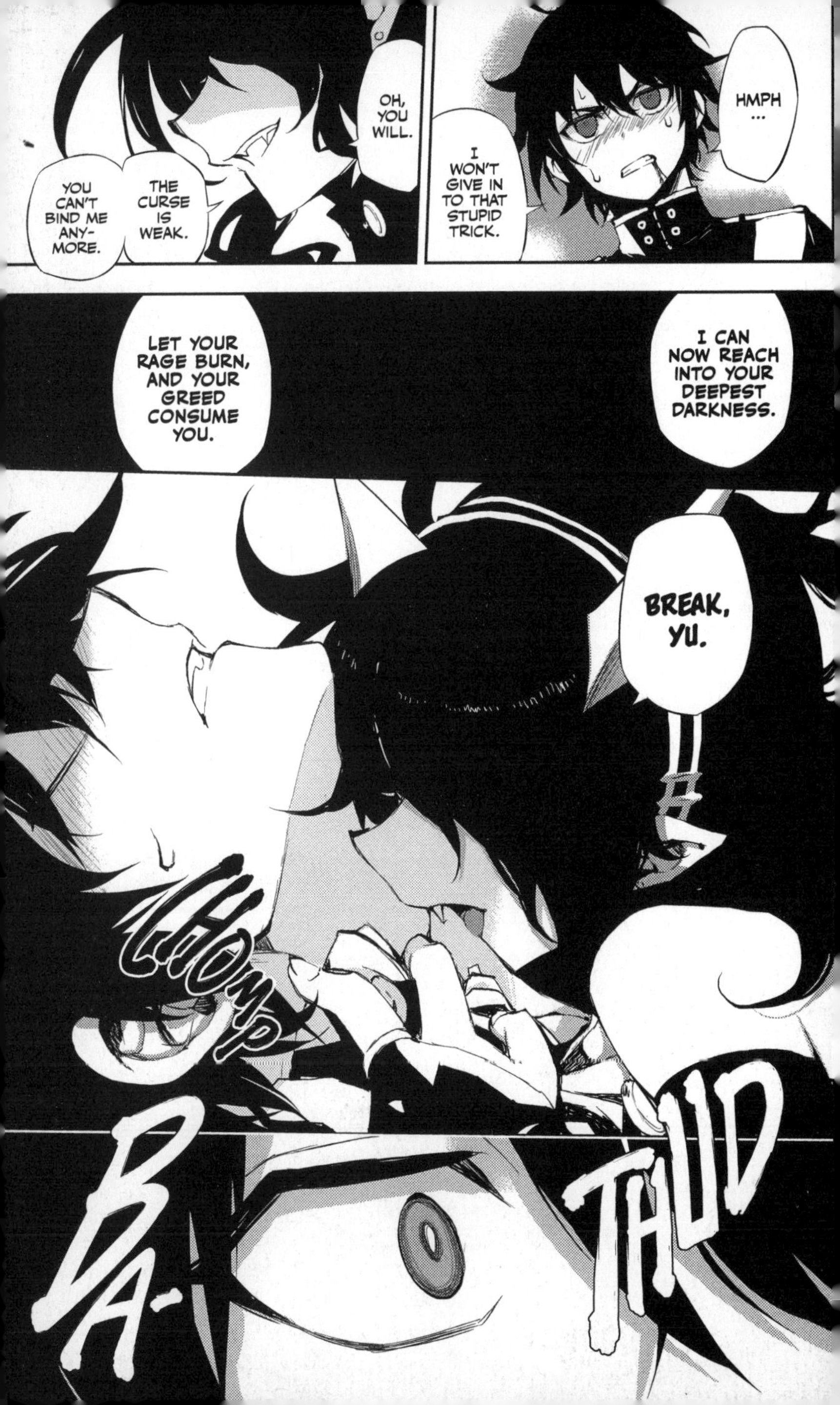
HMPH ...
I WON'T GIVE IN TO THAT STUPID TRICK.
OH, YOU WILL.
THE CURSE IS WEAK.
YOU CAN'T BIND ME ANY-MORE.
I CAN NOW REACH INTO YOUR DEEPEST DARKNESS.
LET YOUR RAGE BURN, AND YOUR GREED CONSUME YOU.
BREAK, YU.
CHOMP
THUD
BA-

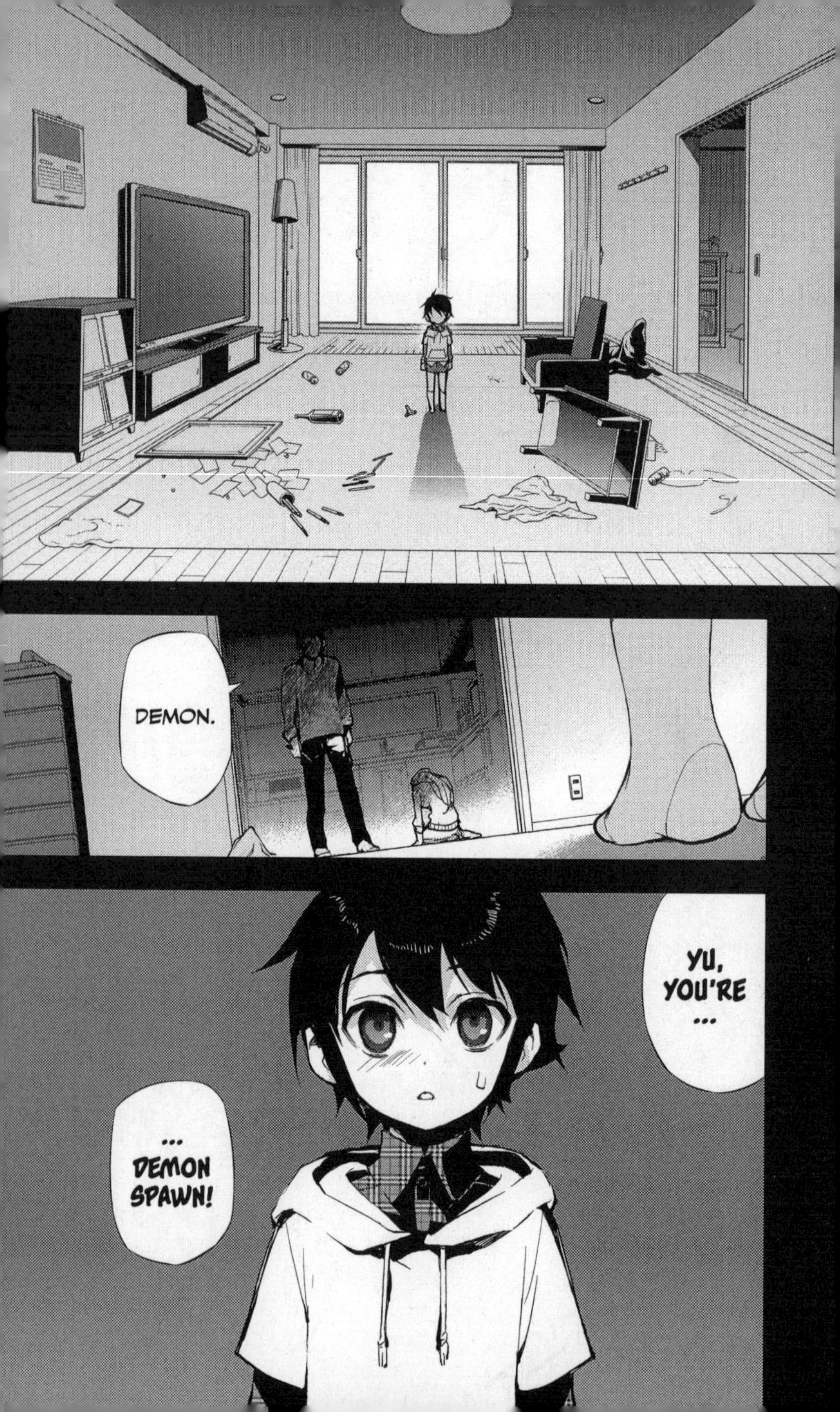
DEMON.
YU, YOU'RE ...
... DEMON SPAWN!

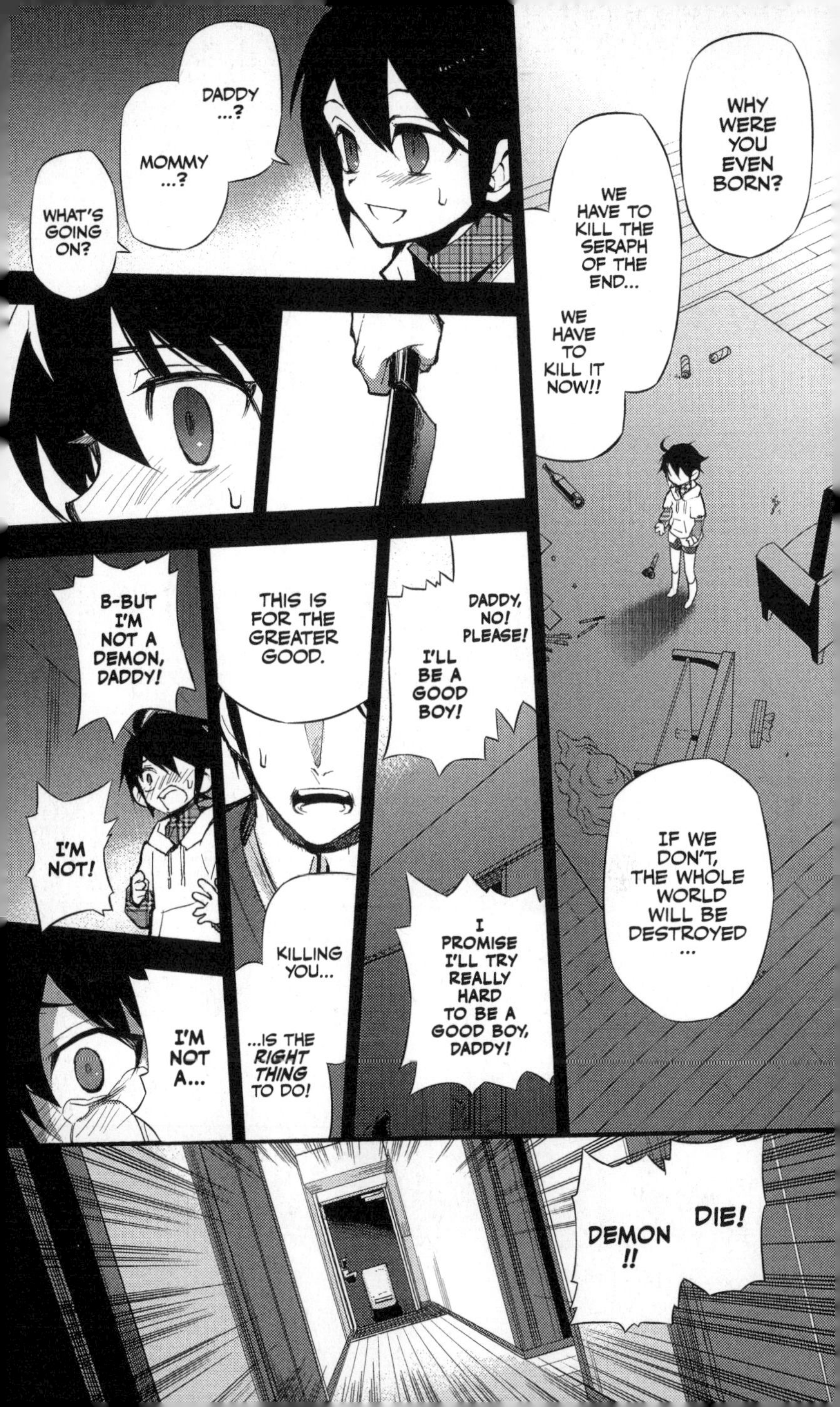

WHY WERE YOU EVEN BORN?
WE HAVE TO KILL THE SERAPH OF THE END...
WE HAVE TO KILL IT NOW!!
IF WE DON'T, THE WHOLE WORLD WILL BE DESTROYED...
DADDY ...?
MOMMY ...?
WHAT'S GOING ON?
DADDY, NO! PLEASE!
I'LL BE A GOOD BOY!
I PROMISE I'LL TRY REALLY HARD TO BE A GOOD BOY, DADDY!
THIS IS FOR THE GREATER GOOD.
KILLING YOU...
...IS THE *RIGHT THING* TO DO!
B-BUT I'M NOT A DEMON, DADDY!
I'M NOT!
I'M NOT A...
DIE!
DEMON !!

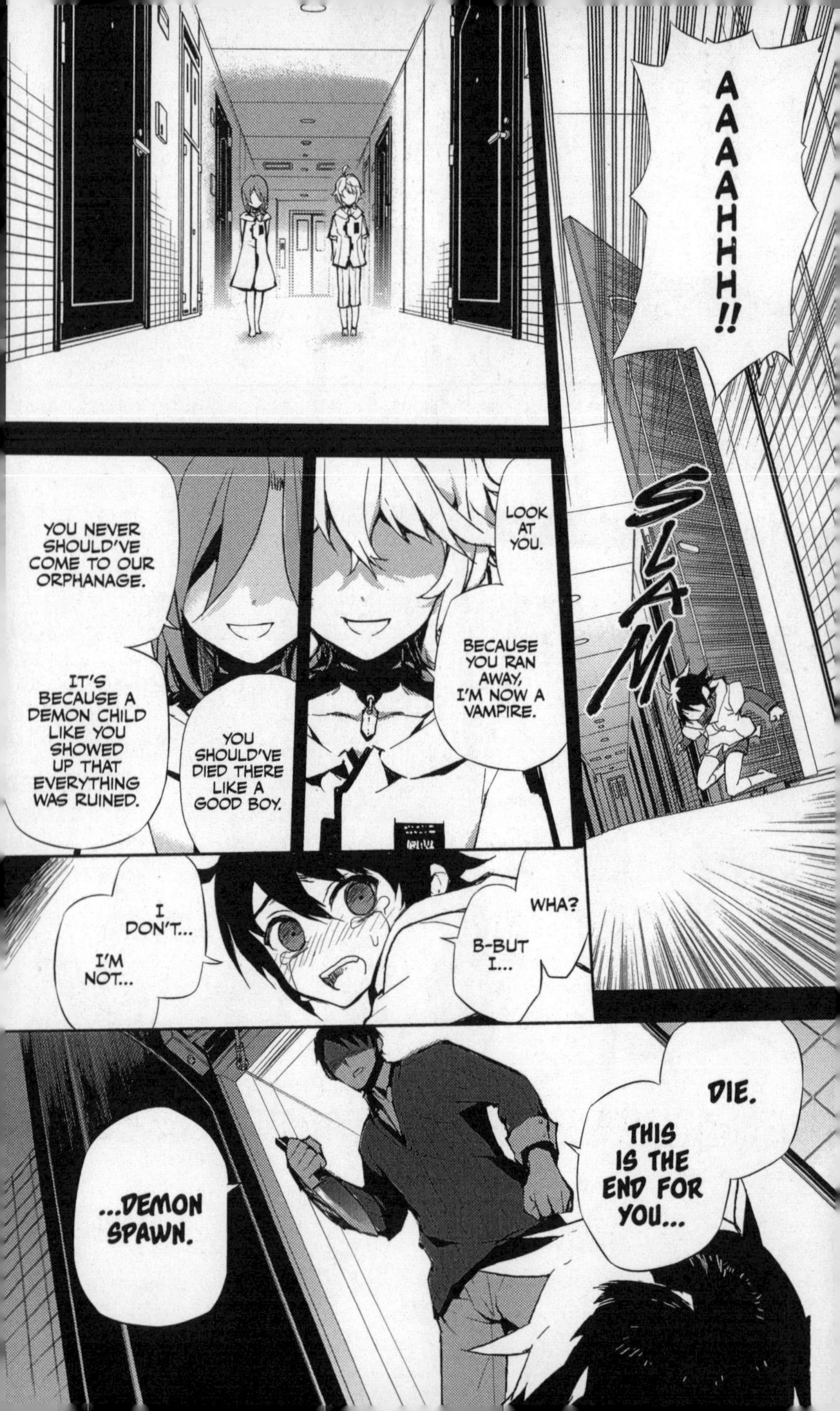
AAAAHHH!!
SLAM
LOOK AT YOU.
BECAUSE YOU RAN AWAY, I'M NOW A VAMPIRE.
YOU NEVER SHOULD'VE COME TO OUR ORPHANAGE.
IT'S BECAUSE A DEMON CHILD LIKE YOU SHOWED UP THAT EVERYTHING WAS RUINED.
YOU SHOULD'VE DIED THERE LIKE A GOOD BOY.
WHA?
B-BUT I...
I DON'T...
I'M NOT...
DIE.
THIS IS THE END FOR YOU...
...DEMON SPAWN.

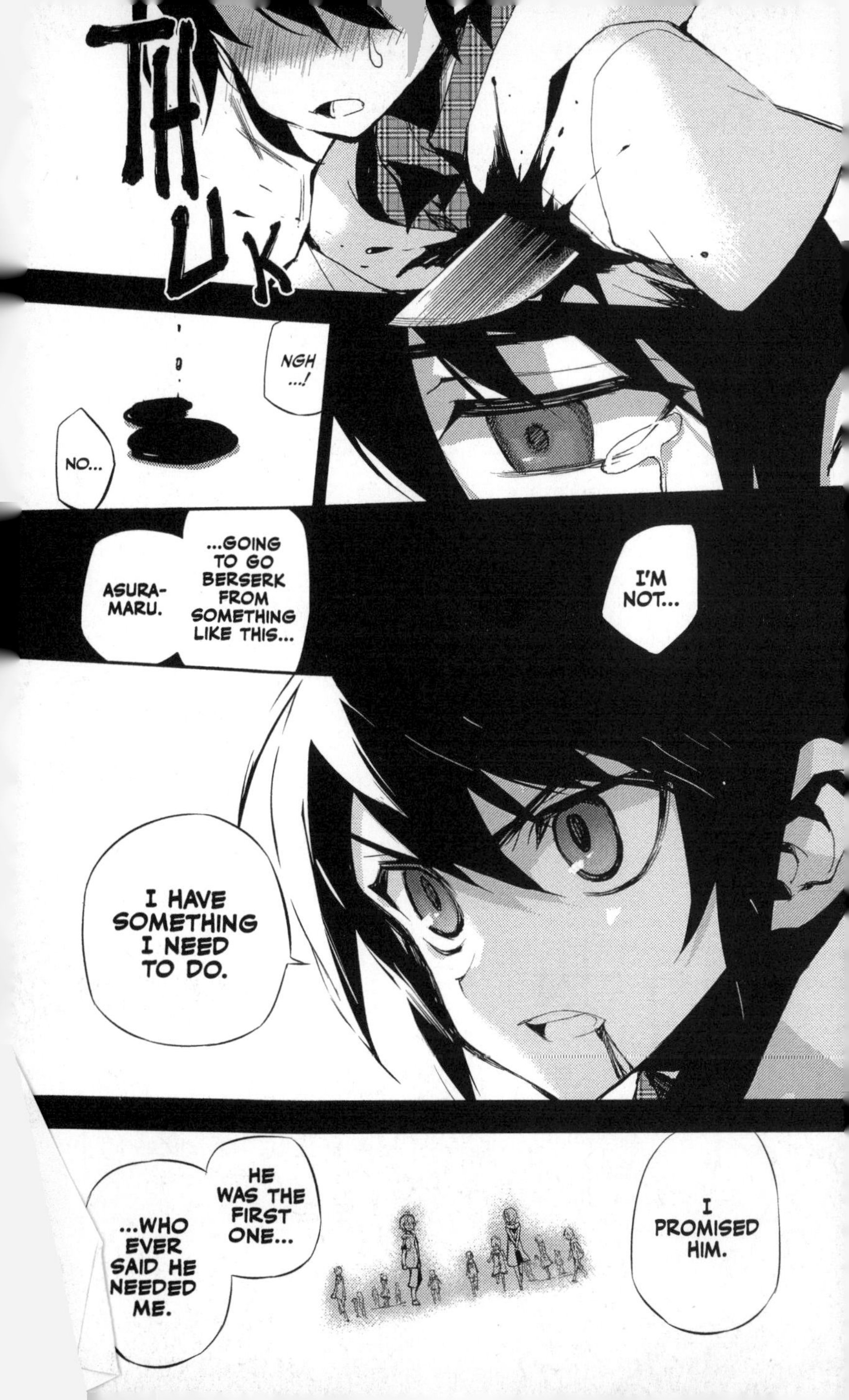
THUK
NGH ...!
NO...
I'M NOT...
...GOING TO GO BERSERK FROM SOMETHING LIKE THIS...
ASURA-MARU.
I HAVE SOMETHING I NEED TO DO.
I PROMISED HIM.
HE WAS THE FIRST ONE...
...WHO EVER SAID HE NEEDED ME.

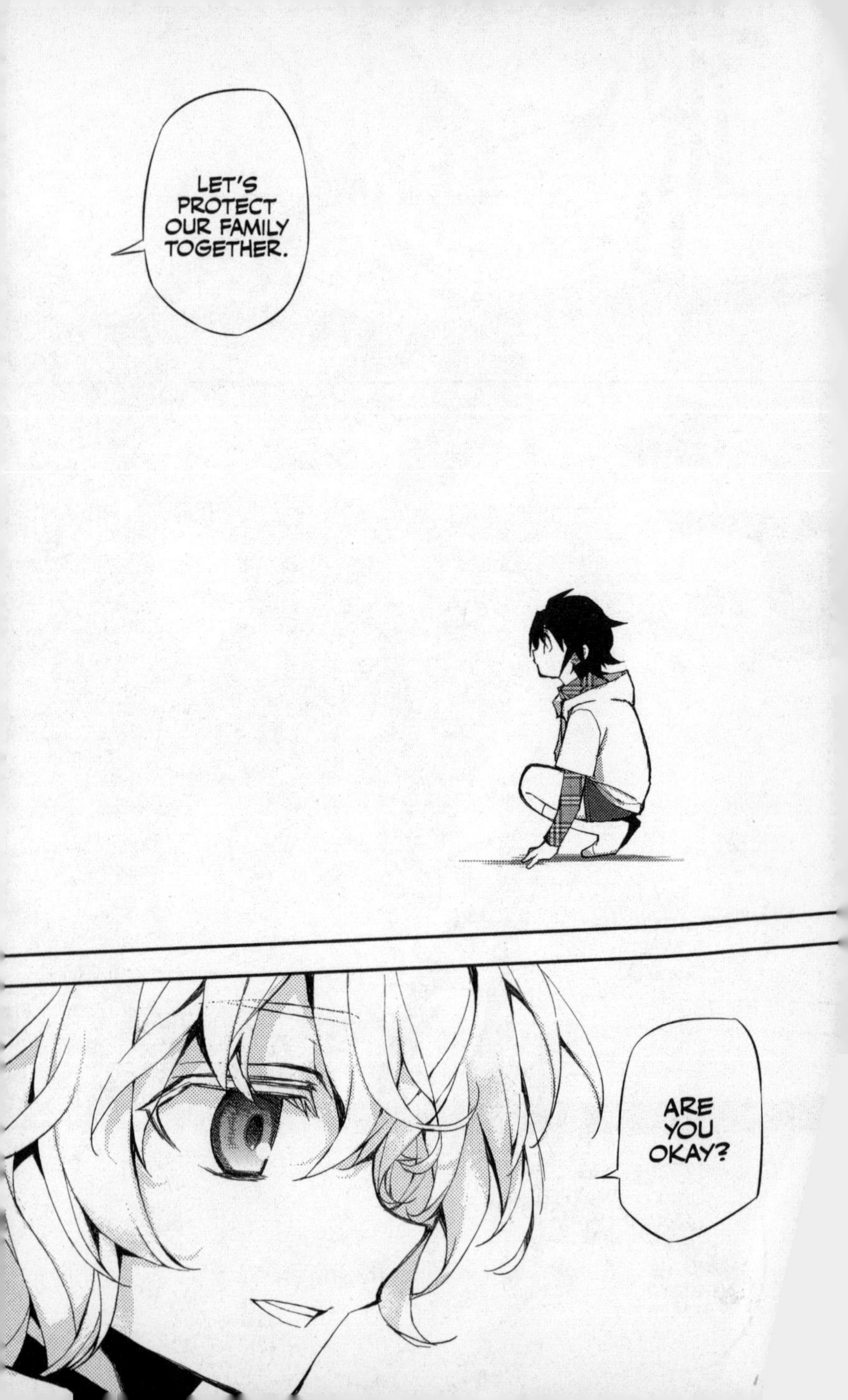
LET'S PROTECT OUR FAMILY TOGETHER.
ARE YOU OKAY?

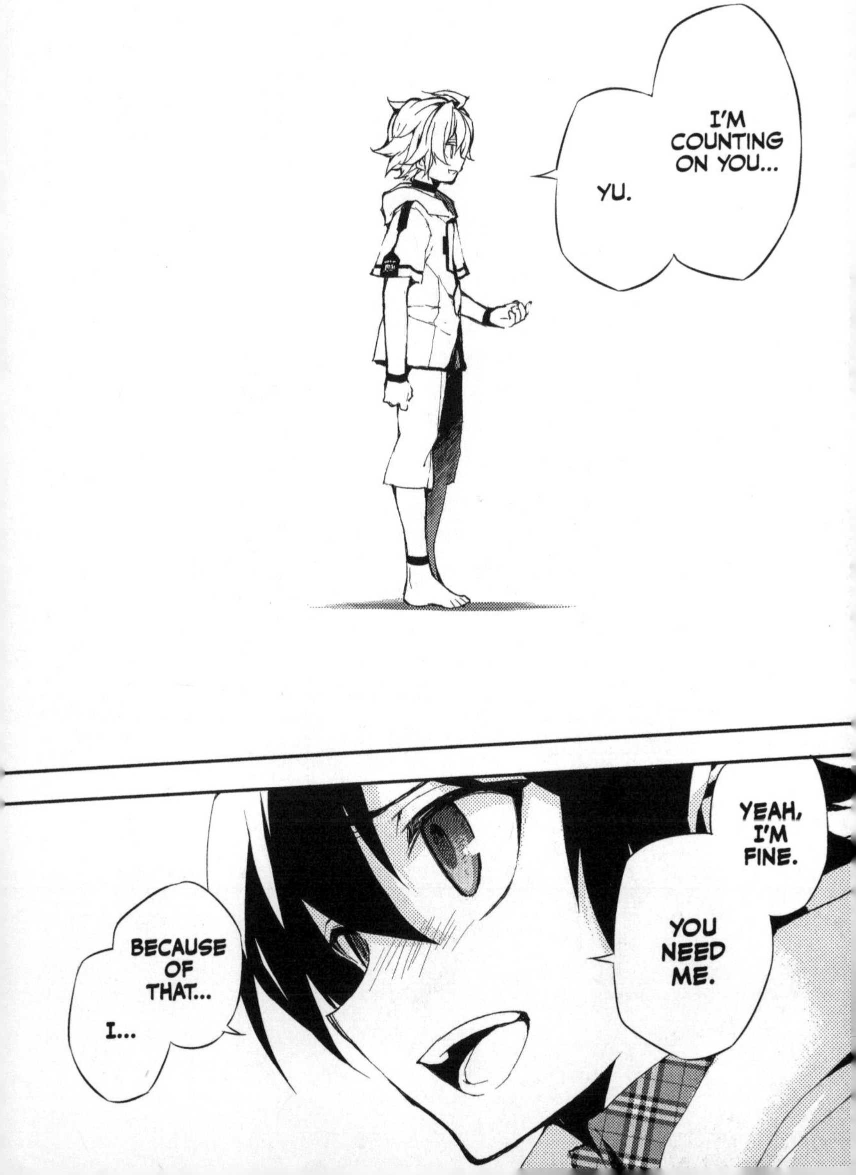
I'M COUNTING ON YOU... YU.
YEAH, I'M FINE.
YOU NEED ME.
BECAUSE OF THAT...
I...

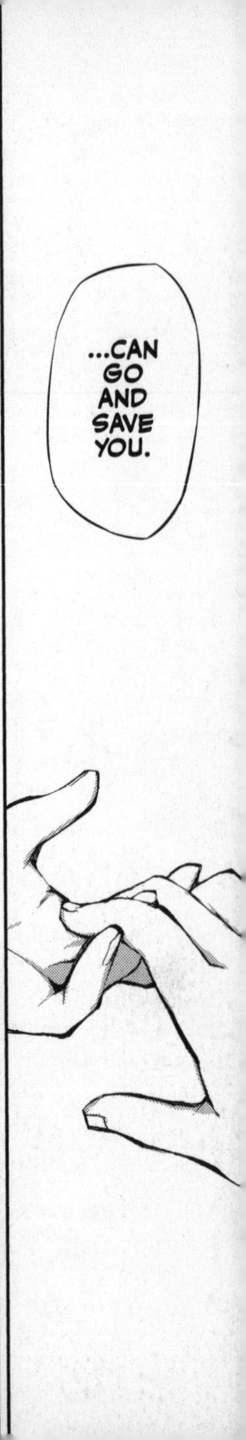
...CAN GO AND SAVE YOU.

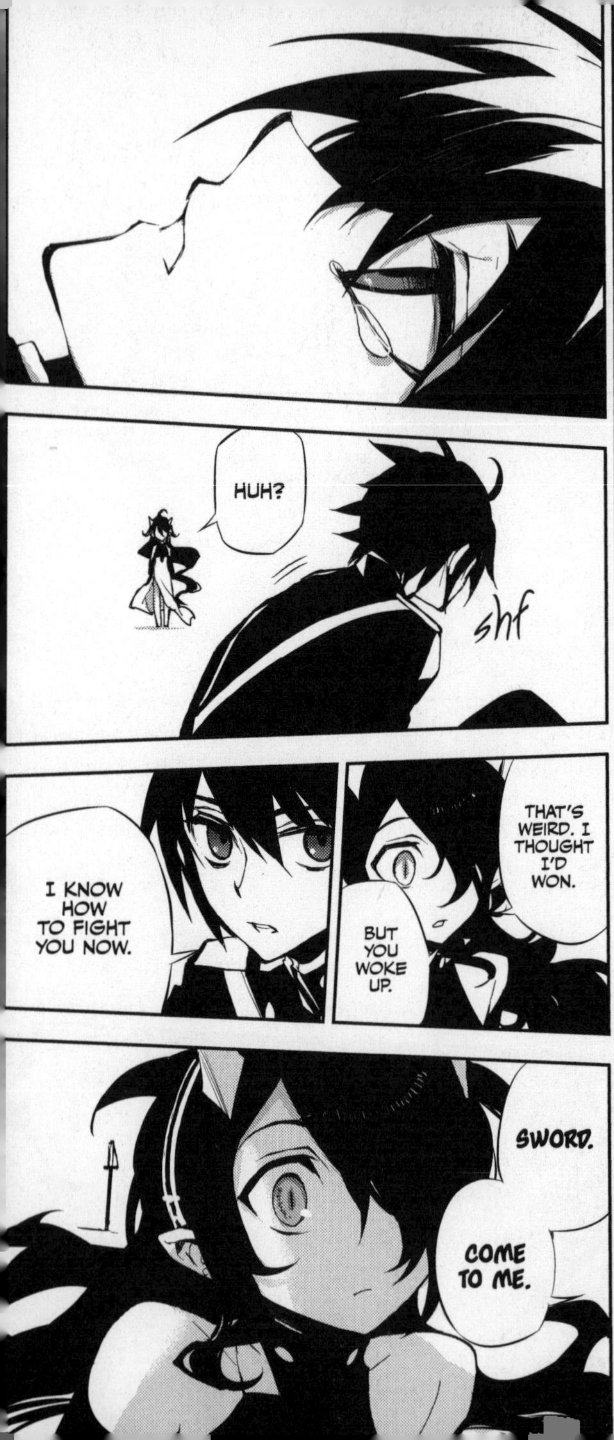
HUH?
shf
THAT'S WEIRD. I THOUGHT I'D WON.
BUT YOU WOKE UP.
I KNOW HOW TO FIGHT YOU NOW.
SWORD.
COME TO ME.

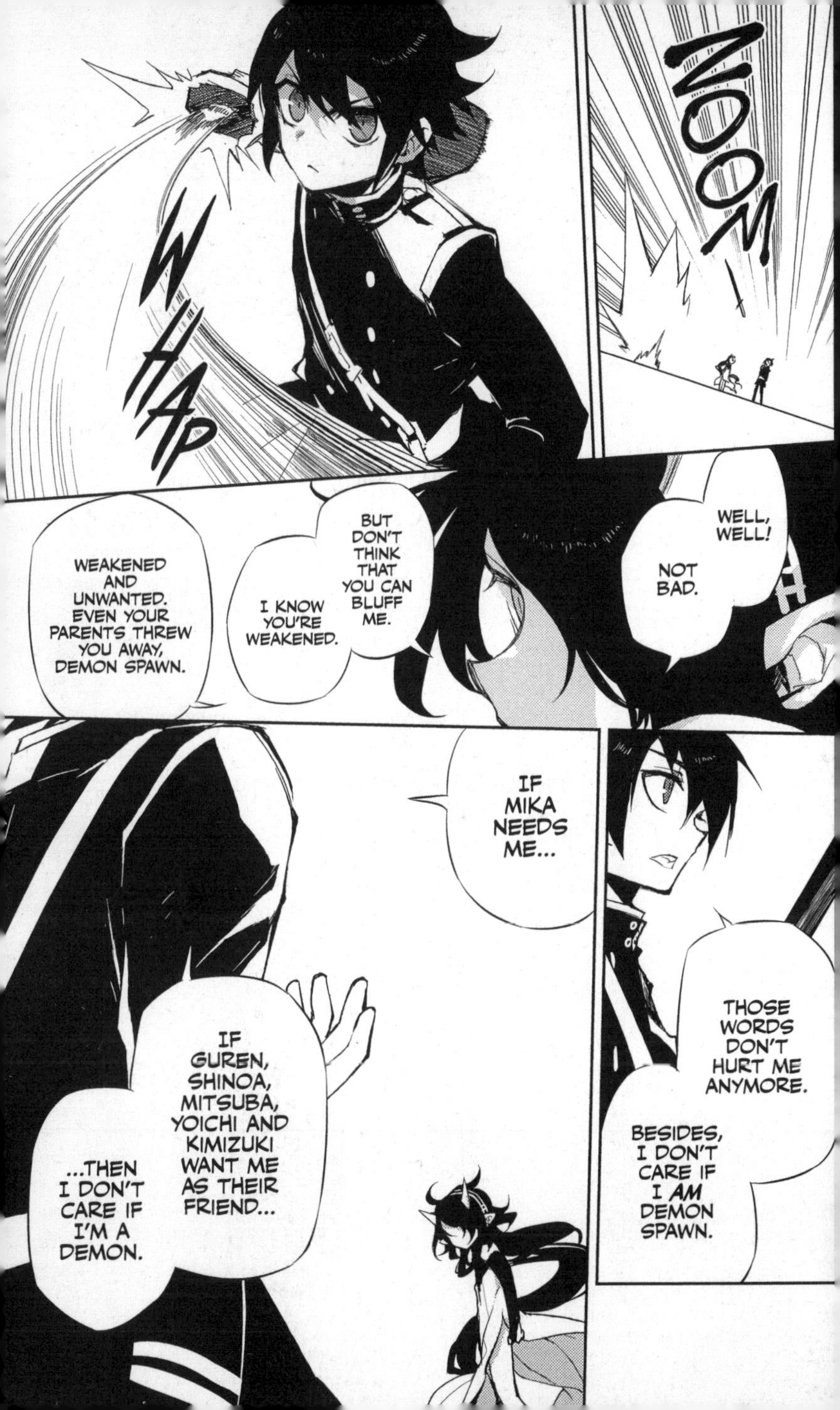
ZOOM
WHAP
WELL, WELL!
NOT BAD.
BUT DON'T THINK THAT YOU CAN BLUFF ME.
I KNOW YOU'RE WEAKENED.
WEAKENED AND UNWANTED. EVEN YOUR PARENTS THREW YOU AWAY, DEMON SPAWN.
THOSE WORDS DON'T HURT ME ANYMORE.
BESIDES, I DON'T CARE IF I *AM* DEMON SPAWN.
IF MIKA NEEDS ME...
IF GUREN, SHINOA, MITSUBA, YOICHI AND KIMIZUKI WANT ME AS THEIR FRIEND...
...THEN I DON'T CARE IF I'M A DEMON.

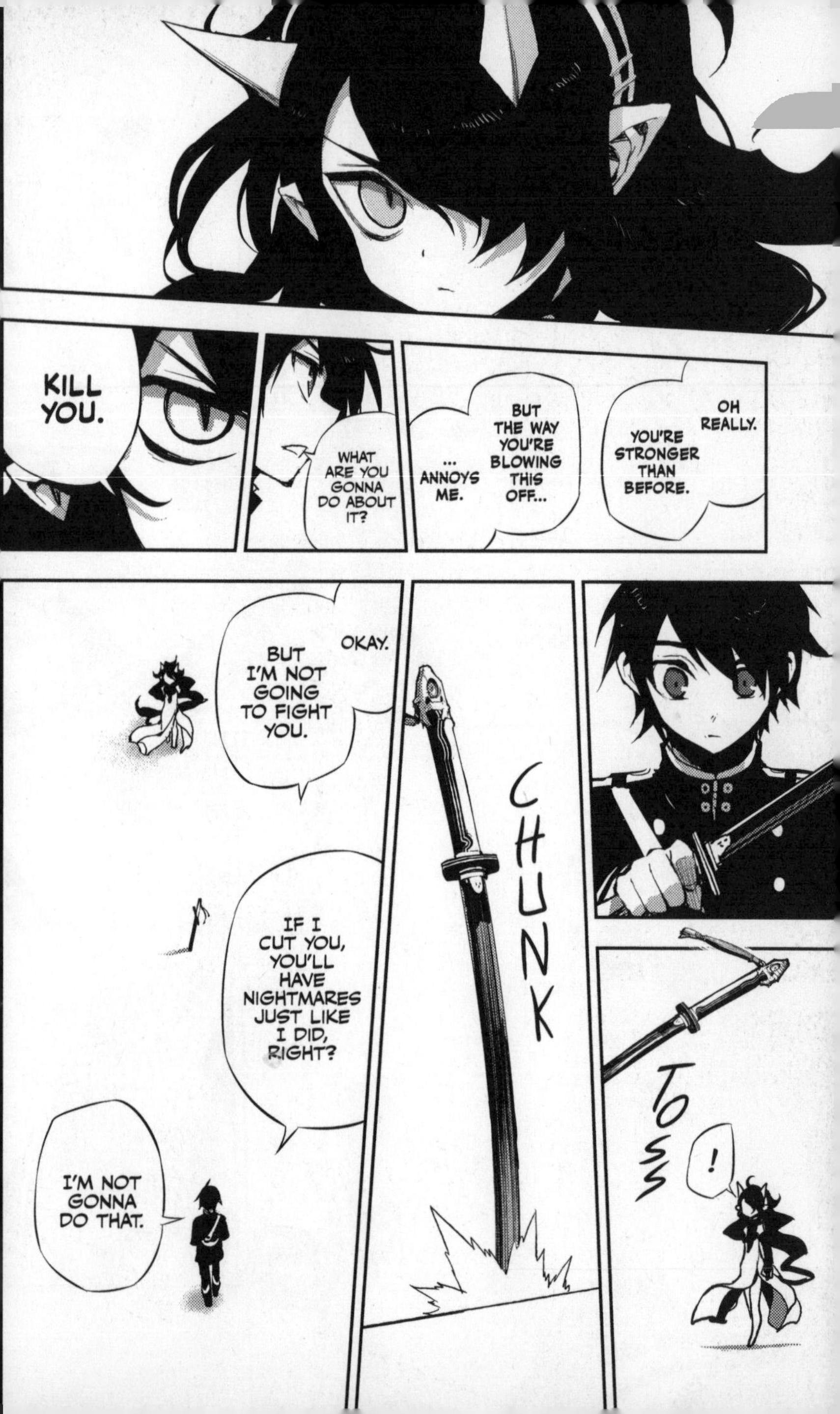
OH REALLY.
YOU'RE STRONGER THAN BEFORE.
BUT THE WAY YOU'RE BLOWING THIS OFF...
...ANNOYS ME.
WHAT ARE YOU GONNA DO ABOUT IT?
KILL YOU.
TOSS
!
CHUNK
OKAY.
BUT I'M NOT GOING TO FIGHT YOU.
IF I CUT YOU, YOU'LL HAVE NIGHTMARES JUST LIKE I DID, RIGHT?
I'M NOT GONNA DO THAT.

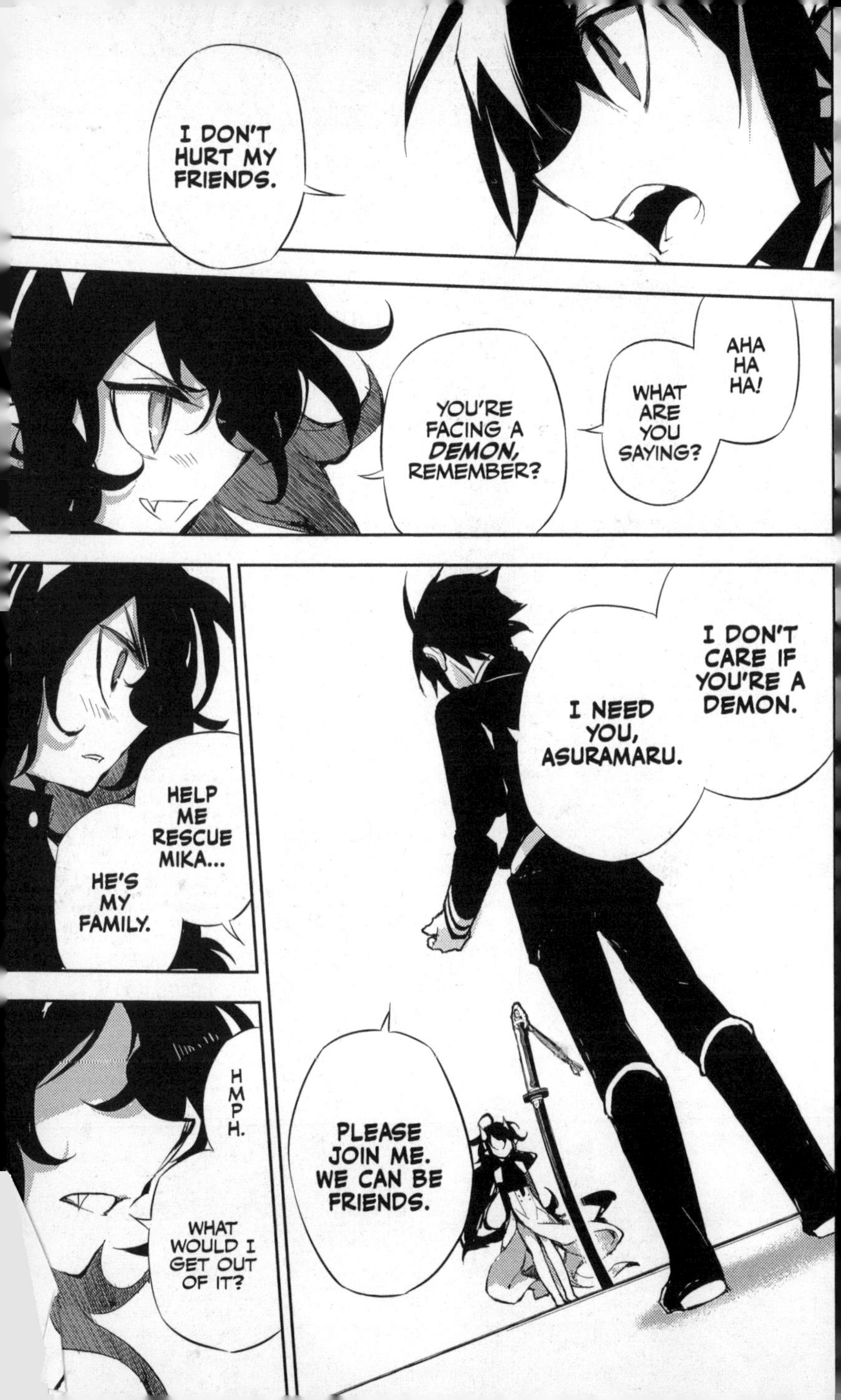
I DON'T HURT MY FRIENDS.
AHA HA HA!
WHAT ARE YOU SAYING?
YOU'RE FACING A *DEMON*, REMEMBER?
I DON'T CARE IF YOU'RE A DEMON.
I NEED YOU, ASURAMARU.
PLEASE JOIN ME. WE CAN BE FRIENDS.
HELP ME RESCUE MIKA...
HE'S MY FAMILY.
HMPH.
WHAT WOULD I GET OUT OF IT?

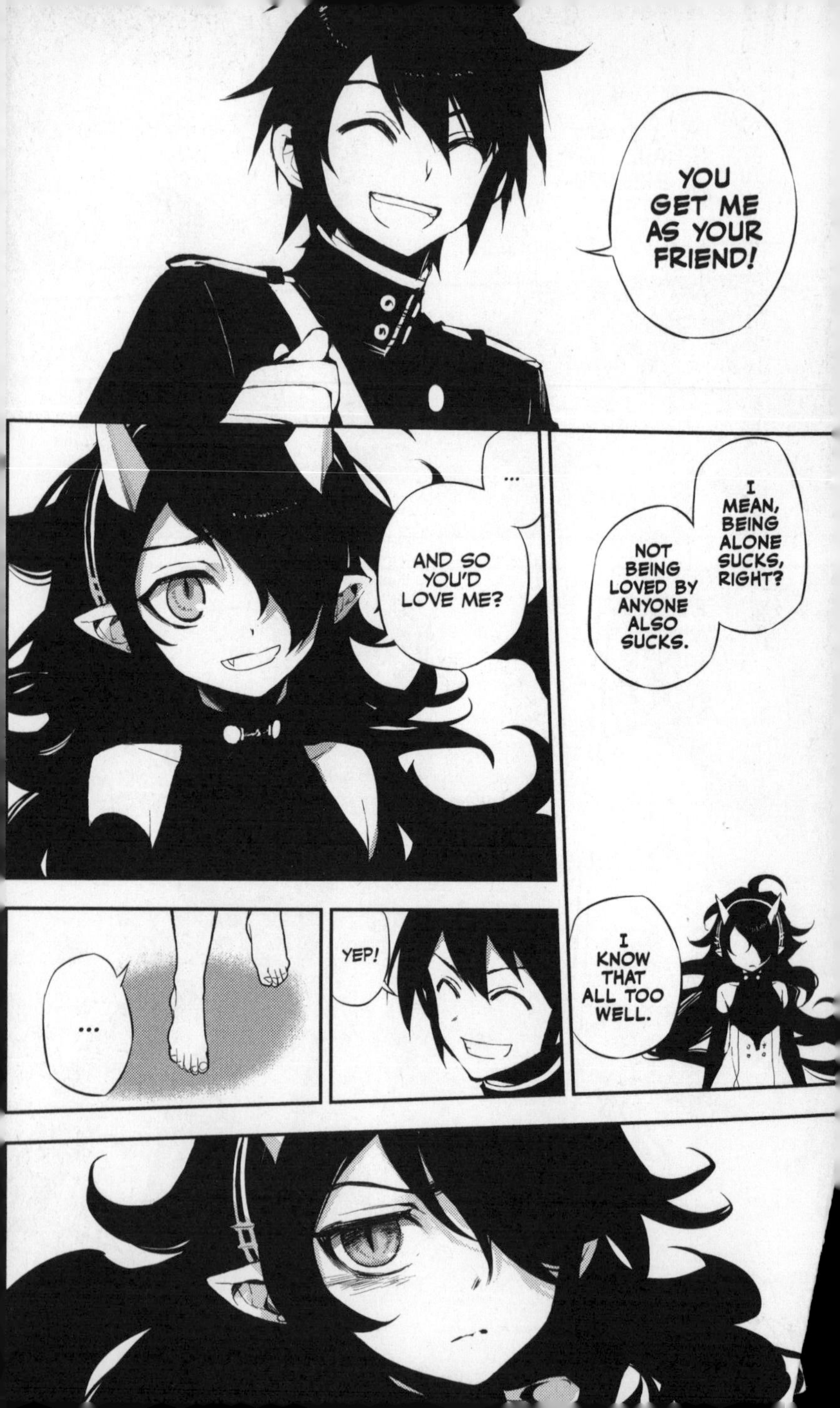
YOU GET ME AS YOUR FRIEND!
I MEAN, BEING ALONE SUCKS, RIGHT?
NOT BEING LOVED BY ANYONE ALSO SUCKS.
I KNOW THAT ALL TOO WELL.
...
AND SO YOU'D LOVE ME?
YEP!
...

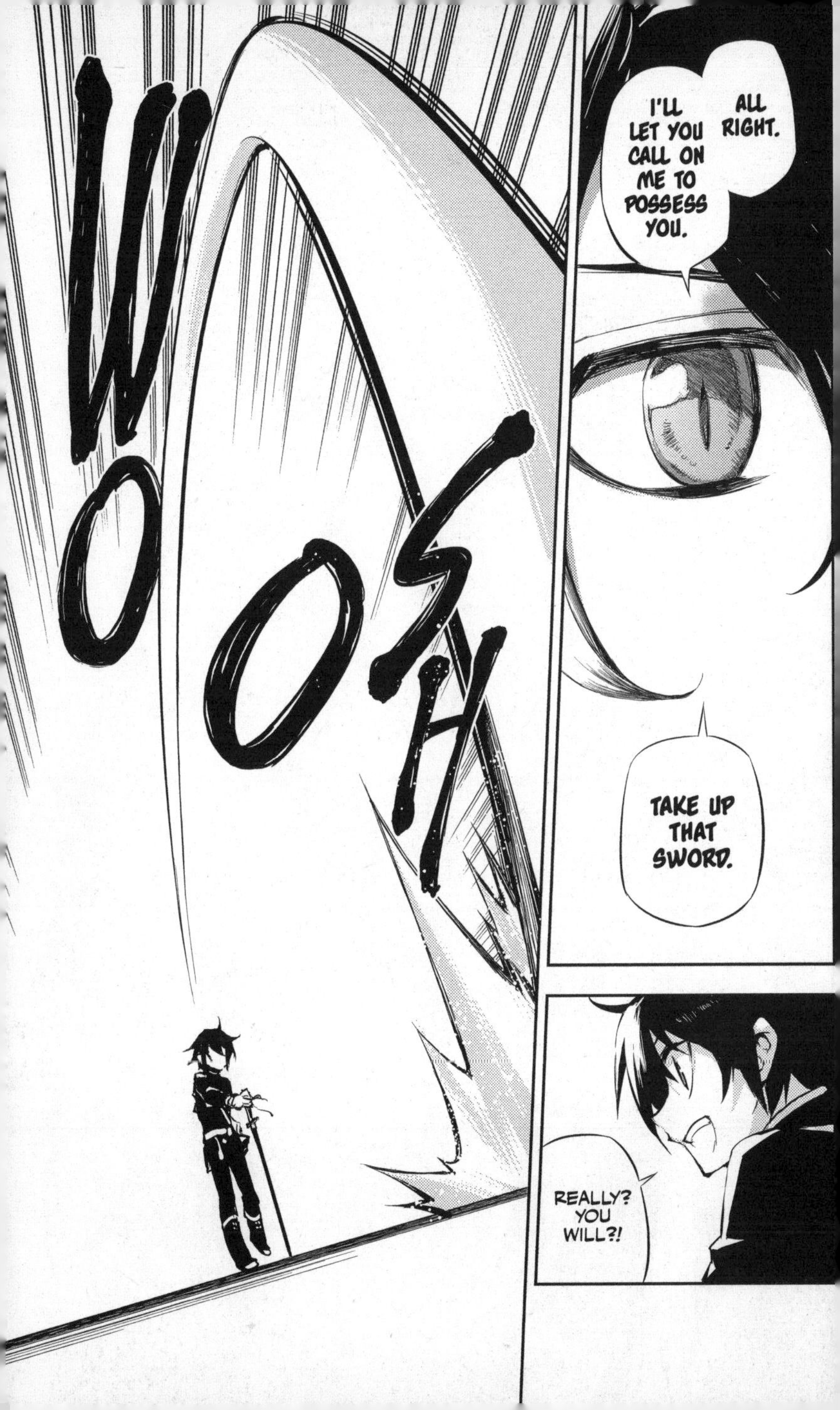
ALL RIGHT.
I'LL LET YOU CALL ON ME TO POSSESS YOU.
TAKE UP THAT SWORD.
REALLY? YOU WILL?!
WOOSH

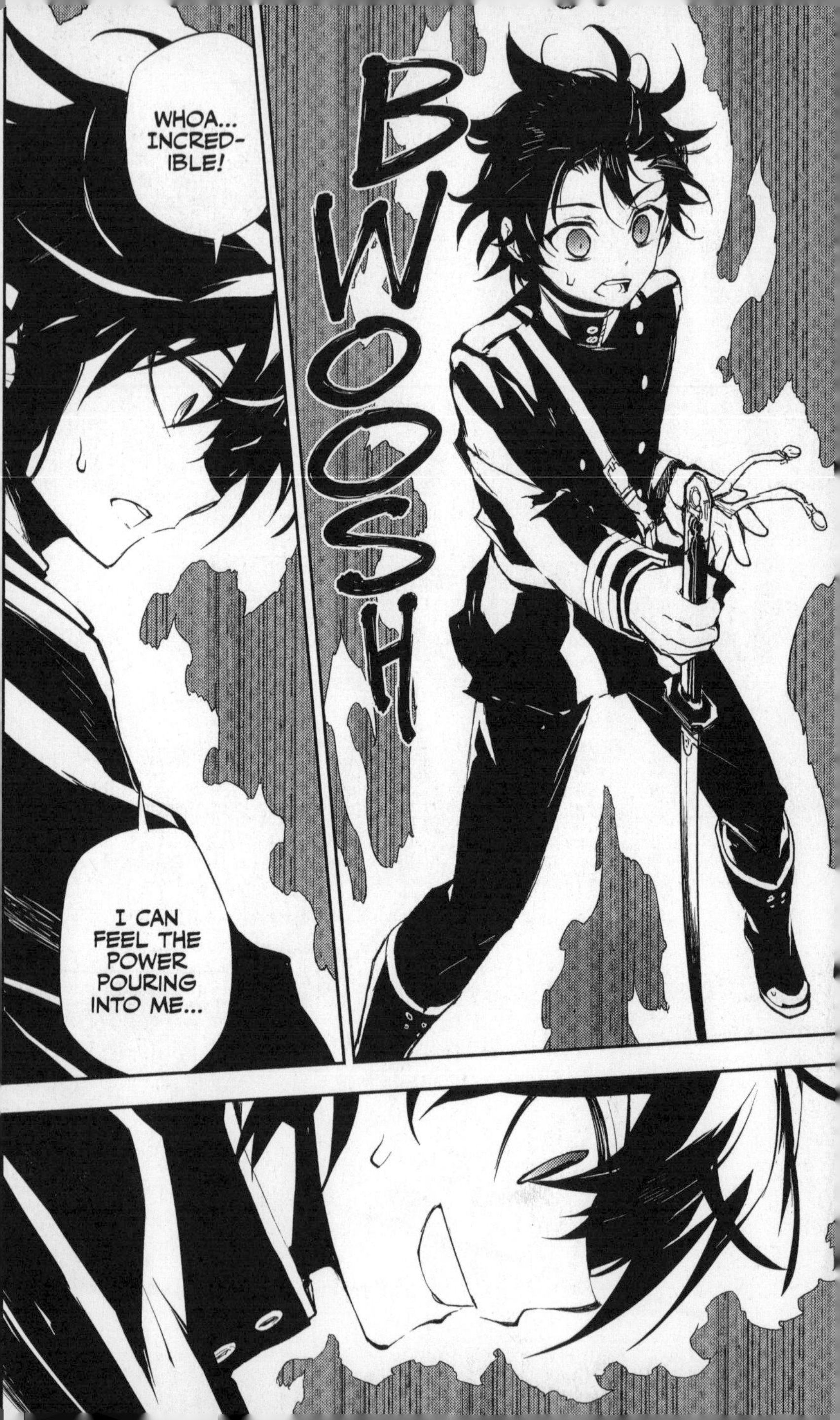
BWOOSH
WHOA... INCRED-IBLE!
I CAN FEEL THE POWER POURING INTO ME...

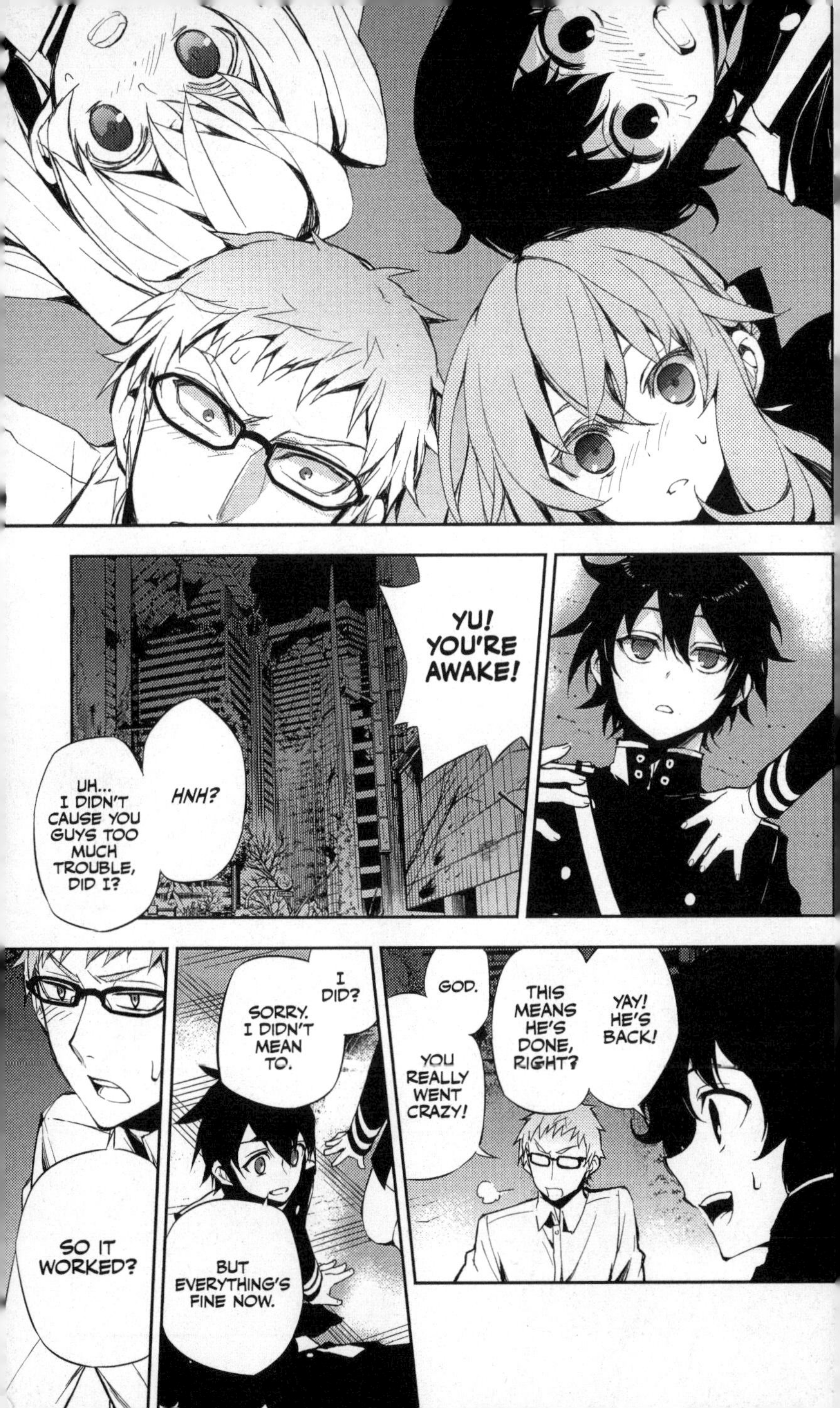
YU! YOU'RE AWAKE!
HNH?
UH... I DIDN'T CAUSE YOU GUYS TOO MUCH TROUBLE, DID I?
YAY! HE'S BACK!
THIS MEANS HE'S DONE, RIGHT?
GOD.
YOU REALLY WENT CRAZY!
I DID?
SORRY. I DIDN'T MEAN TO.
BUT EVERYTHING'S FINE NOW.
SO IT WORKED?

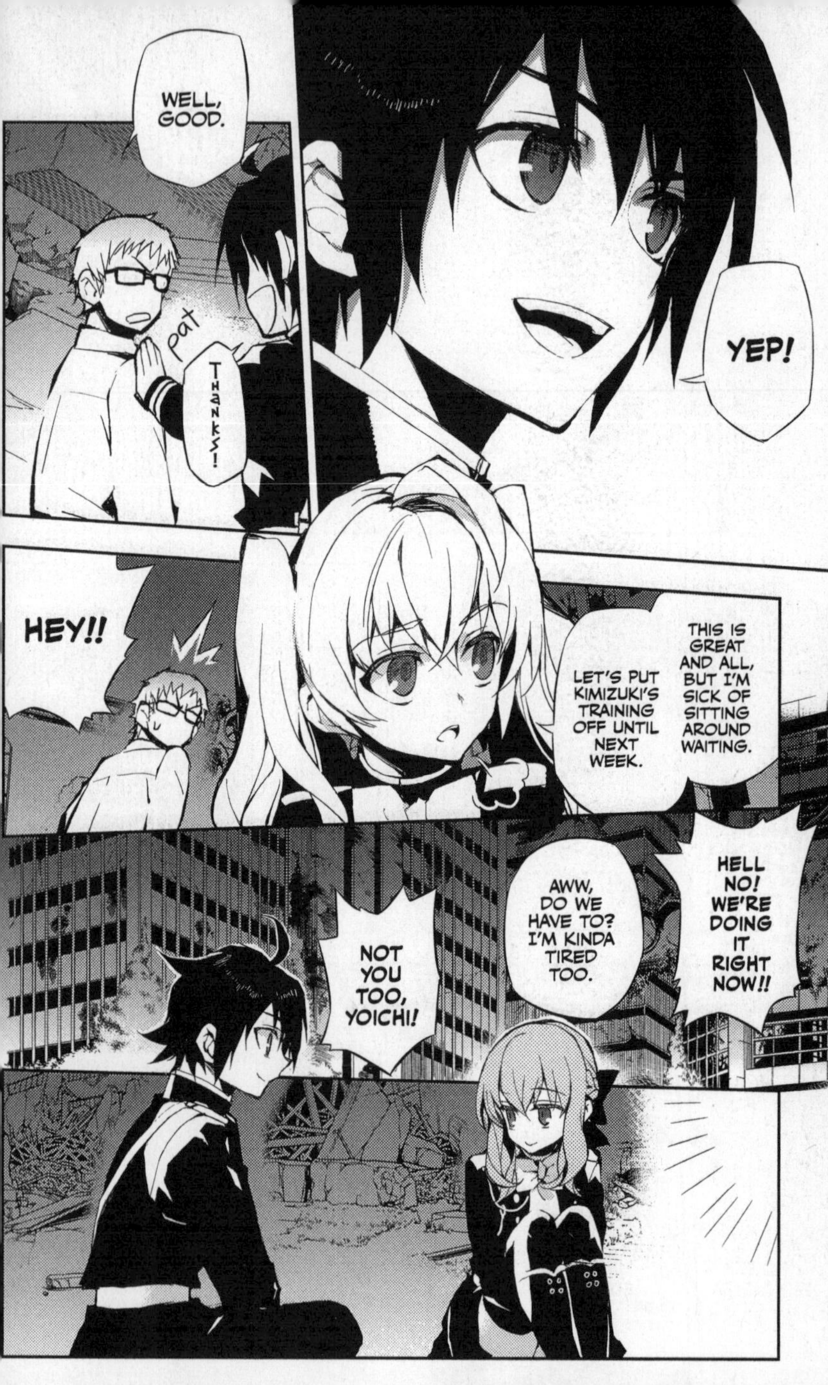
YEP!
WELL, GOOD.
pat
Thanks!
THIS IS GREAT AND ALL, BUT I'M SICK OF SITTING AROUND WAITING.
LET'S PUT KIMIZUKI'S TRAINING OFF UNTIL NEXT WEEK.
HEY!!
HELL NO! WE'RE DOING IT RIGHT NOW!!
AWW, DO WE HAVE TO? I'M KINDA TIRED TOO.
NOT YOU TOO, YOICHI!

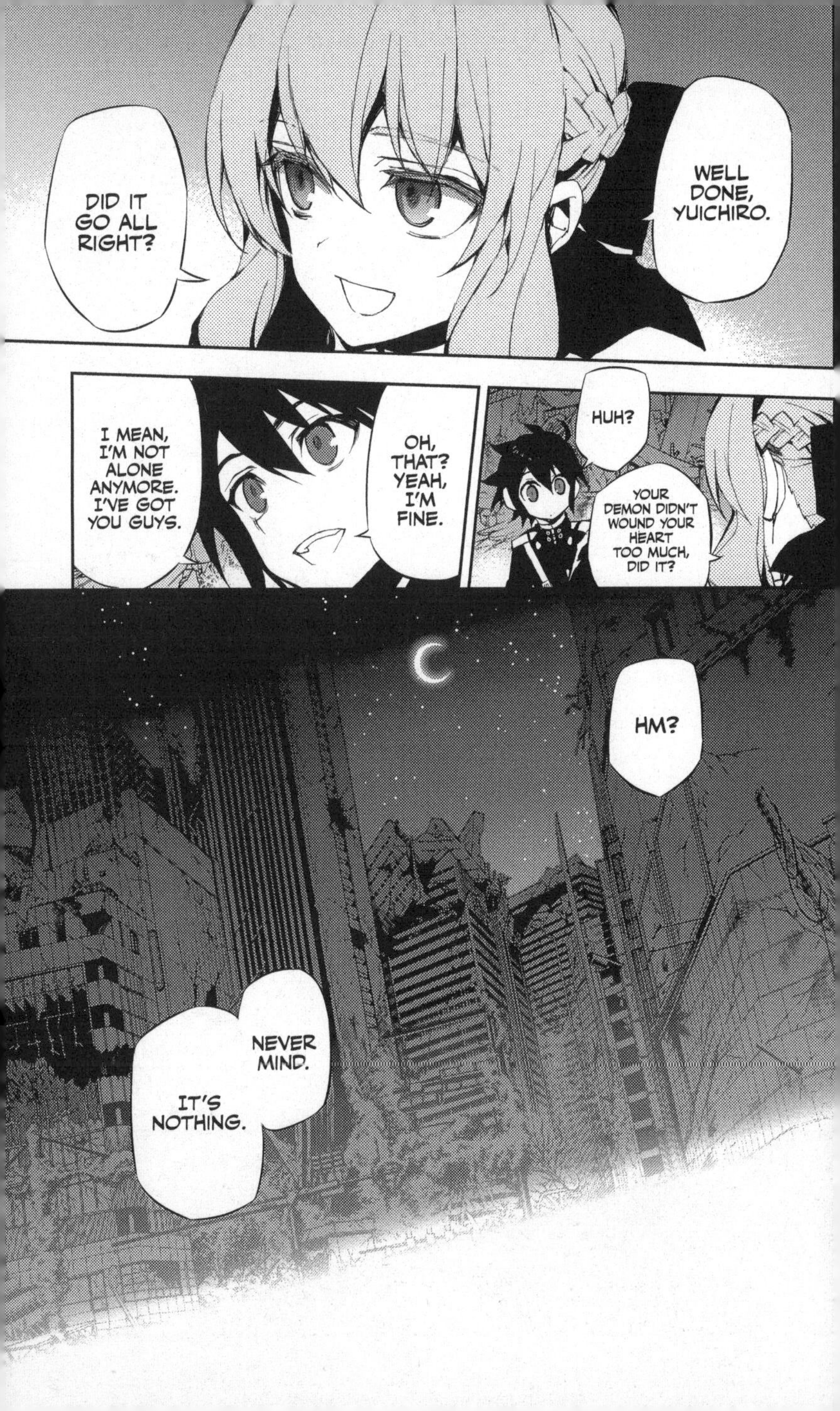
WELL DONE, YUICHIRO.
DID IT GO ALL RIGHT?
HUH?
YOUR DEMON DIDN'T WOUND YOUR HEART TOO MUCH, DID IT?
OH, THAT? YEAH, I'M FINE.
I MEAN, I'M NOT ALONE ANYMORE. I'VE GOT YOU GUYS.
HM?
NEVER MIND.
IT'S NOTHING.

Seraph of the End
—VAMPIRE REIGN—

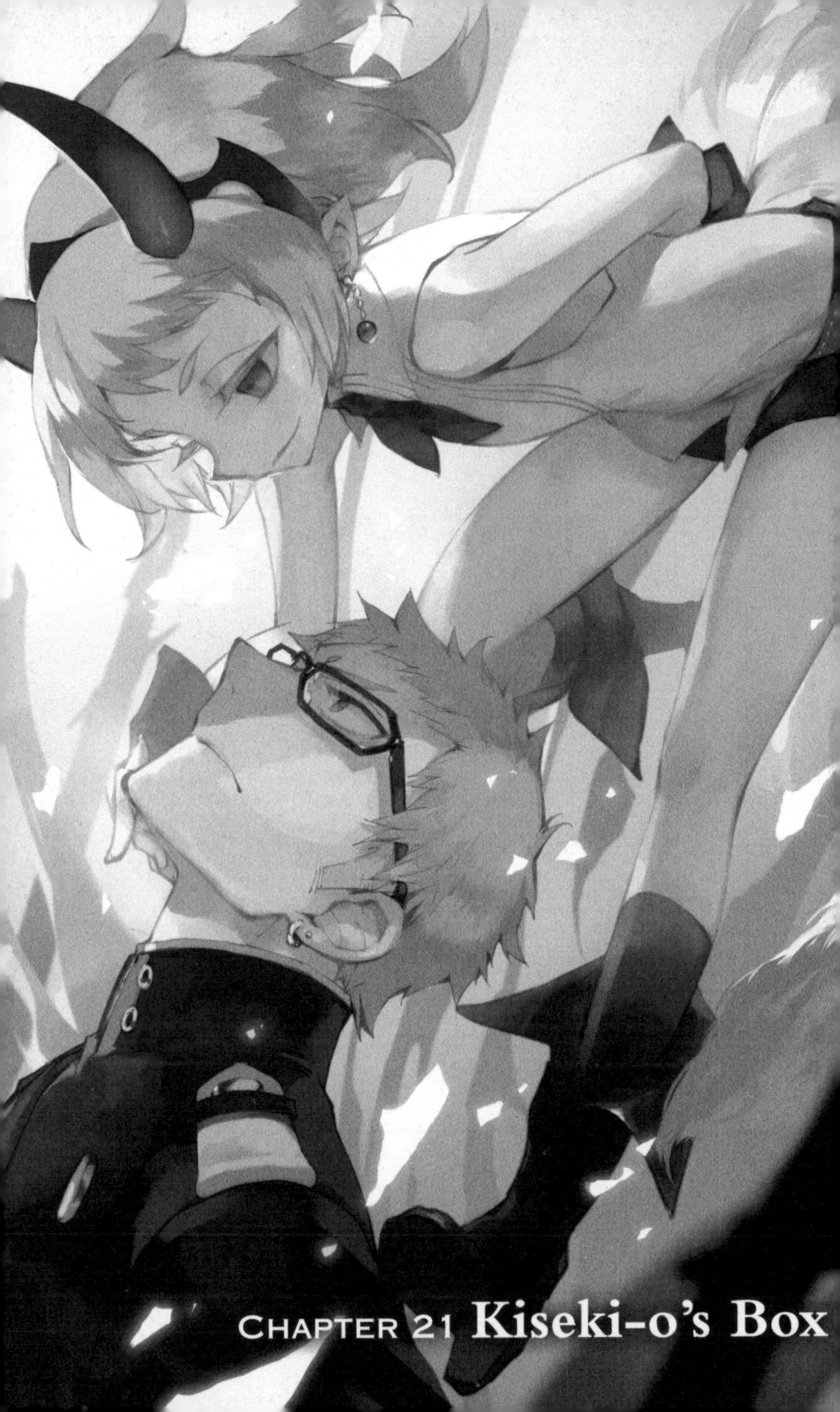

CHAPTER 21 Kiseki-o's Box

Seraph of the End
VAMPIRE REIGN

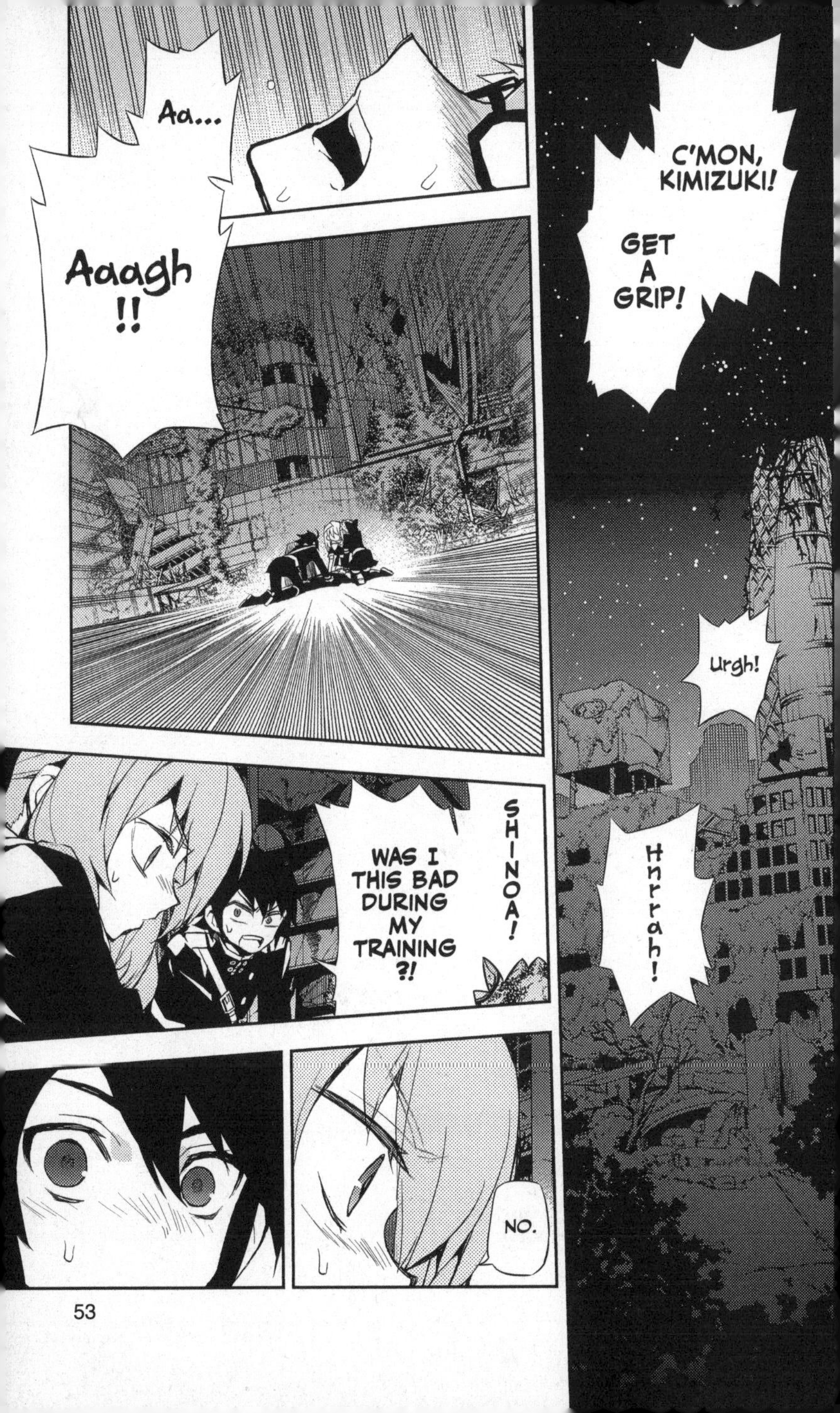
C'MON, KIMIZUKI!
GET A GRIP!
Urgh!
Hnrrah!
Aa...
Aaagh!!
SHINOA!
WAS I THIS BAD DURING MY TRAINING?!
NO.

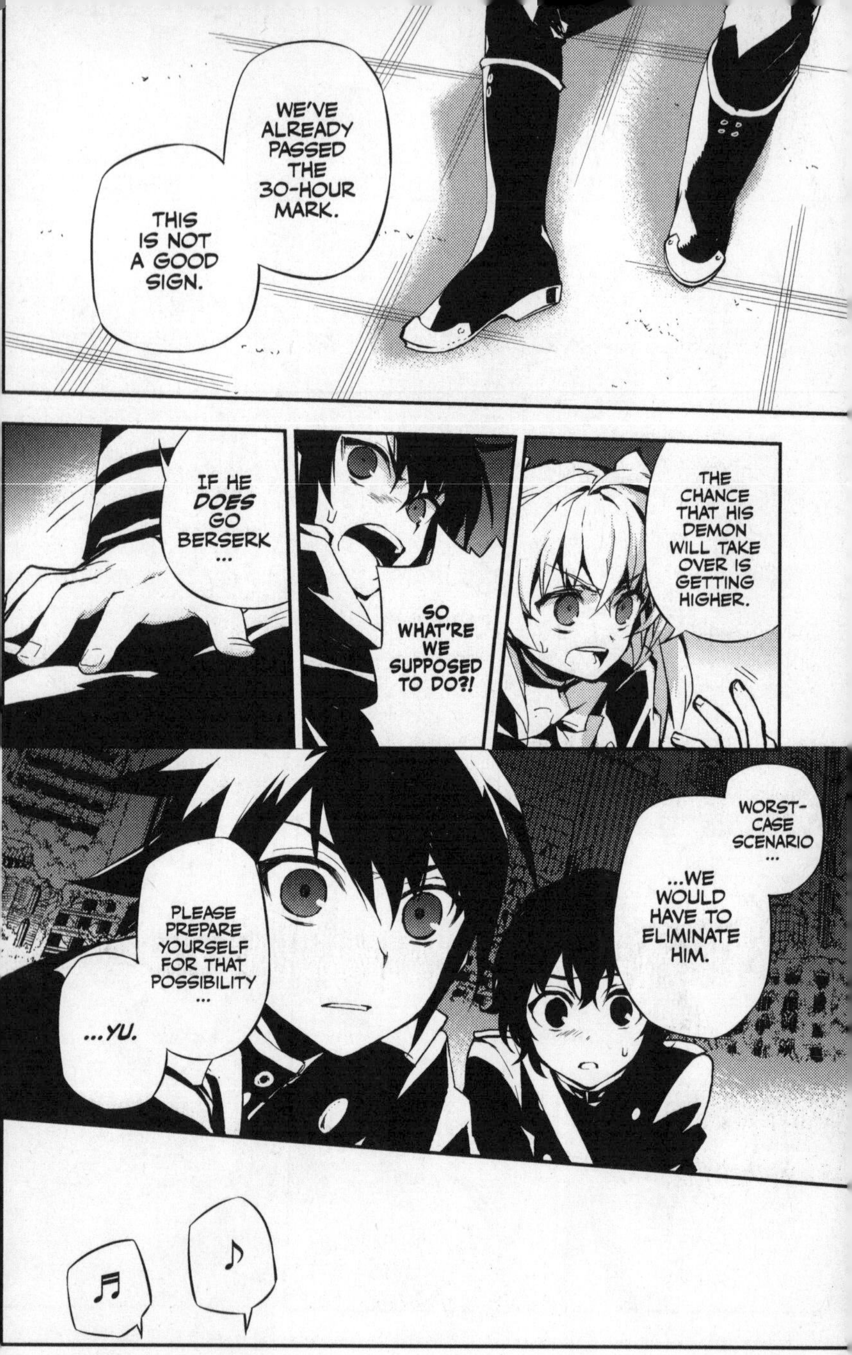
WE'VE ALREADY PASSED THE 30-HOUR MARK.
THIS IS NOT A GOOD SIGN.
THE CHANCE THAT HIS DEMON WILL TAKE OVER IS GETTING HIGHER.
SO WHAT'RE WE SUPPOSED TO DO?!
IF HE *DOES* GO BERSERK...
WORST-CASE SCENARIO...
...WE WOULD HAVE TO ELIMINATE HIM.
PLEASE PREPARE YOURSELF FOR THAT POSSIBILITY...
...YU.
♪
♬

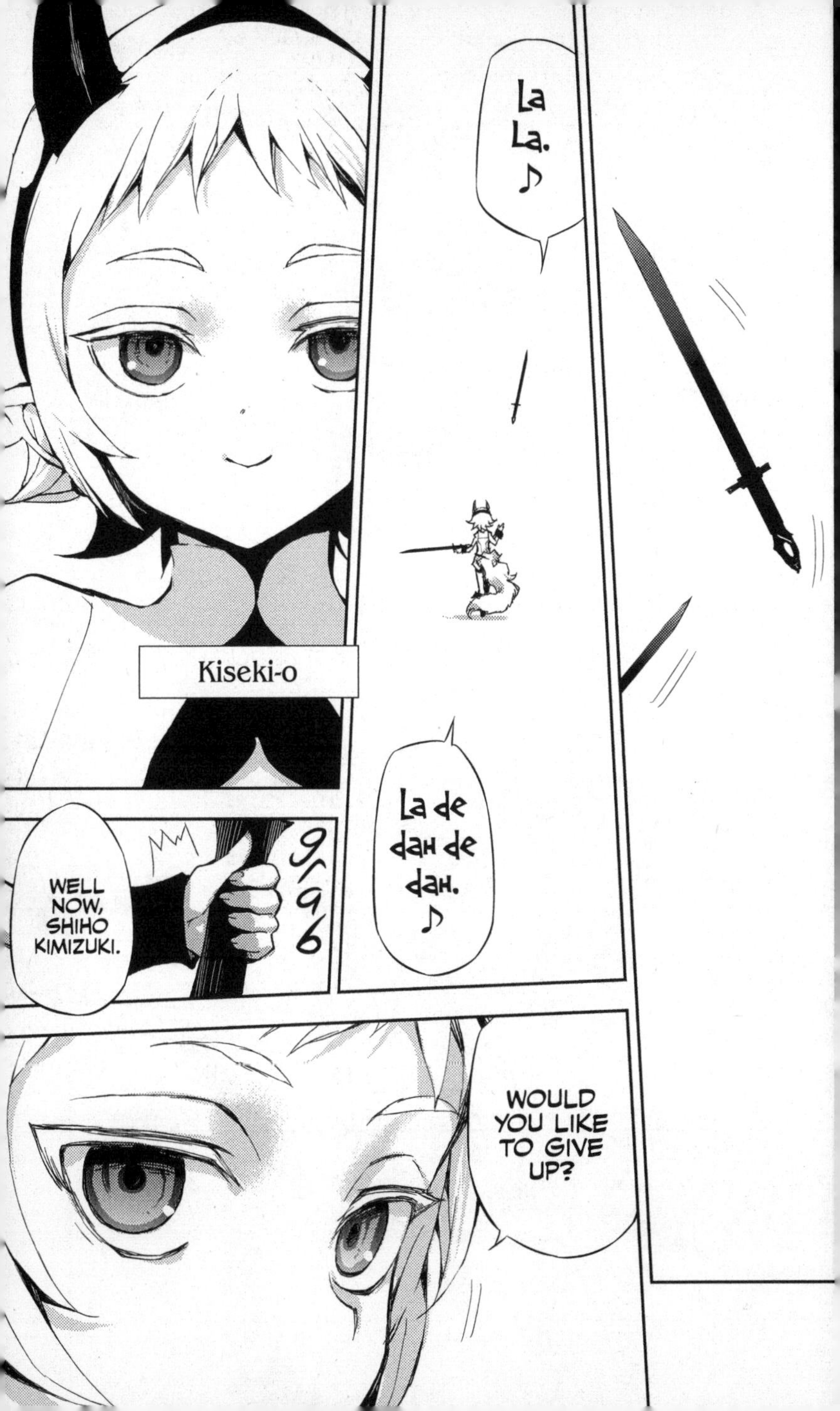
La La. ♪
La de dah de dah. ♪
Kiseki-o
WELL NOW, SHIHO KIMIZUKI.
WOULD YOU LIKE TO GIVE UP?

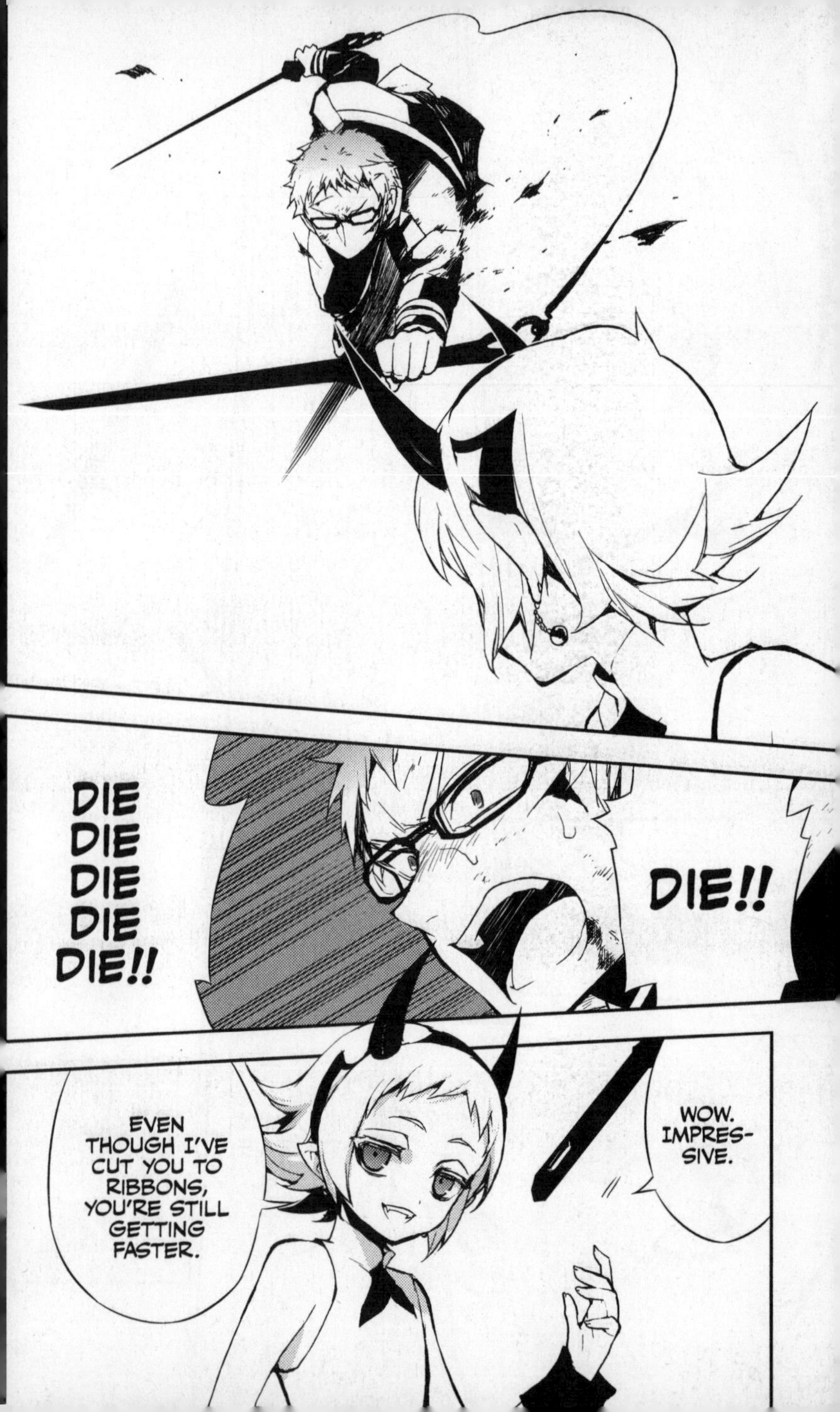
DIE!!
DIE DIE DIE DIE DIE!!
WOW. IMPRES-SIVE.
EVEN THOUGH I'VE CUT YOU TO RIBBONS, YOU'RE STILL GETTING FASTER.

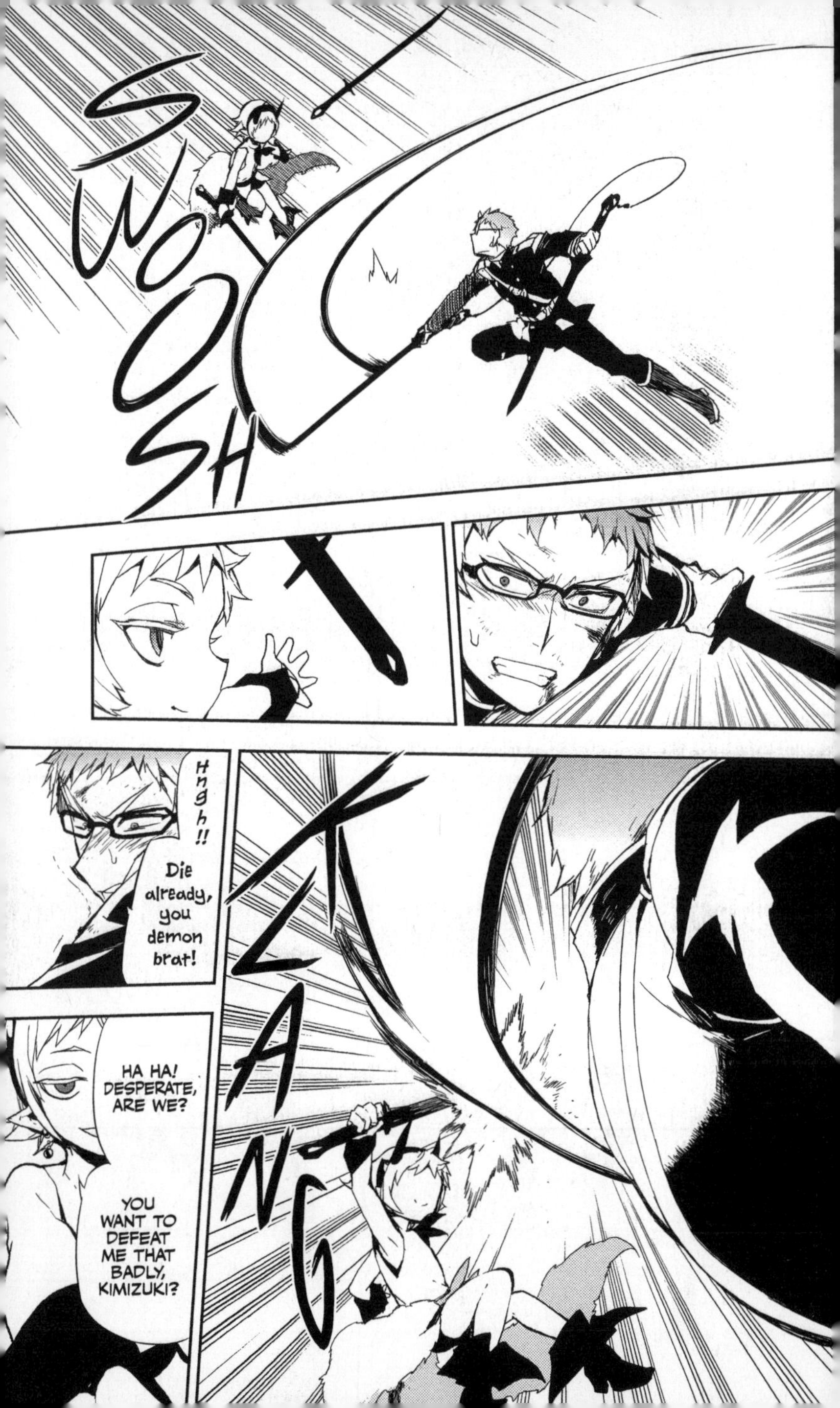
SWOOSH
KLANG
Hngh!!
Die already, you demon brat!
HA HA! DESPERATE, ARE WE?
YOU WANT TO DEFEAT ME THAT BADLY, KIMIZUKI?

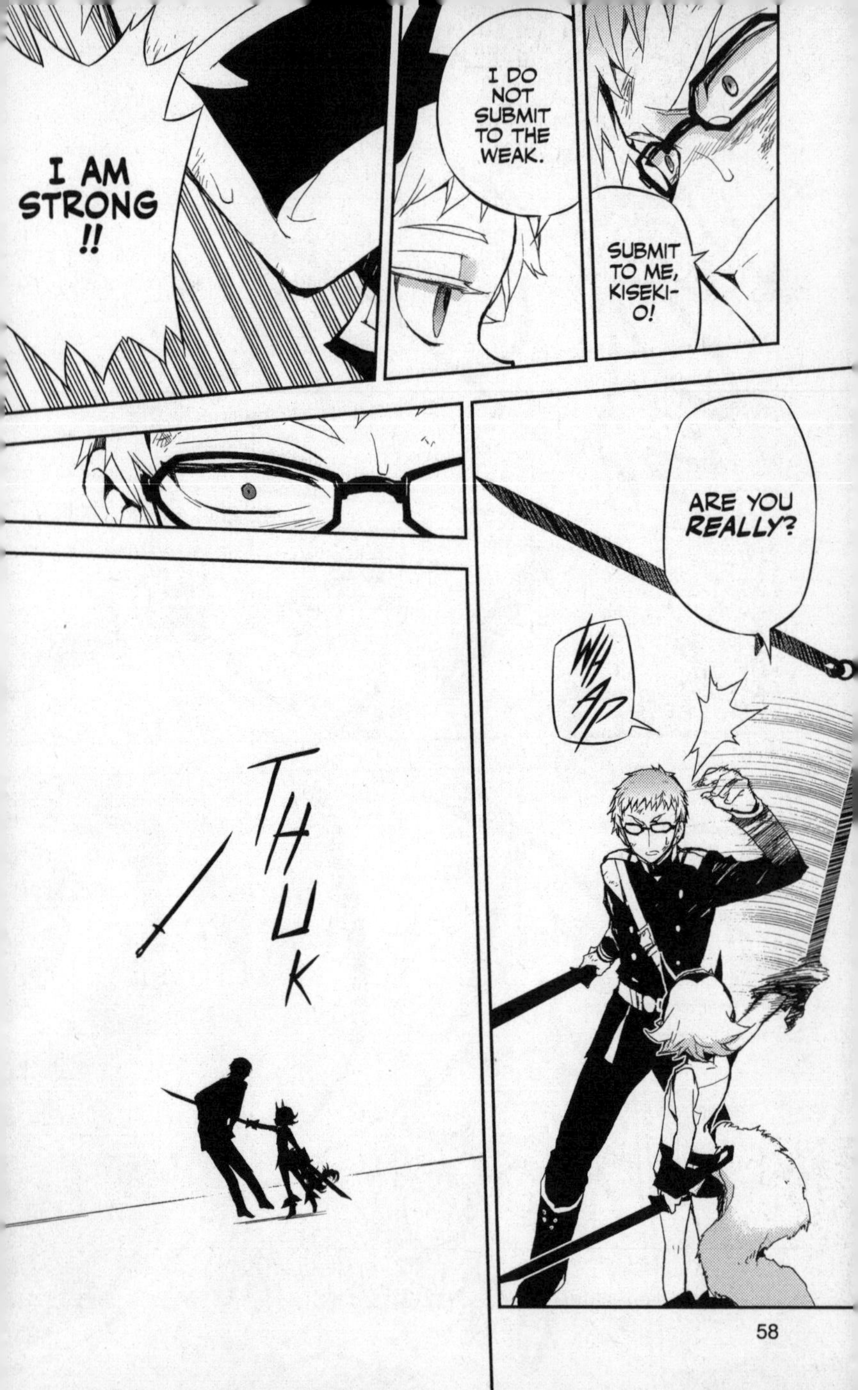
SUBMIT TO ME, KISEKI-O!
I DO NOT SUBMIT TO THE WEAK.
I AM STRONG!!
ARE YOU *REALLY*?
WHAP
THUK

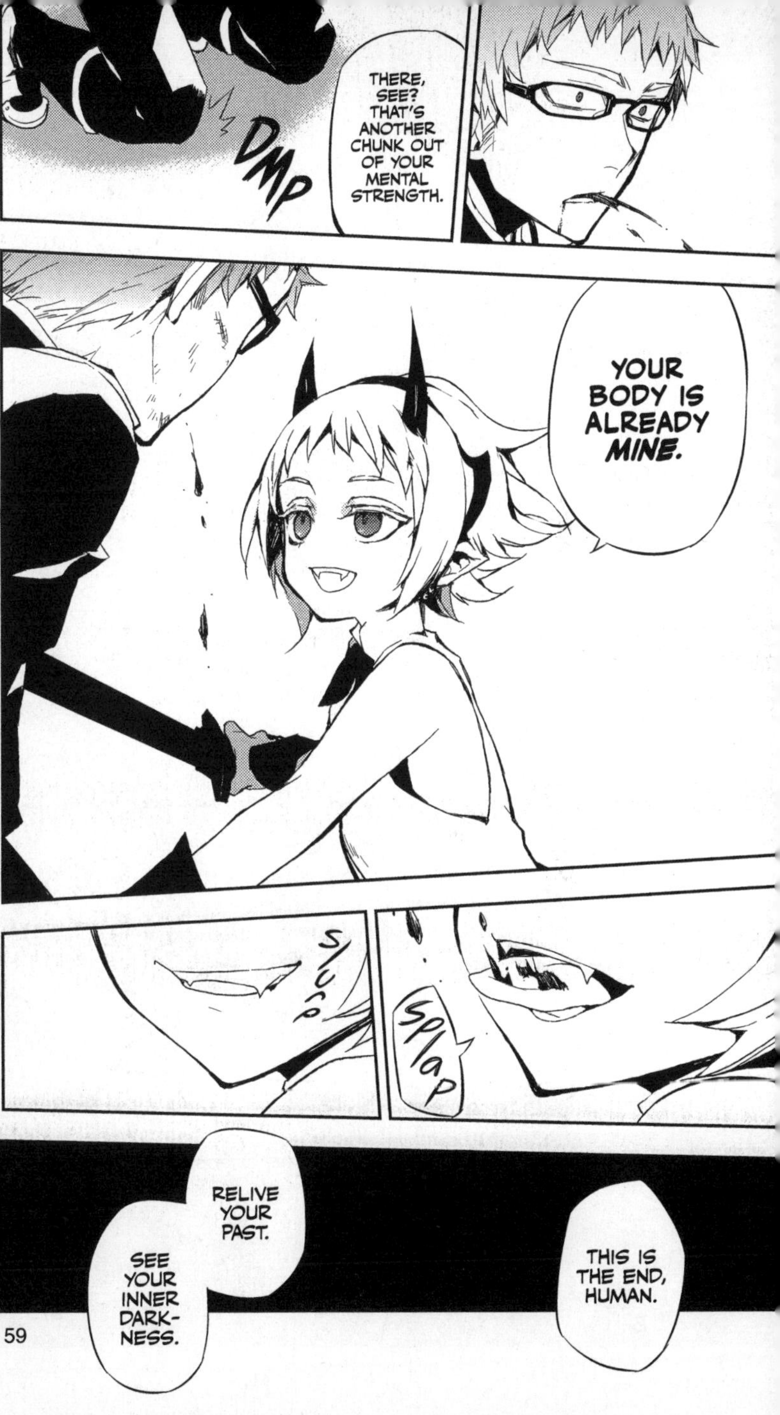
THERE, SEE? THAT'S ANOTHER CHUNK OUT OF YOUR MENTAL STRENGTH.
DMP
YOUR BODY IS ALREADY *MINE.*
Splap
Slurp
THIS IS THE END, HUMAN.
RELIVE YOUR PAST.
SEE YOUR INNER DARK-NESS.

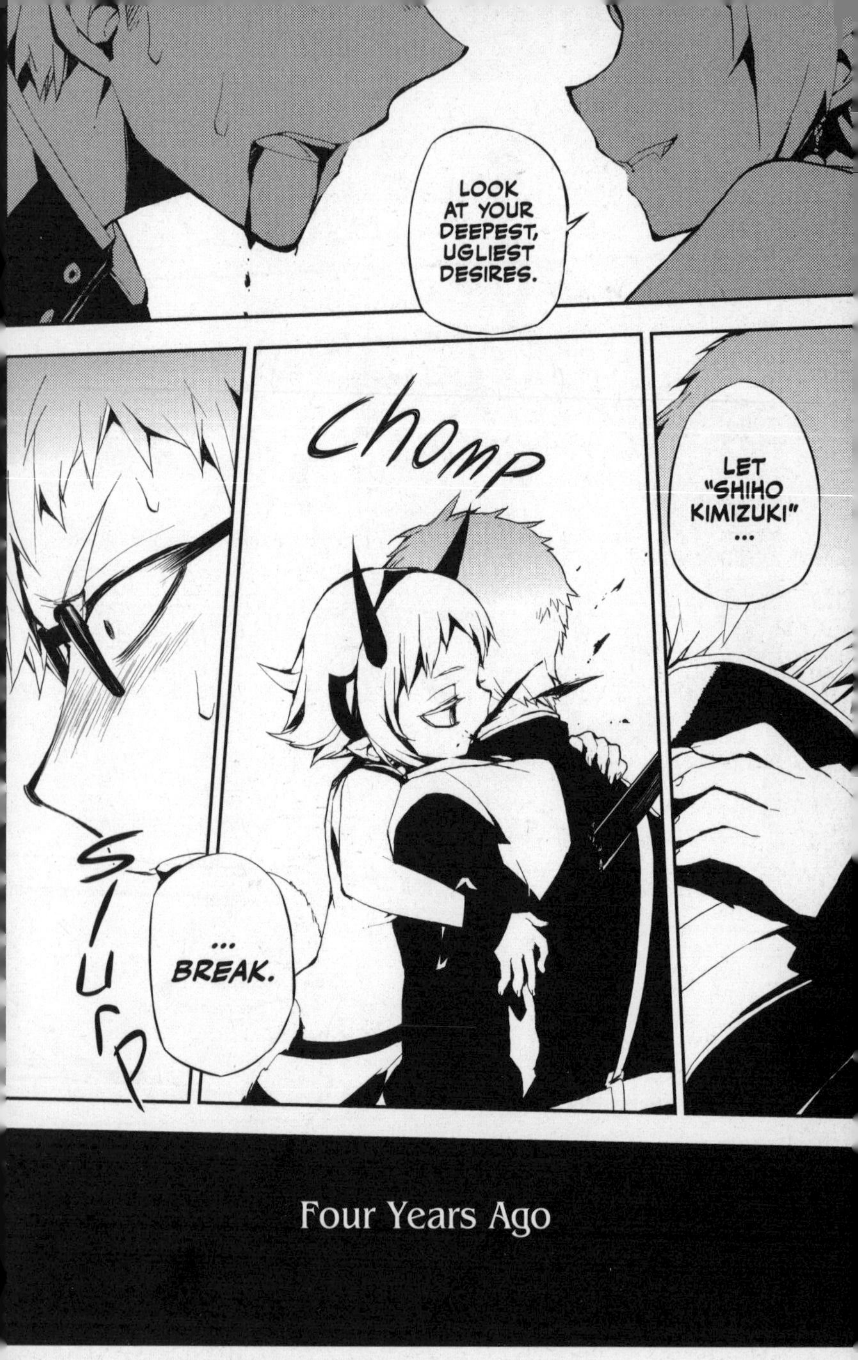
LOOK AT YOUR DEEPEST, UGLIEST DESIRES.
LET "SHIHO KIMIZUKI" ...
CHOMP
SLURP
... BREAK.

Four Years Ago

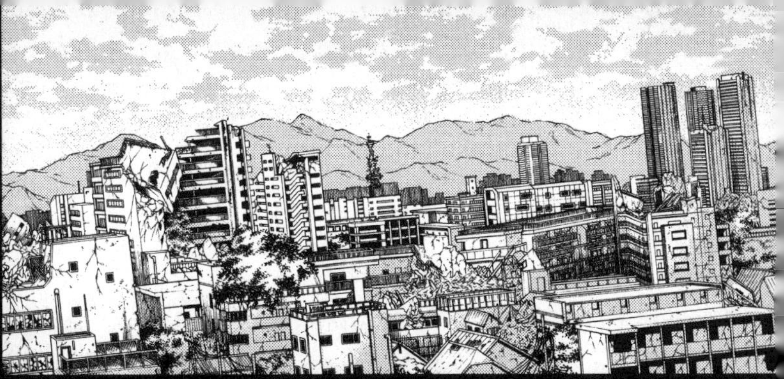

A Prefectural City

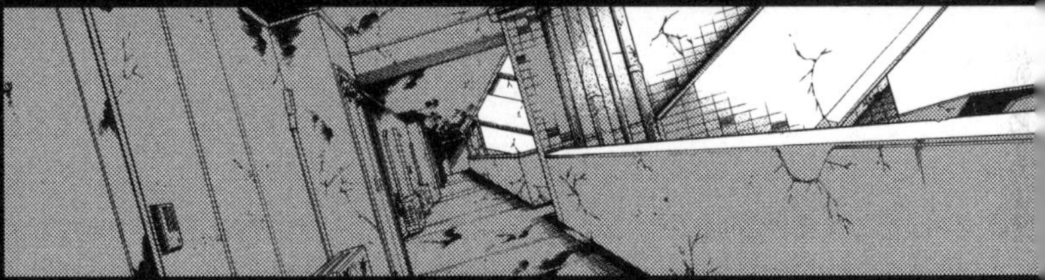

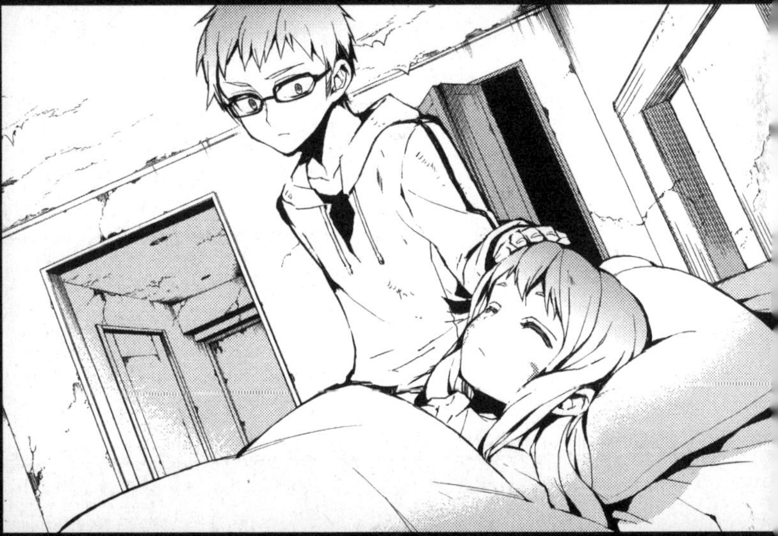

Kimizuki, 11 Years Old

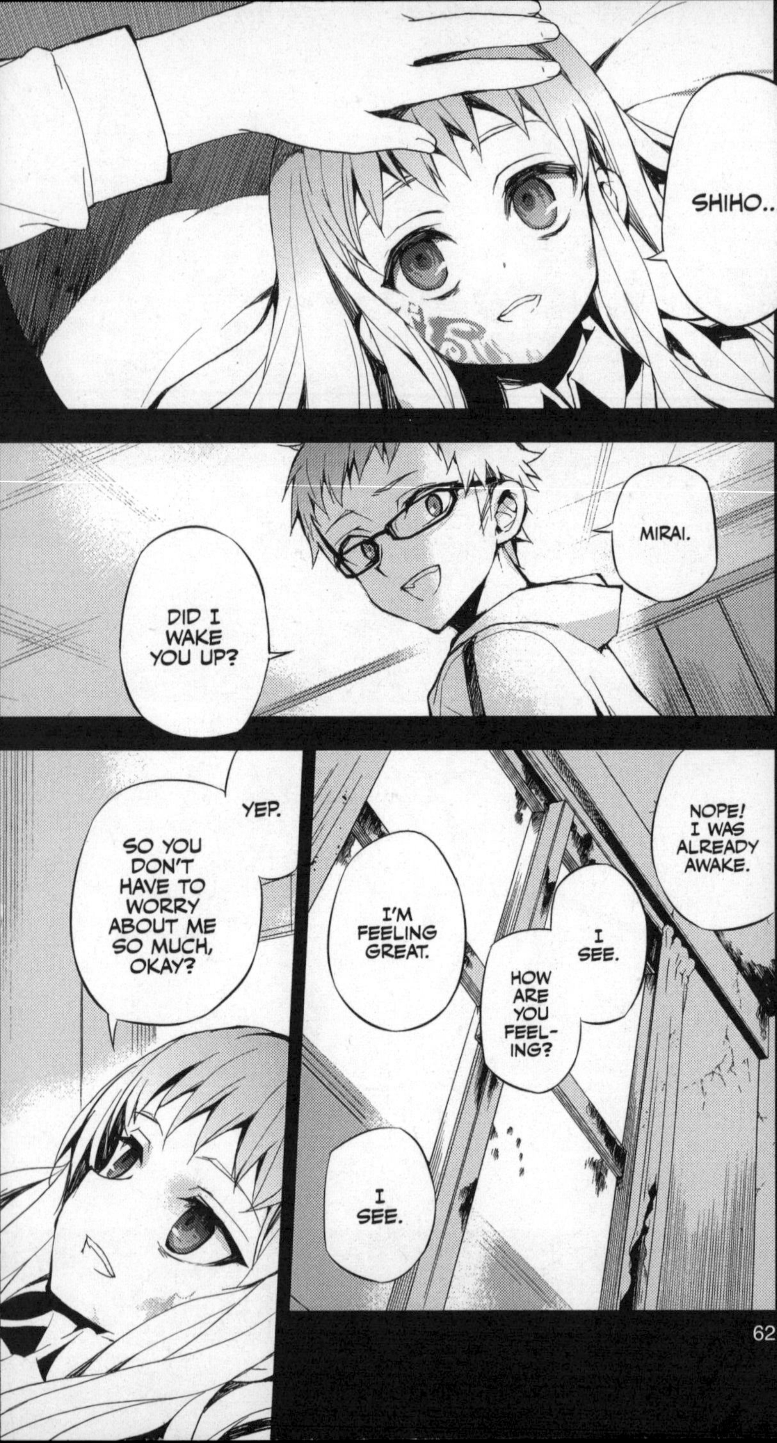
SHIHO...
MIRAI.
DID I WAKE YOU UP?
NOPE! I WAS ALREADY AWAKE.
I SEE.
HOW ARE YOU FEEL-ING?
I'M FEELING GREAT.
I SEE.
YEP.
SO YOU DON'T HAVE TO WORRY ABOUT ME SO MUCH, OKAY?

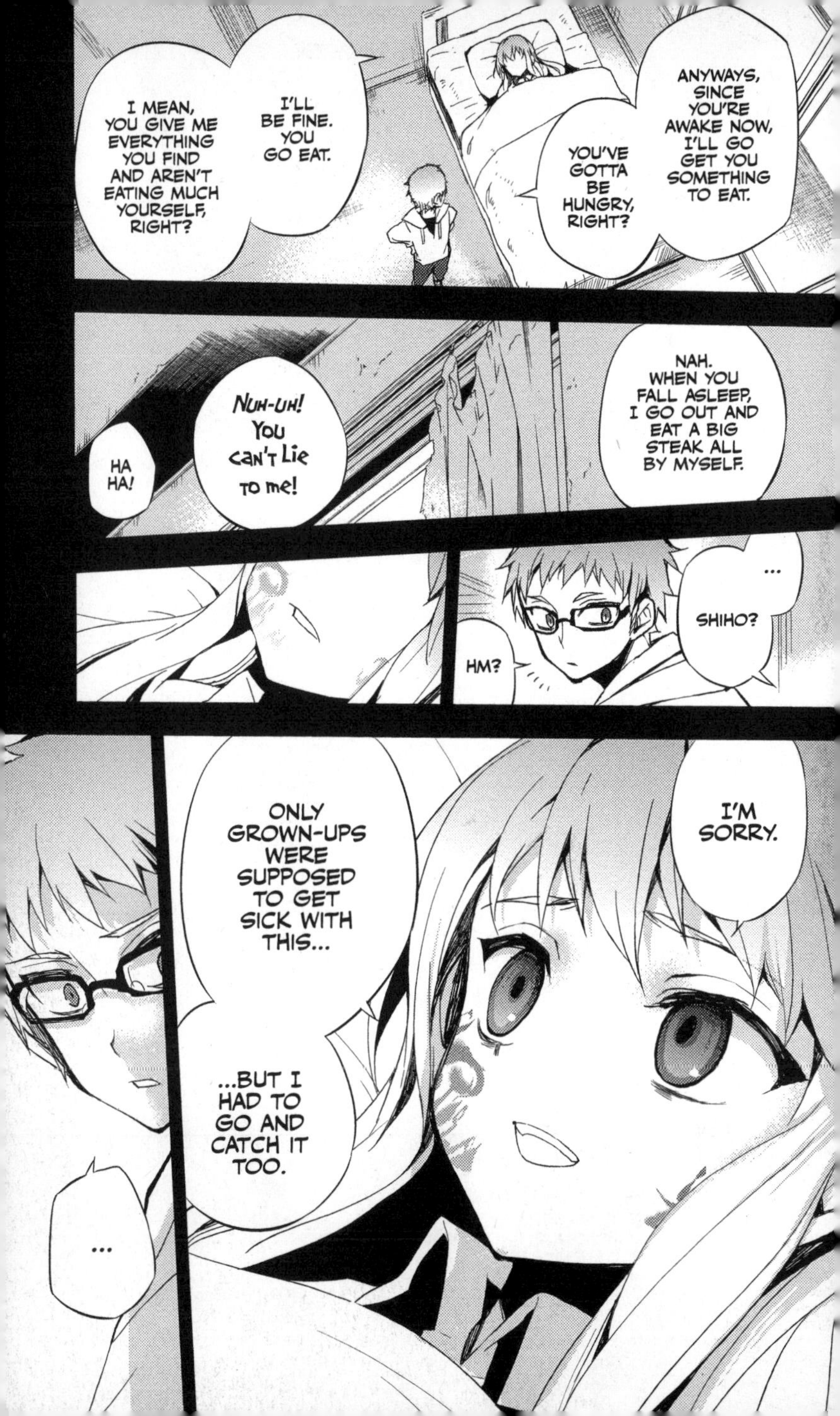
ANYWAYS, SINCE YOU'RE AWAKE NOW, I'LL GO GET YOU SOMETHING TO EAT.
YOU'VE GOTTA BE HUNGRY, RIGHT?
I'LL BE FINE. YOU GO EAT.
I MEAN, YOU GIVE ME EVERYTHING YOU FIND AND AREN'T EATING MUCH YOURSELF, RIGHT?
NAH. WHEN YOU FALL ASLEEP, I GO OUT AND EAT A BIG STEAK ALL BY MYSELF.
Nuh-uh! You can't lie to me!
HA HA!
...
SHIHO?
HM?
I'M SORRY.
ONLY GROWN-UPS WERE SUPPOSED TO GET SICK WITH THIS...
...BUT I HAD TO GO AND CATCH IT TOO.
...

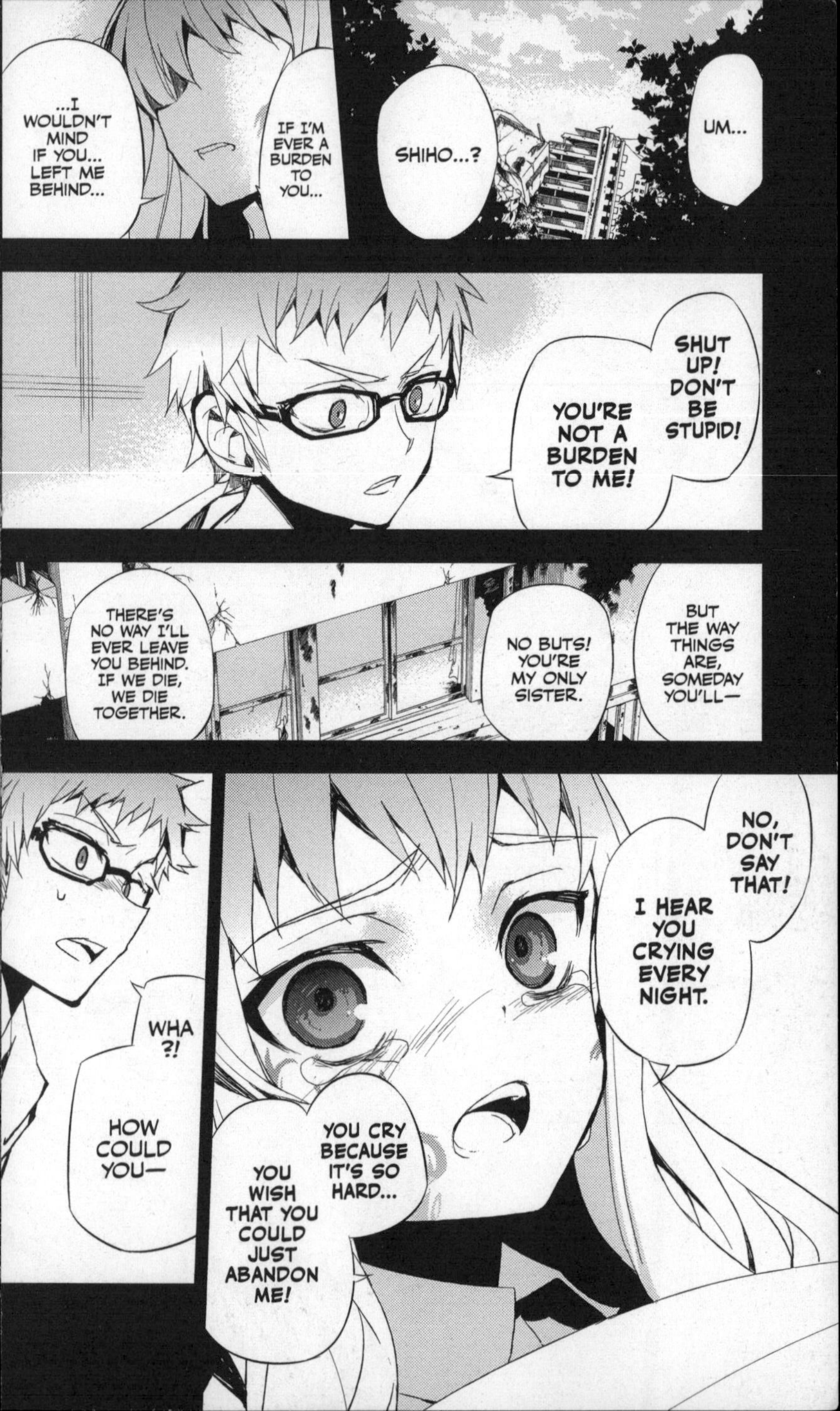
UM...
SHIHO...?
IF I'M EVER A BURDEN TO YOU...
...I WOULDN'T MIND IF YOU... LEFT ME BEHIND...
SHUT UP! DON'T BE STUPID!
YOU'RE NOT A BURDEN TO ME!
BUT THE WAY THINGS ARE, SOMEDAY YOU'LL—
NO BUTS! YOU'RE MY ONLY SISTER.
THERE'S NO WAY I'LL EVER LEAVE YOU BEHIND. IF WE DIE, WE DIE TOGETHER.
NO, DON'T SAY THAT!
I HEAR YOU CRYING EVERY NIGHT.
YOU CRY BECAUSE IT'S SO HARD...
YOU WISH THAT YOU COULD JUST ABANDON ME!
WHA?!
HOW COULD YOU—

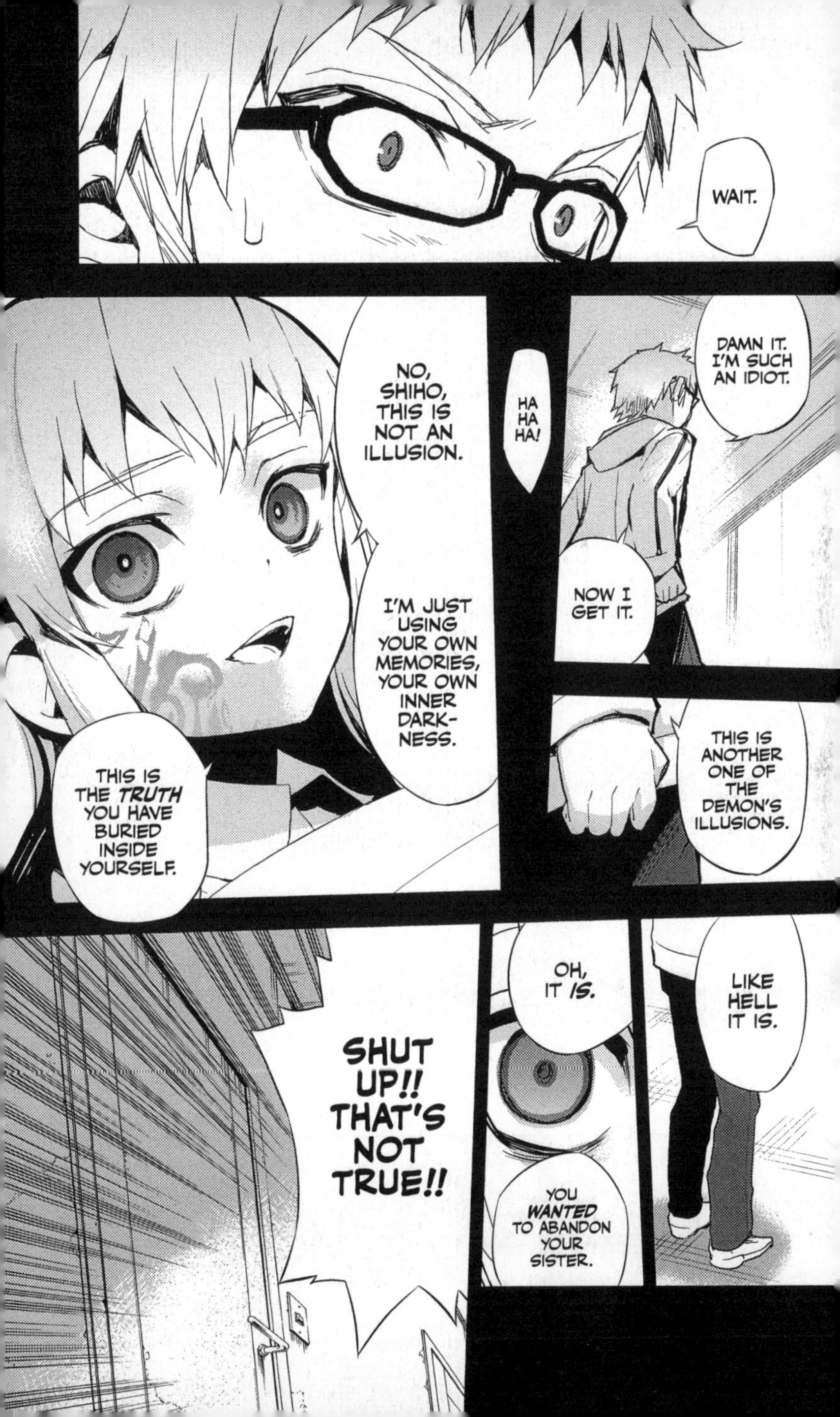
WAIT.
DAMN IT. I'M SUCH AN IDIOT.
NOW I GET IT.
THIS IS ANOTHER ONE OF THE DEMON'S ILLUSIONS.
HA HA HA!
NO, SHIHO, THIS IS NOT AN ILLUSION.
I'M JUST USING YOUR OWN MEMORIES, YOUR OWN INNER DARK-NESS.
THIS IS THE *TRUTH* YOU HAVE BURIED INSIDE YOURSELF.
LIKE HELL IT IS.
OH, IT *IS*.
YOU *WANTED* TO ABANDON YOUR SISTER.
SHUT UP!! THAT'S NOT TRUE!!

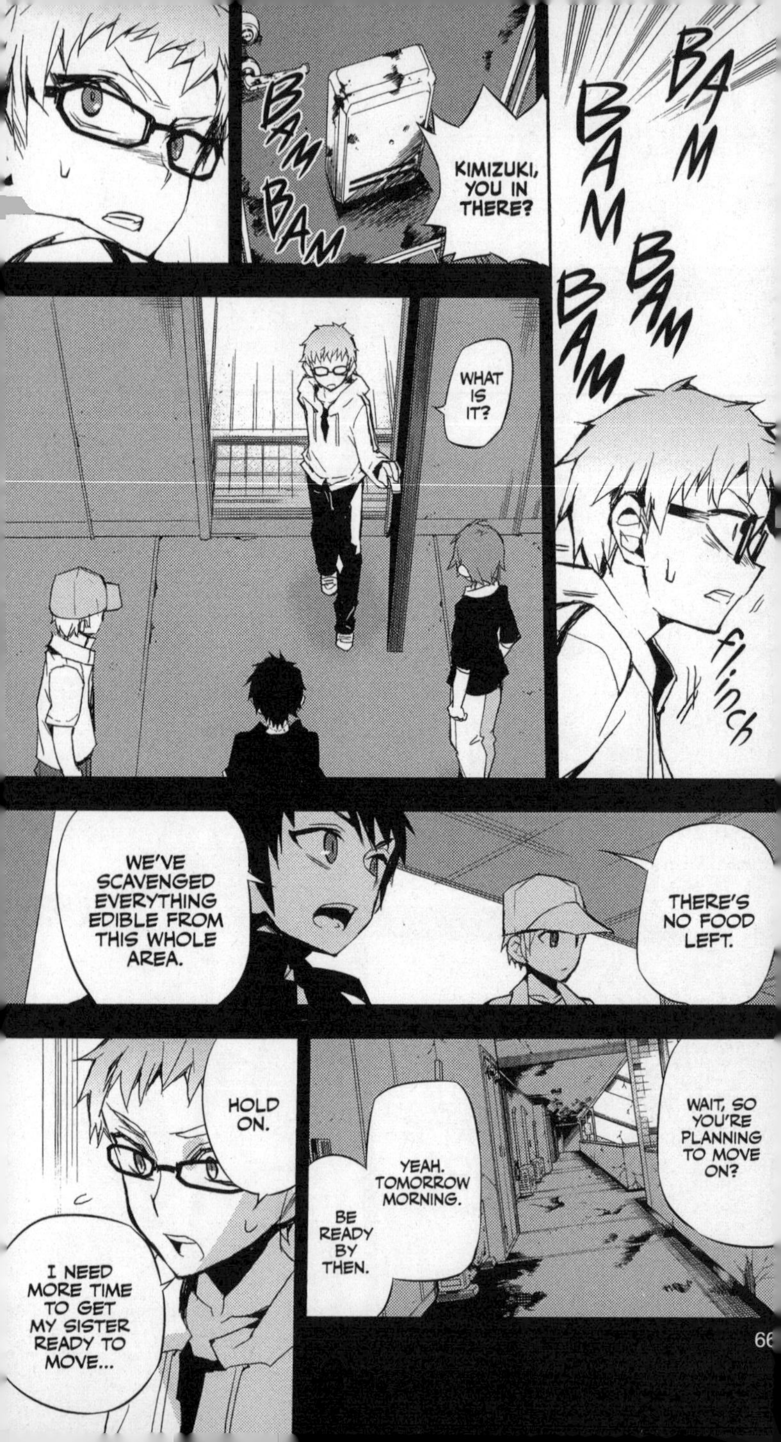
BAM BAM
BAM BAM
BAM BAM
flinch
BAM BAM
KIMIZUKI, YOU IN THERE?
WHAT IS IT?
THERE'S NO FOOD LEFT.
WE'VE SCAVENGED EVERYTHING EDIBLE FROM THIS WHOLE AREA.
WAIT, SO YOU'RE PLANNING TO MOVE ON?
YEAH. TOMORROW MORNING.
BE READY BY THEN.
HOLD ON.
I NEED MORE TIME TO GET MY SISTER READY TO MOVE...

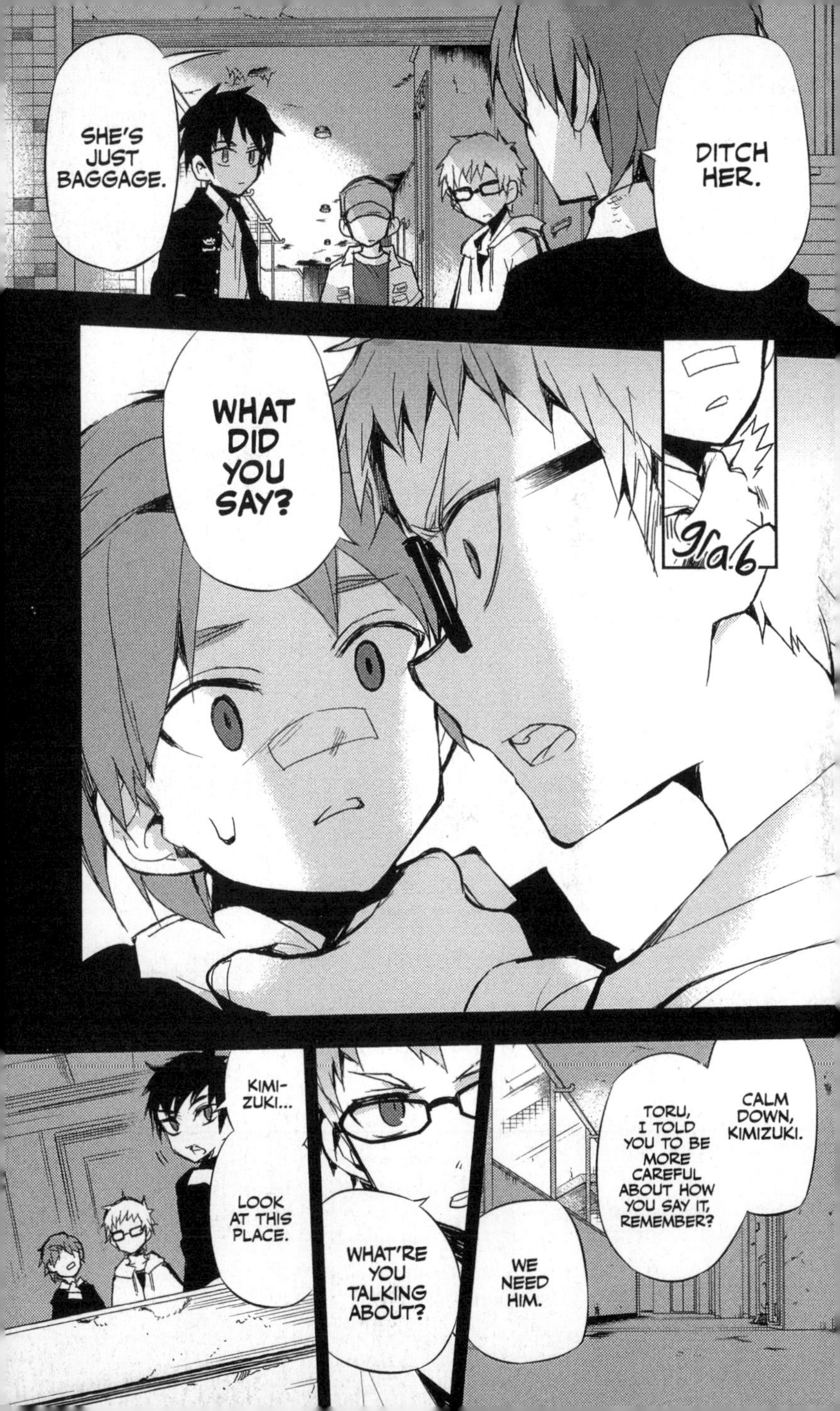
DITCH HER.
SHE'S JUST BAGGAGE.
grab
WHAT DID YOU SAY?
CALM DOWN, KIMIZUKI.
TORU, I TOLD YOU TO BE MORE CAREFUL ABOUT HOW YOU SAY IT, REMEMBER?
WE NEED HIM.
WHAT'RE YOU TALKING ABOUT?
KIMI-ZUKI...
LOOK AT THIS PLACE.

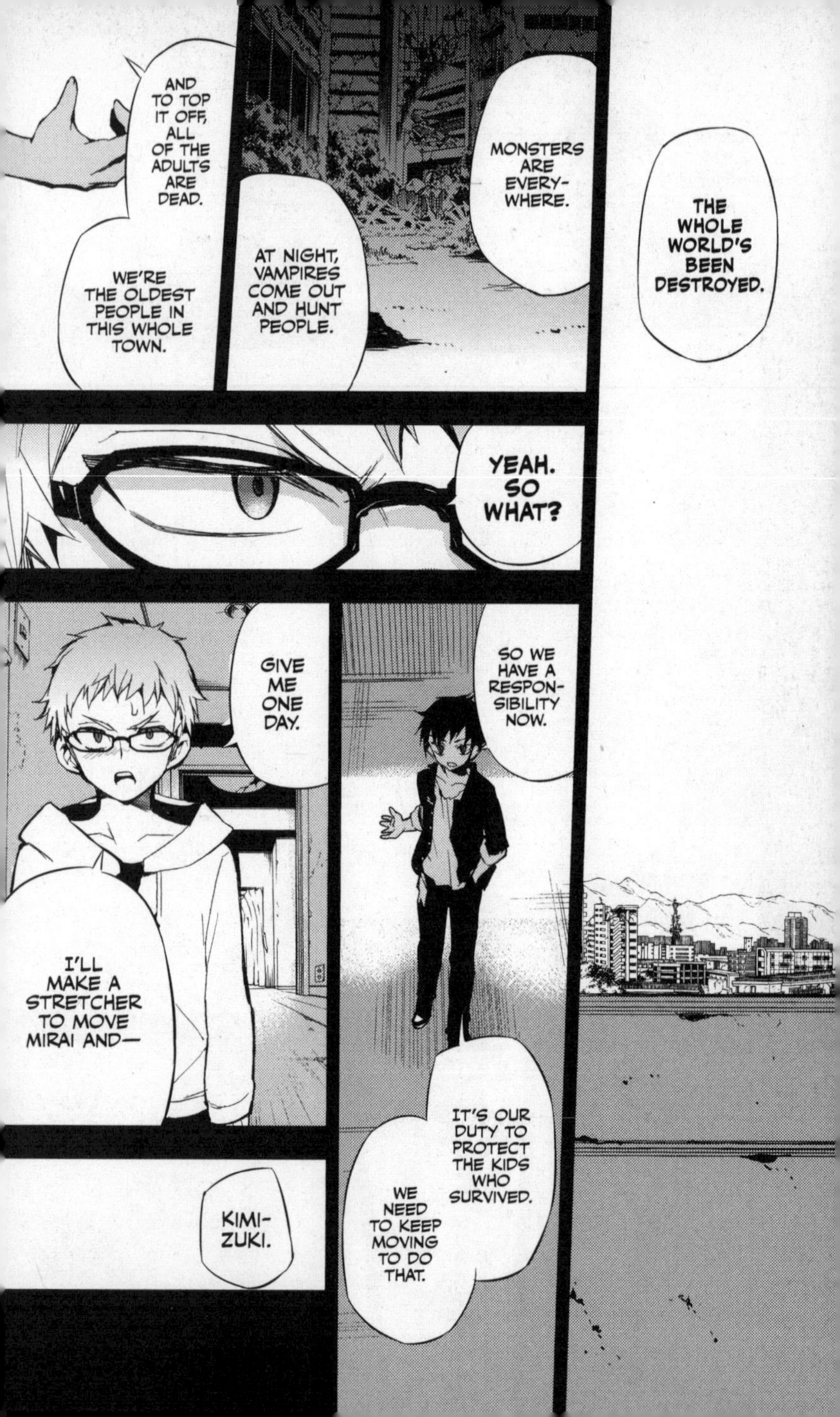
THE WHOLE WORLD'S BEEN DESTROYED.
MONSTERS ARE EVERYWHERE.
AT NIGHT, VAMPIRES COME OUT AND HUNT PEOPLE.
AND TO TOP IT OFF, ALL OF THE ADULTS ARE DEAD.
WE'RE THE OLDEST PEOPLE IN THIS WHOLE TOWN.
YEAH. SO WHAT?
SO WE HAVE A RESPONSIBILITY NOW.
IT'S OUR DUTY TO PROTECT THE KIDS WHO SURVIVED.
WE NEED TO KEEP MOVING TO DO THAT.
GIVE ME ONE DAY.
I'LL MAKE A STRETCHER TO MOVE MIRAI AND—
KIMIZUKI.

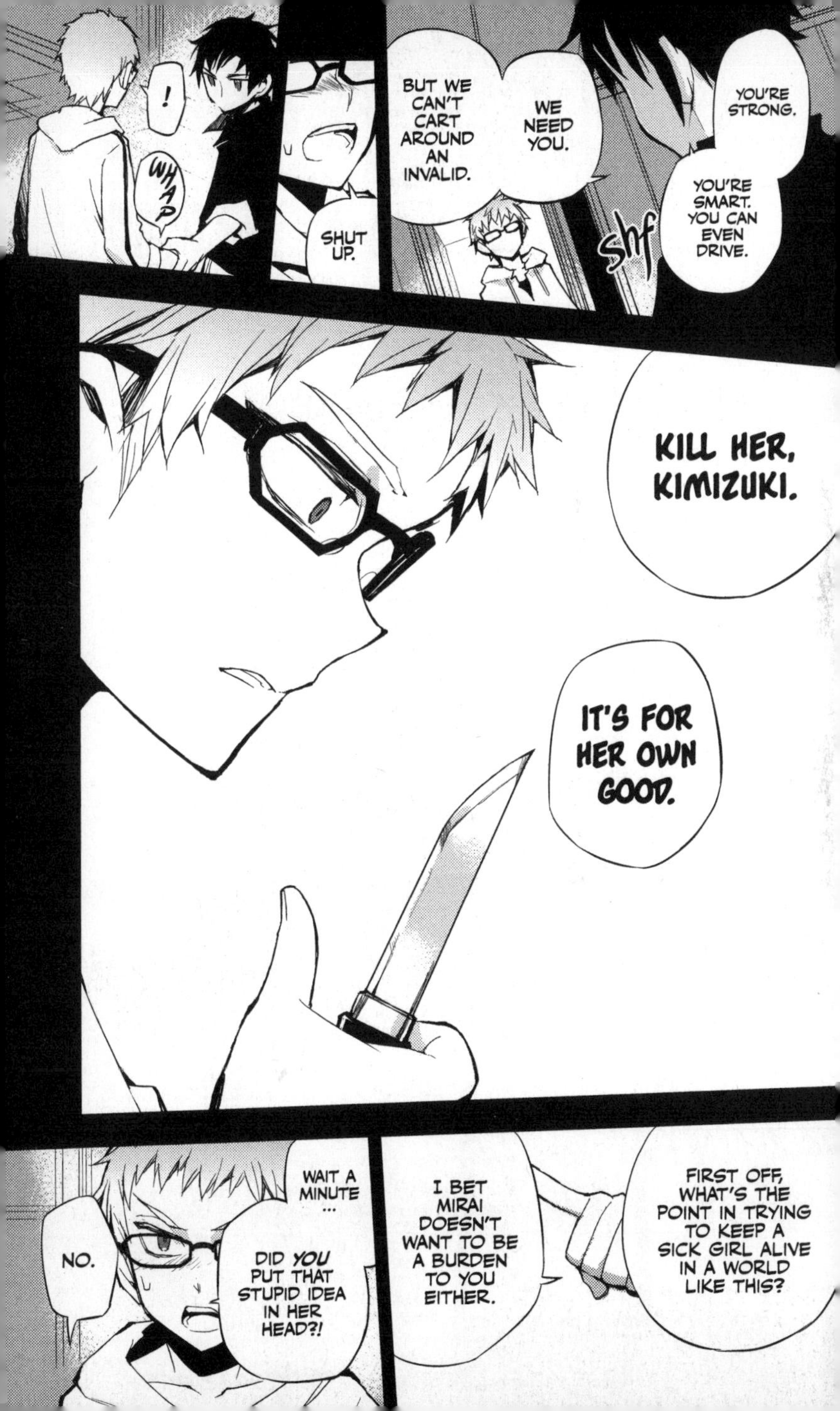
YOU'RE STRONG.
shf
YOU'RE SMART. YOU CAN EVEN DRIVE.
WE NEED YOU.
BUT WE CAN'T CART AROUND AN INVALID.
SHUT UP.
!
WHAP
KILL HER, KIMIZUKI.
IT'S FOR HER OWN GOOD.
FIRST OFF, WHAT'S THE POINT IN TRYING TO KEEP A SICK GIRL ALIVE IN A WORLD LIKE THIS?
I BET MIRAI DOESN'T WANT TO BE A BURDEN TO YOU EITHER.
WAIT A MINUTE ...
DID *YOU* PUT THAT STUPID IDEA IN HER HEAD?!
NO.

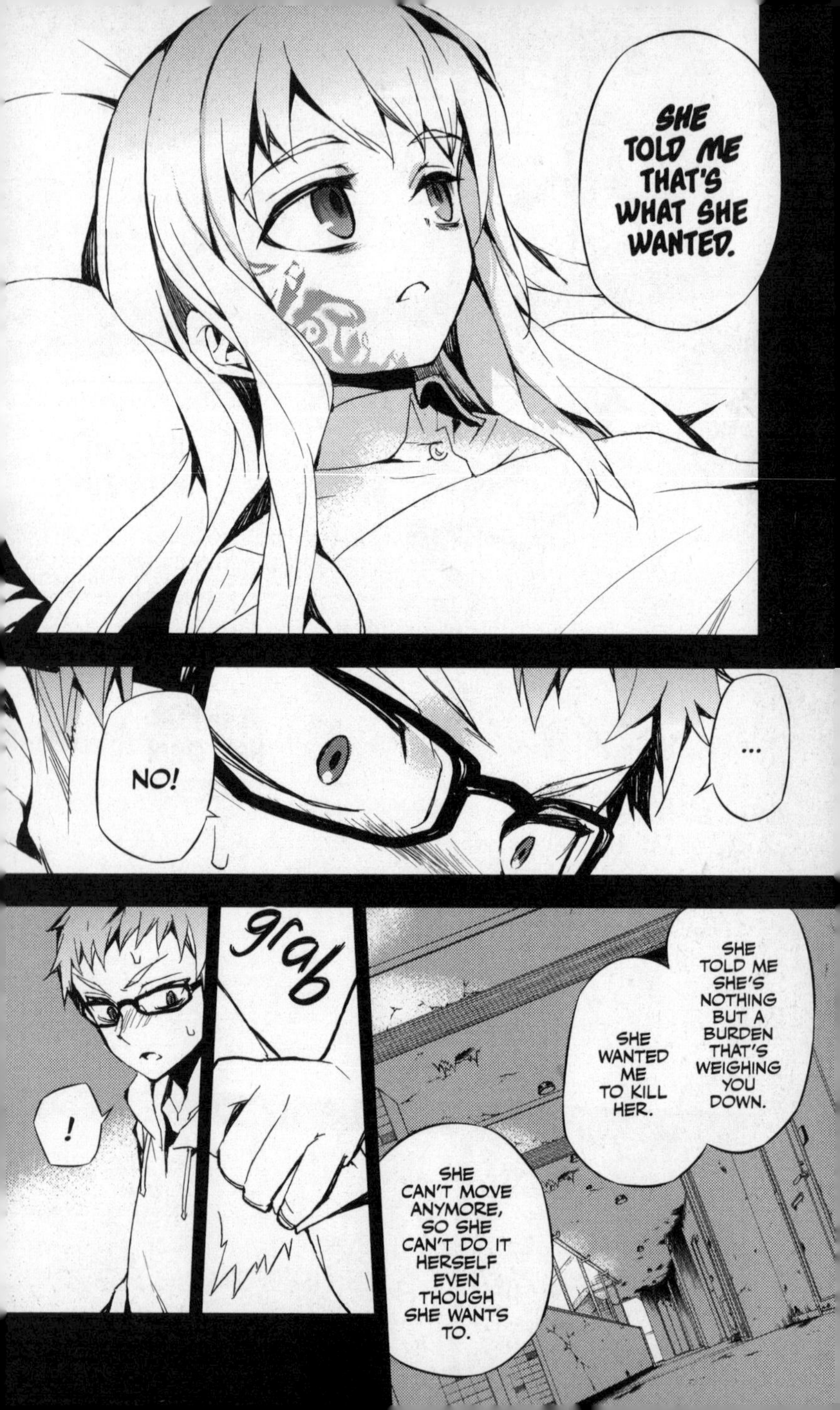

SHE TOLD ME THAT'S WHAT SHE WANTED.
...
NO!
SHE TOLD ME SHE'S NOTHING BUT A BURDEN THAT'S WEIGHING YOU DOWN.
SHE WANTED ME TO KILL HER.
SHE CAN'T MOVE ANYMORE, SO SHE CAN'T DO IT HERSELF EVEN THOUGH SHE WANTS TO.
grab
!

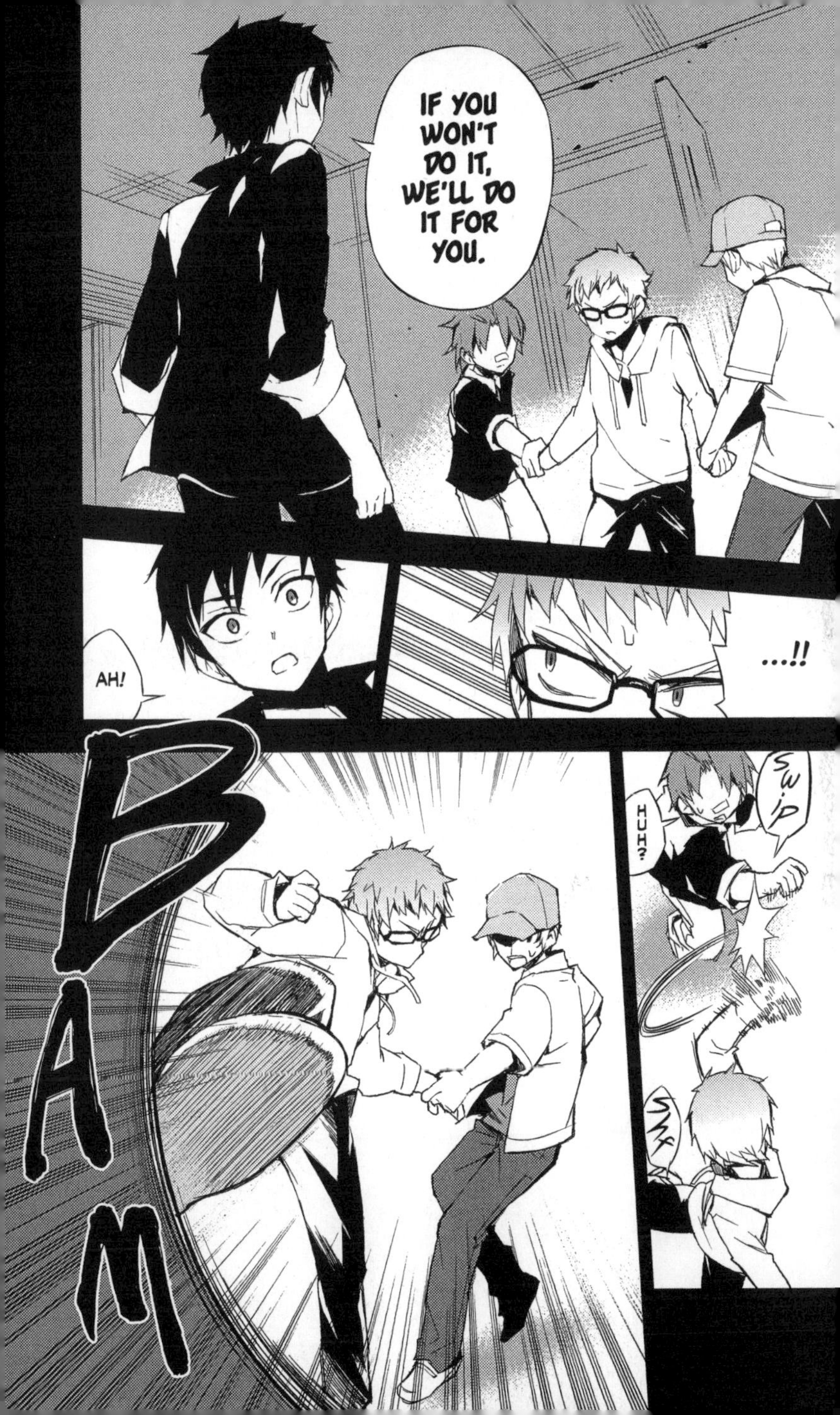
IF YOU WON'T DO IT, WE'LL DO IT FOR YOU.
...!!
AH!
SWIP
HUH?
BAM

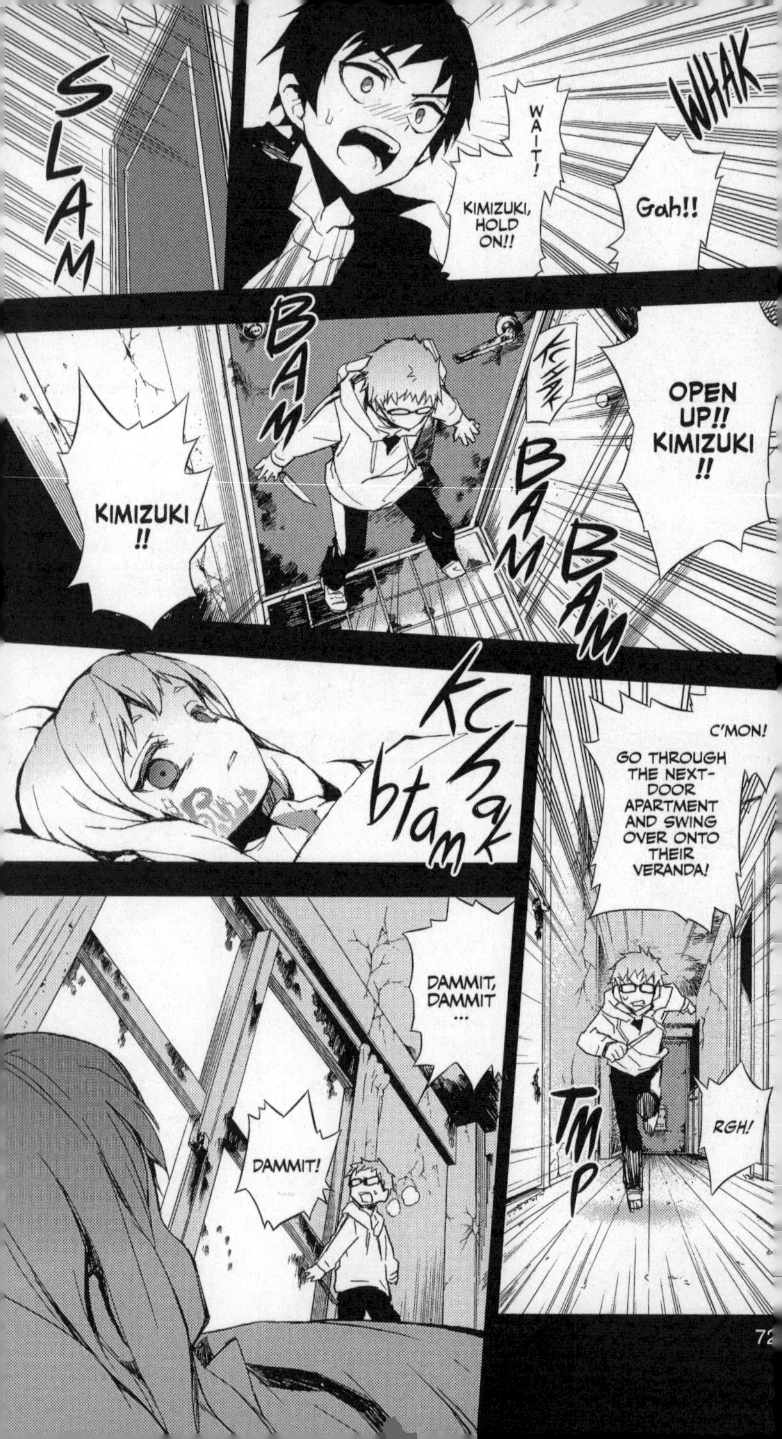
WHAK
Gah!!
WAIT!
KIMIZUKI, HOLD ON!!
SLAM
OPEN UP!! KIMIZUKI !!
KCHAK
BAM BAM BAM
KIMIZUKI !!
C'MON!
GO THROUGH THE NEXT-DOOR APARTMENT AND SWING OVER ONTO THEIR VERANDA!
RGH!
TMP
kchak
btam
DAMMIT, DAMMIT ...
DAMMIT!

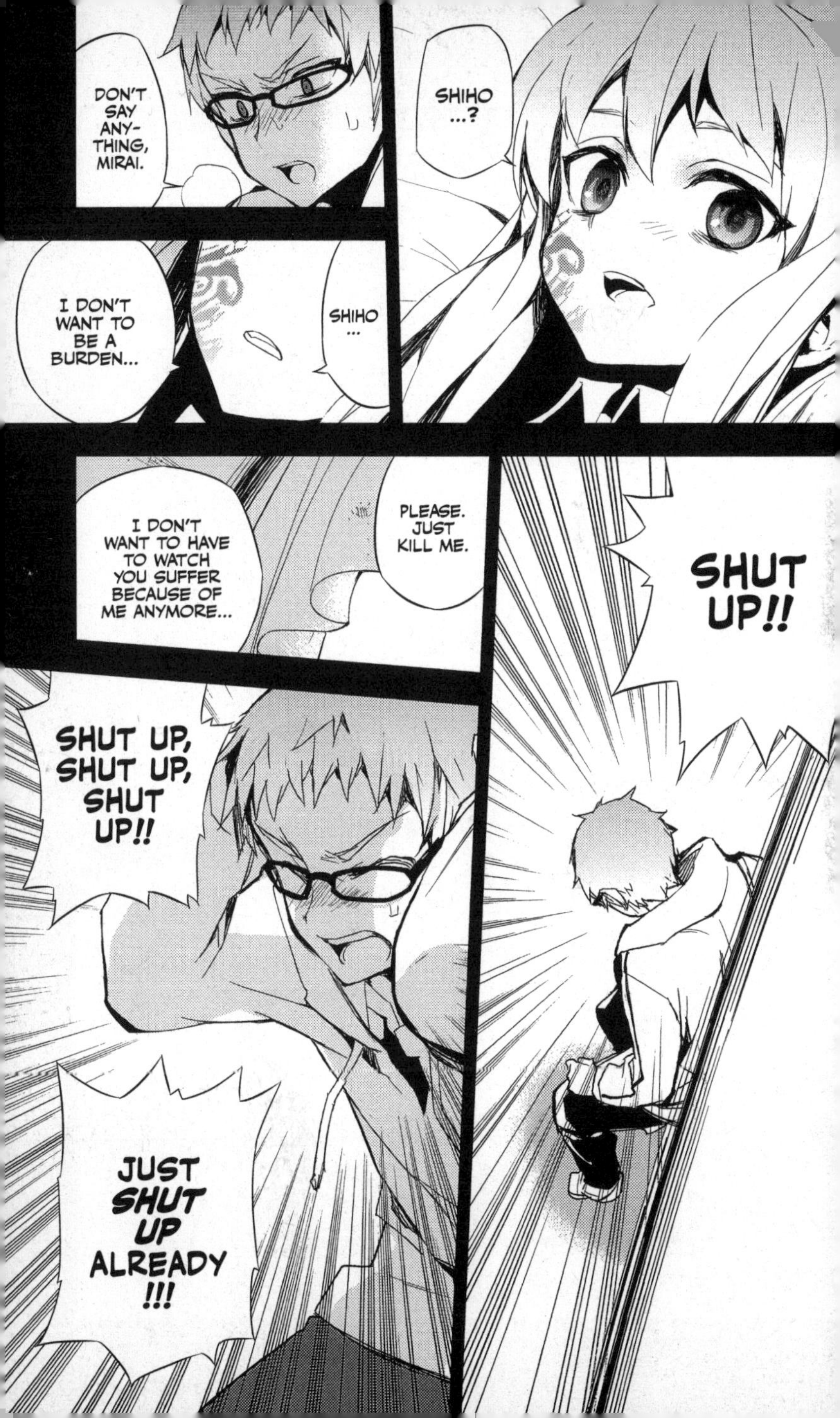
SHIHO ...?
DON'T SAY ANYTHING, MIRAI.
SHIHO ...
I DON'T WANT TO BE A BURDEN...
SHUT UP!!
PLEASE. JUST KILL ME.
I DON'T WANT TO HAVE TO WATCH YOU SUFFER BECAUSE OF ME ANYMORE...
SHUT UP, SHUT UP, SHUT UP!!
JUST SHUT UP ALREADY !!!

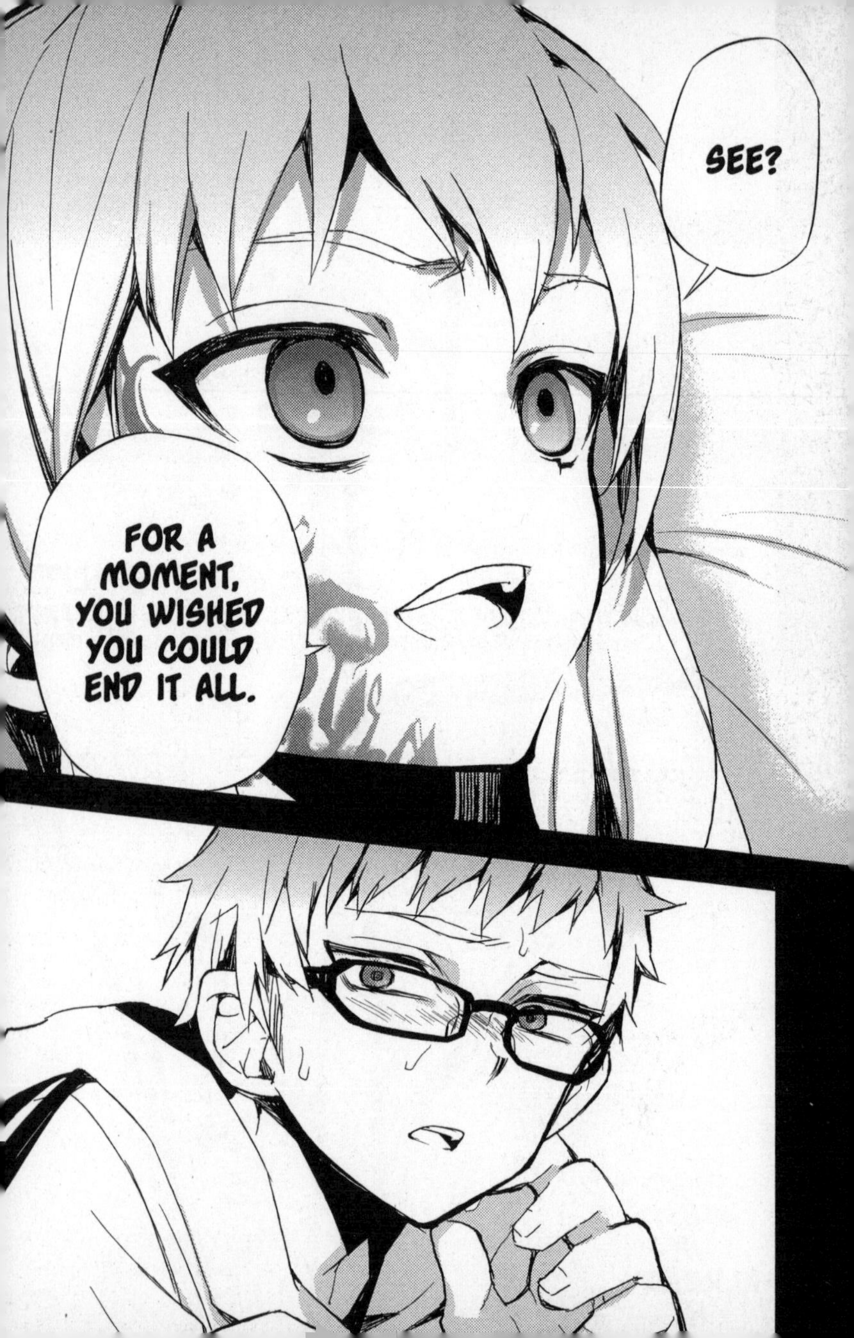
SEE?
FOR A MOMENT, YOU WISHED YOU COULD END IT ALL.

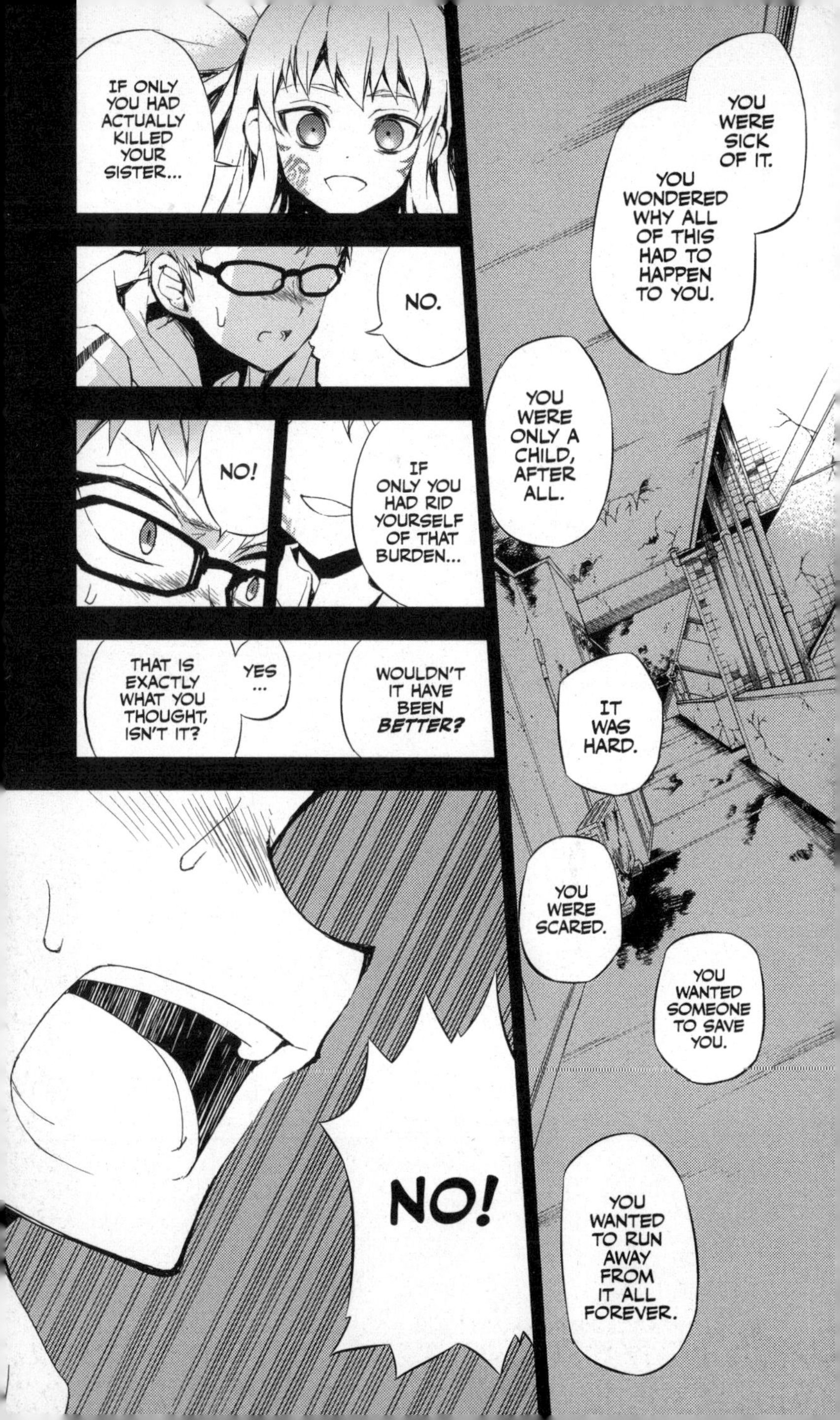
YOU WERE SICK OF IT.
YOU WONDERED WHY ALL OF THIS HAD TO HAPPEN TO YOU.
YOU WERE ONLY A CHILD, AFTER ALL.
IT WAS HARD.
YOU WERE SCARED.
YOU WANTED SOMEONE TO SAVE YOU.
YOU WANTED TO RUN AWAY FROM IT ALL FOREVER.
IF ONLY YOU HAD ACTUALLY KILLED YOUR SISTER...
NO.
IF ONLY YOU HAD RID YOURSELF OF THAT BURDEN...
NO!
WOULDN'T IT HAVE BEEN *BETTER?*
YES ...
THAT IS EXACTLY WHAT YOU THOUGHT, ISN'T IT?
NO!

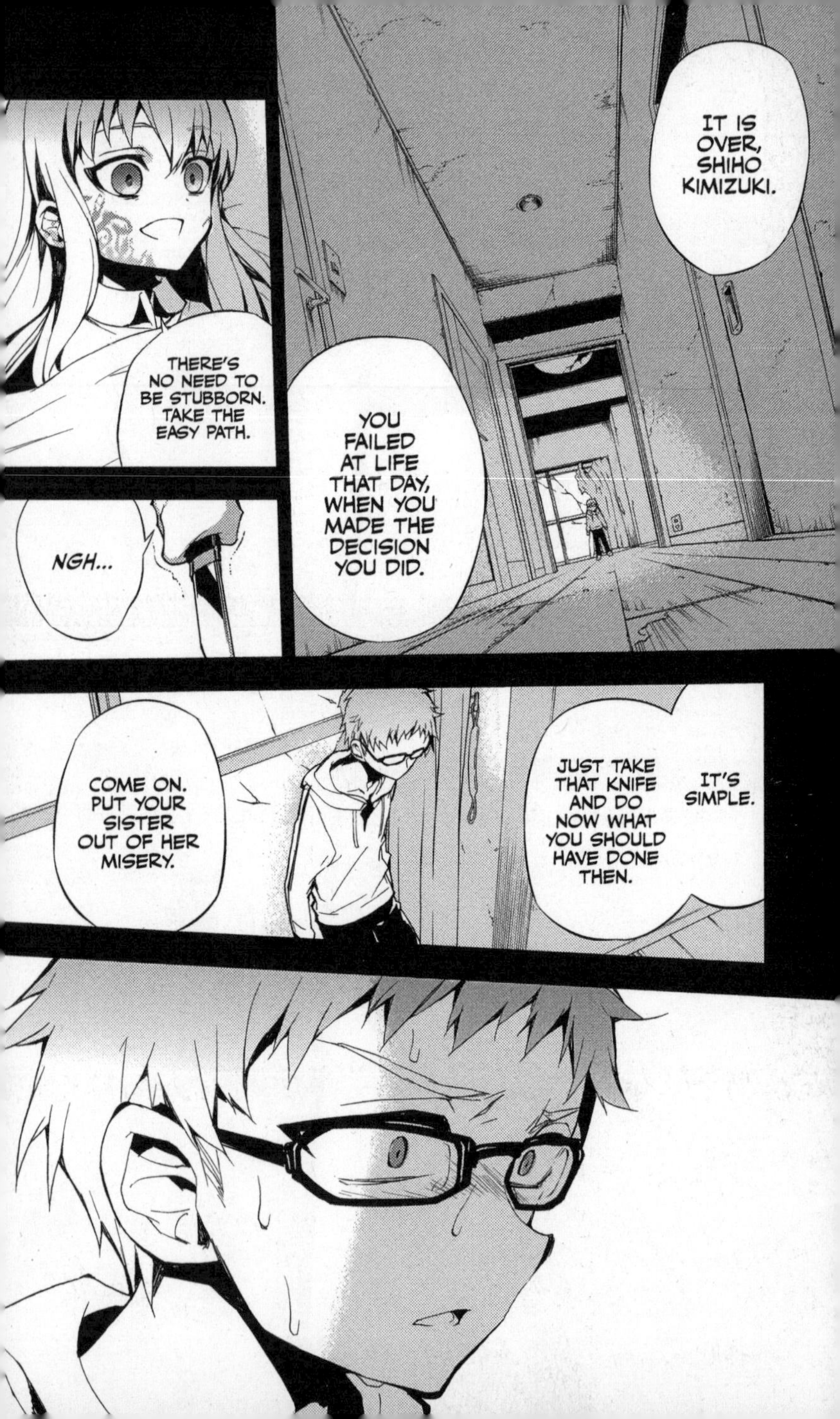
IT IS OVER, SHIHO KIMIZUKI.
YOU FAILED AT LIFE THAT DAY, WHEN YOU MADE THE DECISION YOU DID.
THERE'S NO NEED TO BE STUBBORN. TAKE THE EASY PATH.
NGH...
IT'S SIMPLE.
JUST TAKE THAT KNIFE AND DO NOW WHAT YOU SHOULD HAVE DONE THEN.
COME ON. PUT YOUR SISTER OUT OF HER MISERY.

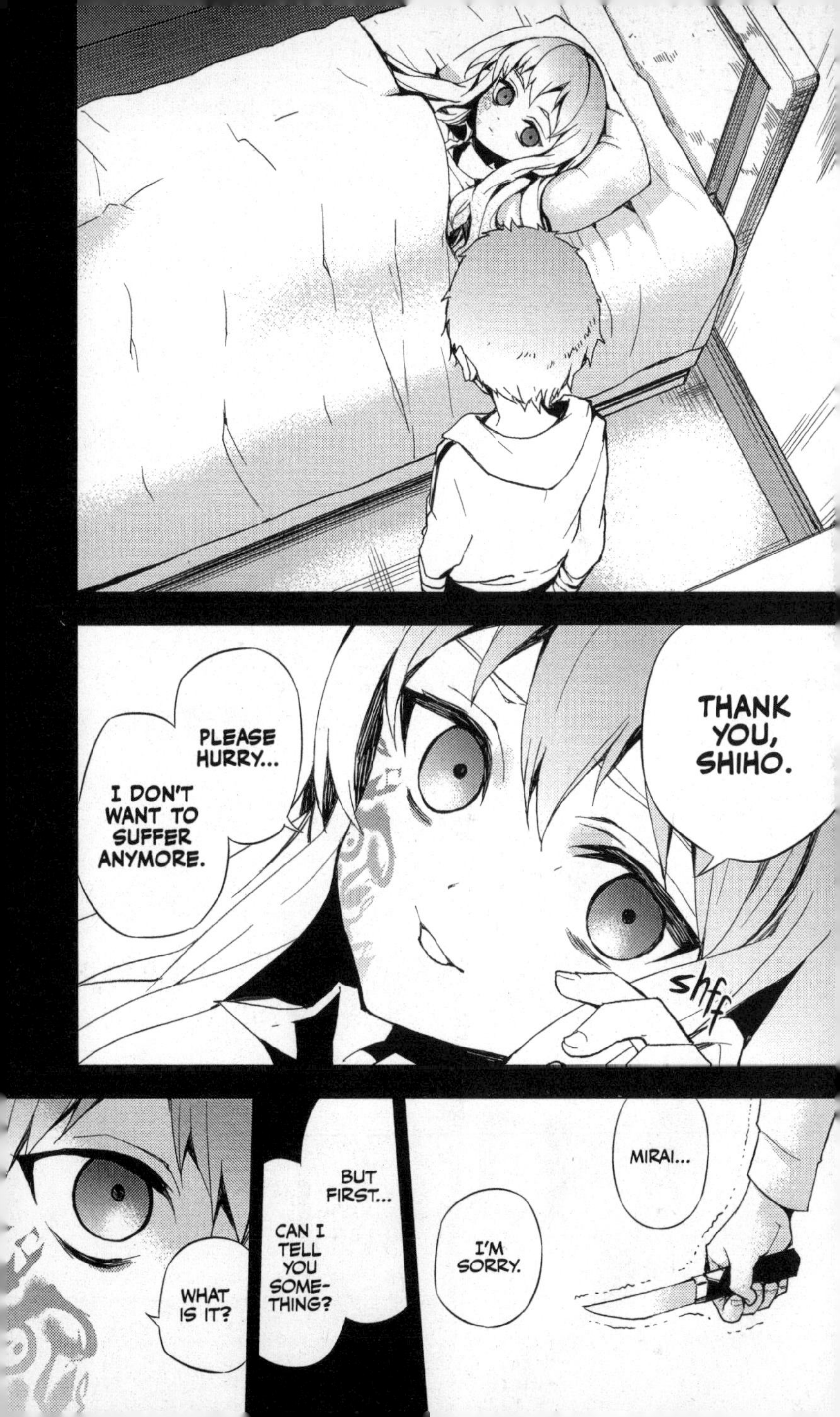
THANK YOU, SHIHO.
PLEASE HURRY...
I DON'T WANT TO SUFFER ANYMORE.
shff
MIRAI...
I'M SORRY.
BUT FIRST...
CAN I TELL YOU SOME-THING?
WHAT IS IT?

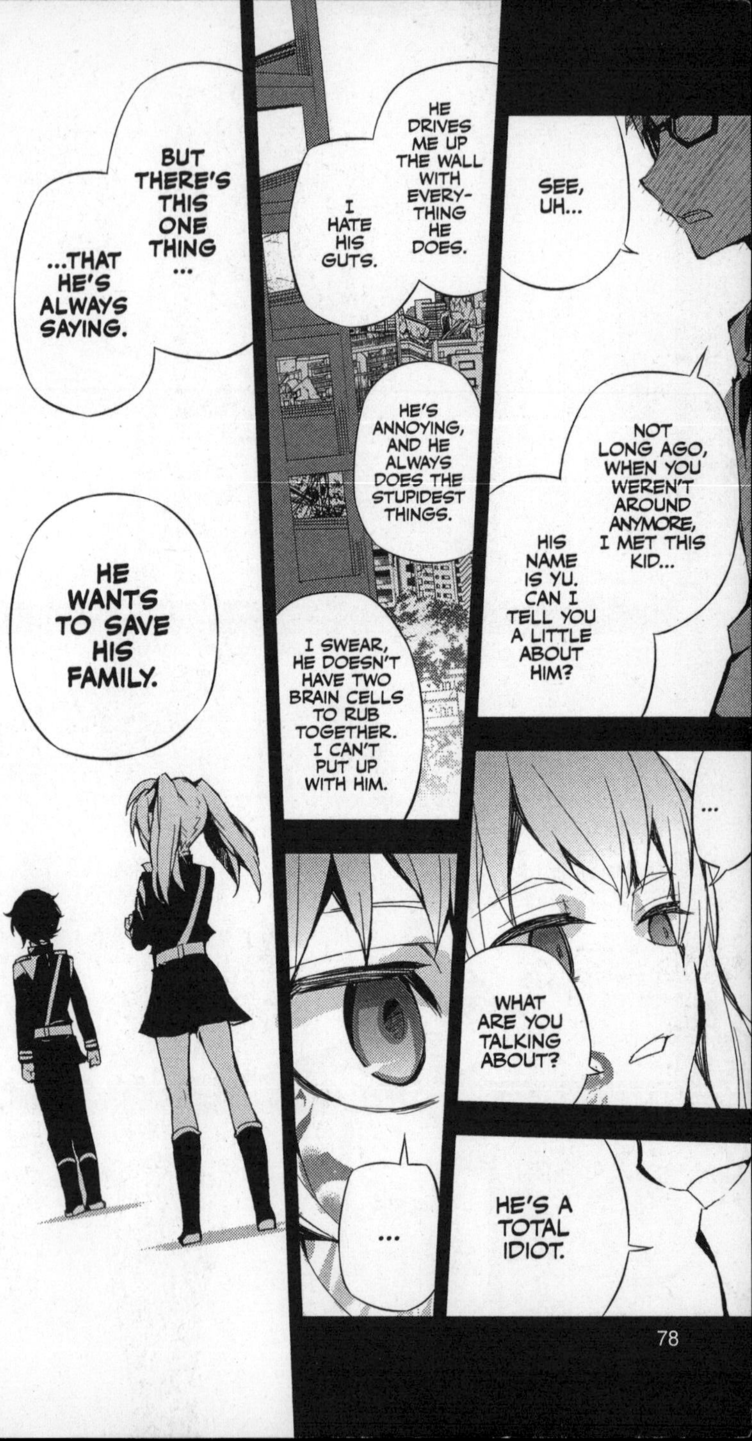
SEE, UH...
NOT LONG AGO, WHEN YOU WEREN'T AROUND ANYMORE, I MET THIS KID...
HIS NAME IS YU. CAN I TELL YOU A LITTLE ABOUT HIM?
HE DRIVES ME UP THE WALL WITH EVERYTHING HE DOES.
I HATE HIS GUTS.
HE'S ANNOYING, AND HE ALWAYS DOES THE STUPIDEST THINGS.
I SWEAR, HE DOESN'T HAVE TWO BRAIN CELLS TO RUB TOGETHER. I CAN'T PUT UP WITH HIM.
...
WHAT ARE YOU TALKING ABOUT?
HE'S A TOTAL IDIOT.
...
BUT THERE'S THIS ONE THING...
...THAT HE'S ALWAYS SAYING.
HE WANTS TO SAVE HIS FAMILY.

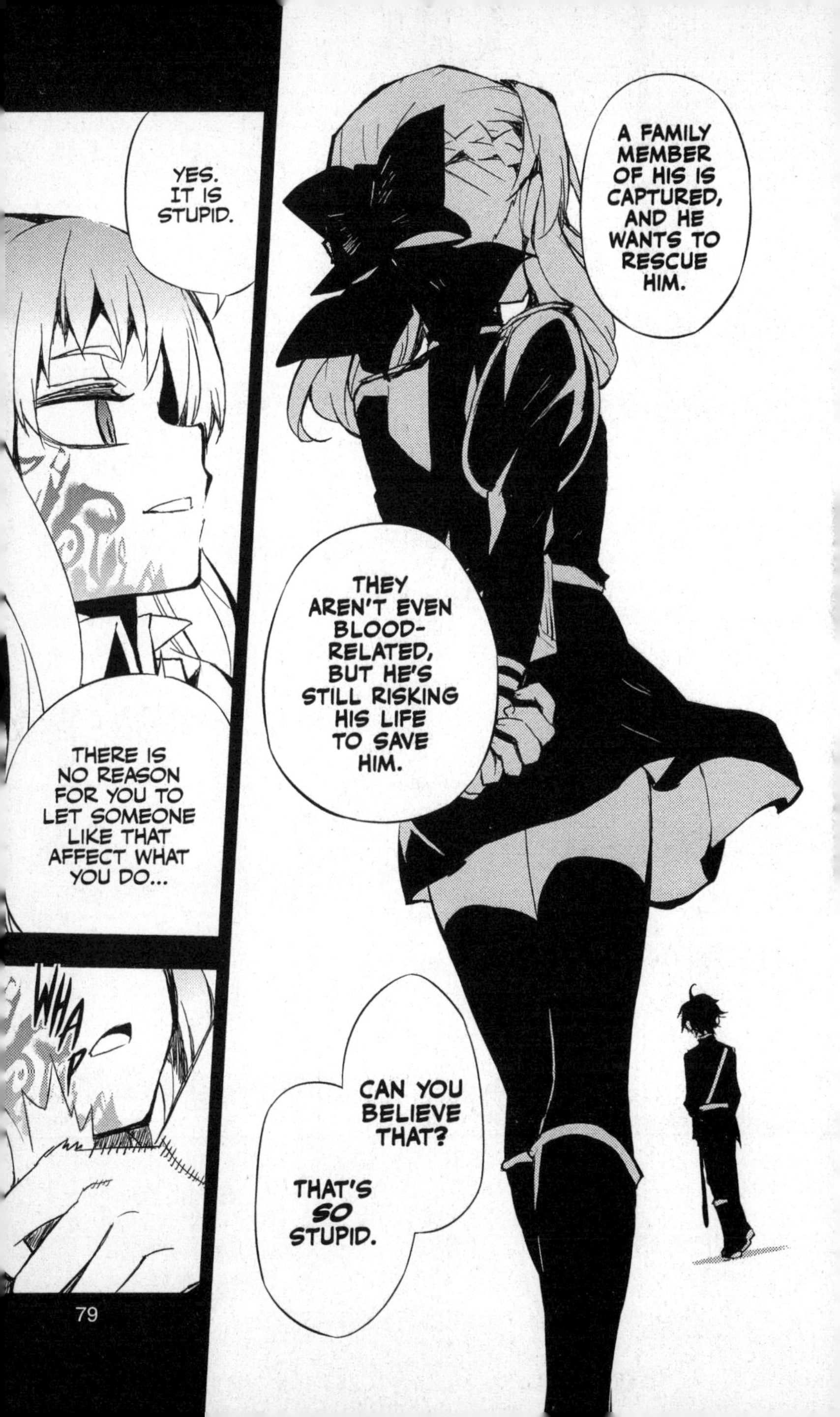
A FAMILY MEMBER OF HIS IS CAPTURED, AND HE WANTS TO RESCUE HIM.
THEY AREN'T EVEN BLOOD-RELATED, BUT HE'S STILL RISKING HIS LIFE TO SAVE HIM.
CAN YOU BELIEVE THAT?
THAT'S *SO* STUPID.
YES. IT IS STUPID.
THERE IS NO REASON FOR YOU TO LET SOMEONE LIKE THAT AFFECT WHAT YOU DO...
WHAP

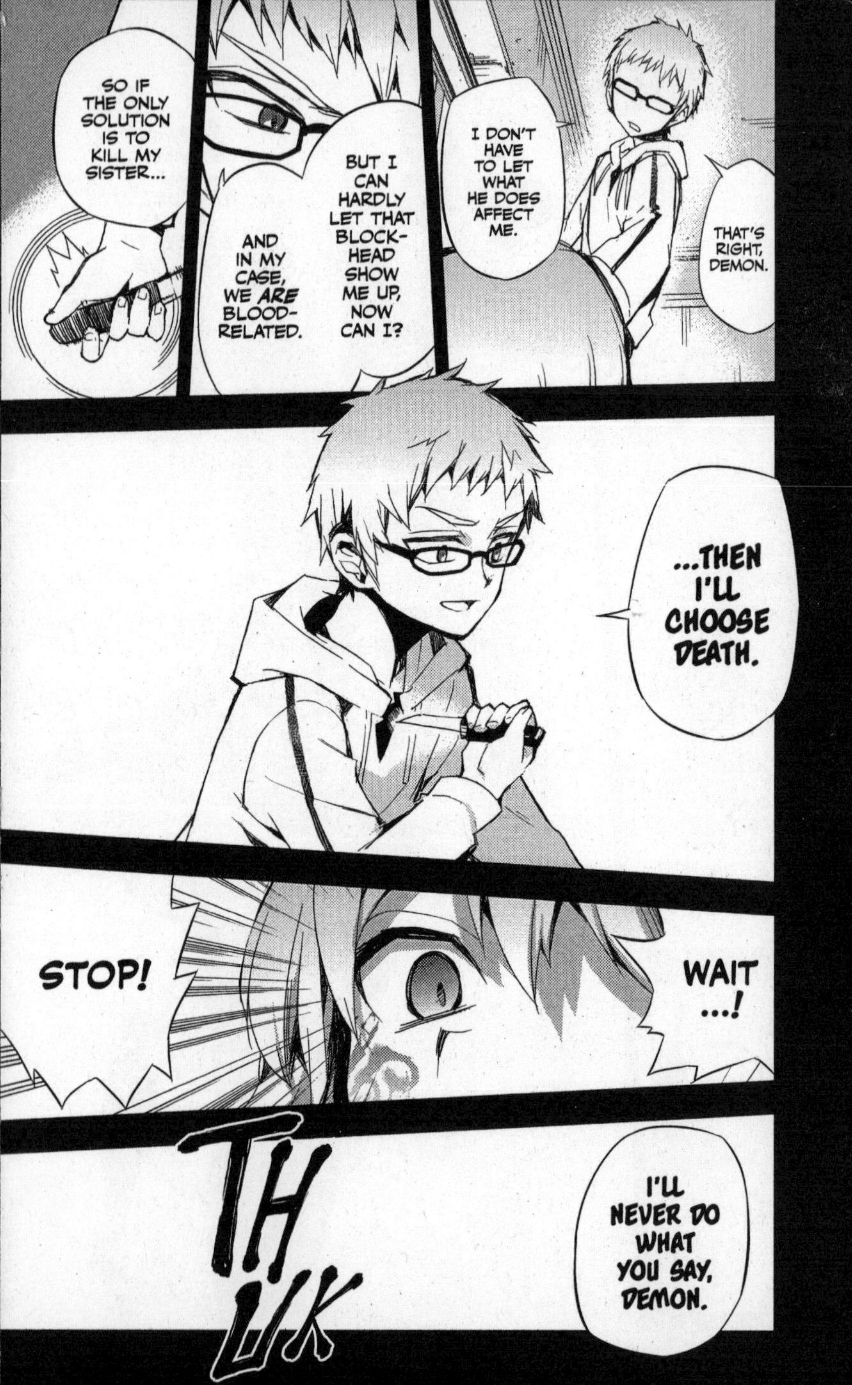
THAT'S RIGHT, DEMON.
I DON'T HAVE TO LET WHAT HE DOES AFFECT ME.
BUT I CAN HARDLY LET THAT BLOCK-HEAD SHOW ME UP, NOW CAN I?
AND IN MY CASE, WE *ARE* BLOOD-RELATED.
SO IF THE ONLY SOLUTION IS TO KILL MY SISTER...
...THEN I'LL CHOOSE DEATH.
WAIT ...!
STOP!
I'LL NEVER DO WHAT YOU SAY, DEMON.
THUK

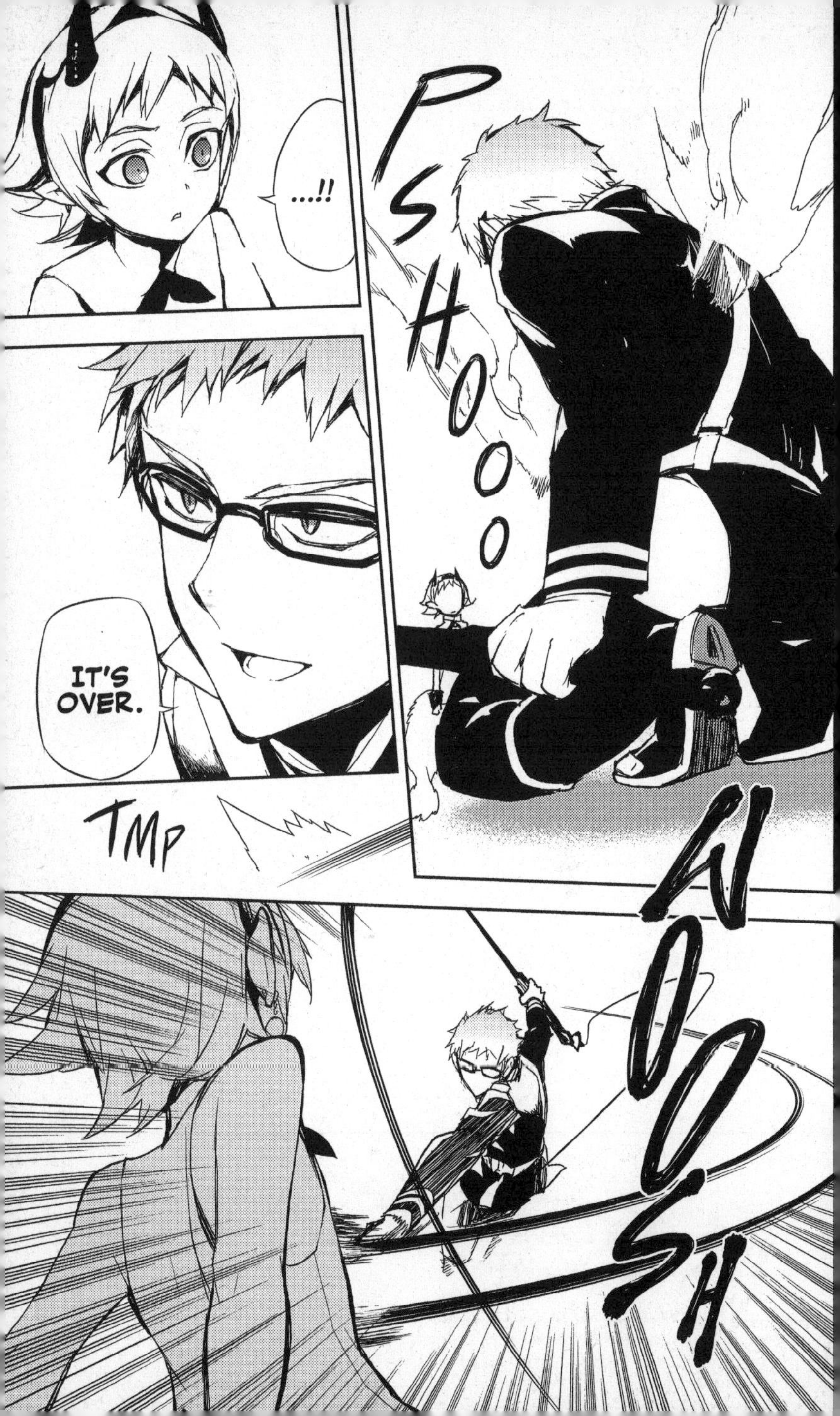
PSHOOOO
...!!
IT'S OVER.
TMP
WHOOSH

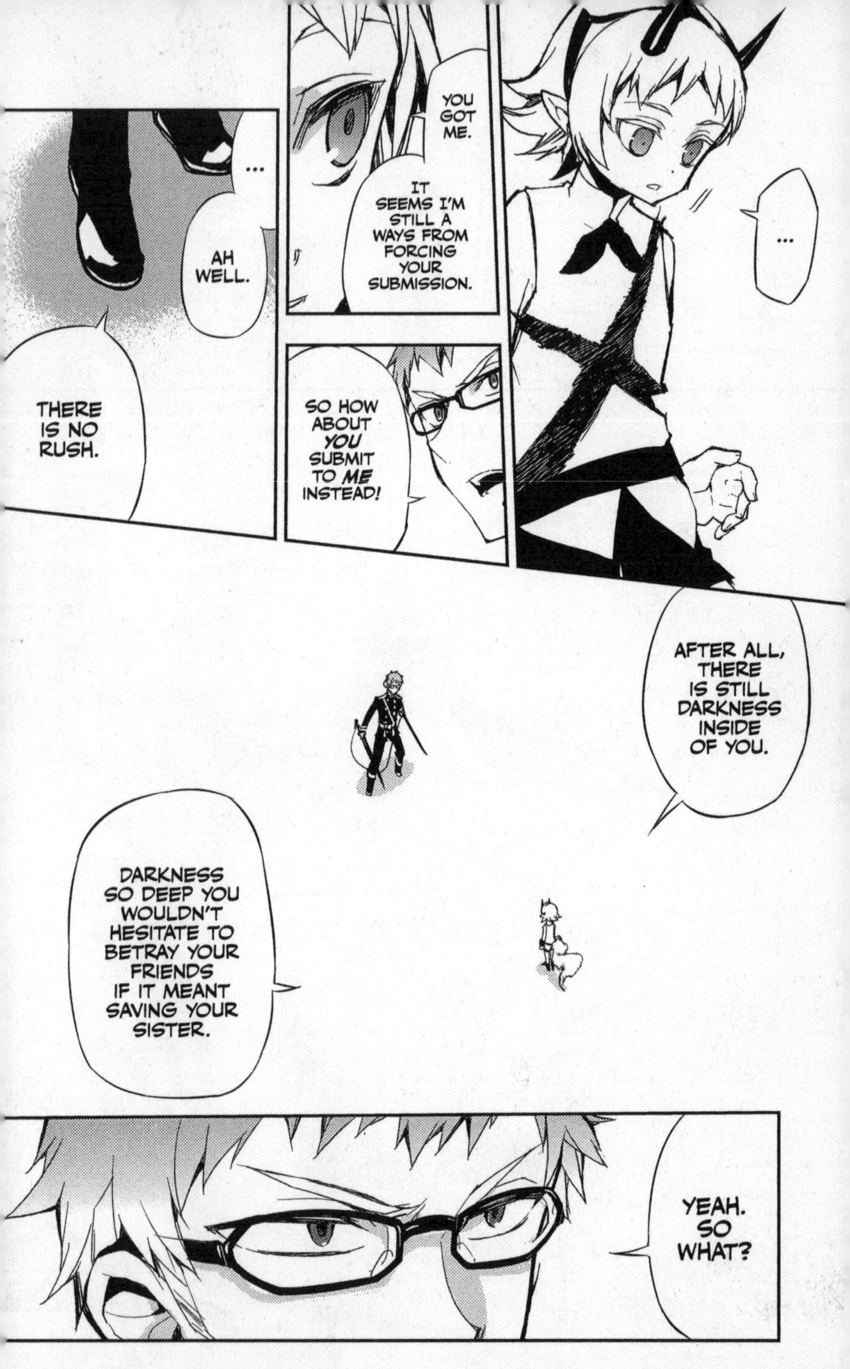
...
YOU GOT ME.
IT SEEMS I'M STILL A WAYS FROM FORCING YOUR SUBMISSION.
SO HOW ABOUT *YOU* SUBMIT TO *ME* INSTEAD!
...
AH WELL.
THERE IS NO RUSH.
AFTER ALL, THERE IS STILL DARKNESS INSIDE OF YOU.
DARKNESS SO DEEP YOU WOULDN'T HESITATE TO BETRAY YOUR FRIENDS IF IT MEANT SAVING YOUR SISTER.
YEAH. SO WHAT?

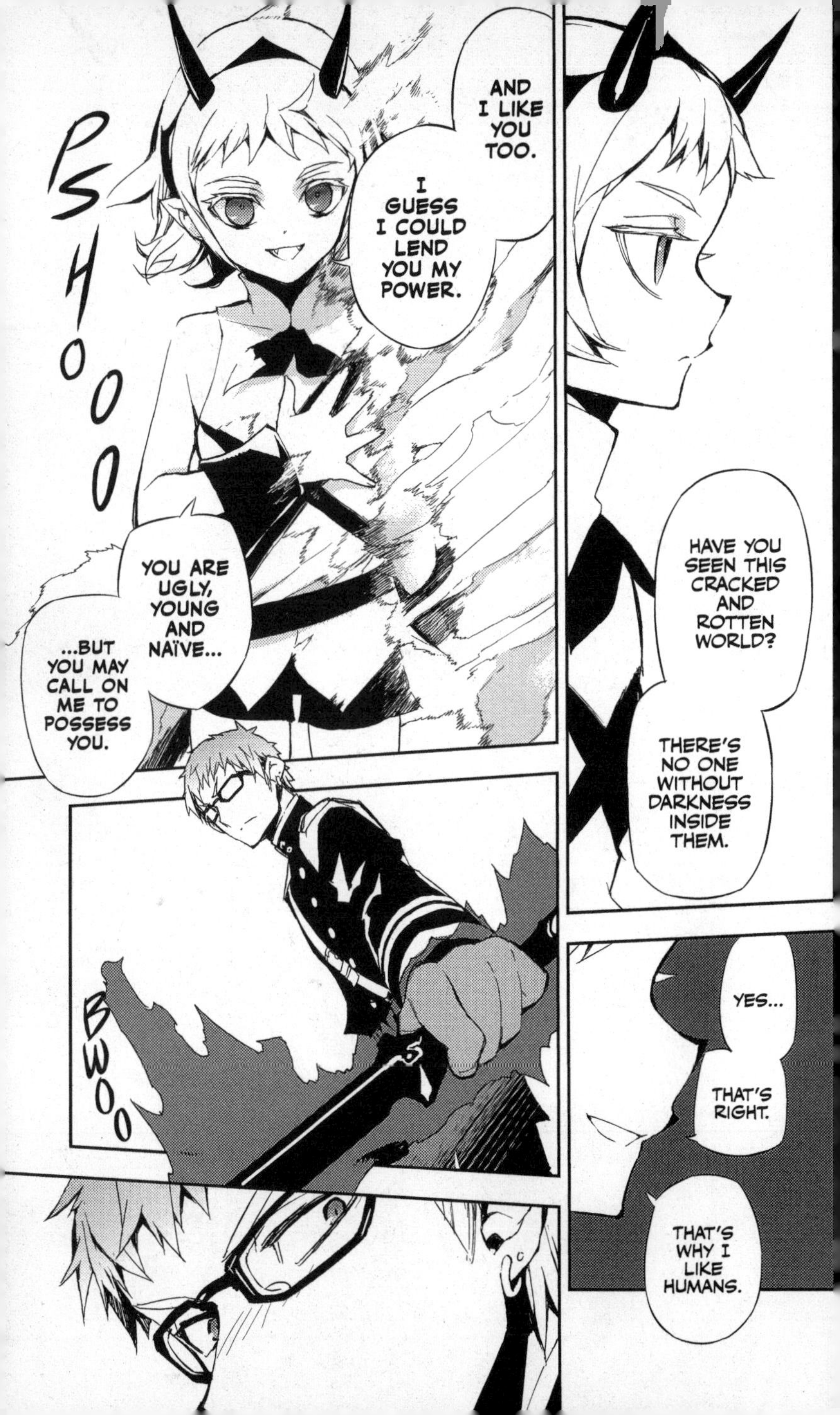
HAVE YOU SEEN THIS CRACKED AND ROTTEN WORLD?
THERE'S NO ONE WITHOUT DARKNESS INSIDE THEM.
YES...
THAT'S RIGHT.
THAT'S WHY I LIKE HUMANS.
AND I LIKE YOU TOO.
I GUESS I COULD LEND YOU MY POWER.
PSHOOO
YOU ARE UGLY, YOUNG AND NAÏVE...
...BUT YOU MAY CALL ON ME TO POSSESS YOU.
BWOOO

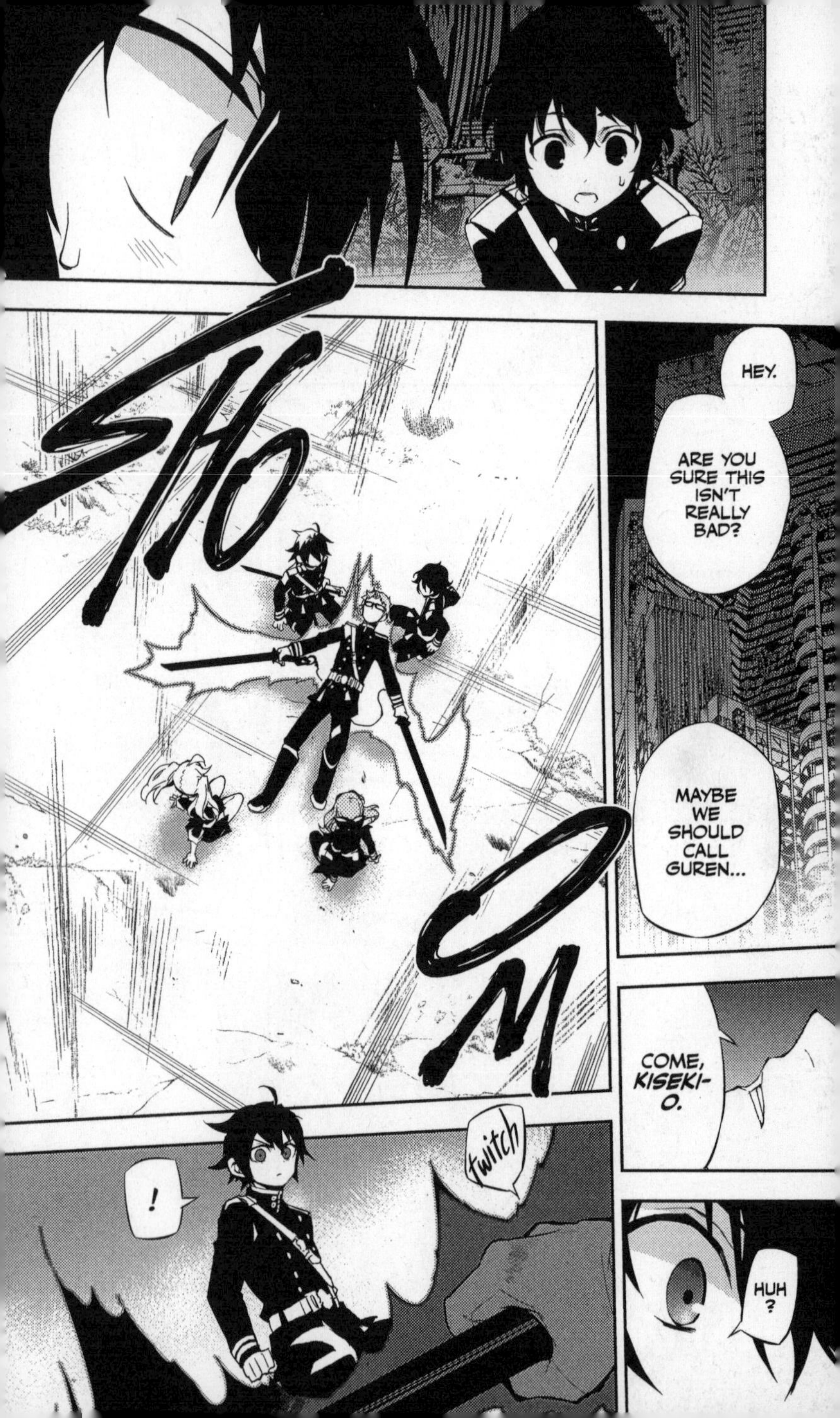

HEY.
ARE YOU SURE THIS ISN'T REALLY BAD?
MAYBE WE SHOULD CALL GUREN...
COME, KISEKI-O.
HUH?
SHOOM
!
twitch

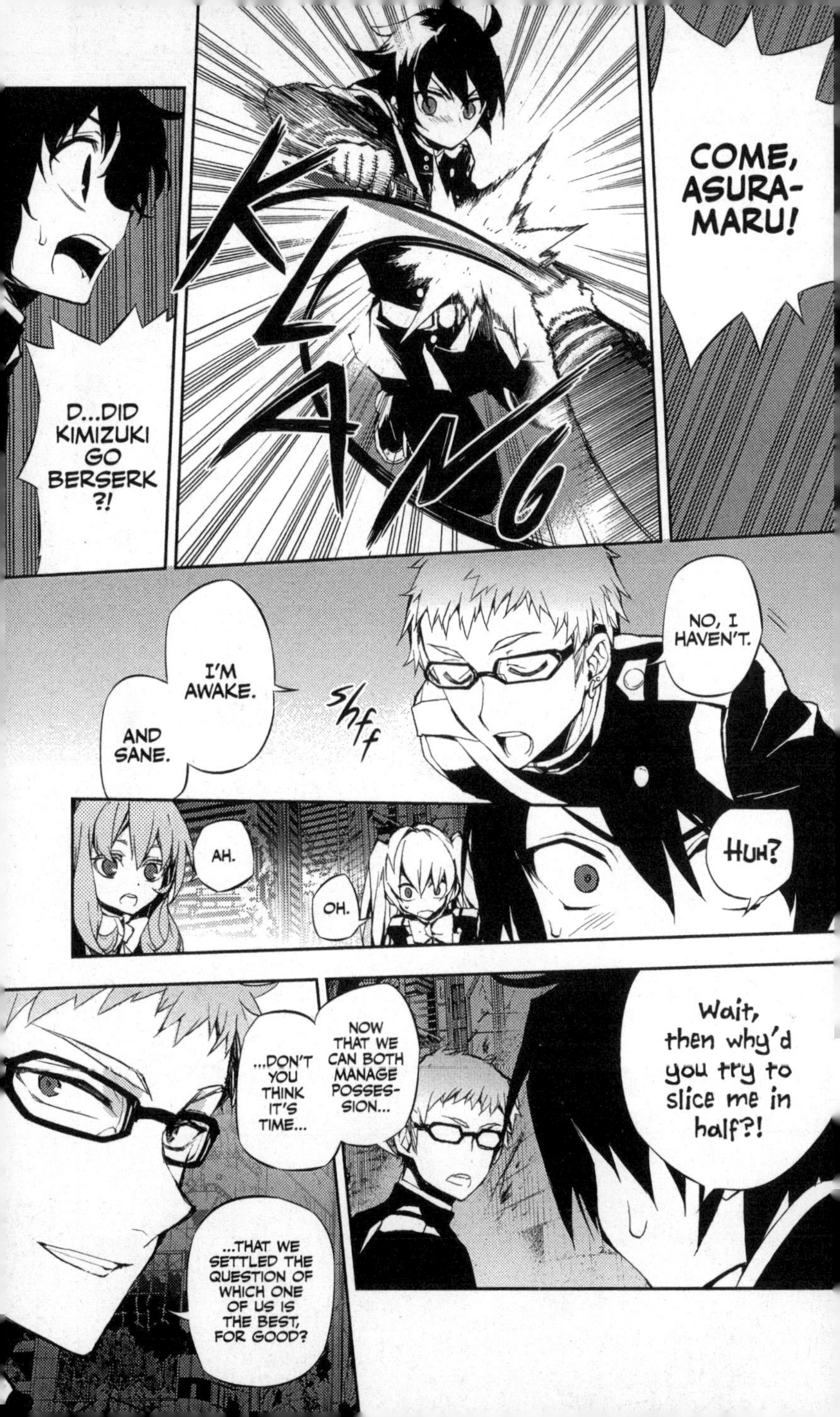
COME, ASURA-MARU!
KLANG
D...DID KIMIZUKI GO BERSERK?!
NO, I HAVEN'T.
I'M AWAKE.
AND SANE.
shff
HUH?
OH.
AH.
Wait, then why'd you try to slice me in half?!
NOW THAT WE CAN BOTH MANAGE POSSESSION...
...DON'T YOU THINK IT'S TIME...
...THAT WE SETTLED THE QUESTION OF WHICH ONE OF US IS THE BEST, FOR GOOD?

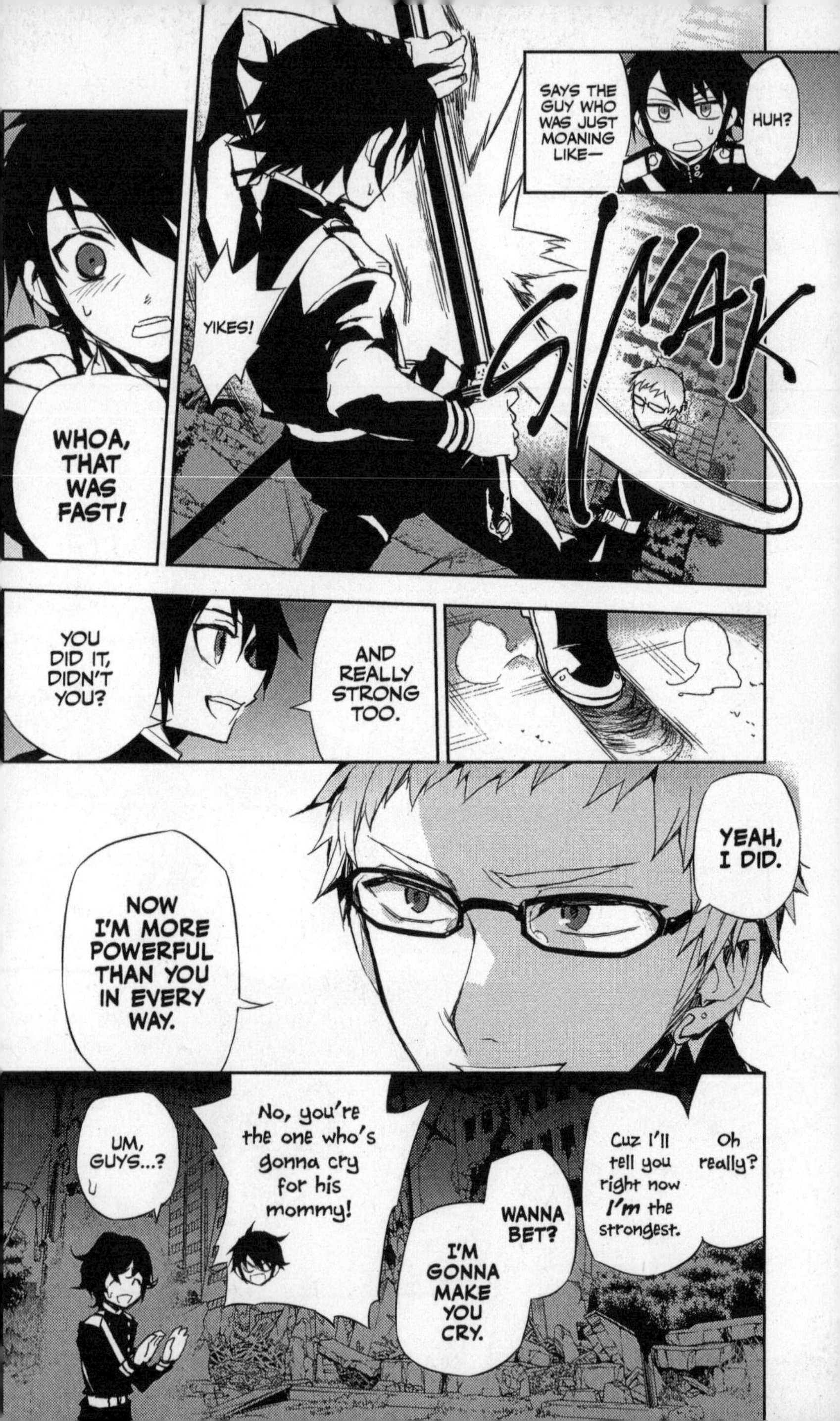
HUH?
SAYS THE GUY WHO WAS JUST MOANING LIKE—
SNAK
YIKES!
WHOA, THAT WAS FAST!
AND REALLY STRONG TOO.
YOU DID IT, DIDN'T YOU?
YEAH, I DID.
NOW I'M MORE POWERFUL THAN YOU IN EVERY WAY.
Oh really?
Cuz I'll tell you right now *I'm* the strongest.
WANNA BET?
I'M GONNA MAKE YOU CRY.
No, you're the one who's gonna cry for his mommy!
UM, GUYS...?

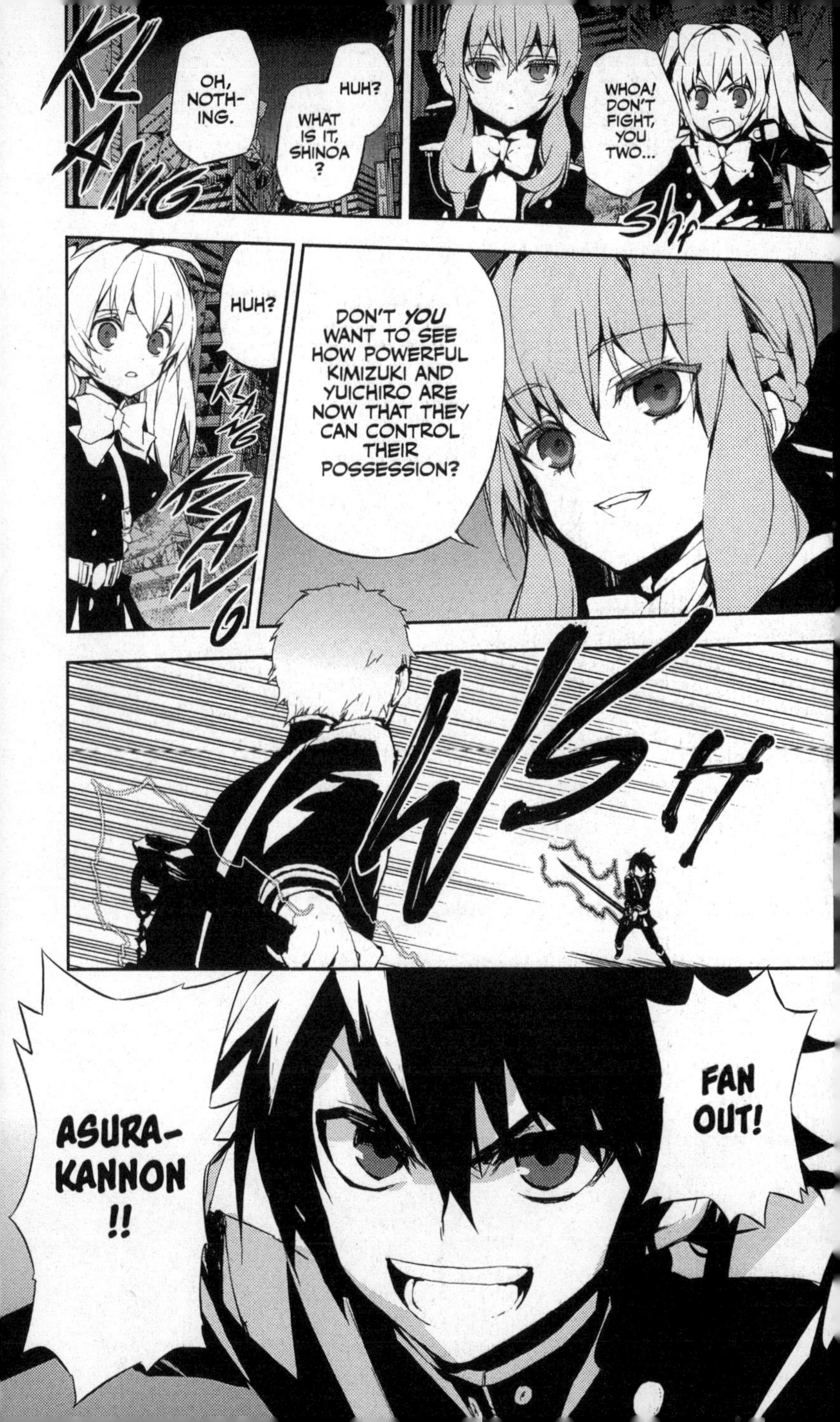
WHOA! DON'T FIGHT, YOU TWO...
SHF
HUH? WHAT IS IT, SHINOA?
OH, NOTHING.
KLANG
DON'T *YOU* WANT TO SEE HOW POWERFUL KIMIZUKI AND YUICHIRO ARE NOW THAT THEY CAN CONTROL THEIR POSSESSION?
HUH?
KLANG
KLANG
WHSH
FAN OUT!
ASURA-KANNON!!

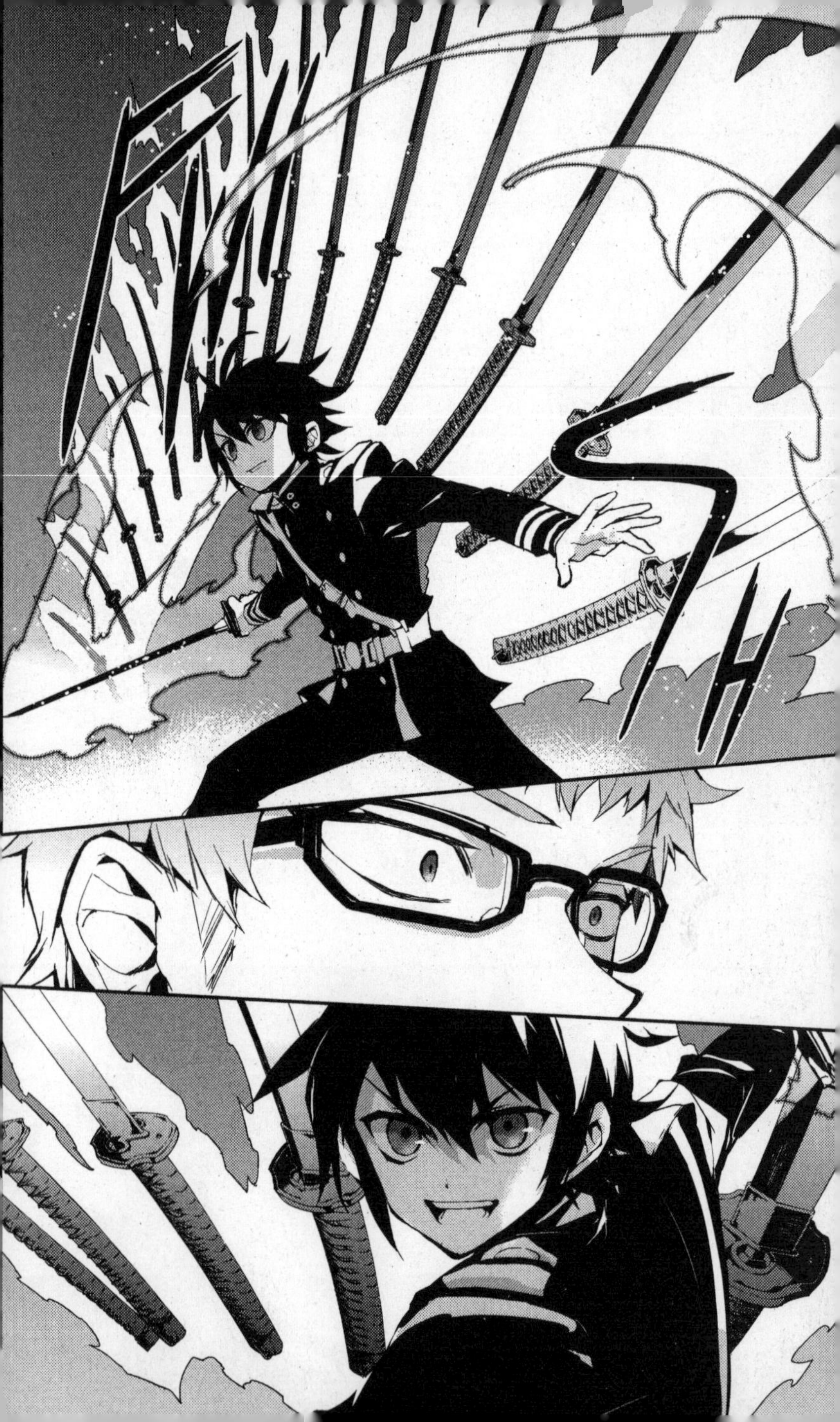

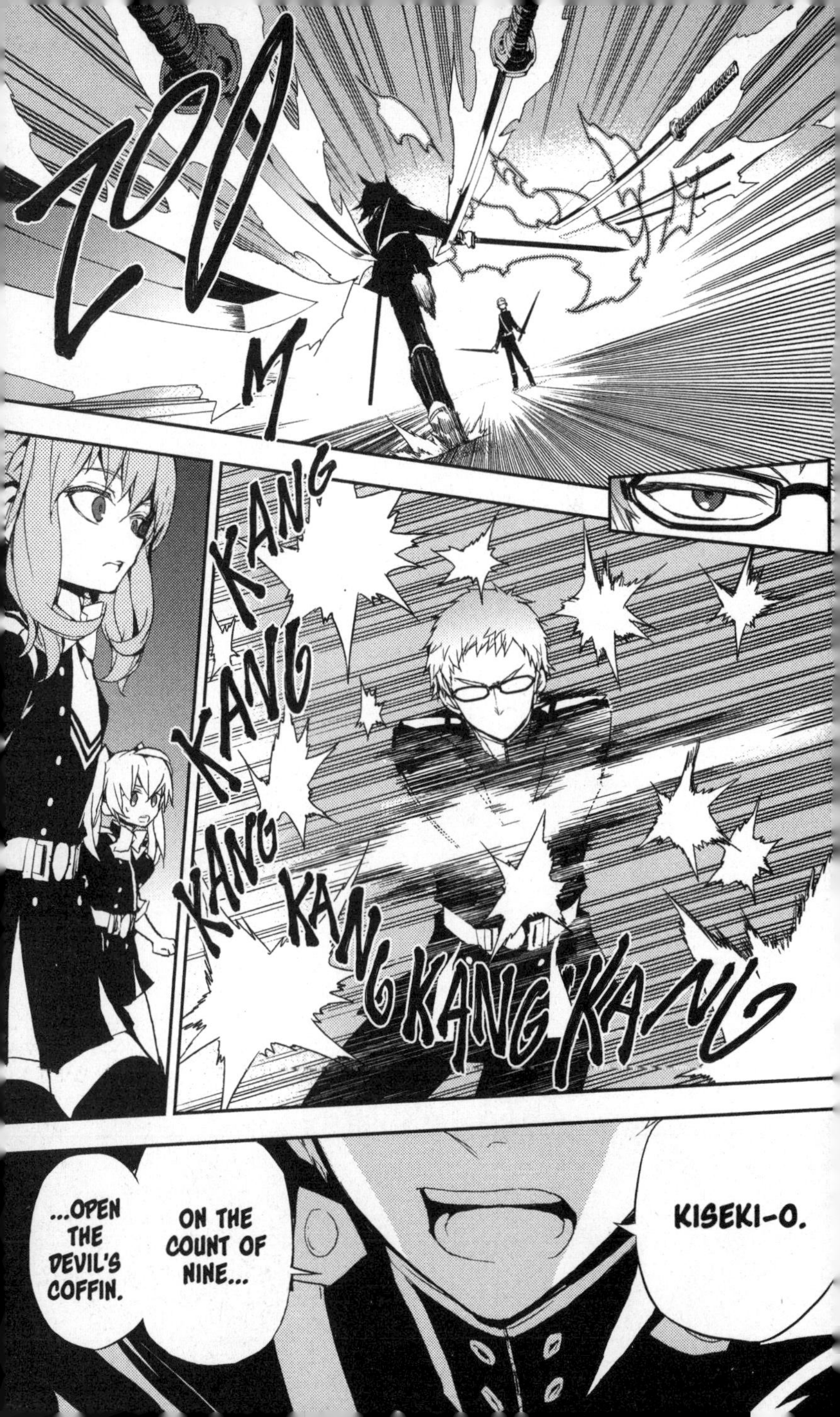
ZOOM
KANG
KANG
KANG
KANG KANG KANG
KISEKI-O.
ON THE COUNT OF NINE...
...OPEN THE DEVIL'S COFFIN.

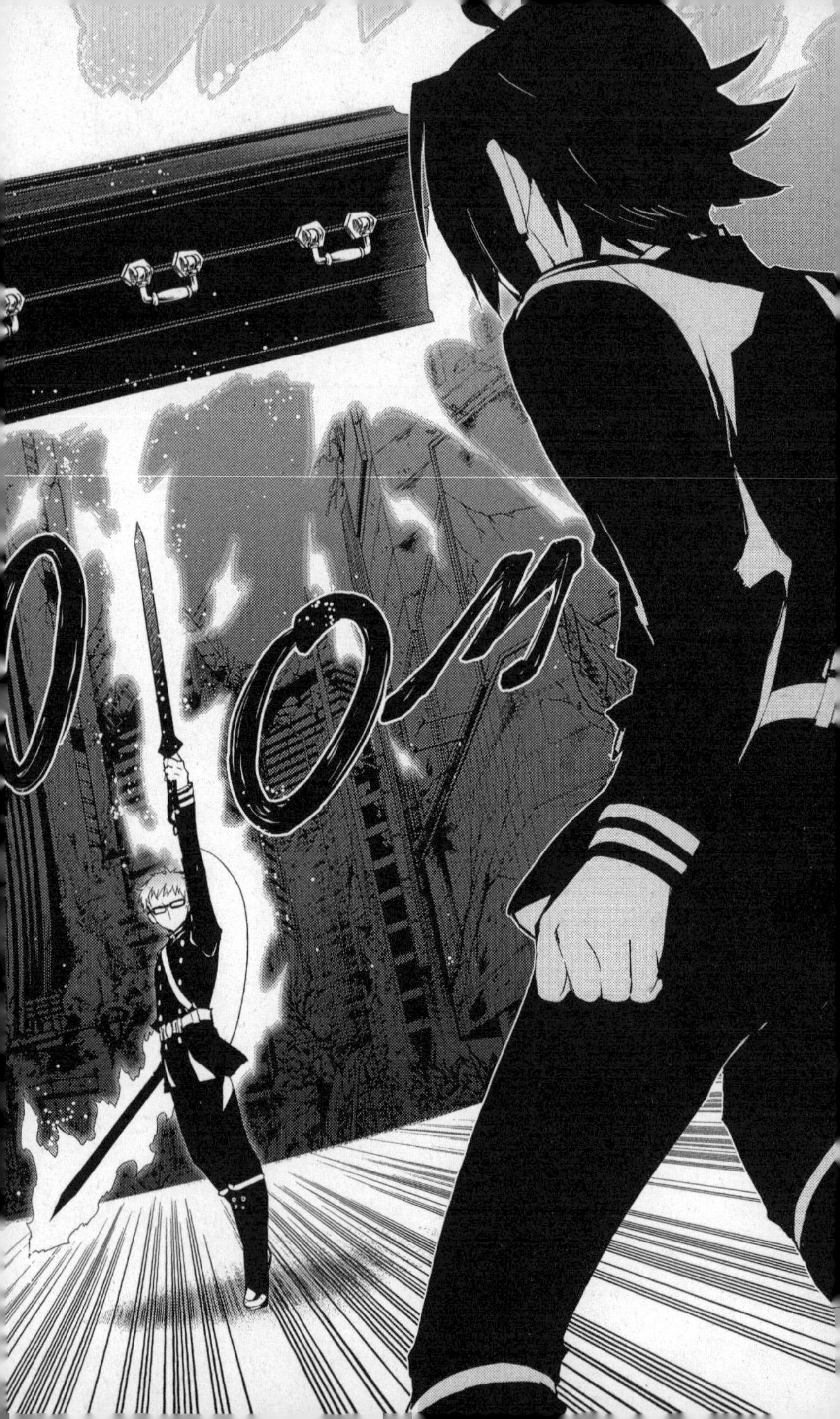
OOM

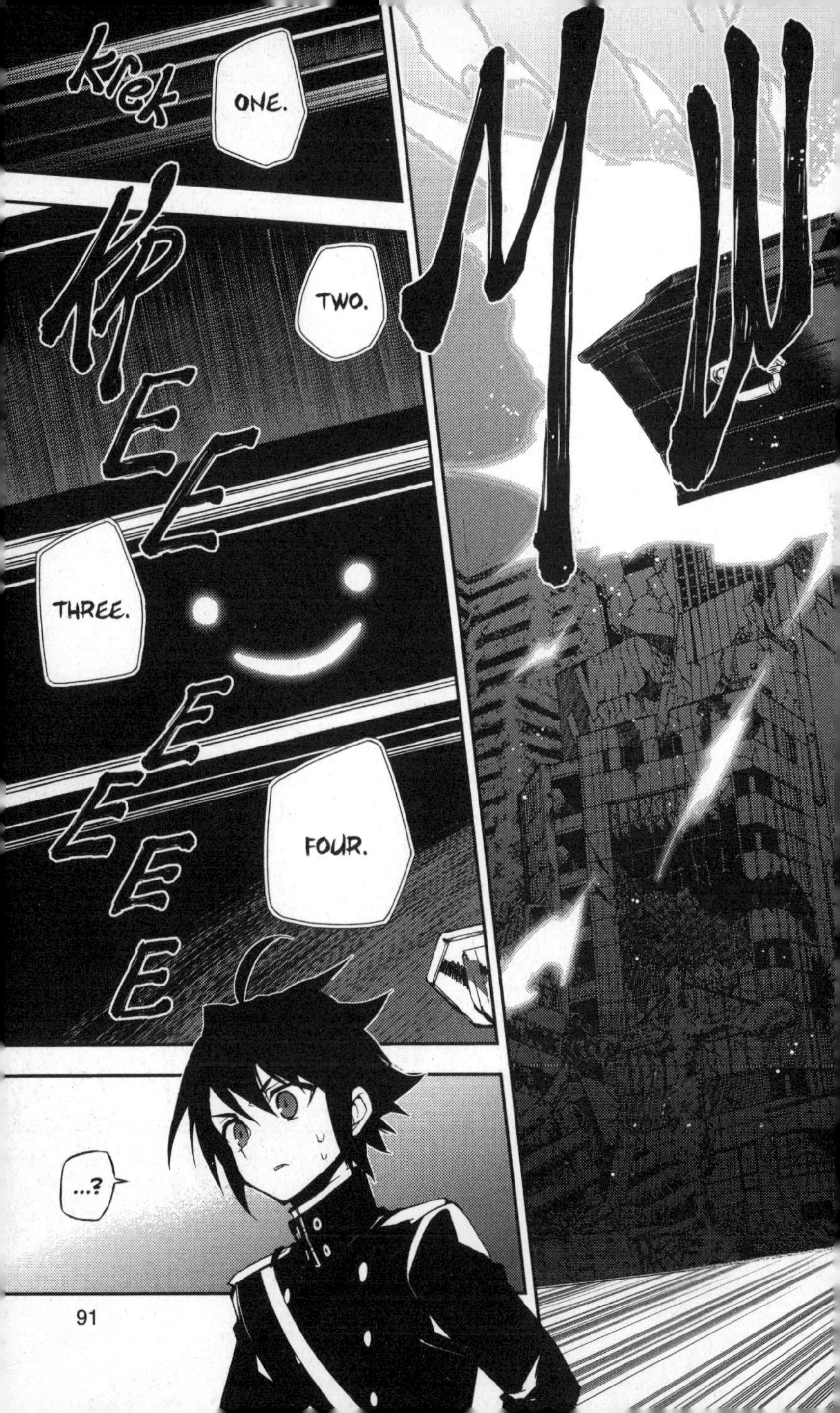
krek
ONE.
TWO.
THREE.
FOUR.
...?

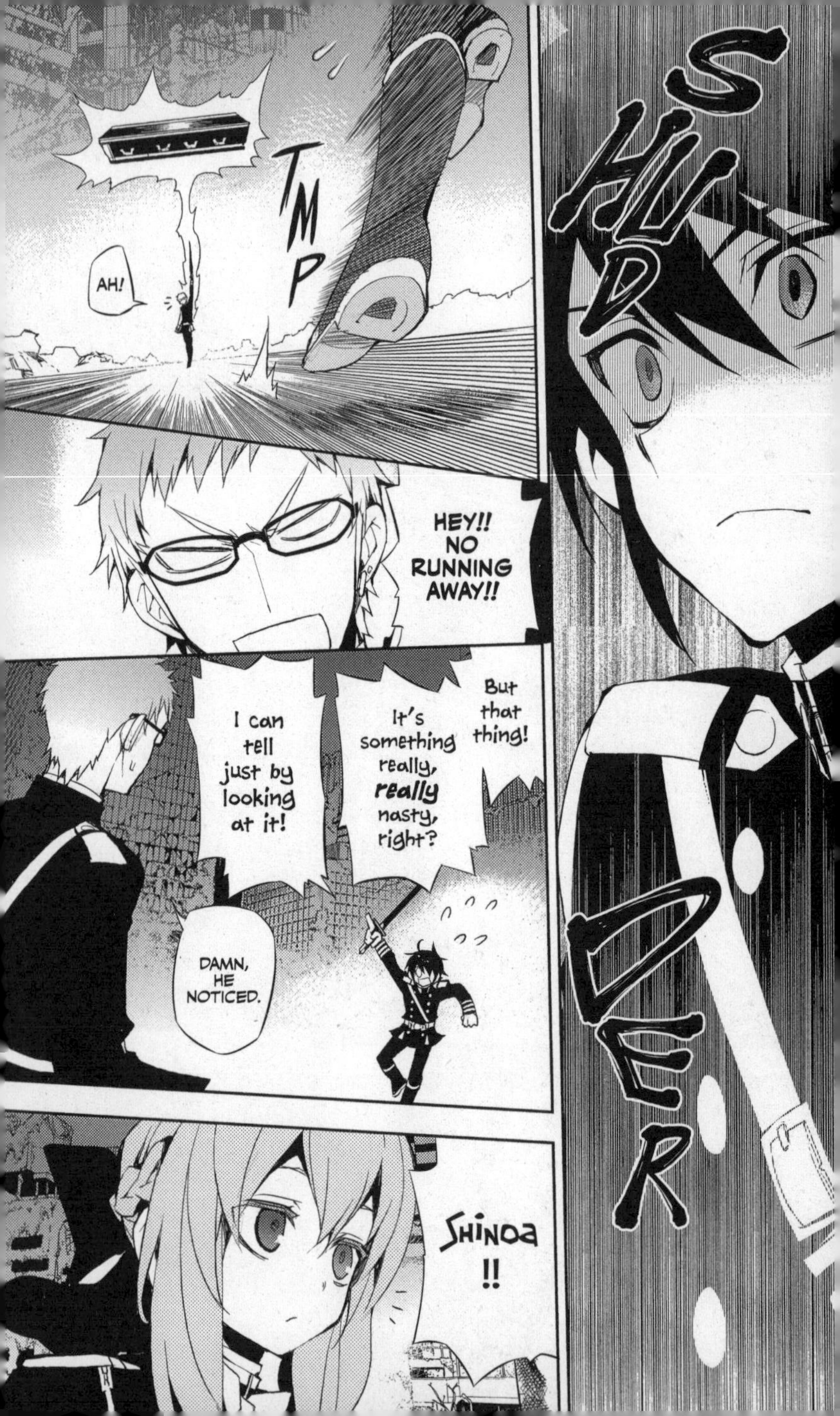
SHUDDER
SHINOA!!
TMP
AH!
HEY!! NO RUNNING AWAY!!
But that thing!
It's something really, ***really*** nasty, right?
I can tell just by looking at it!
DAMN, HE NOTICED.

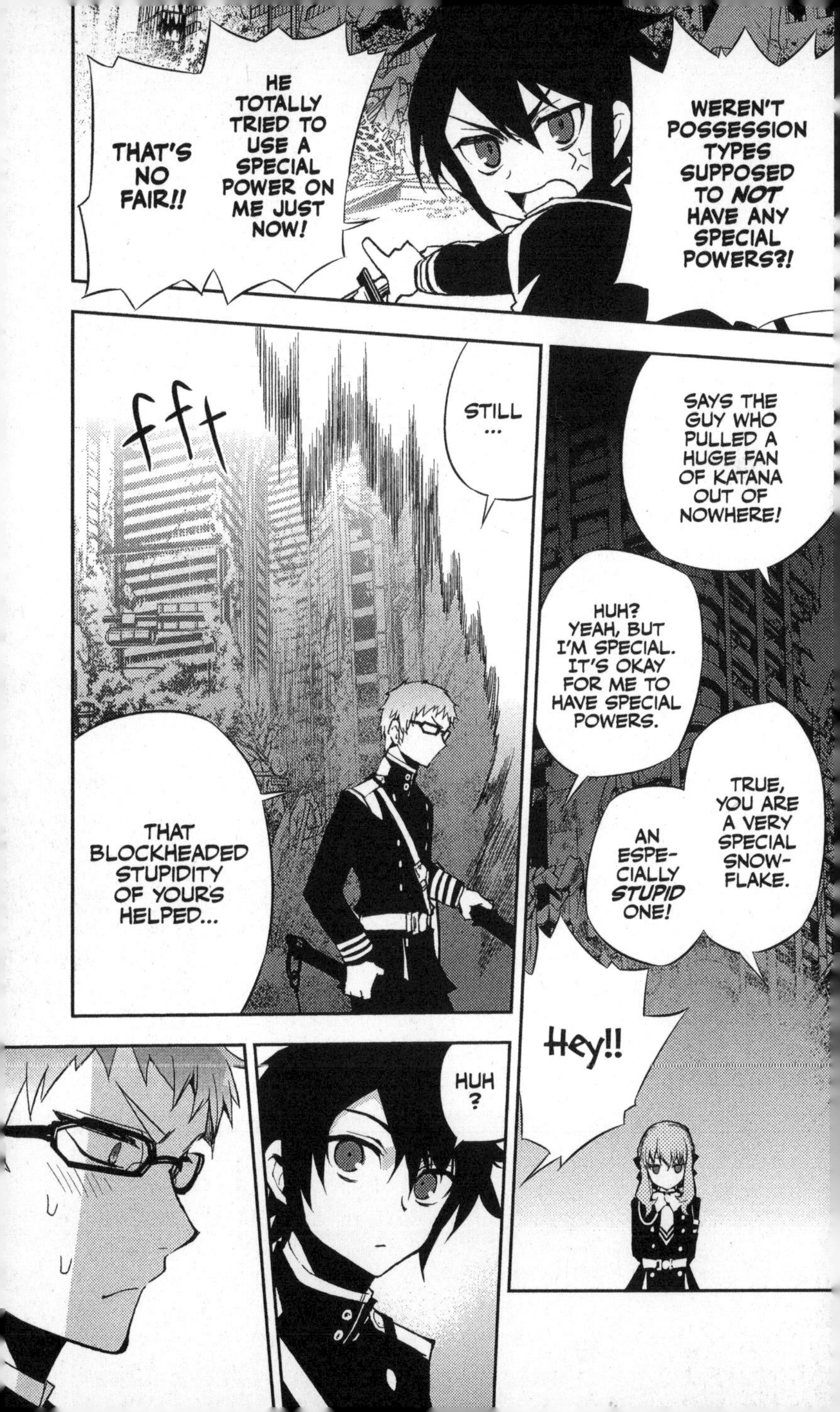
WEREN'T POSSESSION TYPES SUPPOSED TO *NOT* HAVE ANY SPECIAL POWERS?!
HE TOTALLY TRIED TO USE A SPECIAL POWER ON ME JUST NOW!
THAT'S NO FAIR!!
SAYS THE GUY WHO PULLED A HUGE FAN OF KATANA OUT OF NOWHERE!
HUH? YEAH, BUT I'M SPECIAL. IT'S OKAY FOR ME TO HAVE SPECIAL POWERS.
TRUE, YOU ARE A VERY SPECIAL SNOW-FLAKE.
AN ESPE-CIALLY *STUPID* ONE!
Hey!!
STILL ...
fft
THAT BLOCKHEADED STUPIDITY OF YOURS HELPED...
HUH ?

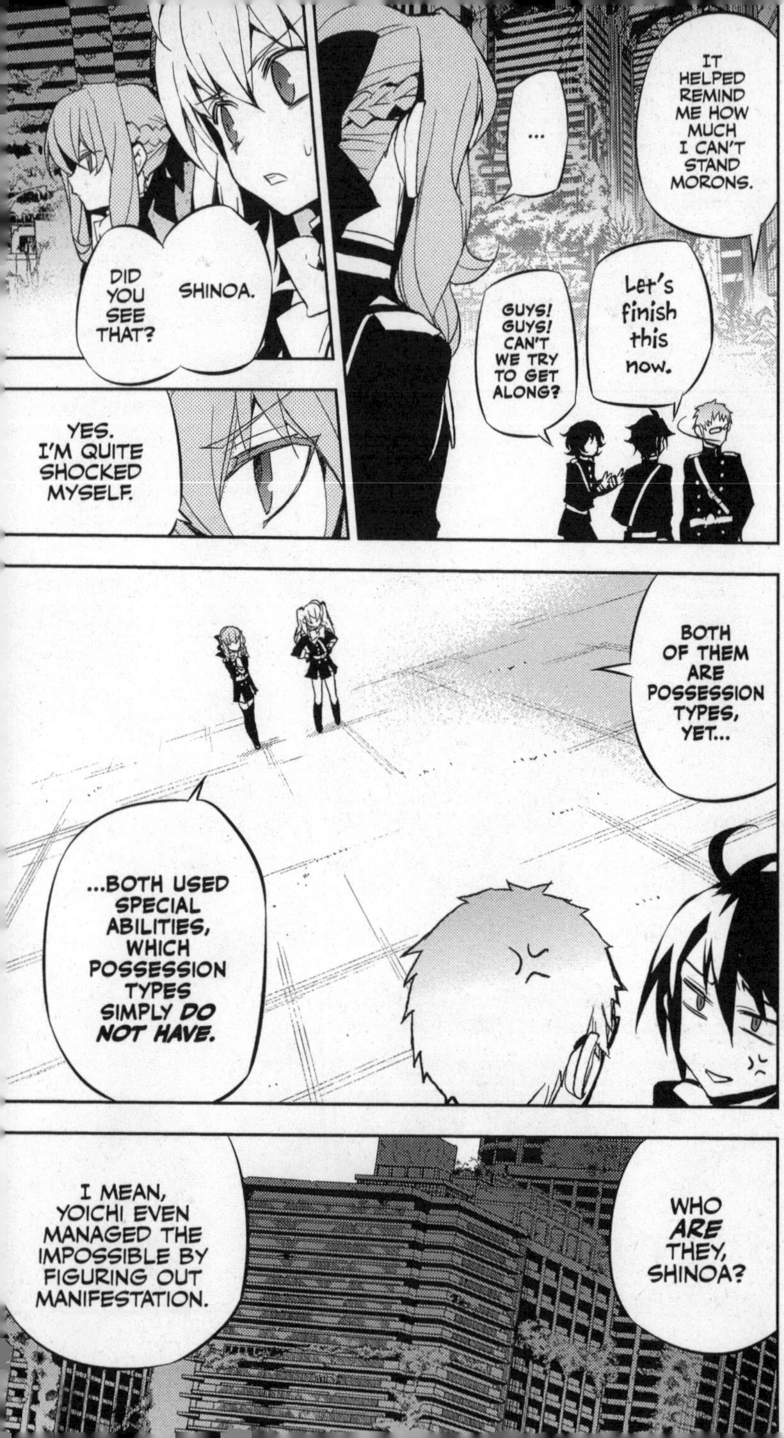
IT HELPED REMIND ME HOW MUCH I CAN'T STAND MORONS.
...
Let's finish this now.
GUYS! GUYS! CAN'T WE TRY TO GET ALONG?
DID YOU SEE THAT? SHINOA.
YES. I'M QUITE SHOCKED MYSELF.
BOTH OF THEM ARE POSSESSION TYPES, YET...
...BOTH USED SPECIAL ABILITIES, WHICH POSSESSION TYPES SIMPLY *DO NOT HAVE.*
WHO *ARE* THEY, SHINOA?
I MEAN, YOICHI EVEN MANAGED THE IMPOSSIBLE BY FIGURING OUT MANIFESTATION.

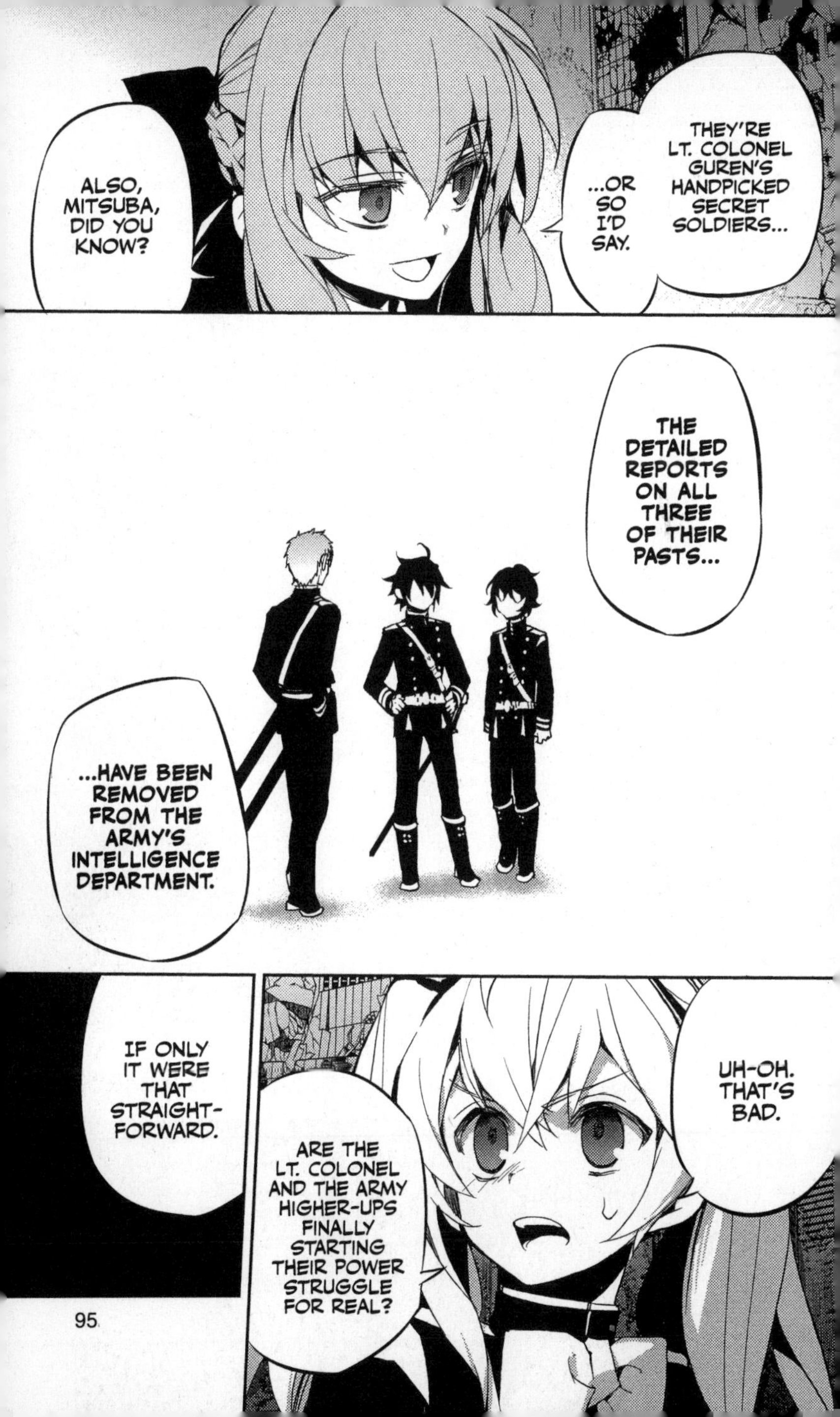
THEY'RE LT. COLONEL GUREN'S HANDPICKED SECRET SOLDIERS...
...OR SO I'D SAY.
ALSO, MITSUBA, DID YOU KNOW?
THE DETAILED REPORTS ON ALL THREE OF THEIR PASTS...
...HAVE BEEN REMOVED FROM THE ARMY'S INTELLIGENCE DEPARTMENT.
UH-OH. THAT'S BAD.
ARE THE LT. COLONEL AND THE ARMY HIGHER-UPS FINALLY STARTING THEIR POWER STRUGGLE FOR REAL?
IF ONLY IT WERE THAT STRAIGHT-FORWARD.

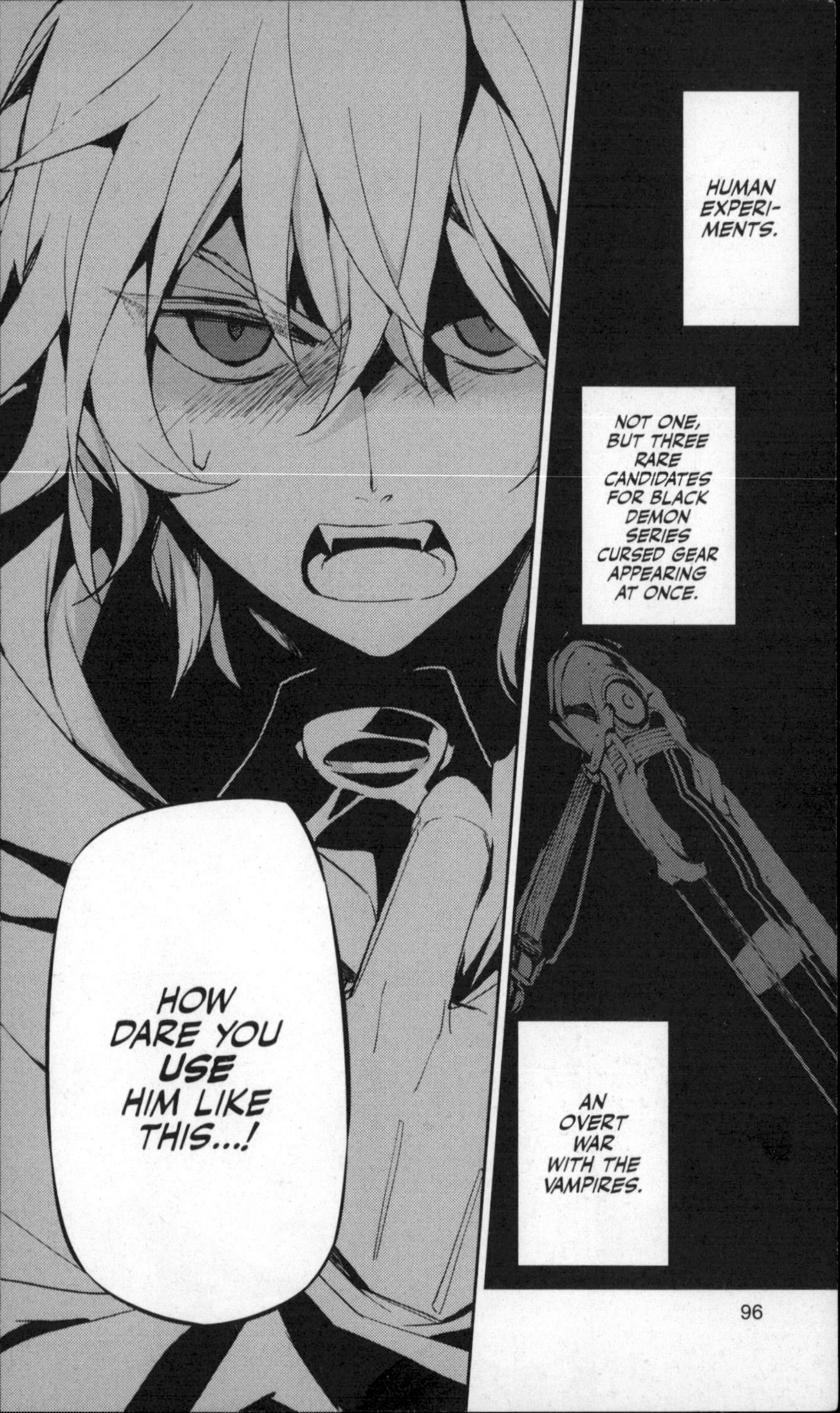
HUMAN EXPERI-MENTS.
NOT ONE, BUT THREE RARE CANDIDATES FOR BLACK DEMON SERIES CURSED GEAR APPEARING AT ONCE.
AN OVERT WAR WITH THE VAMPIRES.
HOW DARE YOU USE HIM LIKE THIS...!

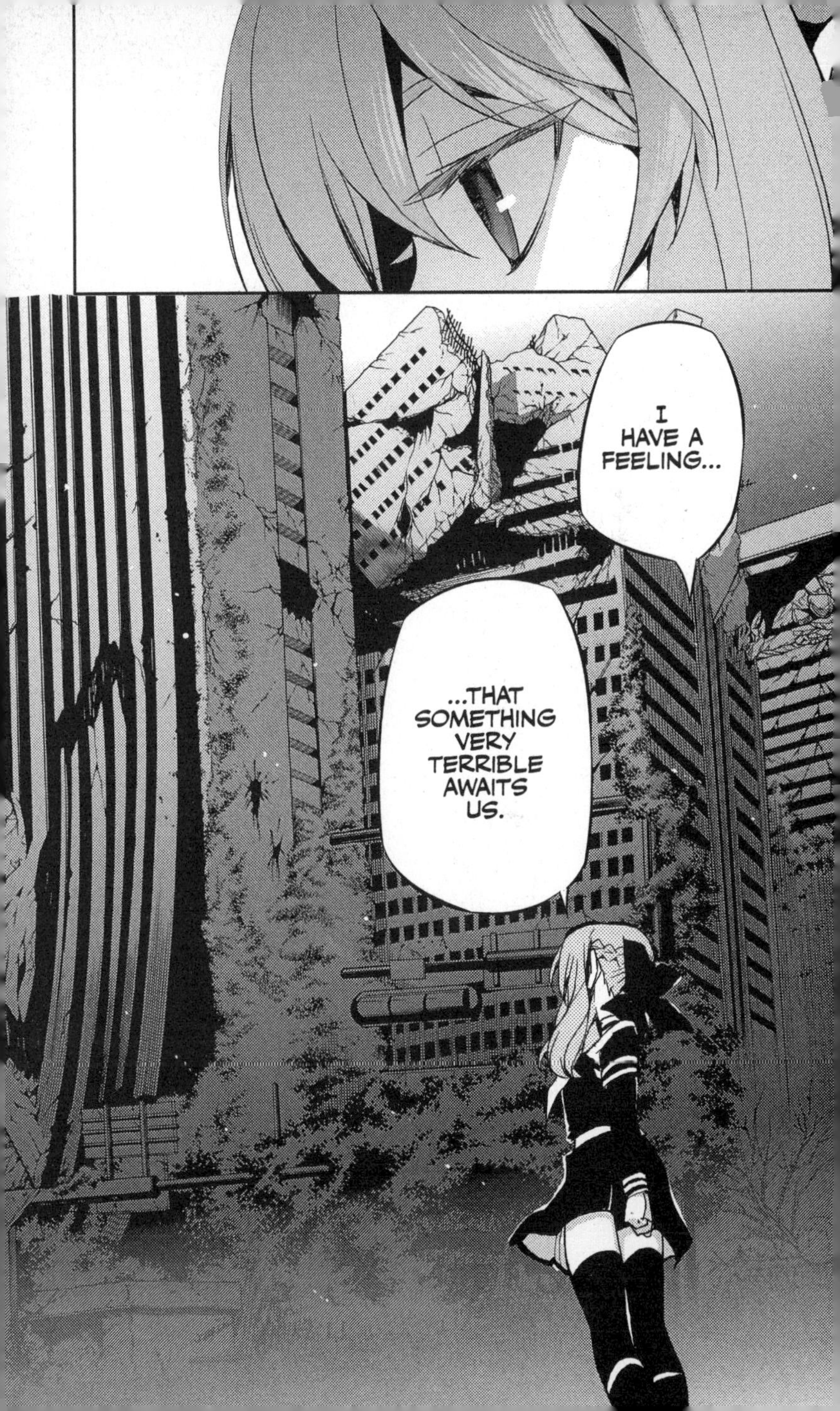
I HAVE A FEELING...
...THAT SOMETHING VERY TERRIBLE AWAITS US.

Seraph of the End
—VAMPIRE REIGN—

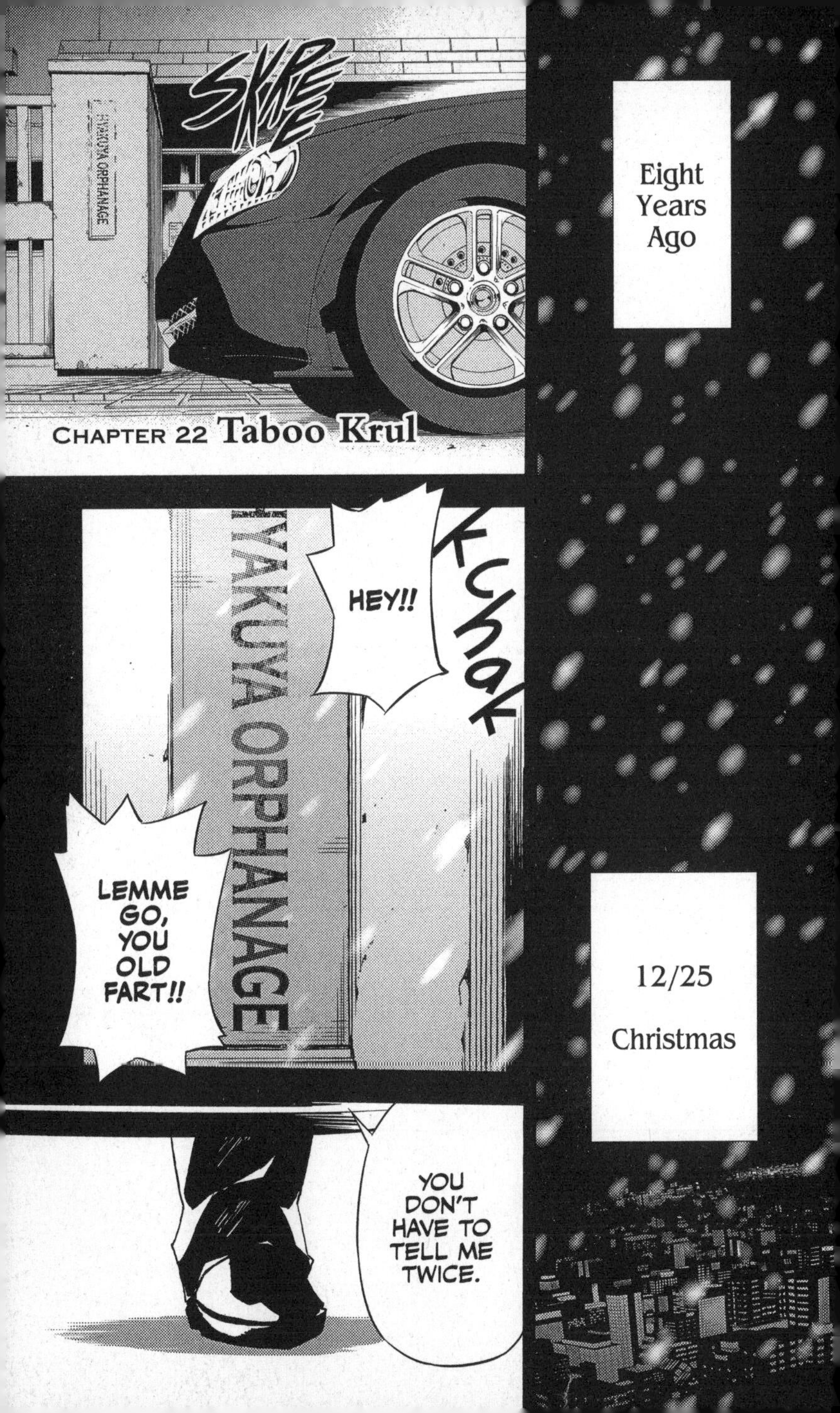

Eight Years Ago
12/25
Christmas
SKREE
HYAKUYA ORPHANAGE
CHAPTER 22 Taboo Krul
KCHAK
HEY!!
YAKUYA ORPHANAGE
LEMME GO, YOU OLD FART!!
YOU DON'T HAVE TO TELL ME TWICE.

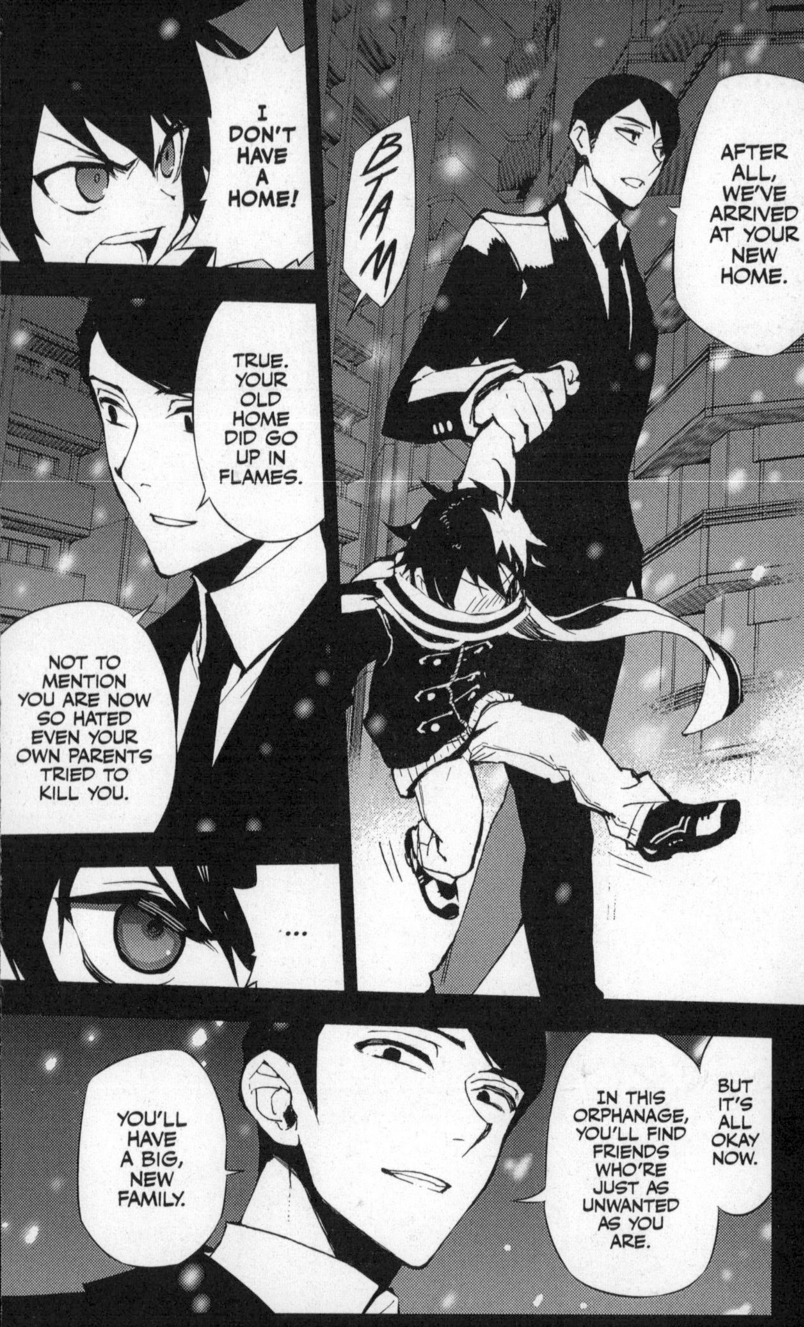
AFTER ALL, WE'VE ARRIVED AT YOUR NEW HOME.
BTAM
I DON'T HAVE A HOME!
TRUE. YOUR OLD HOME DID GO UP IN FLAMES.
NOT TO MENTION YOU ARE NOW SO HATED EVEN YOUR OWN PARENTS TRIED TO KILL YOU.
...
BUT IT'S ALL OKAY NOW.
IN THIS ORPHANAGE, YOU'LL FIND FRIENDS WHO'RE JUST AS UNWANTED AS YOU ARE.
YOU'LL HAVE A BIG, NEW FAMILY.

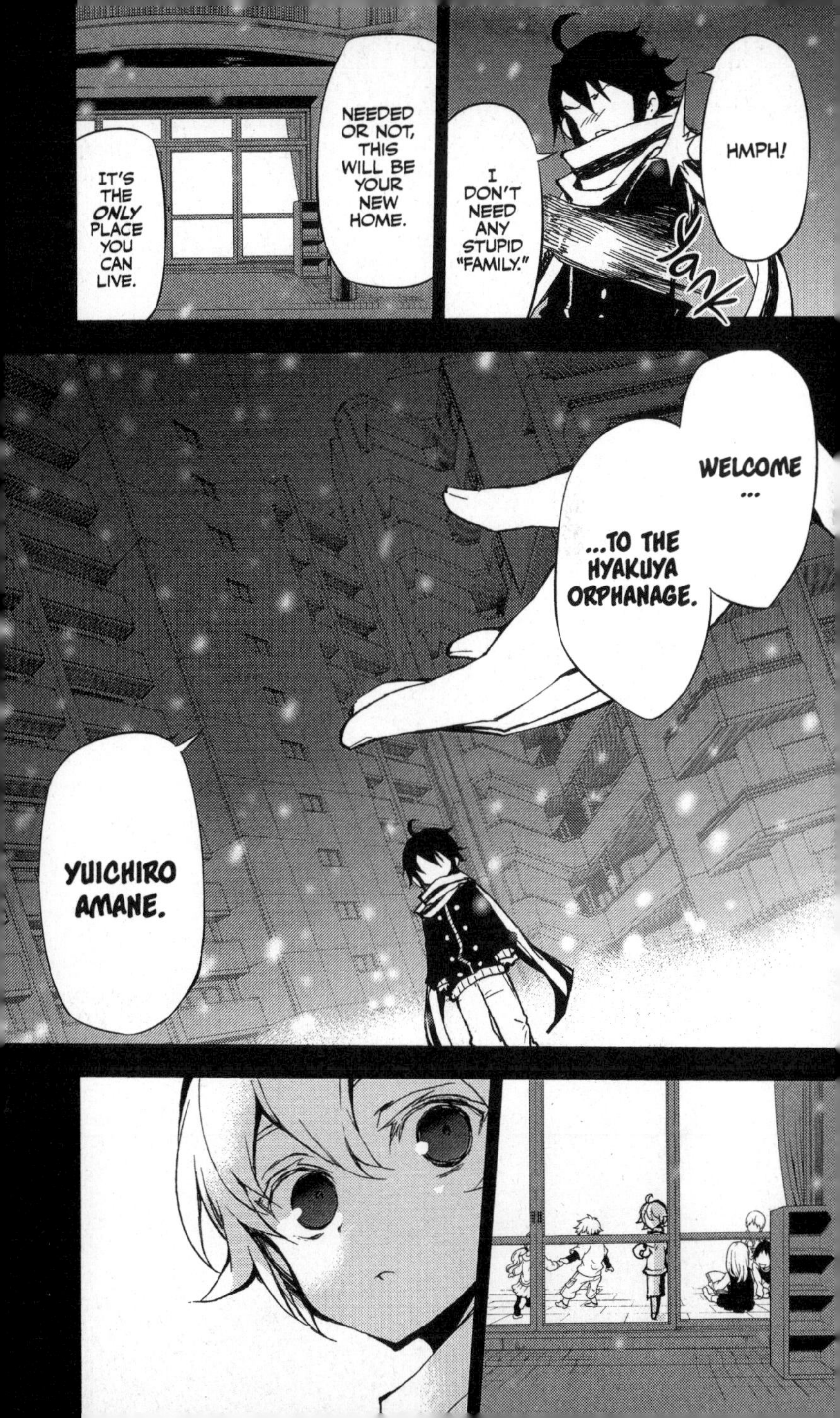
HMPH!
YANK
I DON'T NEED ANY STUPID "FAMILY."
NEEDED OR NOT, THIS WILL BE YOUR NEW HOME.
IT'S THE *ONLY* PLACE YOU CAN LIVE.
WELCOME...
...TO THE HYAKUYA ORPHANAGE.
YUICHIRO AMANE.

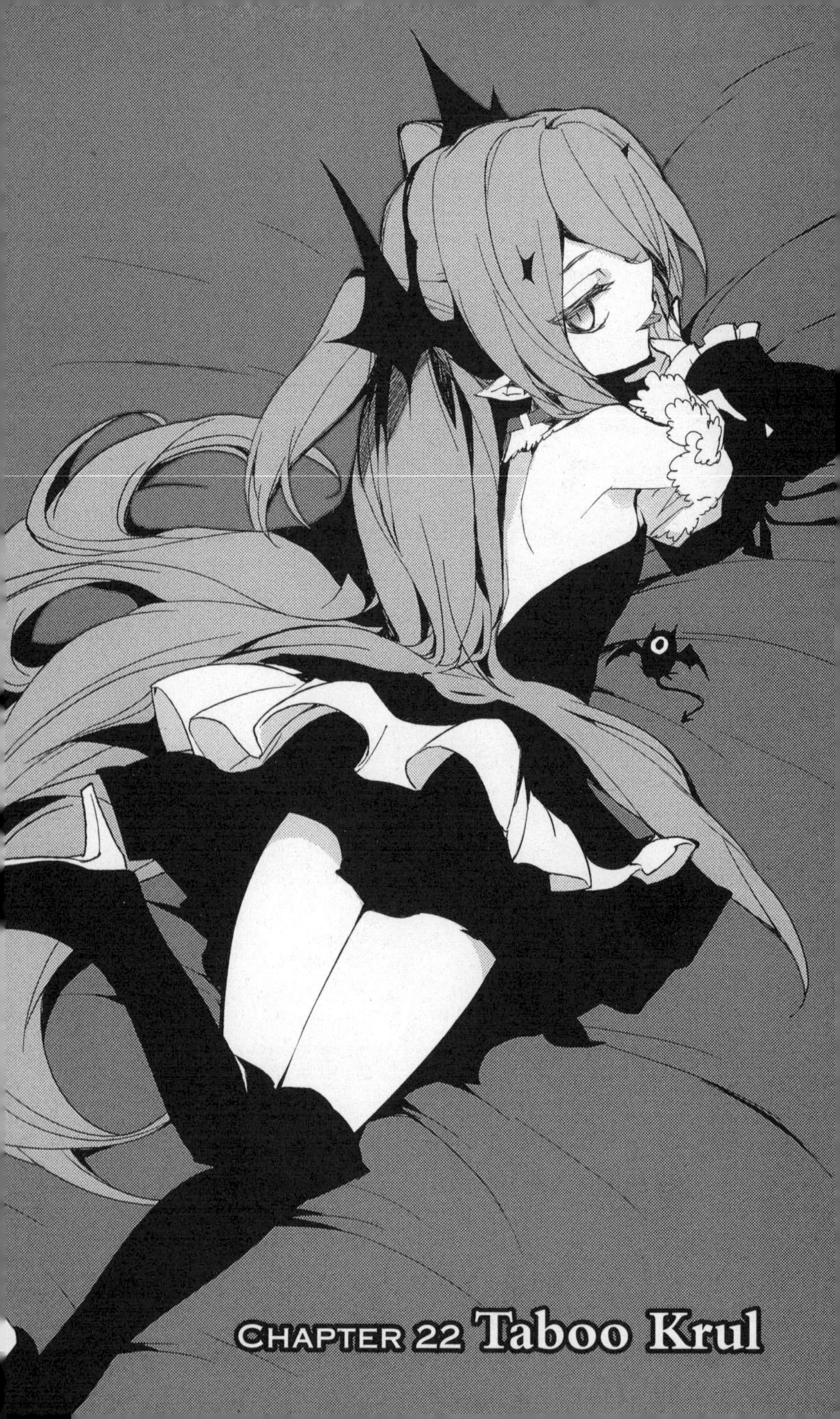

CHAPTER 22 Taboo Krul

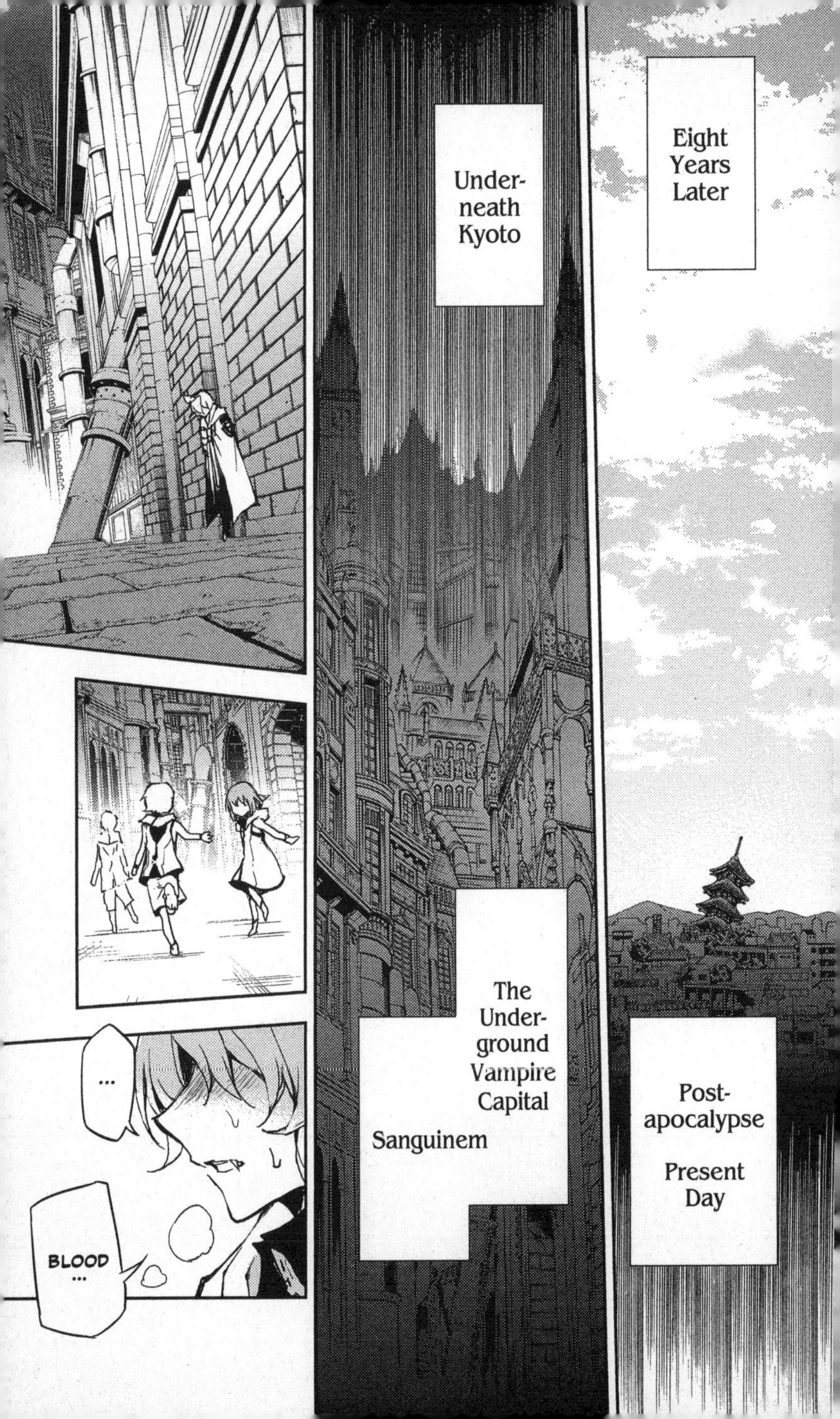
Eight Years Later
Post-apocalypse
Present Day
Underneath Kyoto
The Underground Vampire Capital
Sanguinem
...
BLOOD ...

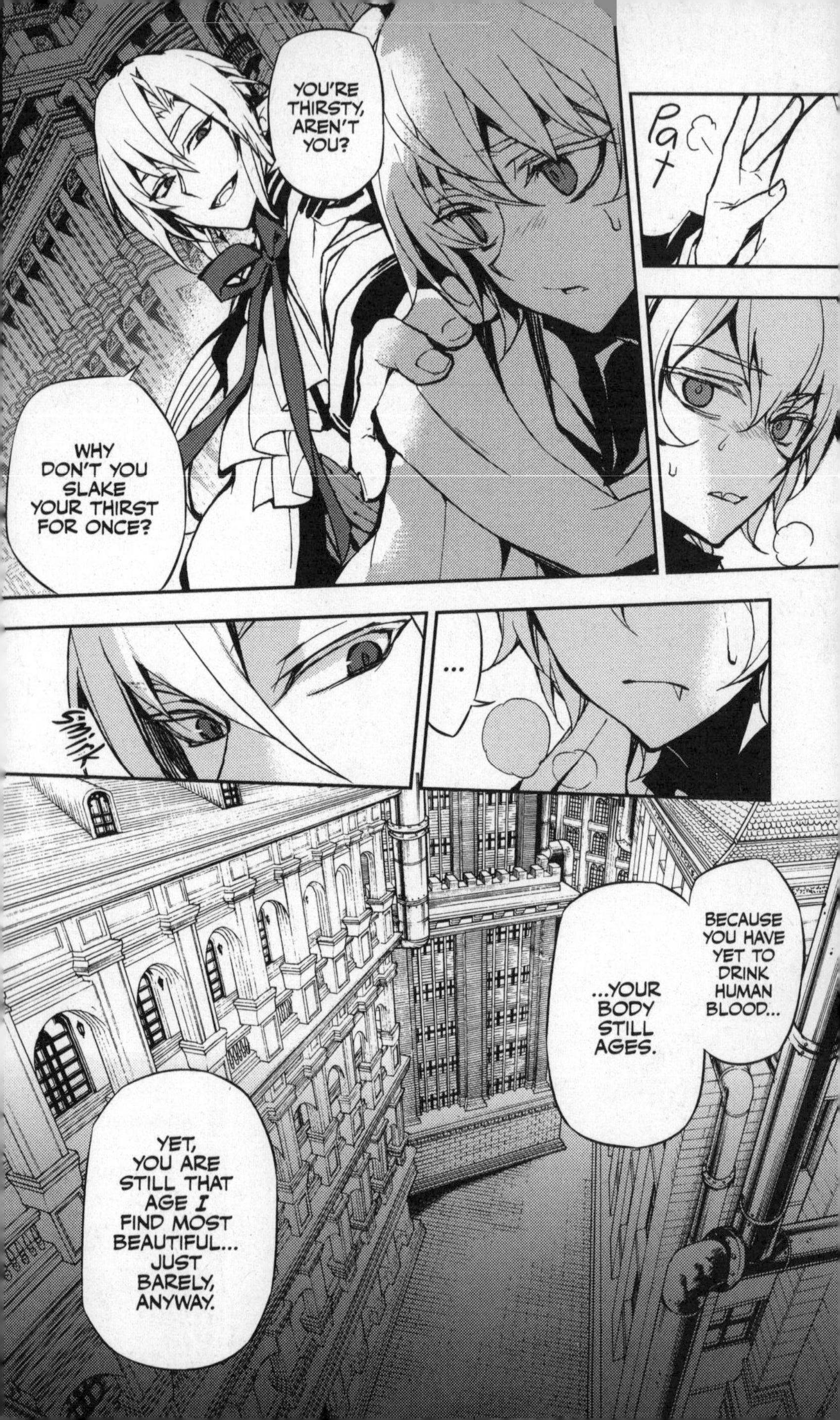
Pat
YOU'RE THIRSTY, AREN'T YOU?
WHY DON'T YOU SLAKE YOUR THIRST FOR ONCE?
...
Smirk
BECAUSE YOU HAVE YET TO DRINK HUMAN BLOOD...
...YOUR BODY STILL AGES.
YET, YOU ARE STILL THAT AGE *I* FIND MOST BEAUTIFUL... JUST BARELY, ANYWAY.

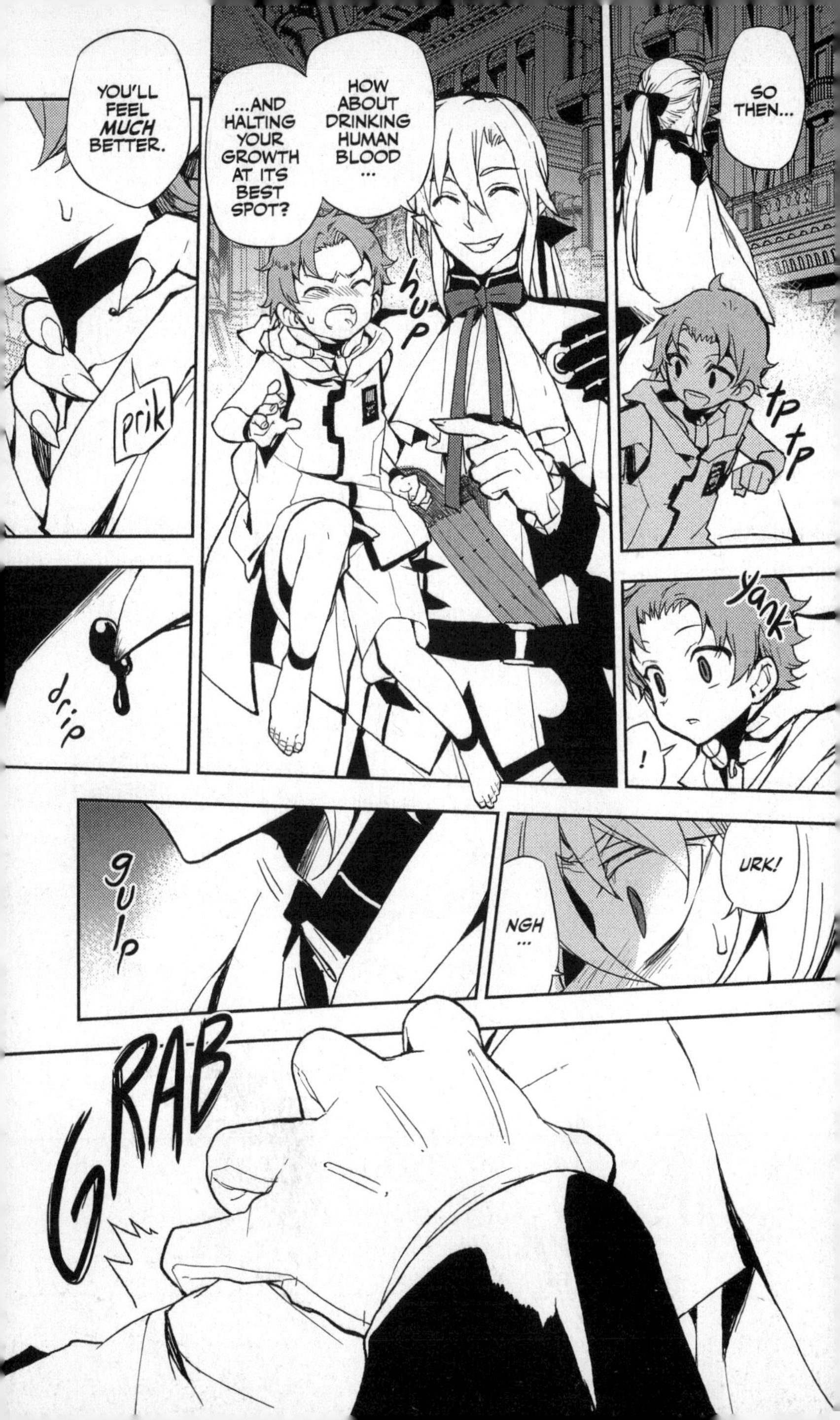
SO THEN...
tp tp
yank
!
HOW ABOUT DRINKING HUMAN BLOOD...
...AND HALTING YOUR GROWTH AT ITS BEST SPOT?
hup
YOU'LL FEEL *MUCH* BETTER.
prik
drip
URK!
NGH...
gulp
GRAB

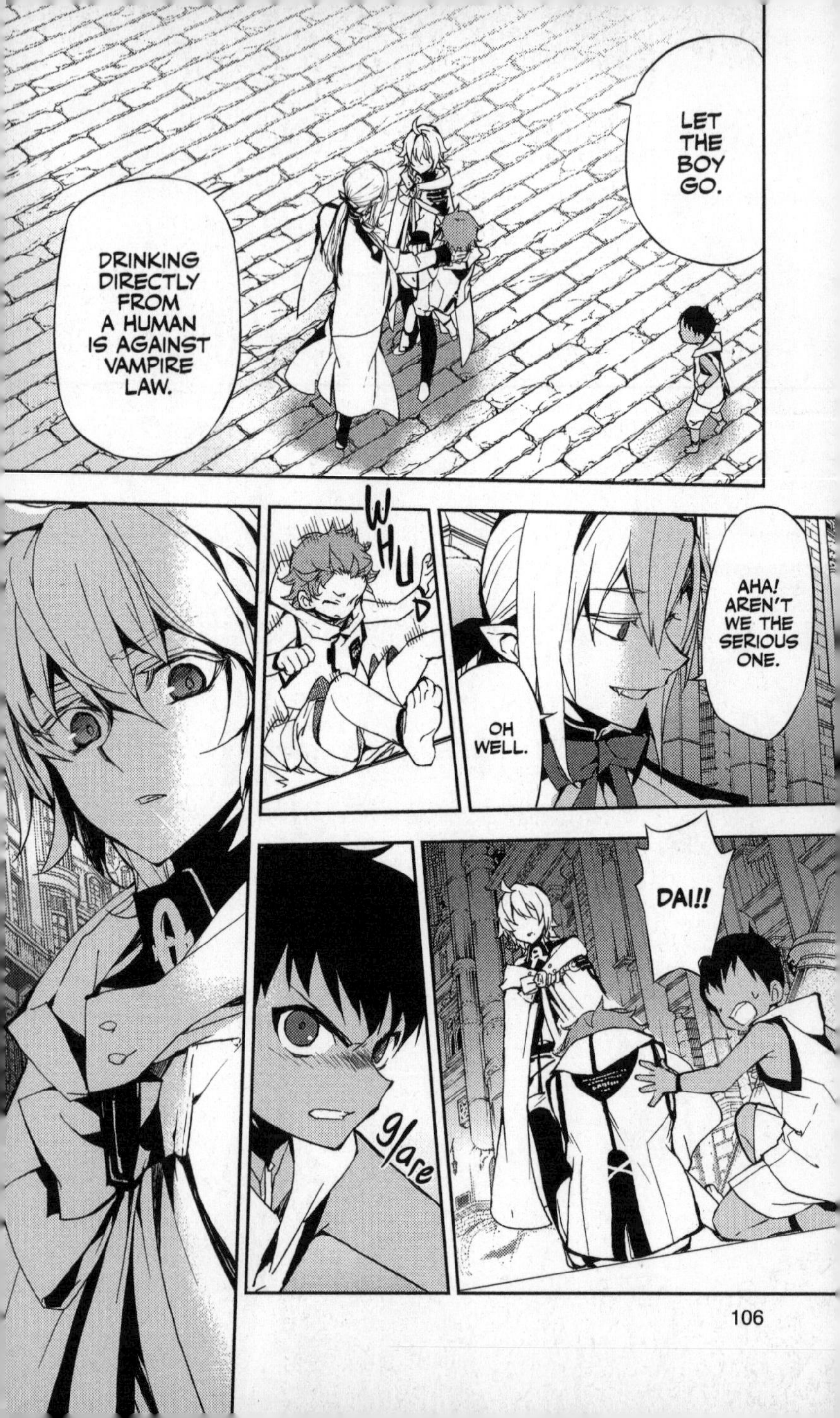

LET THE BOY GO.
DRINKING DIRECTLY FROM A HUMAN IS AGAINST VAMPIRE LAW.
AHA! AREN'T WE THE SERIOUS ONE.
OH WELL.
WHUD
DAI!!
glare

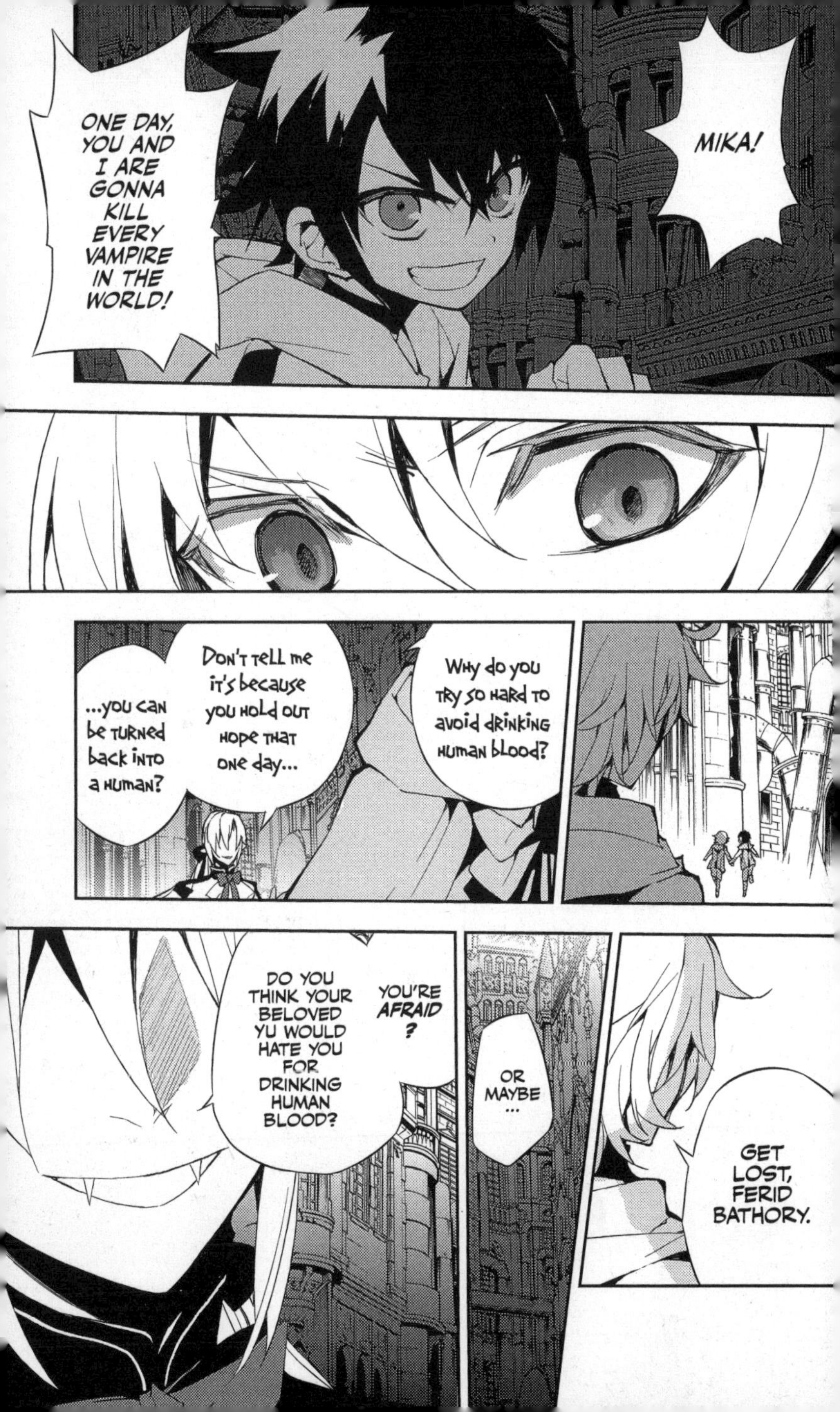
MIKA!
ONE DAY, YOU AND I ARE GONNA KILL EVERY VAMPIRE IN THE WORLD!
Why do you try so hard to avoid drinking human blood?
Don't tell me it's because you hold out hope that one day...
...you can be turned back into a human?
GET LOST, FERID BATHORY.
OR MAYBE ...
YOU'RE *AFRAID* ?
DO YOU THINK YOUR BELOVED YU WOULD HATE YOU FOR DRINKING HUMAN BLOOD?

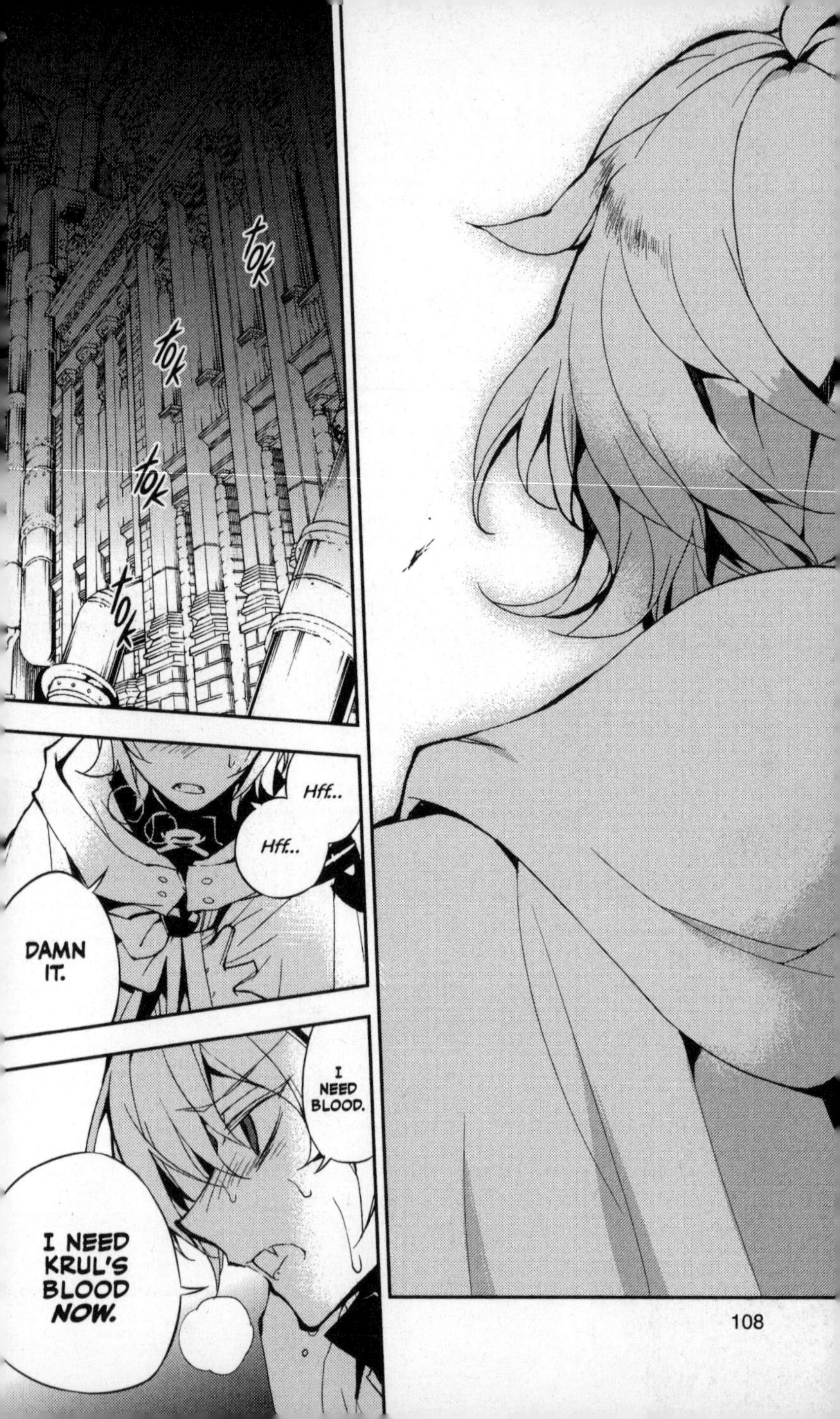
tok
tok
tok
tok
Hff...
Hff...
DAMN IT.
I NEED BLOOD.
I NEED KRUL'S BLOOD NOW.

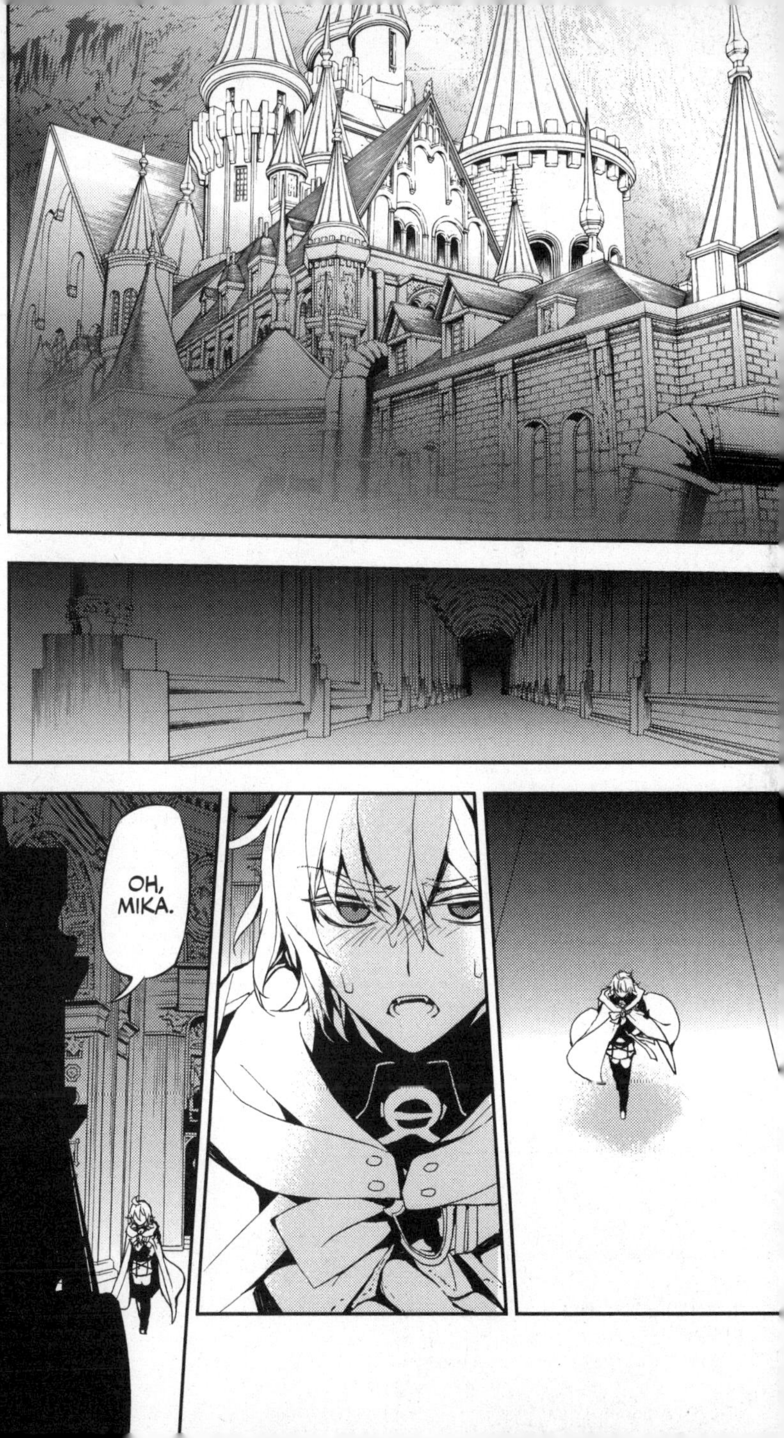
OH, MIKA.

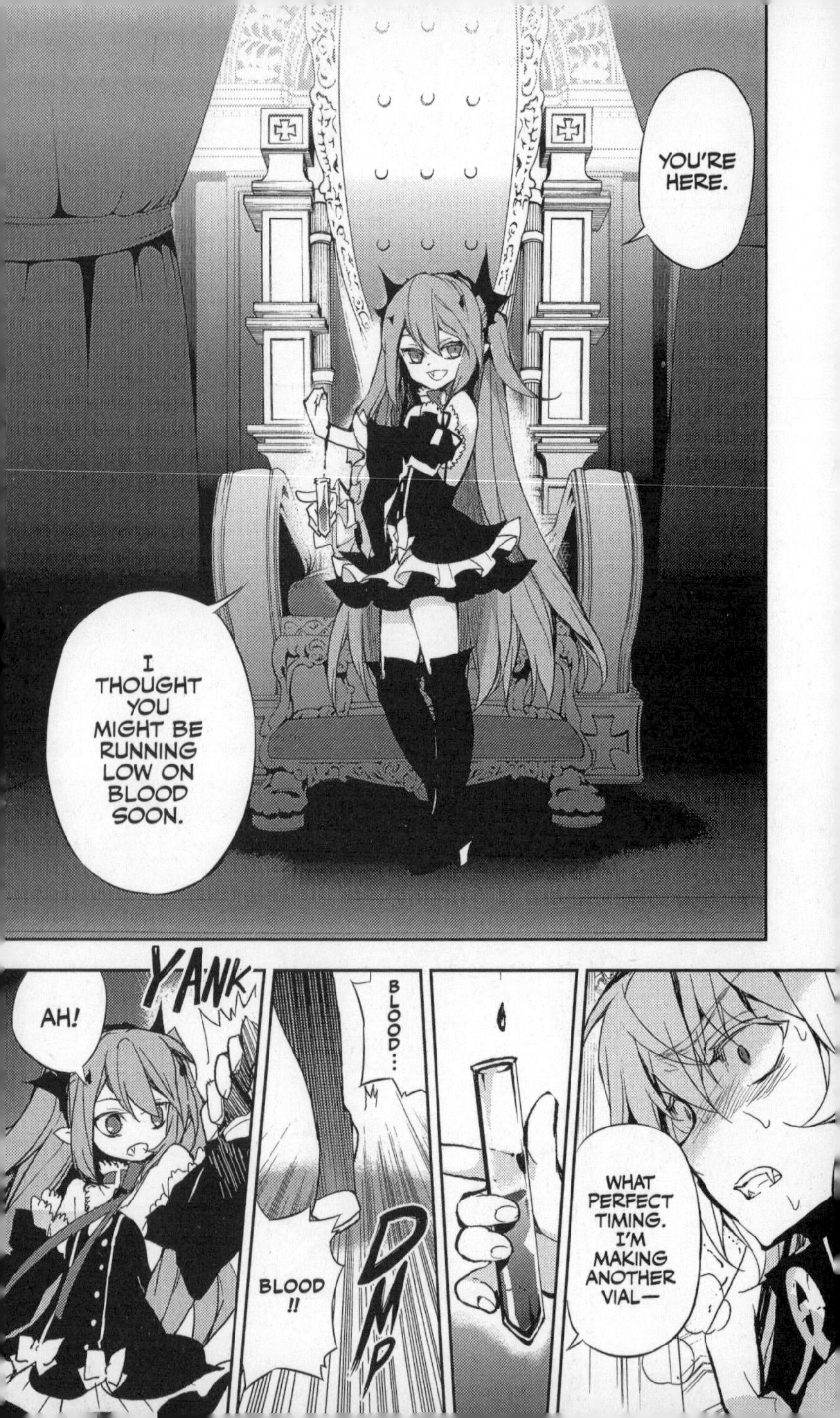
YOU'RE HERE.
I THOUGHT YOU MIGHT BE RUNNING LOW ON BLOOD SOON.
WHAT PERFECT TIMING. I'M MAKING ANOTHER VIAL—
BLOOD...
BLOOD!!
DMP
YANK
AH!

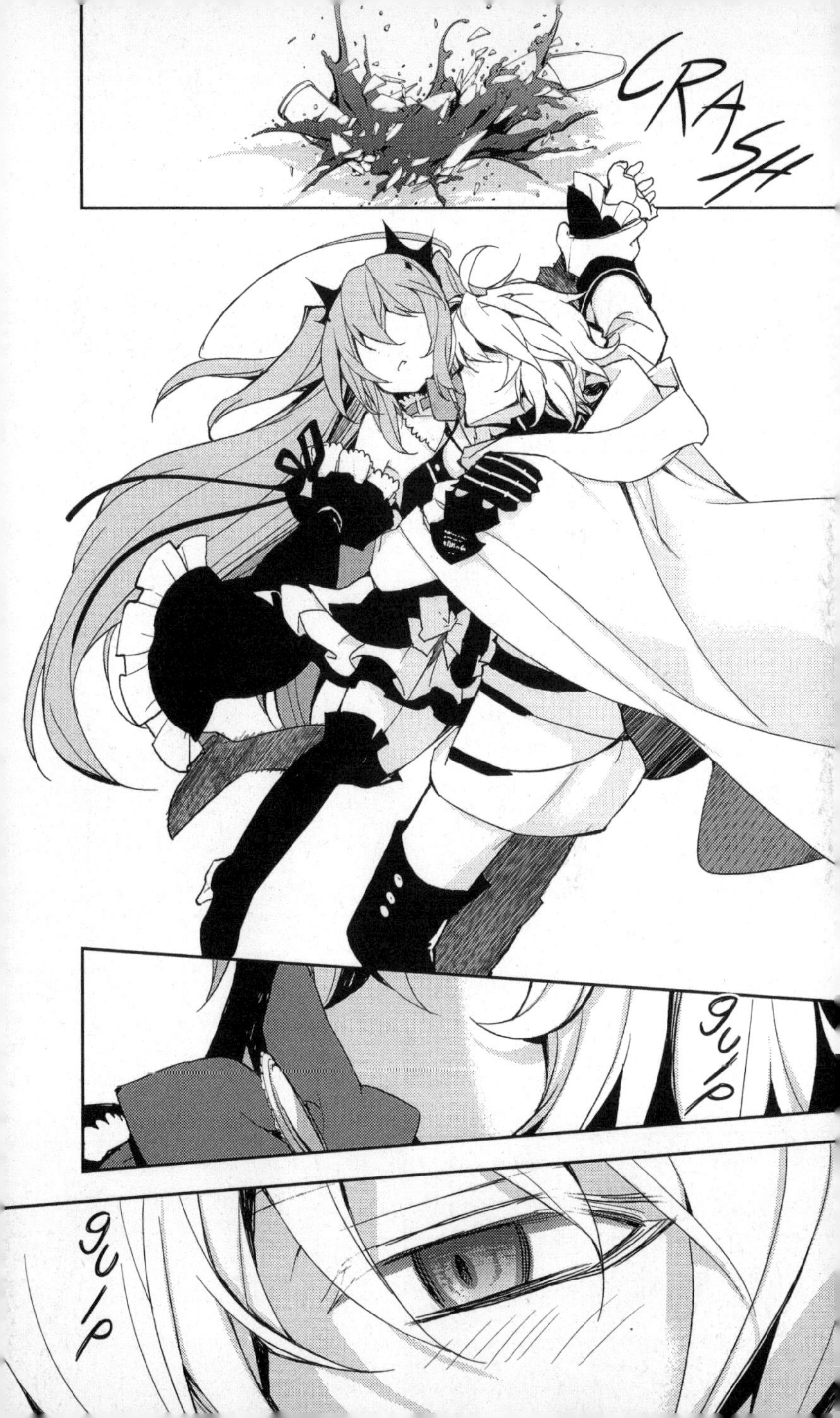
CRASH
gulp
gulp

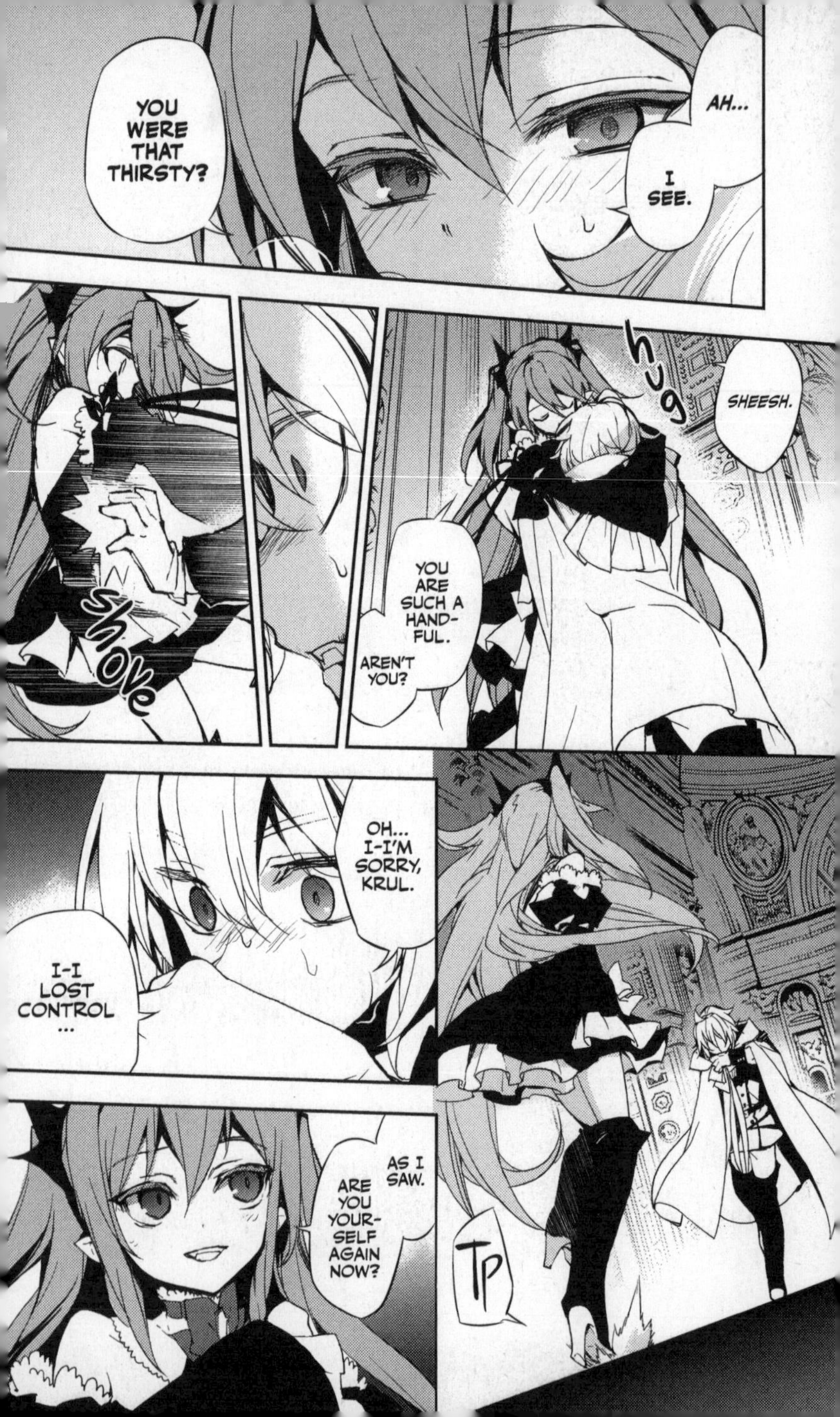
AH...
I SEE.
YOU WERE THAT THIRSTY?
hug
SHEESH.
YOU ARE SUCH A HANDFUL-
AREN'T YOU?
shove
TP
OH... I-I'M SORRY, KRUL.
I-I LOST CONTROL ...
AS I SAW.
ARE YOU YOURSELF AGAIN NOW?

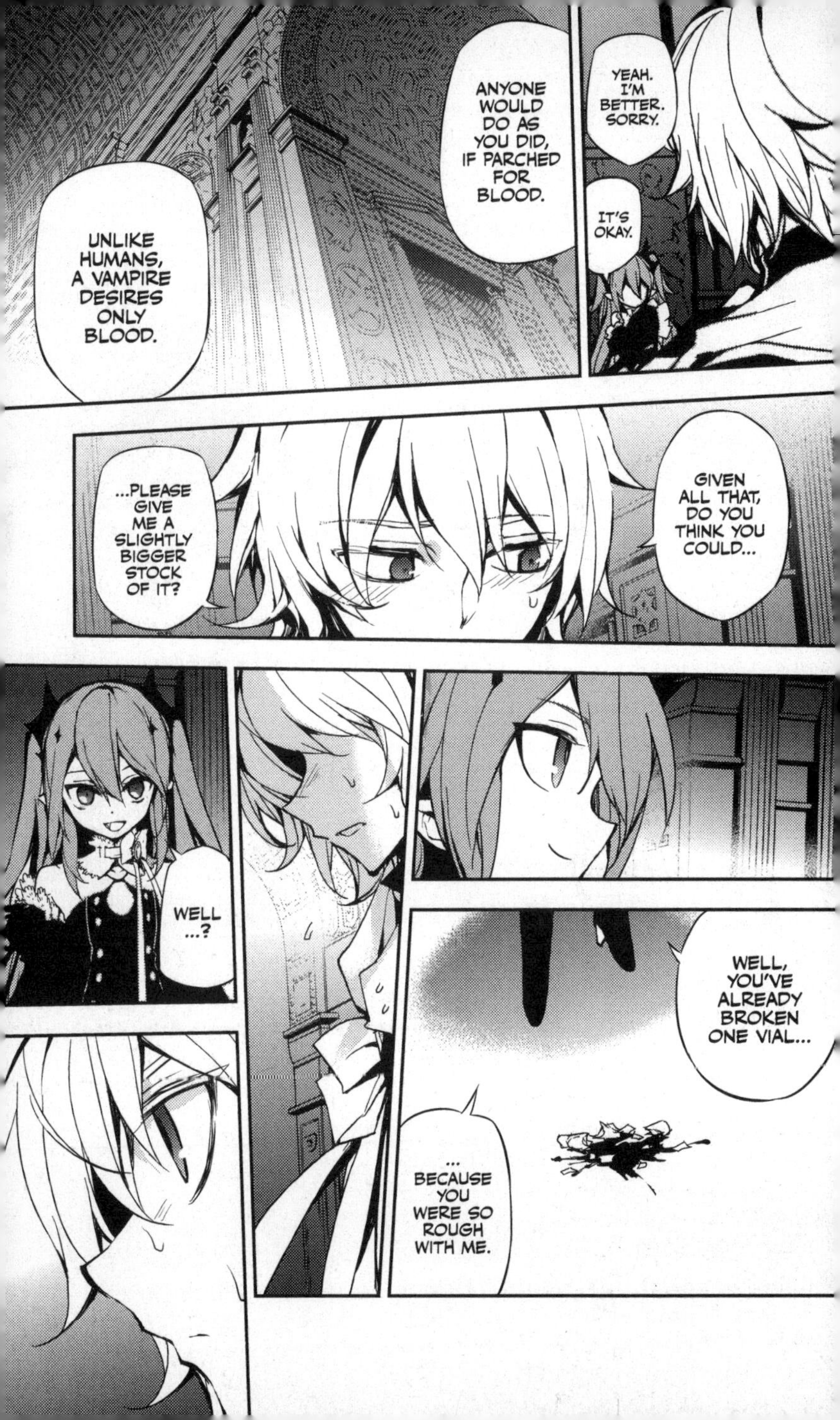
YEAH. I'M BETTER. SORRY.
IT'S OKAY.
ANYONE WOULD DO AS YOU DID, IF PARCHED FOR BLOOD.
UNLIKE HUMANS, A VAMPIRE DESIRES ONLY BLOOD.
GIVEN ALL THAT, DO YOU THINK YOU COULD...
...PLEASE GIVE ME A SLIGHTLY BIGGER STOCK OF IT?
WELL ...?
WELL, YOU'VE ALREADY BROKEN ONE VIAL...
... BECAUSE YOU WERE SO ROUGH WITH ME.

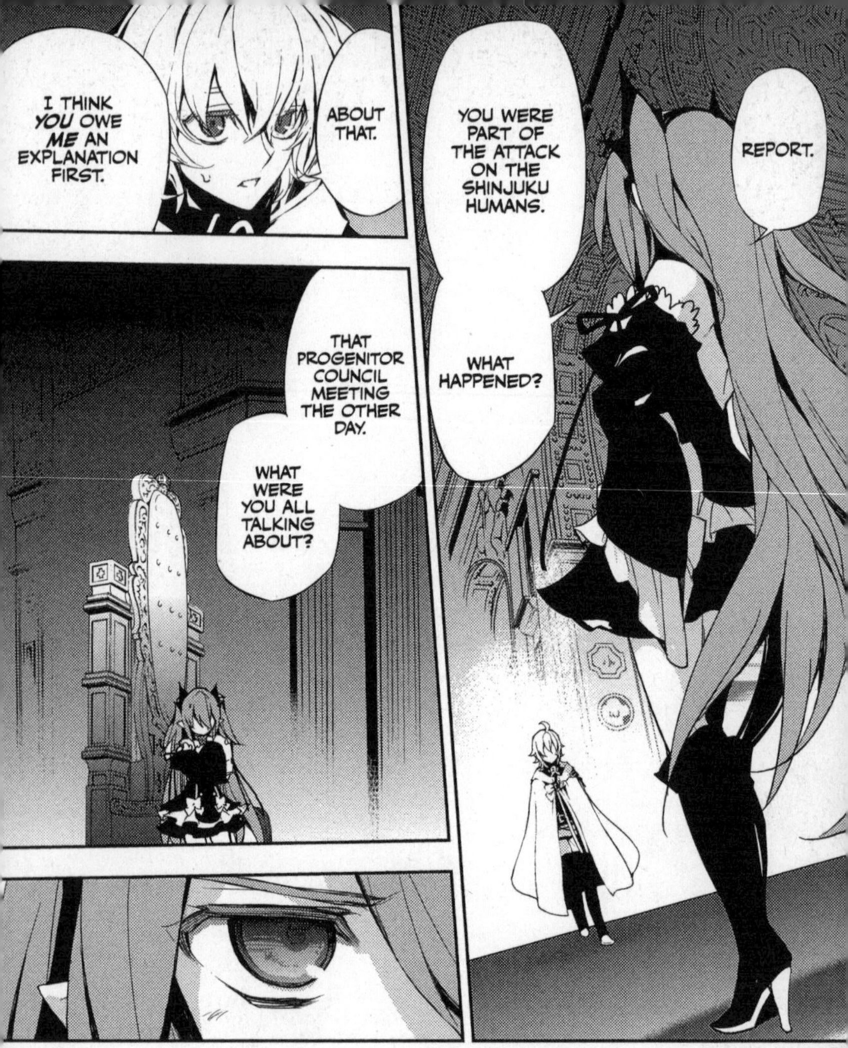
REPORT.
YOU WERE PART OF THE ATTACK ON THE SHINJUKU HUMANS.
WHAT HAPPENED?
ABOUT THAT.
I THINK *YOU* OWE *ME* AN EXPLANATION FIRST.
THAT PROGENITOR COUNCIL MEETING THE OTHER DAY.
WHAT WERE YOU ALL TALKING ABOUT?

The Progenitor Council

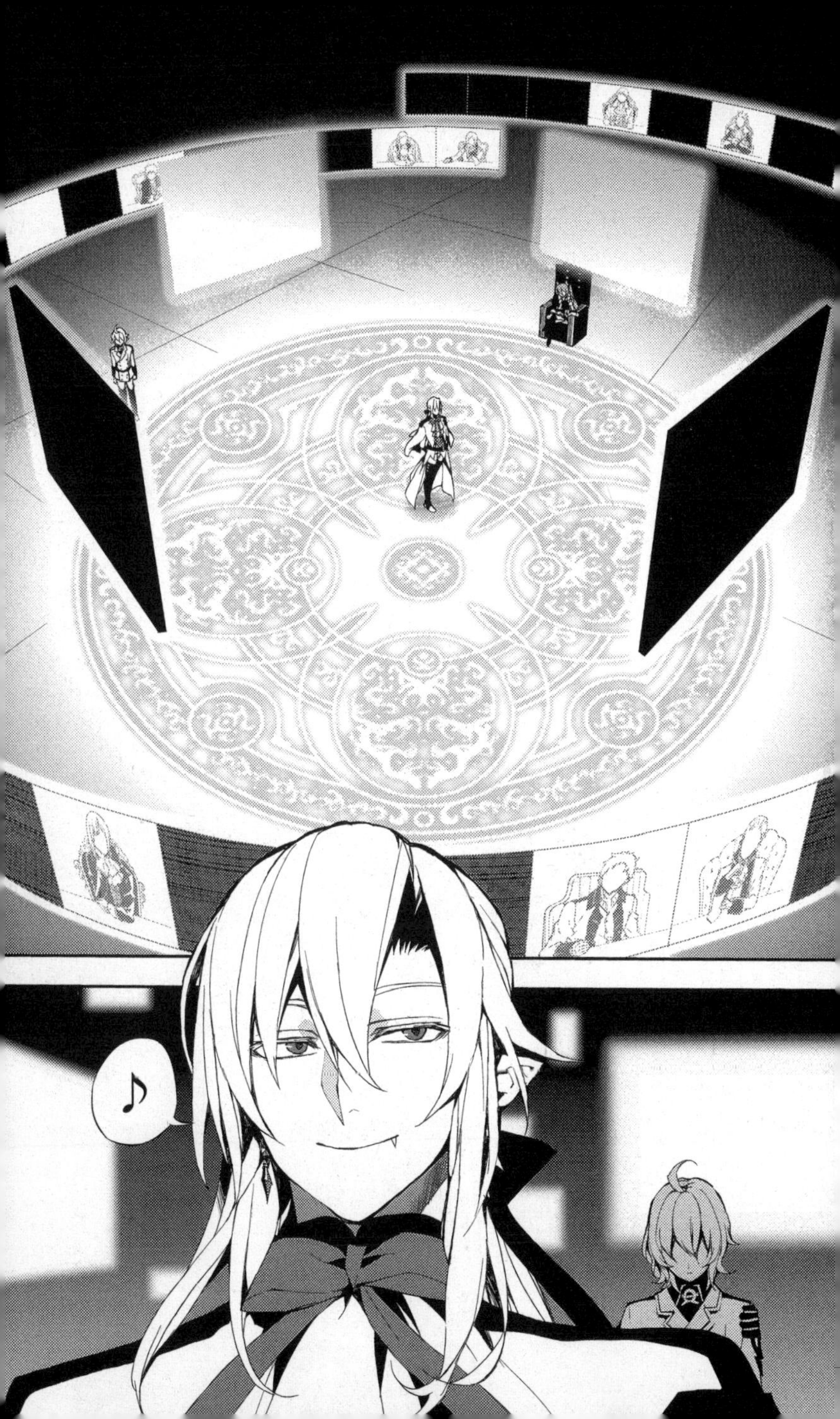
♪

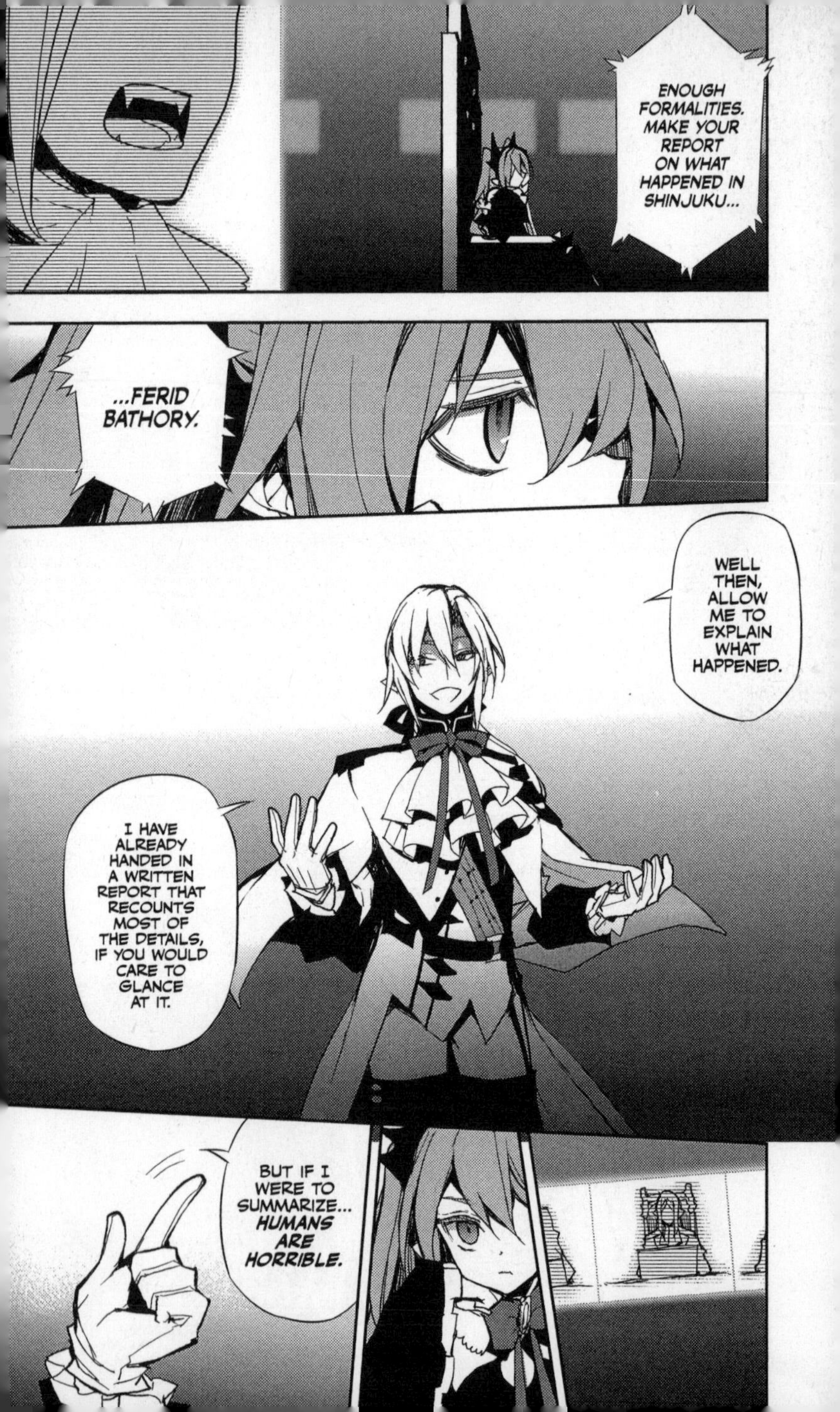
ENOUGH FORMALITIES. MAKE YOUR REPORT ON WHAT HAPPENED IN SHINJUKU...
...FERID BATHORY.
WELL THEN, ALLOW ME TO EXPLAIN WHAT HAPPENED.
I HAVE ALREADY HANDED IN A WRITTEN REPORT THAT RECOUNTS MOST OF THE DETAILS, IF YOU WOULD CARE TO GLANCE AT IT.
BUT IF I WERE TO SUMMARIZE... *HUMANS ARE HORRIBLE.*

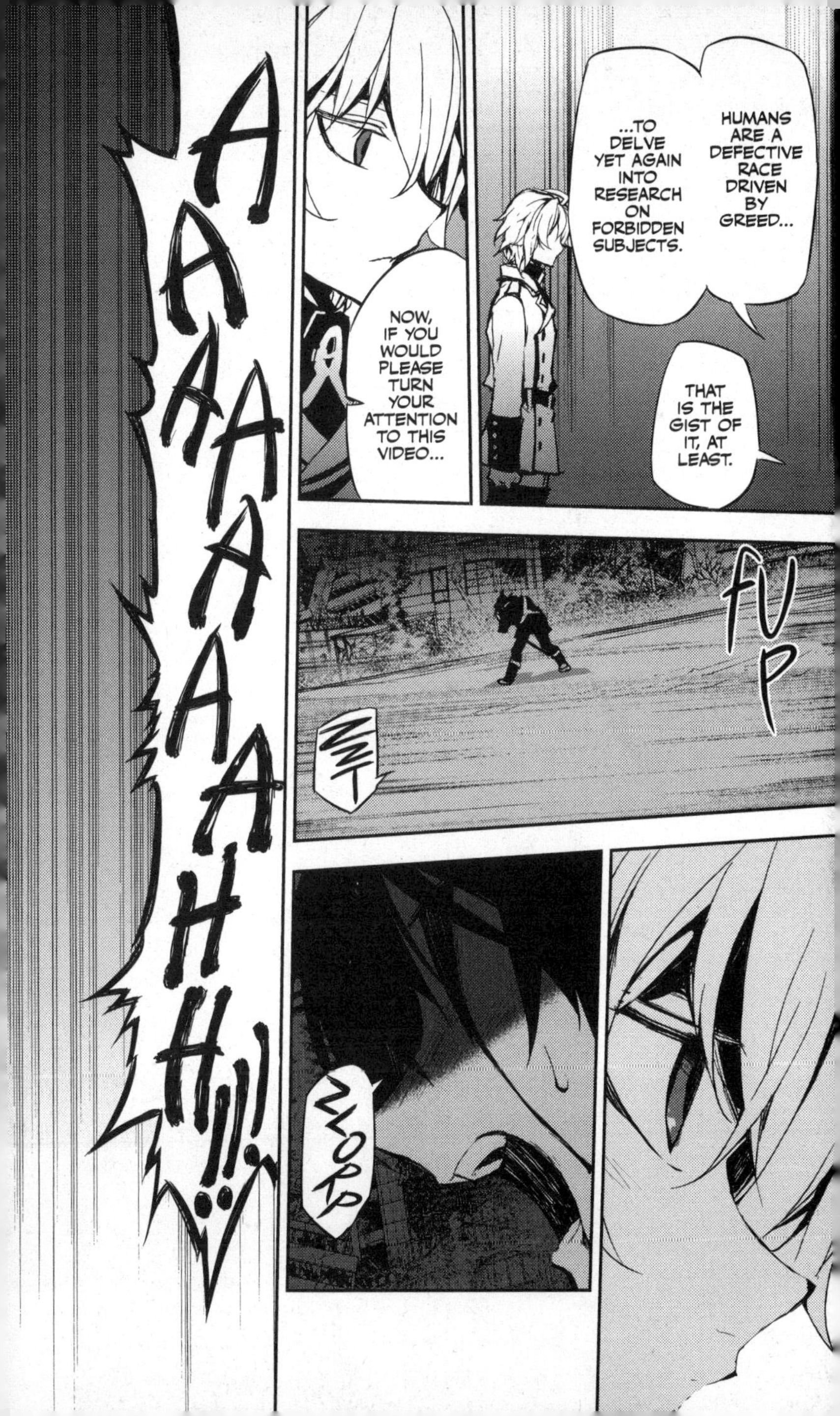
HUMANS ARE A DEFECTIVE RACE DRIVEN BY GREED...
...TO DELVE YET AGAIN INTO RESEARCH ON FORBIDDEN SUBJECTS.
THAT IS THE GIST OF IT, AT LEAST.
NOW, IF YOU WOULD PLEASE TURN YOUR ATTENTION TO THIS VIDEO...
FUP
ZZZT
ZLORP
AAAAAAAHHH!!!

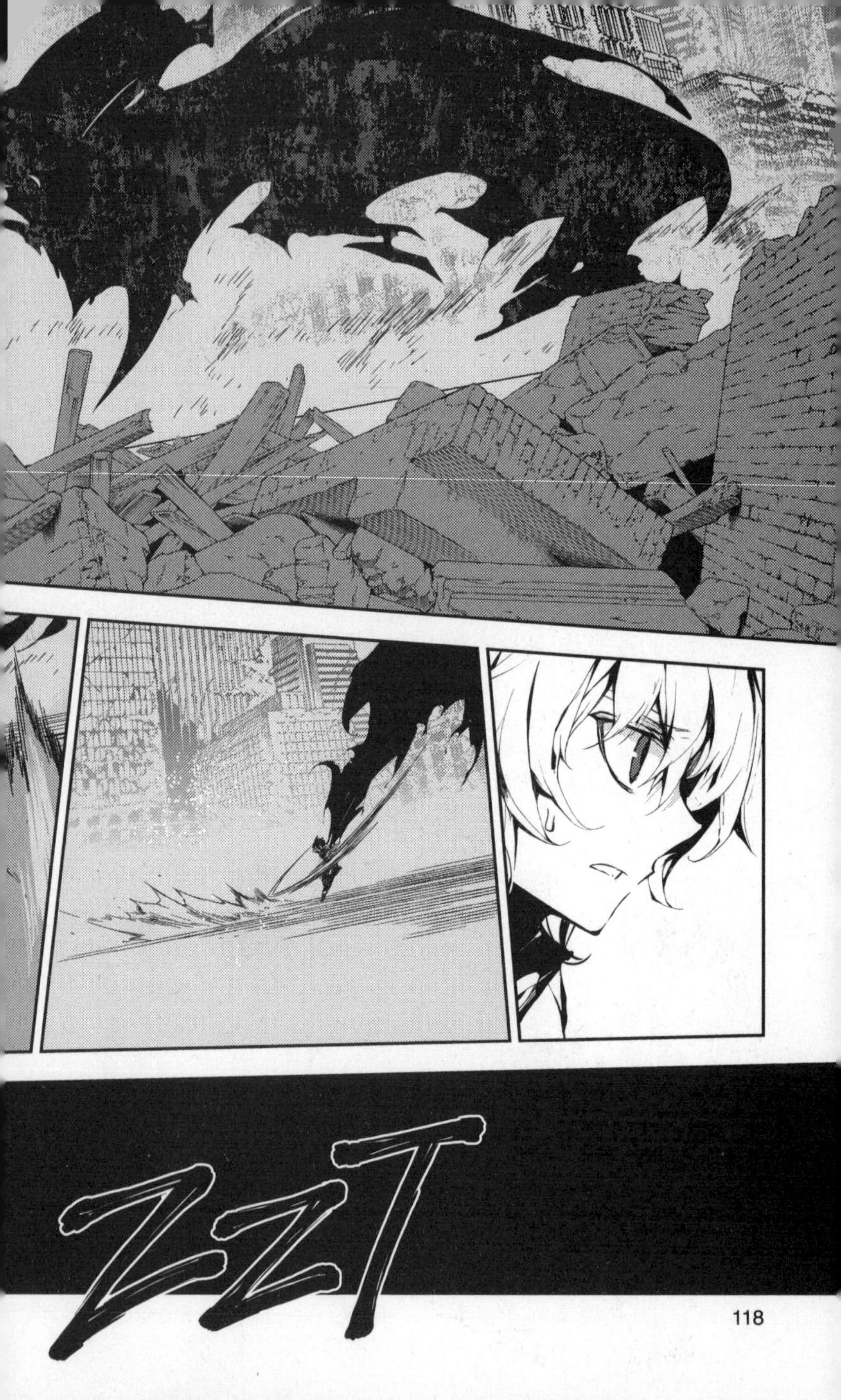
ZZT

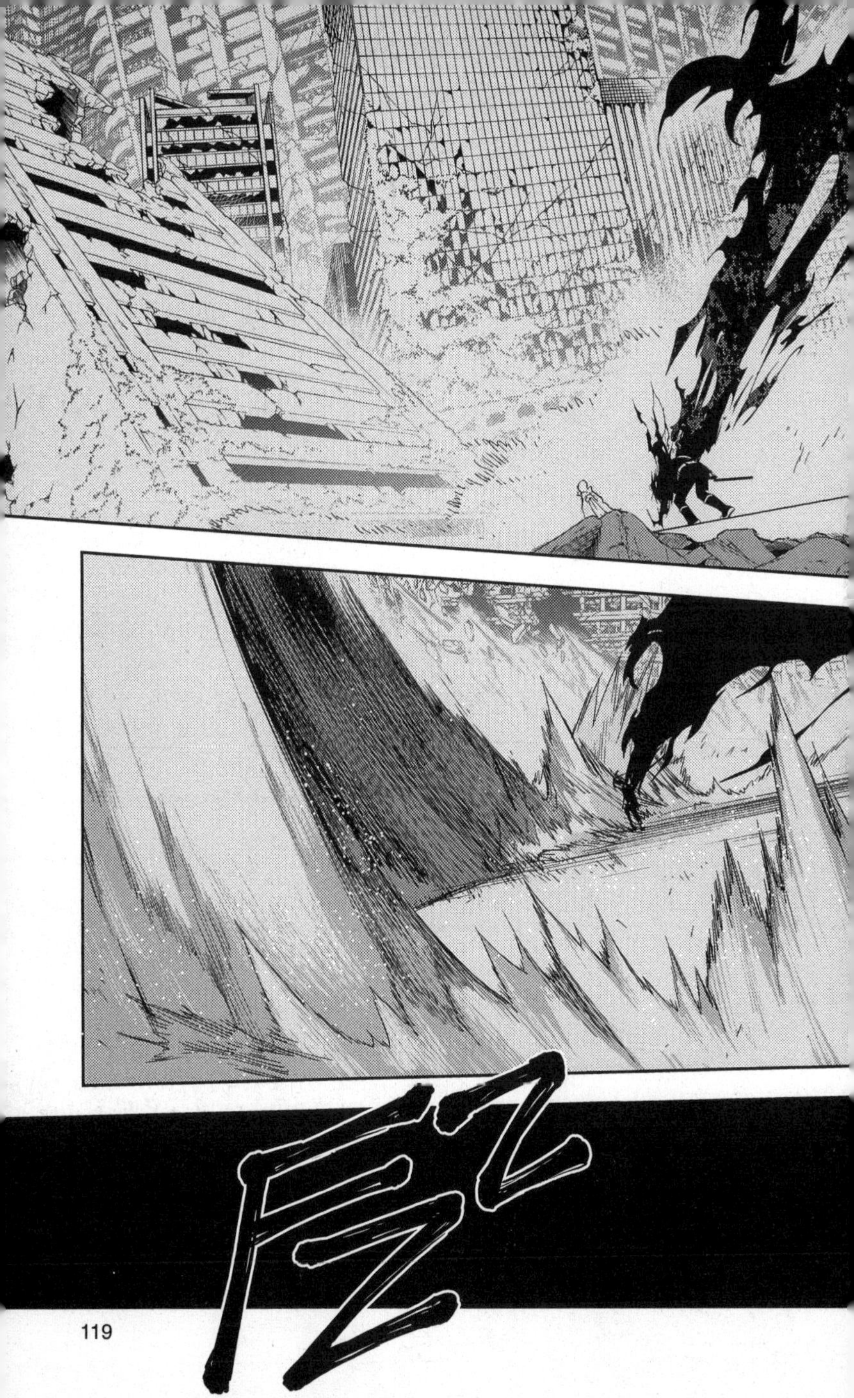
FZZ

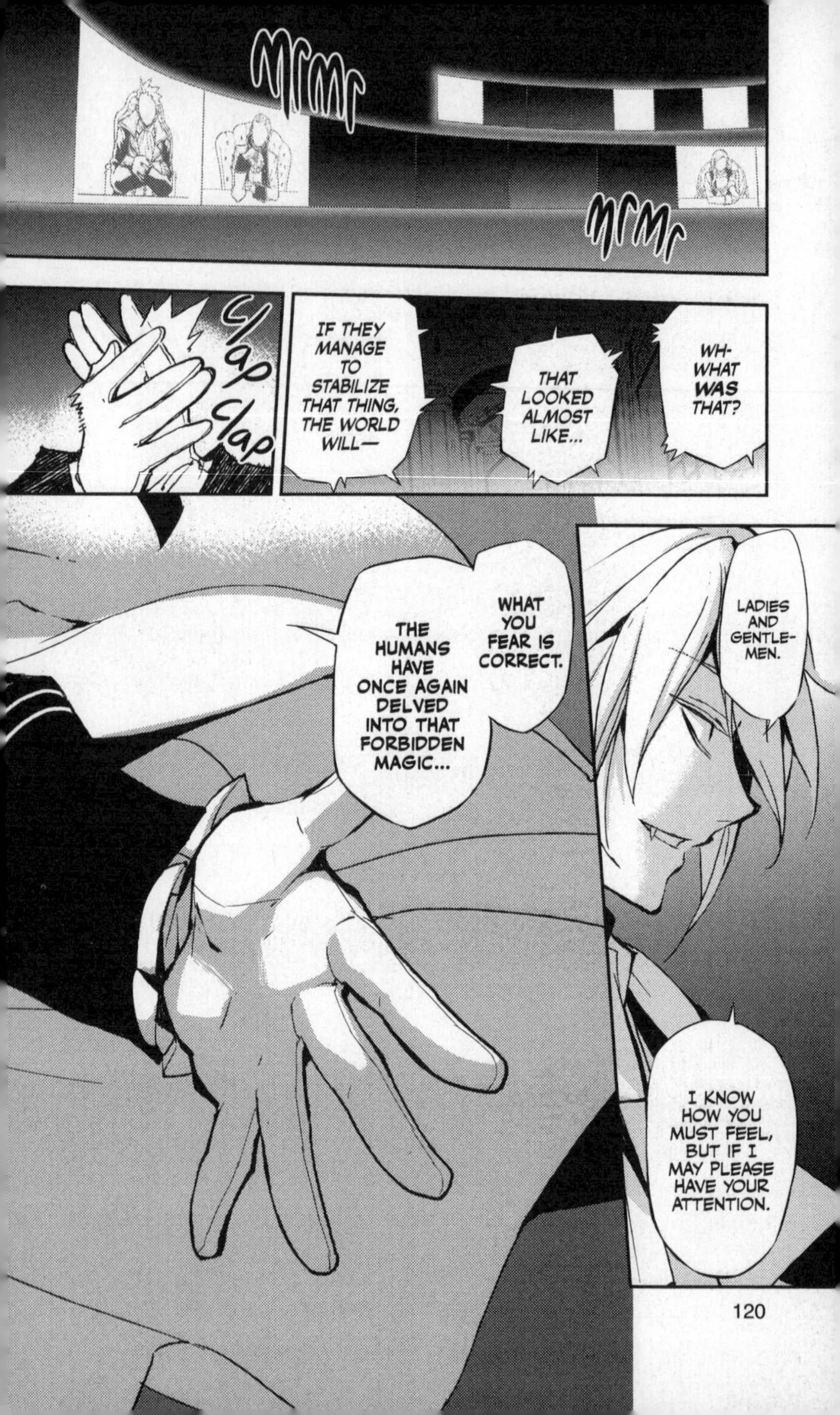
mrmr
mrmr
WH- WHAT WAS THAT?
THAT LOOKED ALMOST LIKE...
IF THEY MANAGE TO STABILIZE THAT THING, THE WORLD WILL—
clap clap
LADIES AND GENTLEMEN.
I KNOW HOW YOU MUST FEEL, BUT IF I MAY PLEASE HAVE YOUR ATTENTION.
WHAT YOU FEAR IS CORRECT.
THE HUMANS HAVE ONCE AGAIN DELVED INTO THAT FORBIDDEN MAGIC...

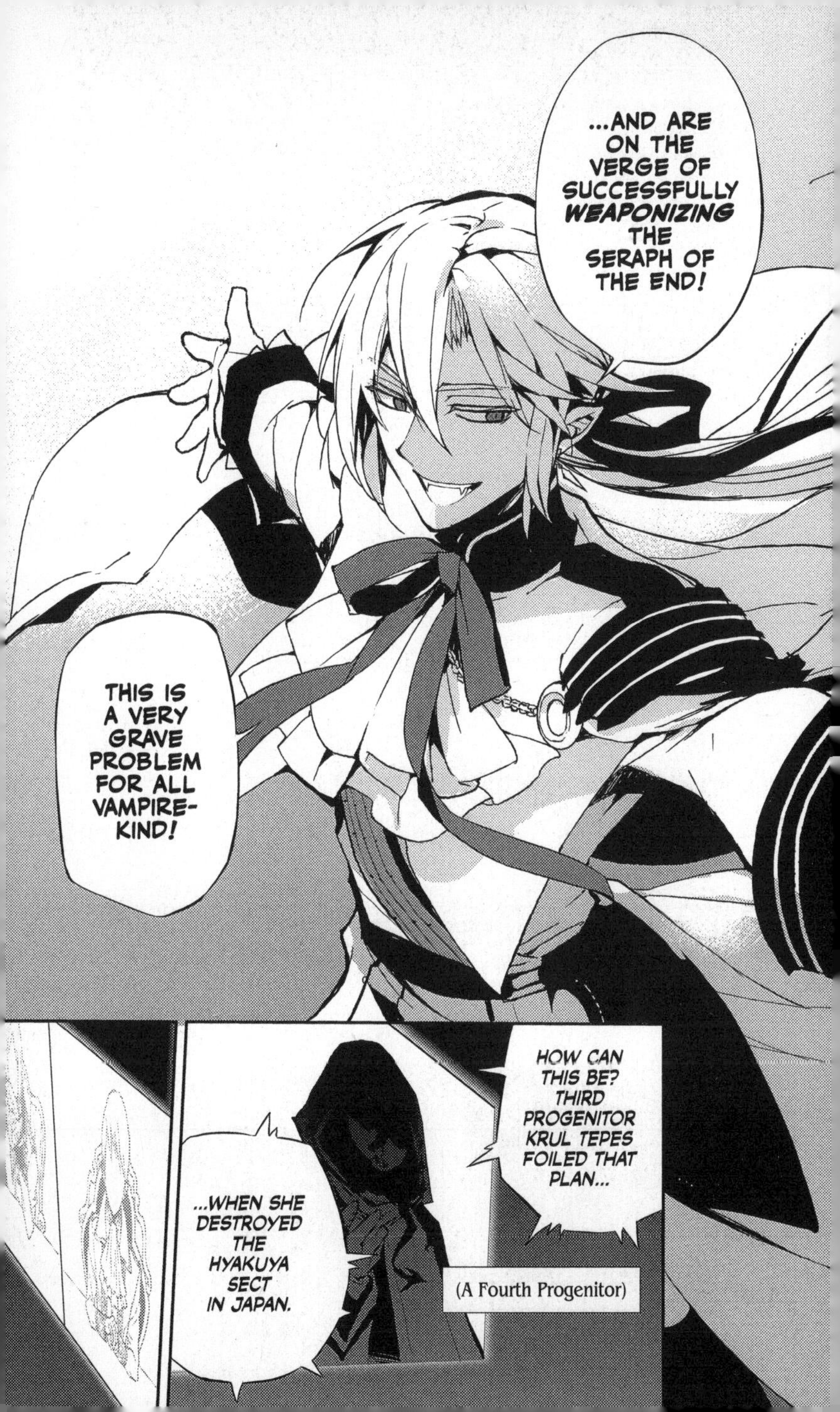
...AND ARE ON THE VERGE OF SUCCESSFULLY ***WEAPONIZING*** THE SERAPH OF THE END!
THIS IS A VERY GRAVE PROBLEM FOR ALL VAMPIRE-KIND!
HOW CAN THIS BE? THIRD PROGENITOR KRUL TEPES FOILED THAT PLAN...
...WHEN SHE DESTROYED THE HYAKUYA SECT IN JAPAN.
(A Fourth Progenitor)

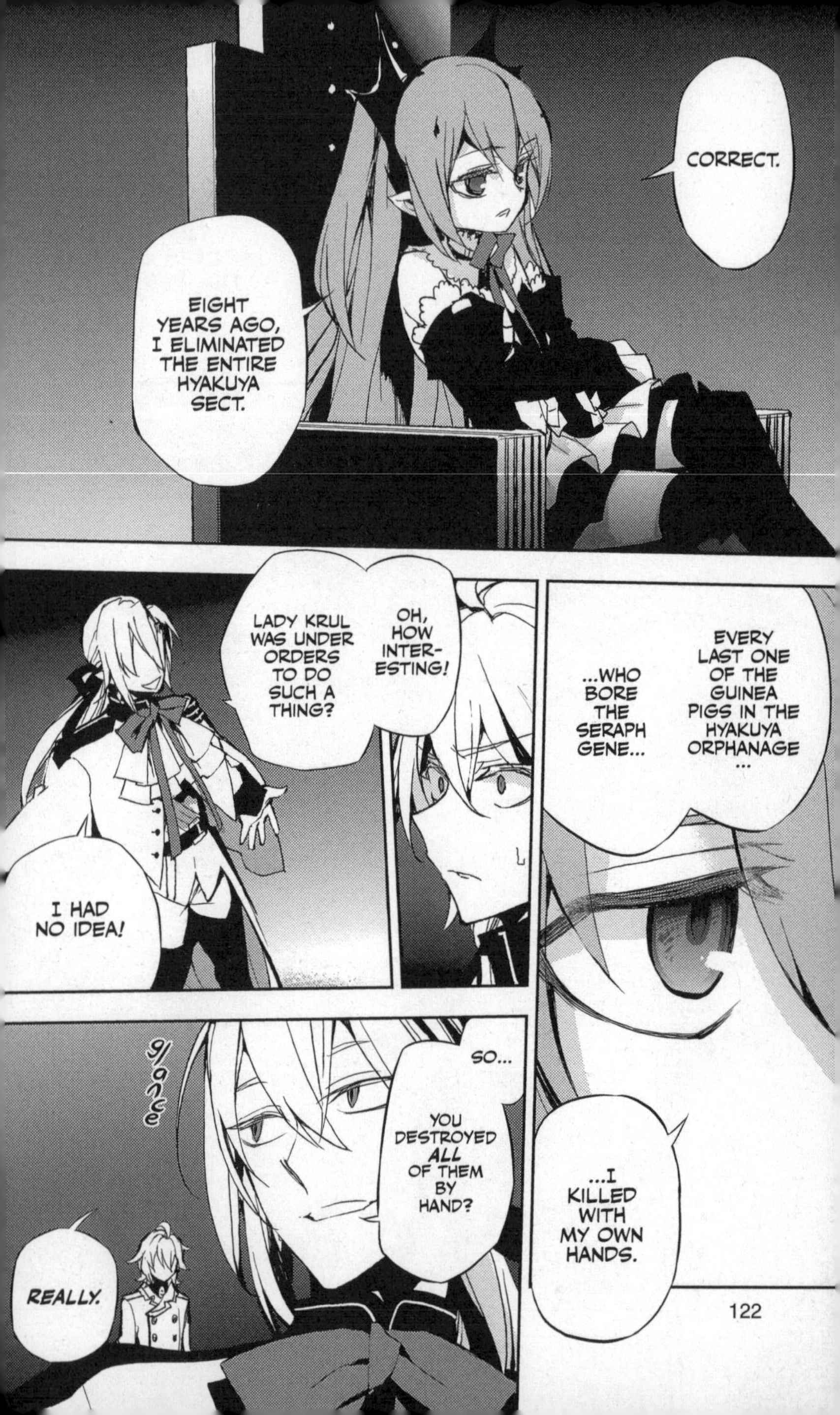

CORRECT.
EIGHT YEARS AGO, I ELIMINATED THE ENTIRE HYAKUYA SECT.
EVERY LAST ONE OF THE GUINEA PIGS IN THE HYAKUYA ORPHANAGE...
...WHO BORE THE SERAPH GENE...
...I KILLED WITH MY OWN HANDS.
OH, HOW INTER-ESTING!
LADY KRUL WAS UNDER ORDERS TO DO SUCH A THING?
I HAD NO IDEA!
SO...
YOU DESTROYED *ALL* OF THEM BY HAND?
glance
REALLY.

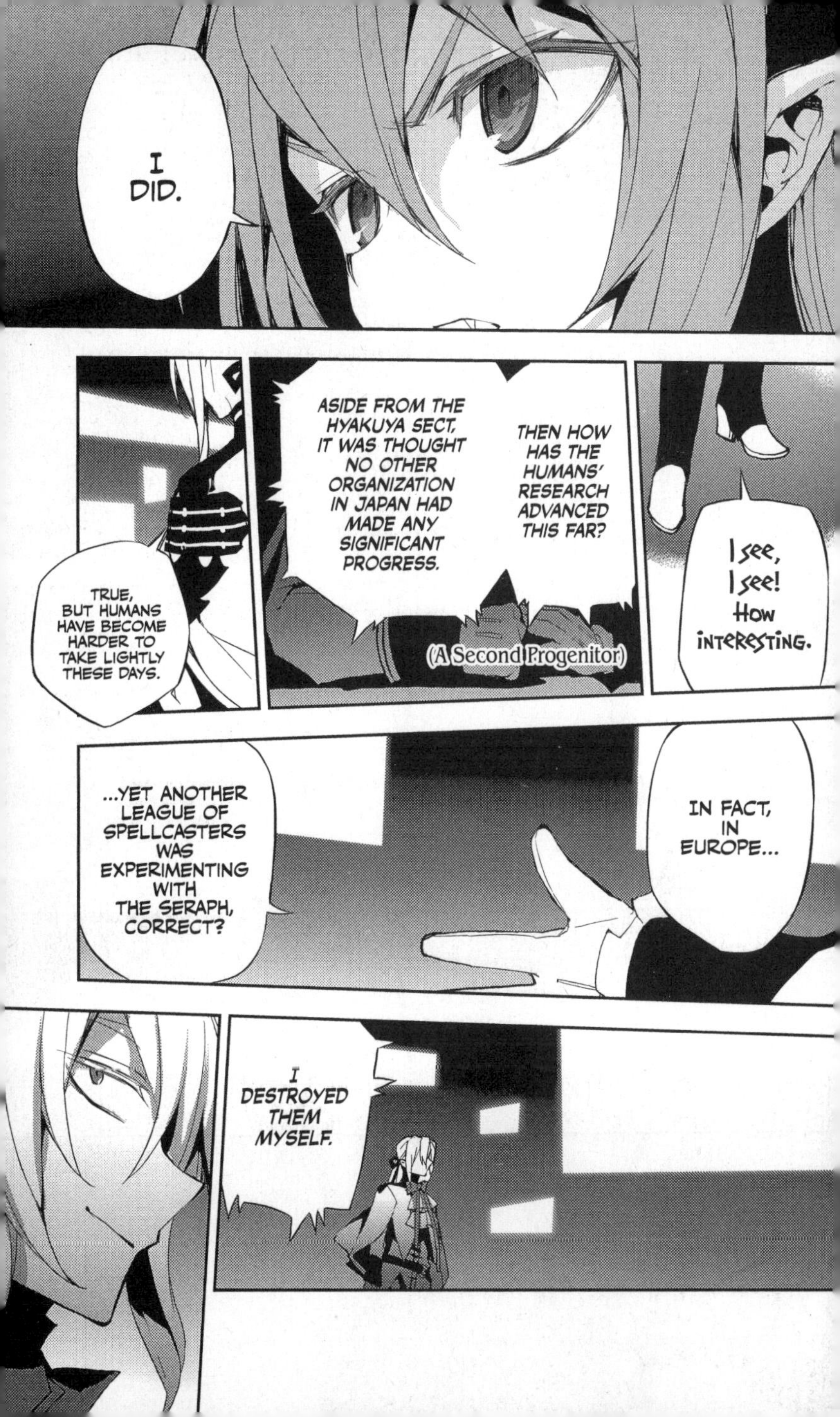
I DID.
I see, I see! How interesting.
THEN HOW HAS THE HUMANS' RESEARCH ADVANCED THIS FAR?
ASIDE FROM THE HYAKUYA SECT, IT WAS THOUGHT NO OTHER ORGANIZATION IN JAPAN HAD MADE ANY SIGNIFICANT PROGRESS.
(A Second Progenitor)
TRUE, BUT HUMANS HAVE BECOME HARDER TO TAKE LIGHTLY THESE DAYS.
IN FACT, IN EUROPE...
...YET ANOTHER LEAGUE OF SPELLCASTERS WAS EXPERIMENTING WITH THE SERAPH, CORRECT?
I DESTROYED THEM MYSELF.

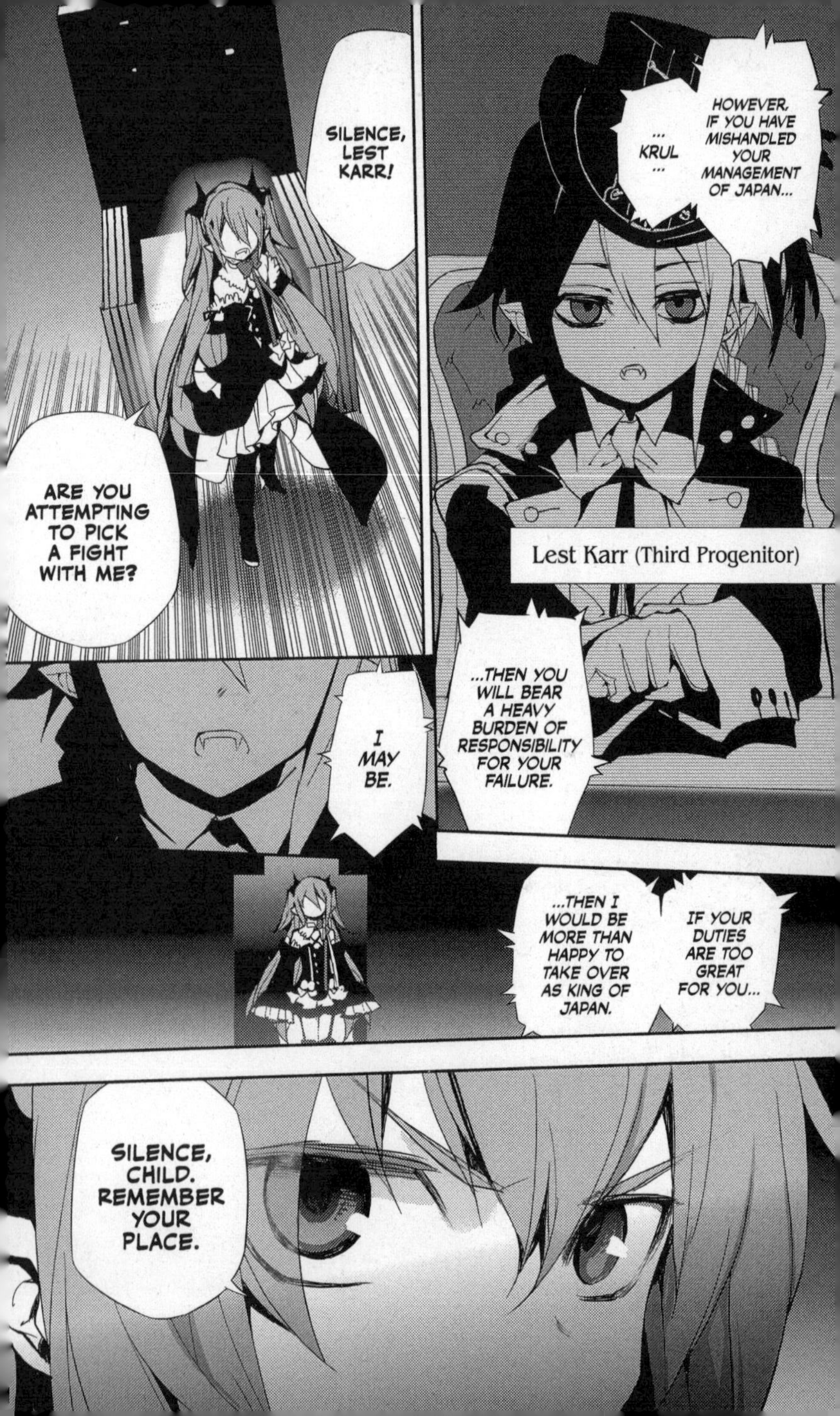
HOWEVER, IF YOU HAVE MISHANDLED YOUR MANAGEMENT OF JAPAN...
...KRUL...
Lest Karr (Third Progenitor)
...THEN YOU WILL BEAR A HEAVY BURDEN OF RESPONSIBILITY FOR YOUR FAILURE.
SILENCE, LEST KARR!
ARE YOU ATTEMPTING TO PICK A FIGHT WITH ME?
I MAY BE.
IF YOUR DUTIES ARE TOO GREAT FOR YOU...
...THEN I WOULD BE MORE THAN HAPPY TO TAKE OVER AS KING OF JAPAN.
SILENCE, CHILD. REMEMBER YOUR PLACE.

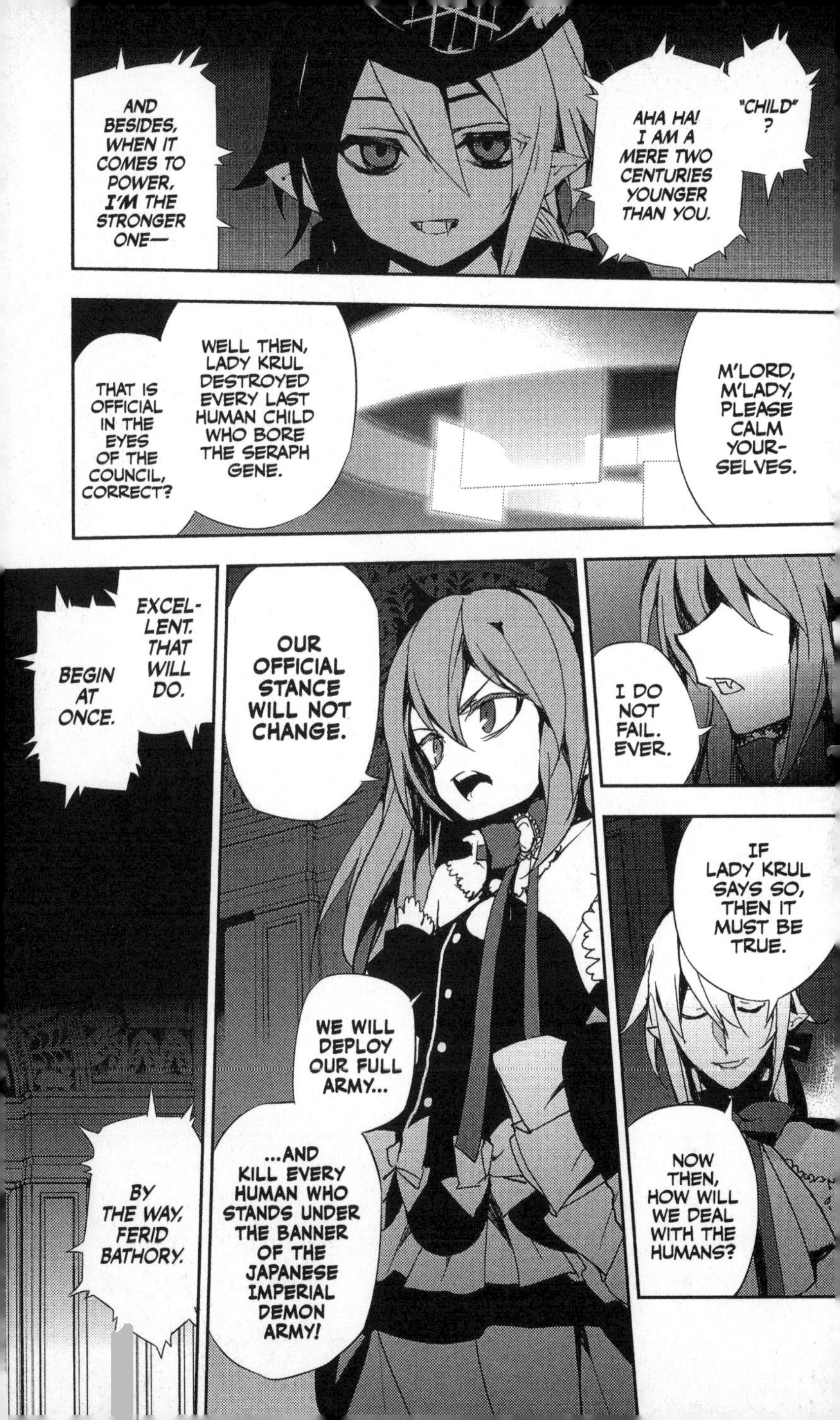
"CHILD"?
AHA HA! I AM A MERE TWO CENTURIES YOUNGER THAN YOU.
AND BESIDES, WHEN IT COMES TO POWER, I'M THE STRONGER ONE—
M'LORD, M'LADY, PLEASE CALM YOURSELVES.
WELL THEN, LADY KRUL DESTROYED EVERY LAST HUMAN CHILD WHO BORE THE SERAPH GENE.
THAT IS OFFICIAL IN THE EYES OF THE COUNCIL, CORRECT?
I DO NOT FAIL. EVER.
IF LADY KRUL SAYS SO, THEN IT MUST BE TRUE.
NOW THEN, HOW WILL WE DEAL WITH THE HUMANS?
OUR OFFICIAL STANCE WILL NOT CHANGE.
WE WILL DEPLOY OUR FULL ARMY...
...AND KILL EVERY HUMAN WHO STANDS UNDER THE BANNER OF THE JAPANESE IMPERIAL DEMON ARMY!
EXCEL-LENT. THAT WILL DO.
BEGIN AT ONCE.
BY THE WAY, FERID BATHORY.

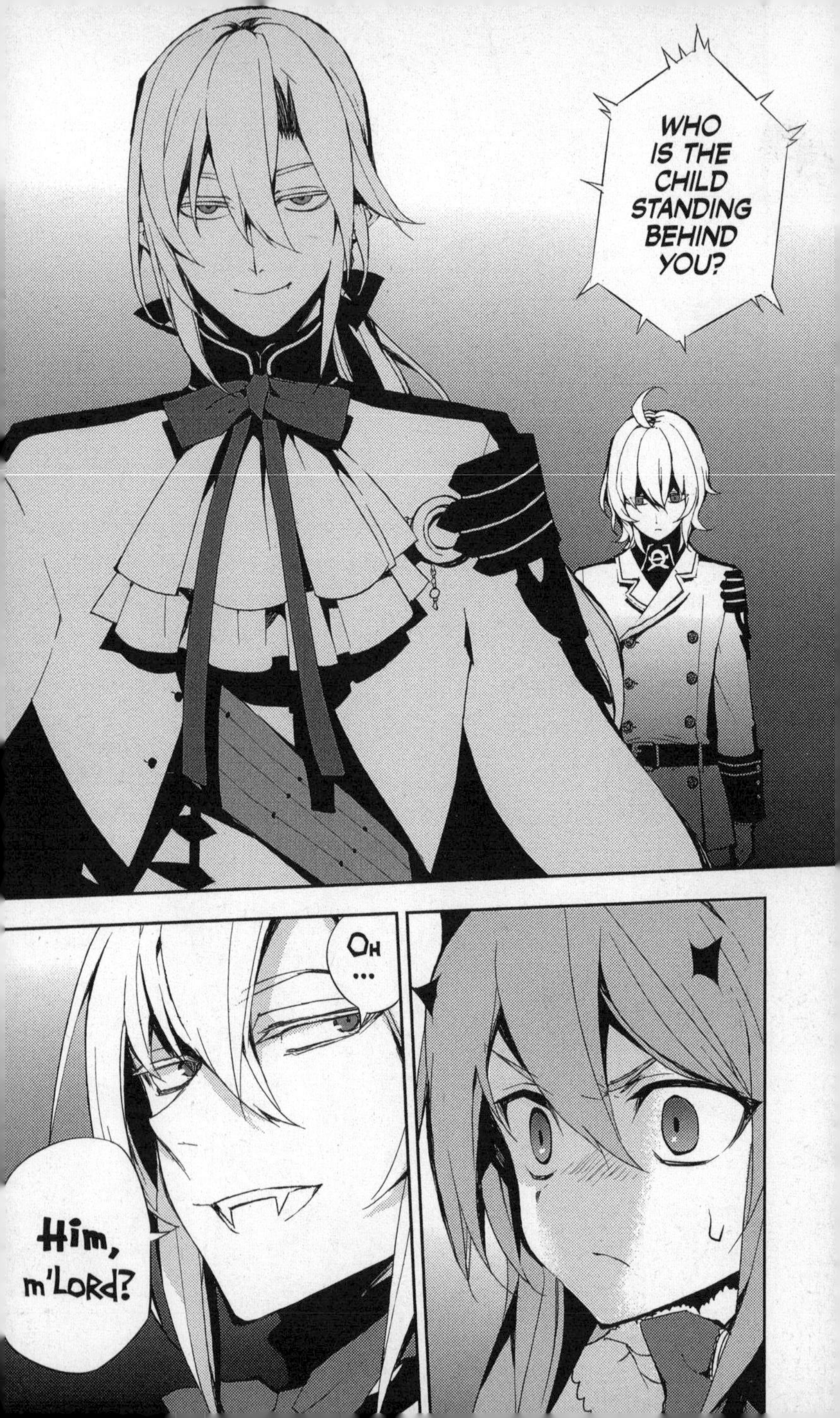
WHO IS THE CHILD STANDING BEHIND YOU?
OH ...
Him, m'LORD?

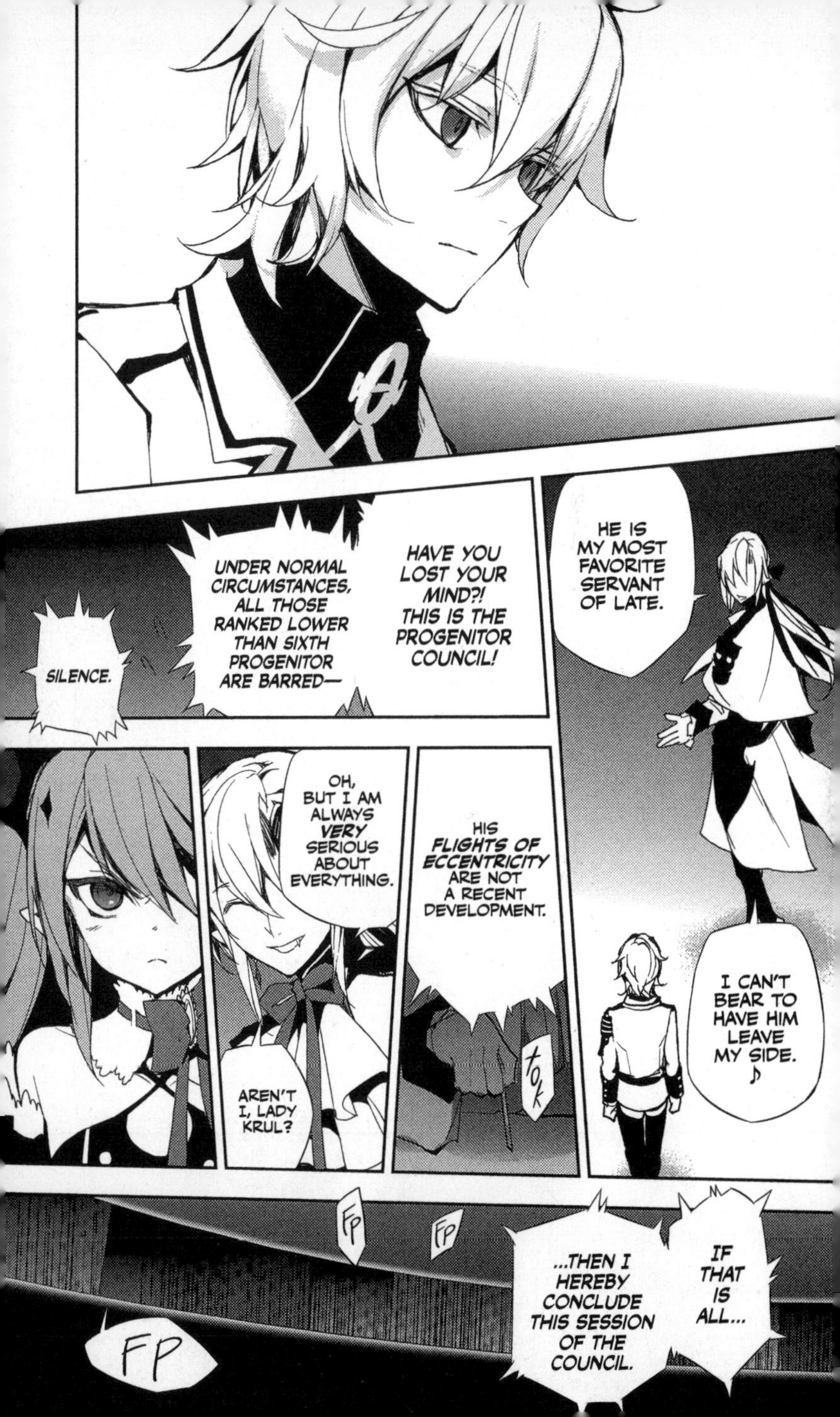
HE IS MY MOST FAVORITE SERVANT OF LATE.
I CAN'T BEAR TO HAVE HIM LEAVE MY SIDE. ♪
HAVE YOU LOST YOUR MIND?! THIS IS THE PROGENITOR COUNCIL!
UNDER NORMAL CIRCUMSTANCES, ALL THOSE RANKED LOWER THAN SIXTH PROGENITOR ARE BARRED—
SILENCE.
HIS *FLIGHTS OF ECCENTRICITY* ARE NOT A RECENT DEVELOPMENT.
TOK
OH, BUT I AM ALWAYS *VERY* SERIOUS ABOUT EVERYTHING.
AREN'T I, LADY KRUL?
IF THAT IS ALL...
...THEN I HEREBY CONCLUDE THIS SESSION OF THE COUNCIL.
FP
FP
FP

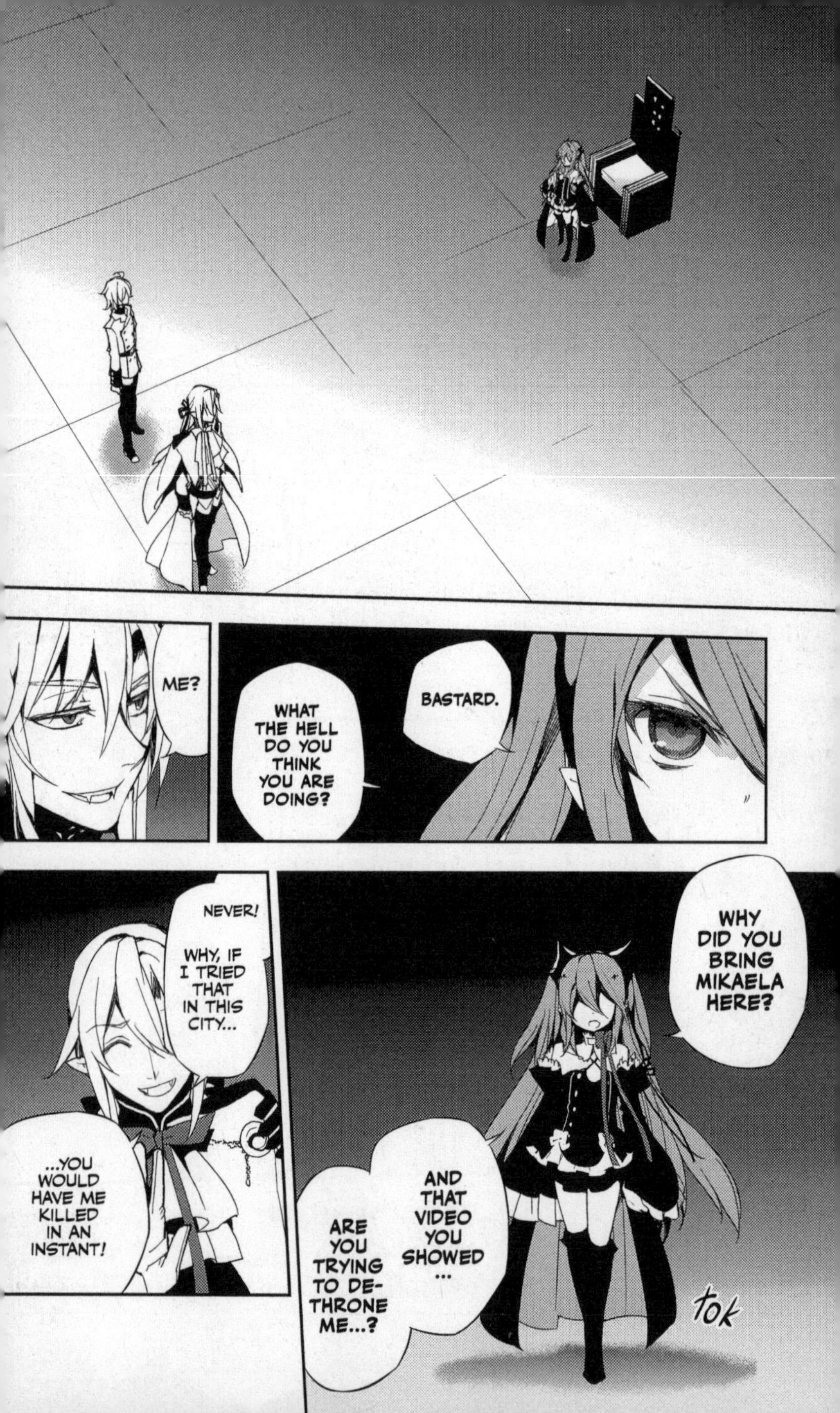
BASTARD.
WHAT THE HELL DO YOU THINK YOU ARE DOING?
ME?
WHY DID YOU BRING MIKAELA HERE?
AND THAT VIDEO YOU SHOWED...
ARE YOU TRYING TO DE-THRONE ME...?
tok
NEVER!
WHY, IF I TRIED THAT IN THIS CITY...
...YOU WOULD HAVE ME KILLED IN AN INSTANT!

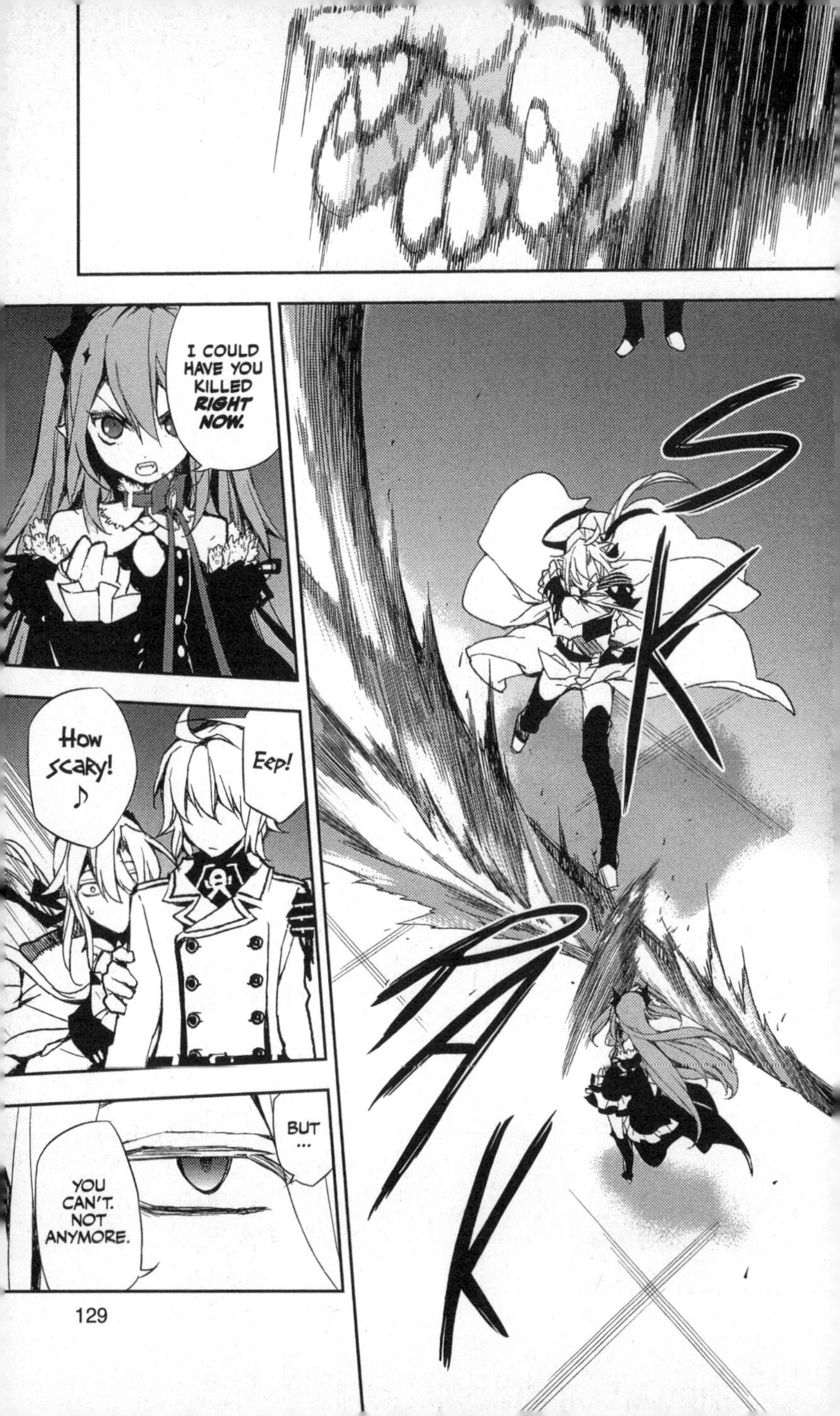
SKRAKK
I COULD HAVE YOU KILLED **RIGHT NOW.**
Eep!
How scary! ♪
BUT...
YOU CAN'T. NOT ANYMORE.

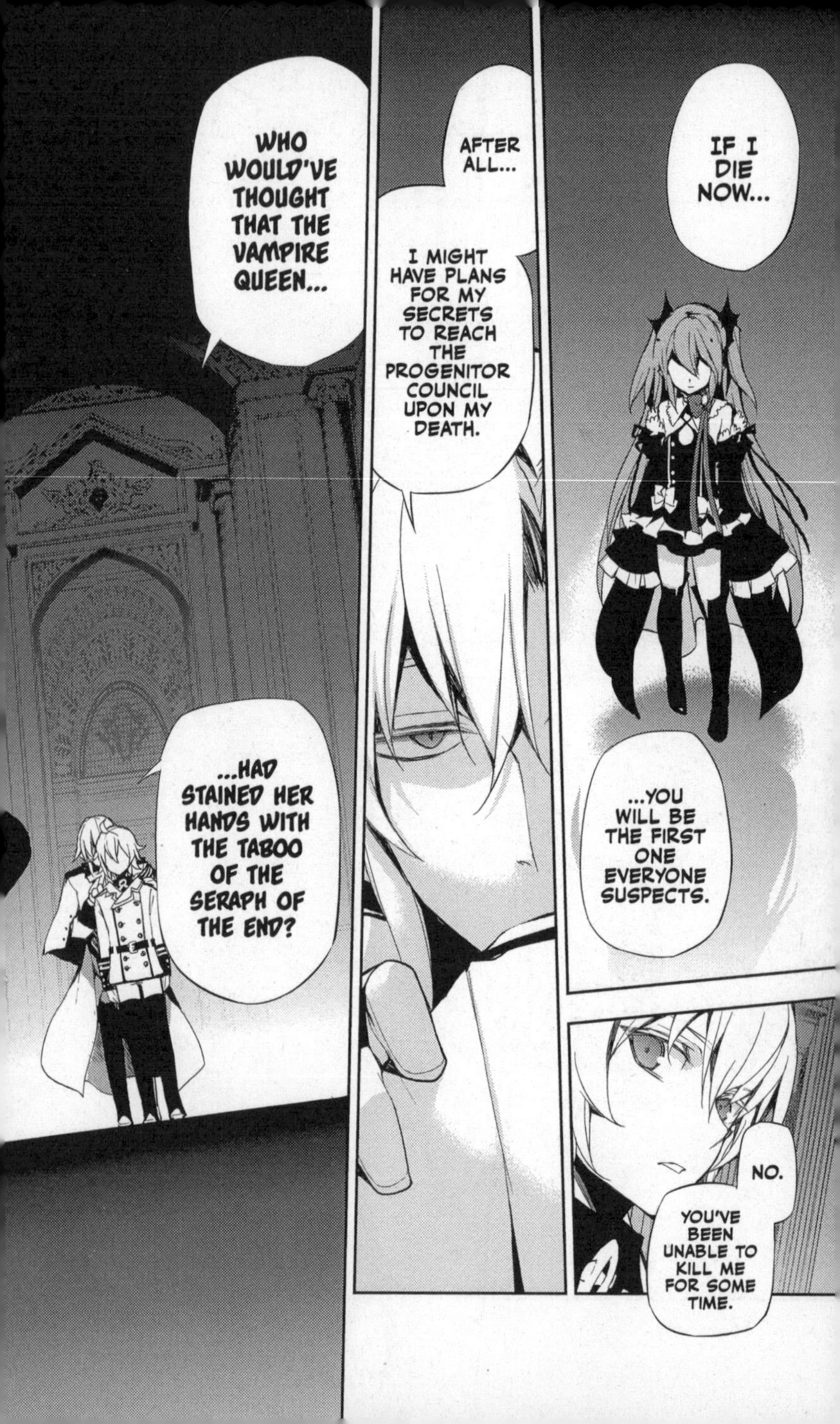
IF I DIE NOW...
...YOU WILL BE THE FIRST ONE EVERYONE SUSPECTS.
NO.
YOU'VE BEEN UNABLE TO KILL ME FOR SOME TIME.
AFTER ALL...
I MIGHT HAVE PLANS FOR MY SECRETS TO REACH THE PROGENITOR COUNCIL UPON MY DEATH.
WHO WOULD'VE THOUGHT THAT THE VAMPIRE QUEEN...
...HAD STAINED HER HANDS WITH THE TABOO OF THE SERAPH OF THE END?

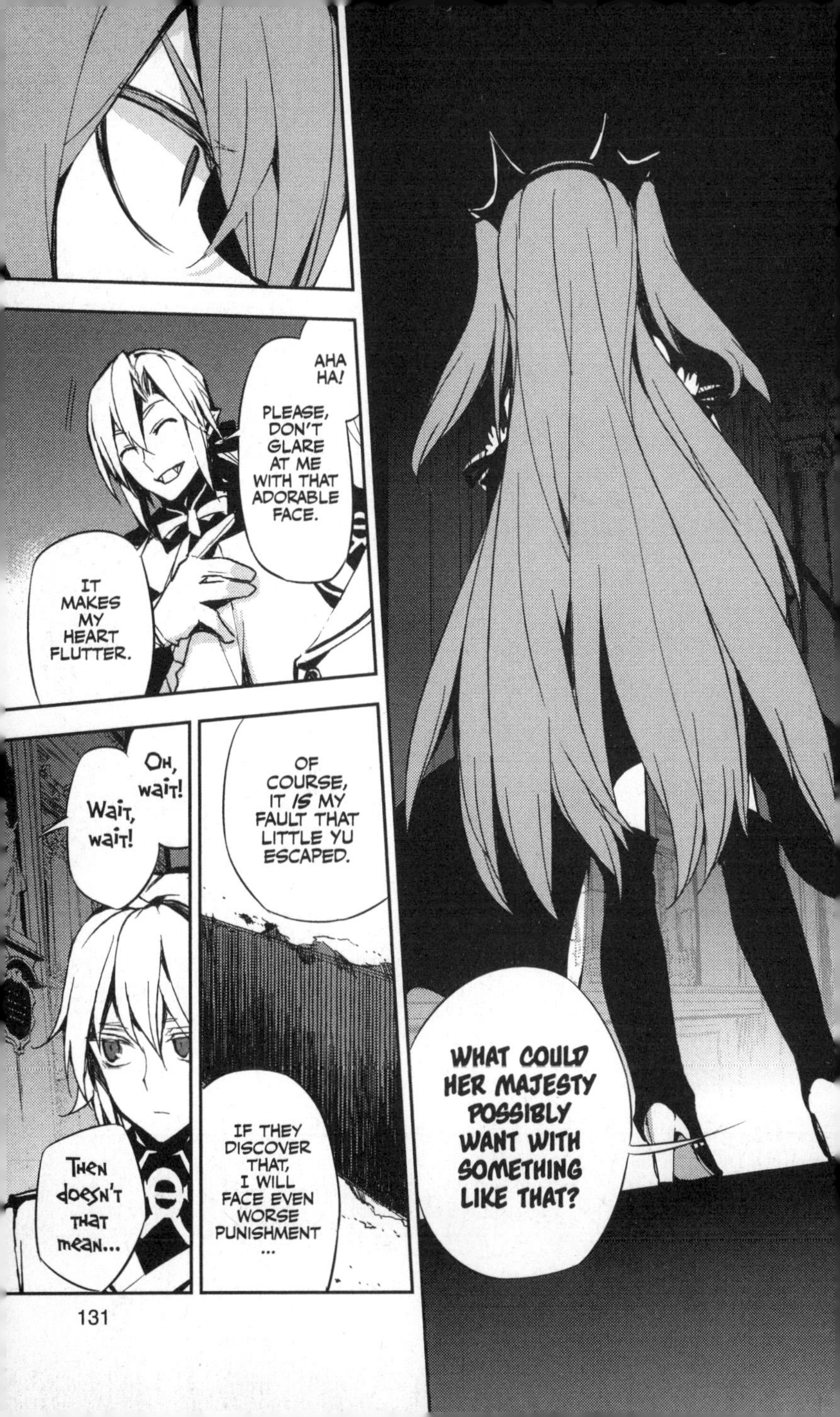
WHAT COULD HER MAJESTY POSSIBLY WANT WITH SOMETHING LIKE THAT?
AHA HA!
PLEASE, DON'T GLARE AT ME WITH THAT ADORABLE FACE.
IT MAKES MY HEART FLUTTER.
OF COURSE, IT *IS* MY FAULT THAT LITTLE YU ESCAPED.
IF THEY DISCOVER THAT, I WILL FACE EVEN WORSE PUNISHMENT...
Oh, wait!
Wait, wait!
Then doesn't that mean...

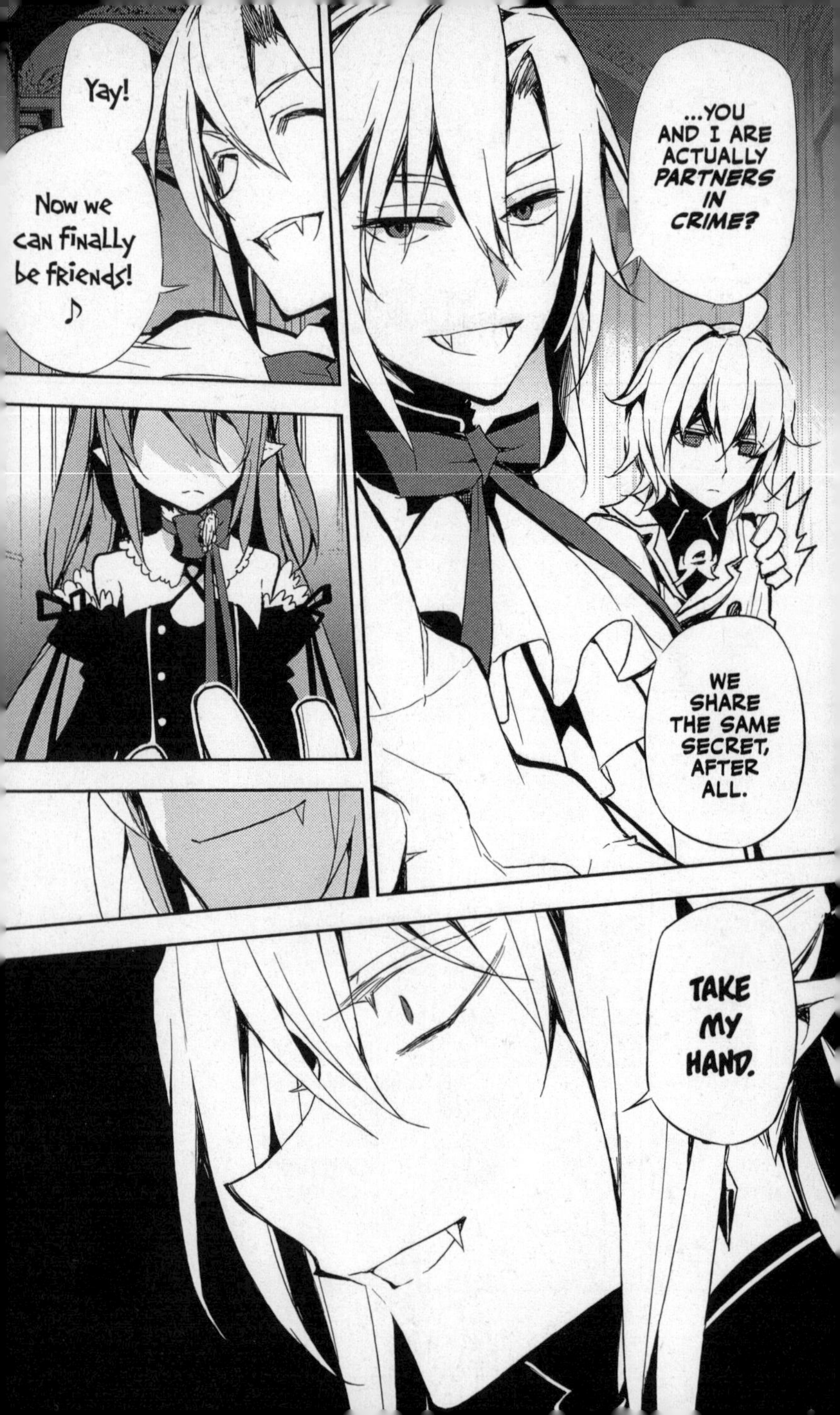
...YOU AND I ARE ACTUALLY PARTNERS IN CRIME?
WE SHARE THE SAME SECRET, AFTER ALL.
Yay!
Now we can finally be friends! ♪
TAKE MY HAND.

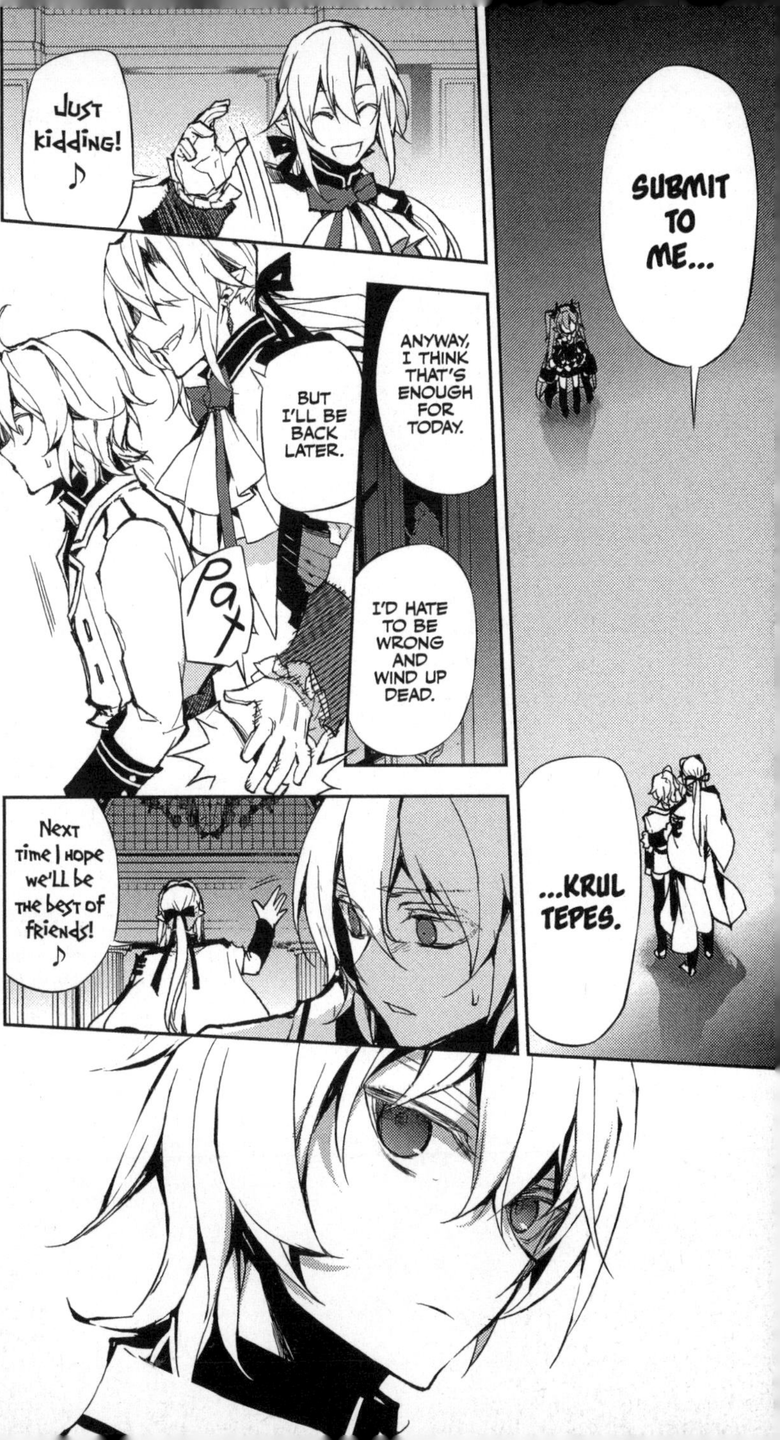
SUBMIT TO ME...
...KRUL TEPES.
JUST kidding! ♪
ANYWAY, I THINK THAT'S ENOUGH FOR TODAY.
BUT I'LL BE BACK LATER.
I'D HATE TO BE WRONG AND WIND UP DEAD.
Pat
Next time I hope we'll be the best of friends! ♪

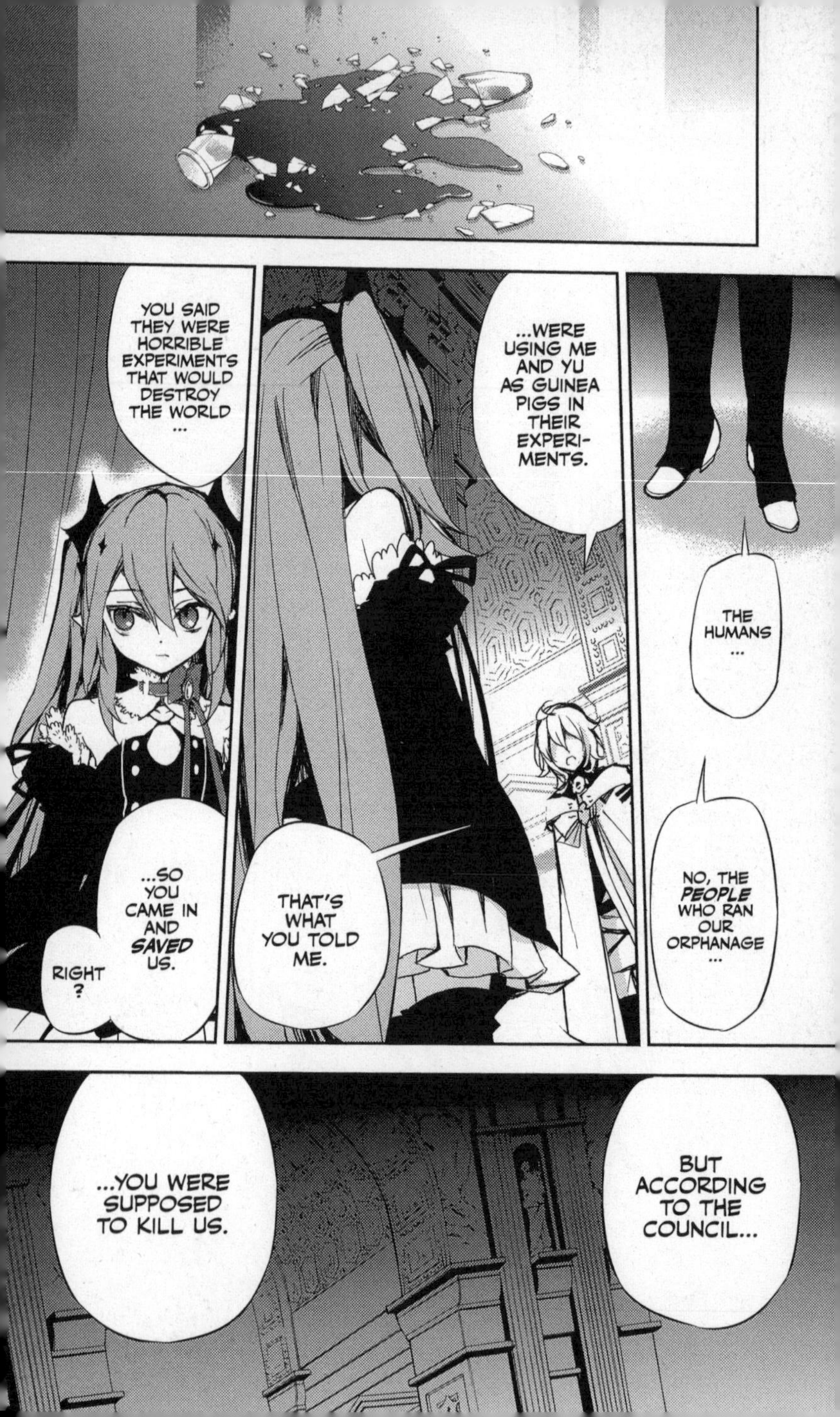
THE HUMANS ...
NO, THE *PEOPLE* WHO RAN OUR ORPHANAGE ...
...WERE USING ME AND YU AS GUINEA PIGS IN THEIR EXPERI-MENTS.
THAT'S WHAT YOU TOLD ME.
YOU SAID THEY WERE HORRIBLE EXPERIMENTS THAT WOULD DESTROY THE WORLD ...
...SO YOU CAME IN AND *SAVED* US.
RIGHT?
BUT ACCORDING TO THE COUNCIL...
...YOU WERE SUPPOSED TO KILL US.

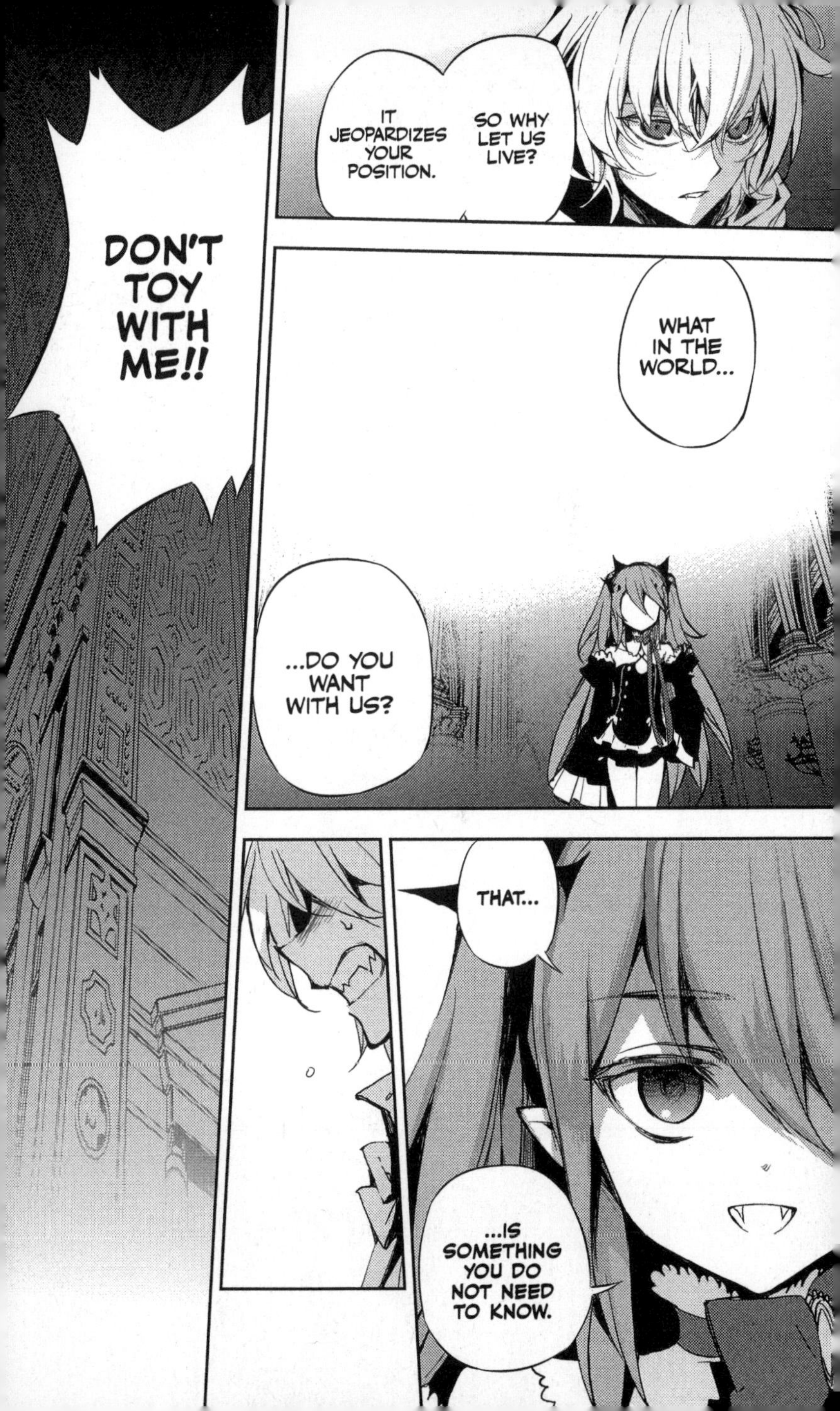
IT JEOPARDIZES YOUR POSITION.
SO WHY LET US LIVE?
WHAT IN THE WORLD...
...DO YOU WANT WITH US?
THAT...
...IS SOMETHING YOU DO NOT NEED TO KNOW.
DON'T TOY WITH ME!!

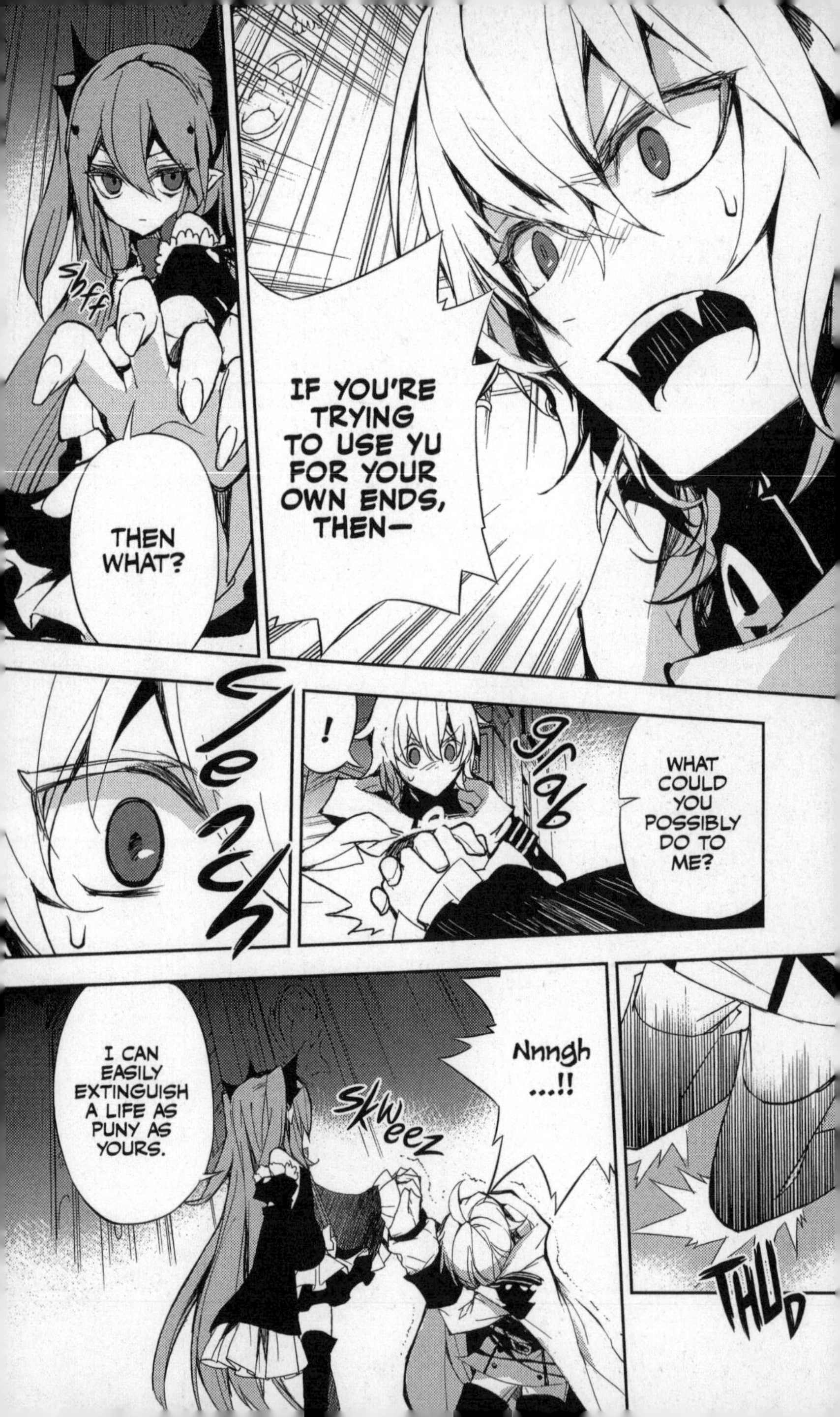
IF YOU'RE TRYING TO USE YU FOR YOUR OWN ENDS, THEN—
shff
THEN WHAT?
WHAT COULD YOU POSSIBLY DO TO ME?
grab
!
Clench
THUD
Nnngh ...!!
skweez
I CAN EASILY EXTINGUISH A LIFE AS PUNY AS YOURS.

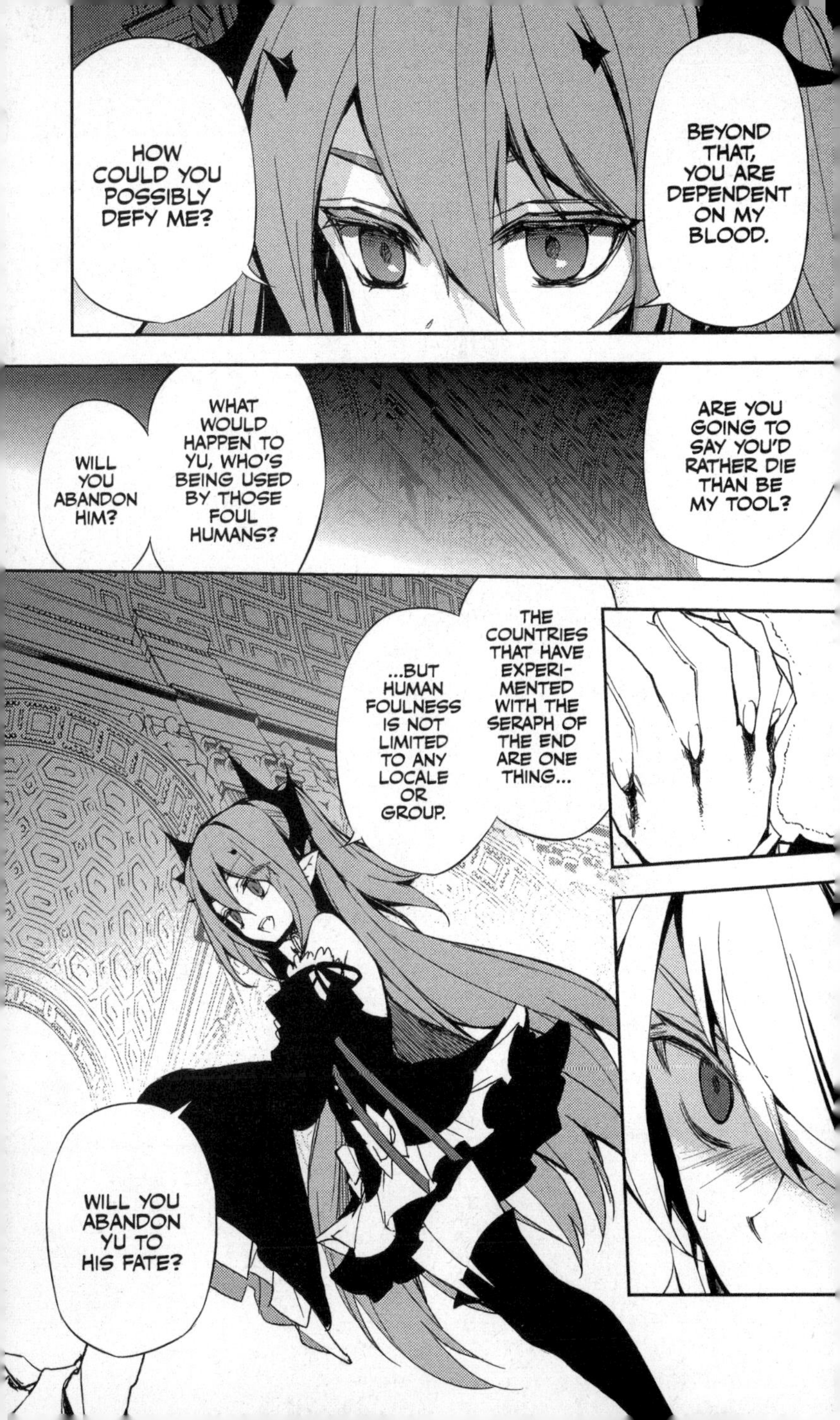
BEYOND THAT, YOU ARE DEPENDENT ON MY BLOOD.
HOW COULD YOU POSSIBLY DEFY ME?
ARE YOU GOING TO SAY YOU'D RATHER DIE THAN BE MY TOOL?
WHAT WOULD HAPPEN TO YU, WHO'S BEING USED BY THOSE FOUL HUMANS?
WILL YOU ABANDON HIM?
THE COUNTRIES THAT HAVE EXPERI-MENTED WITH THE SERAPH OF THE END ARE ONE THING...
...BUT HUMAN FOULNESS IS NOT LIMITED TO ANY LOCALE OR GROUP.
WILL YOU ABANDON YU TO HIS FATE?

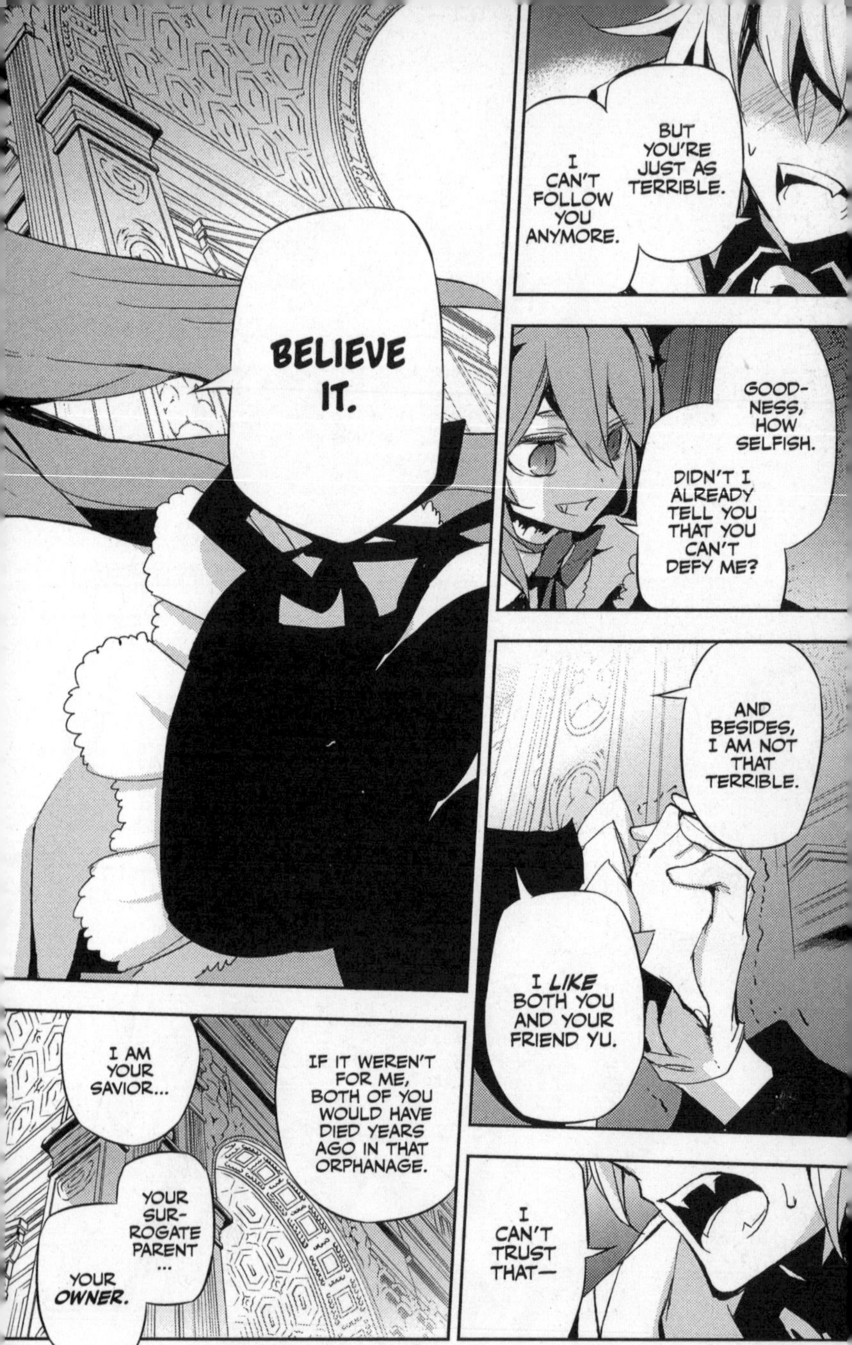
BUT YOU'RE JUST AS TERRIBLE.
I CAN'T FOLLOW YOU ANYMORE.
GOODNESS, HOW SELFISH.
DIDN'T I ALREADY TELL YOU THAT YOU CAN'T DEFY ME?
AND BESIDES, I AM NOT THAT TERRIBLE.
I *LIKE* BOTH YOU AND YOUR FRIEND YU.
I CAN'T TRUST THAT—
BELIEVE IT.
IF IT WEREN'T FOR ME, BOTH OF YOU WOULD HAVE DIED YEARS AGO IN THAT ORPHANAGE.
I AM YOUR SAVIOR...
YOUR SURROGATE PARENT...
YOUR *OWNER*.

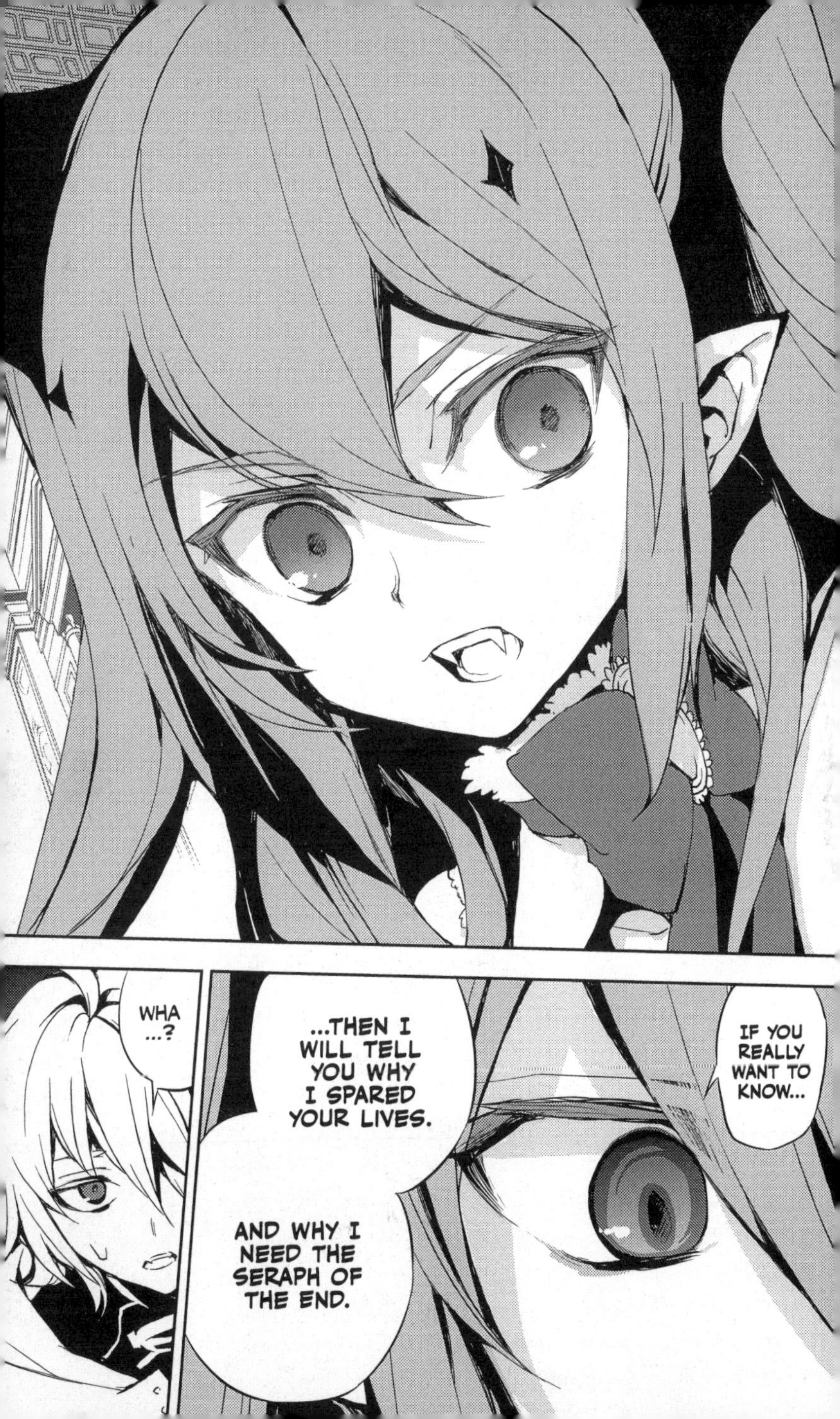
IF YOU REALLY WANT TO KNOW...
...THEN I WILL TELL YOU WHY I SPARED YOUR LIVES.
AND WHY I NEED THE SERAPH OF THE END.
WHA ...?

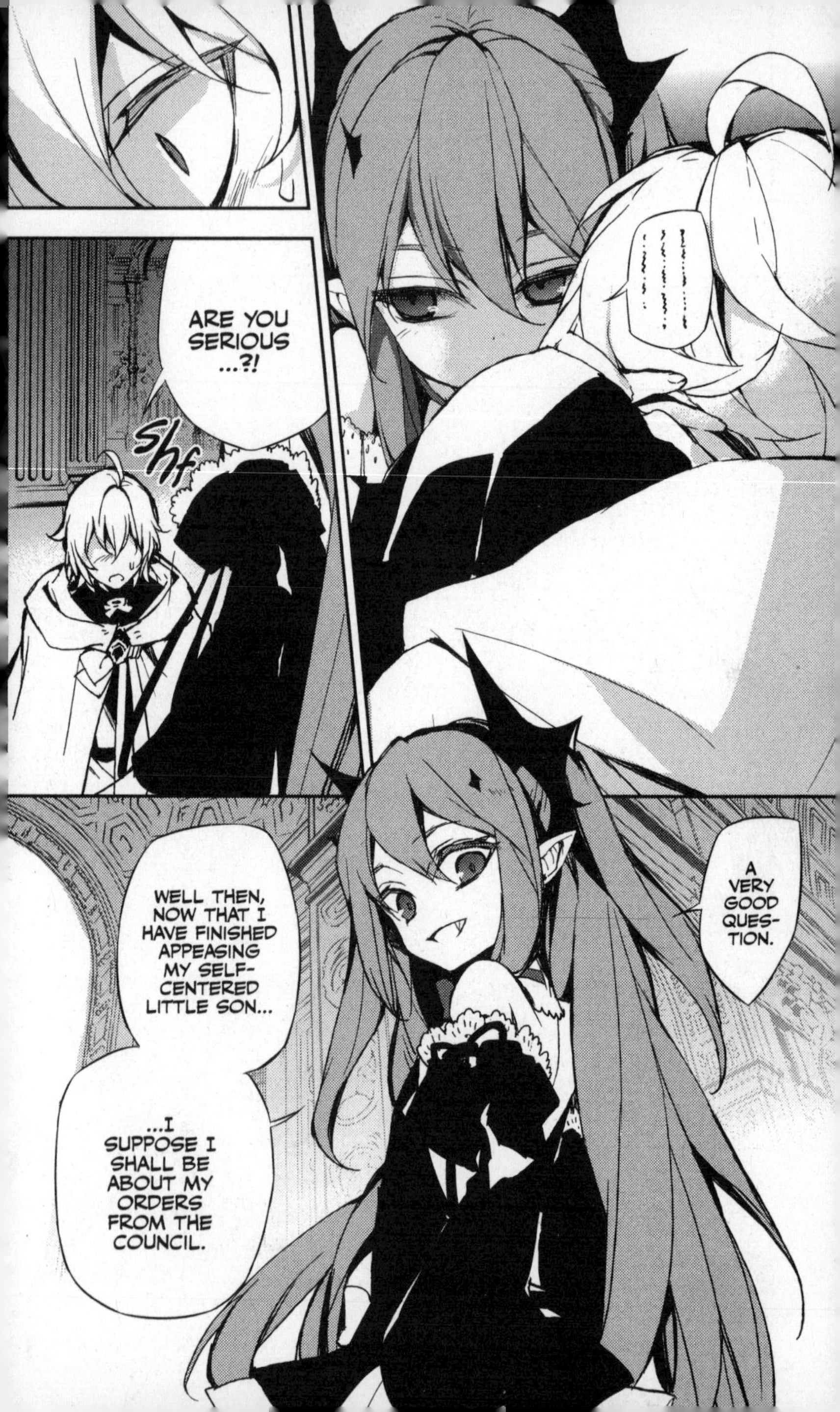
……
ARE YOU SERIOUS ...?!
Shf
A VERY GOOD QUES- TION.
WELL THEN, NOW THAT I HAVE FINISHED APPEASING MY SELF- CENTERED LITTLE SON...
...I SUPPOSE I SHALL BE ABOUT MY ORDERS FROM THE COUNCIL.

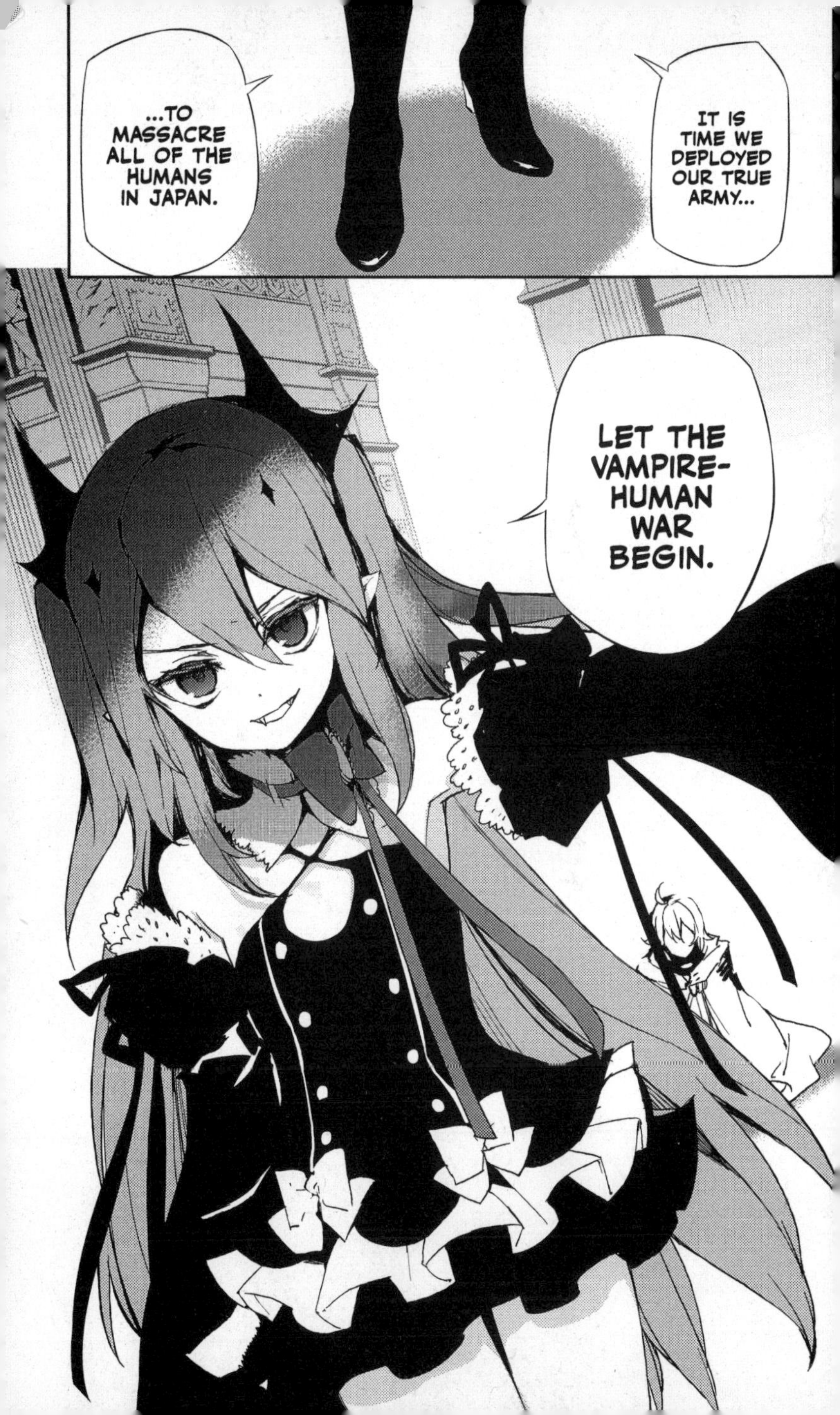
IT IS TIME WE DEPLOYED OUR TRUE ARMY...
...TO MASSACRE ALL OF THE HUMANS IN JAPAN.
LET THE VAMPIRE-HUMAN WAR BEGIN.

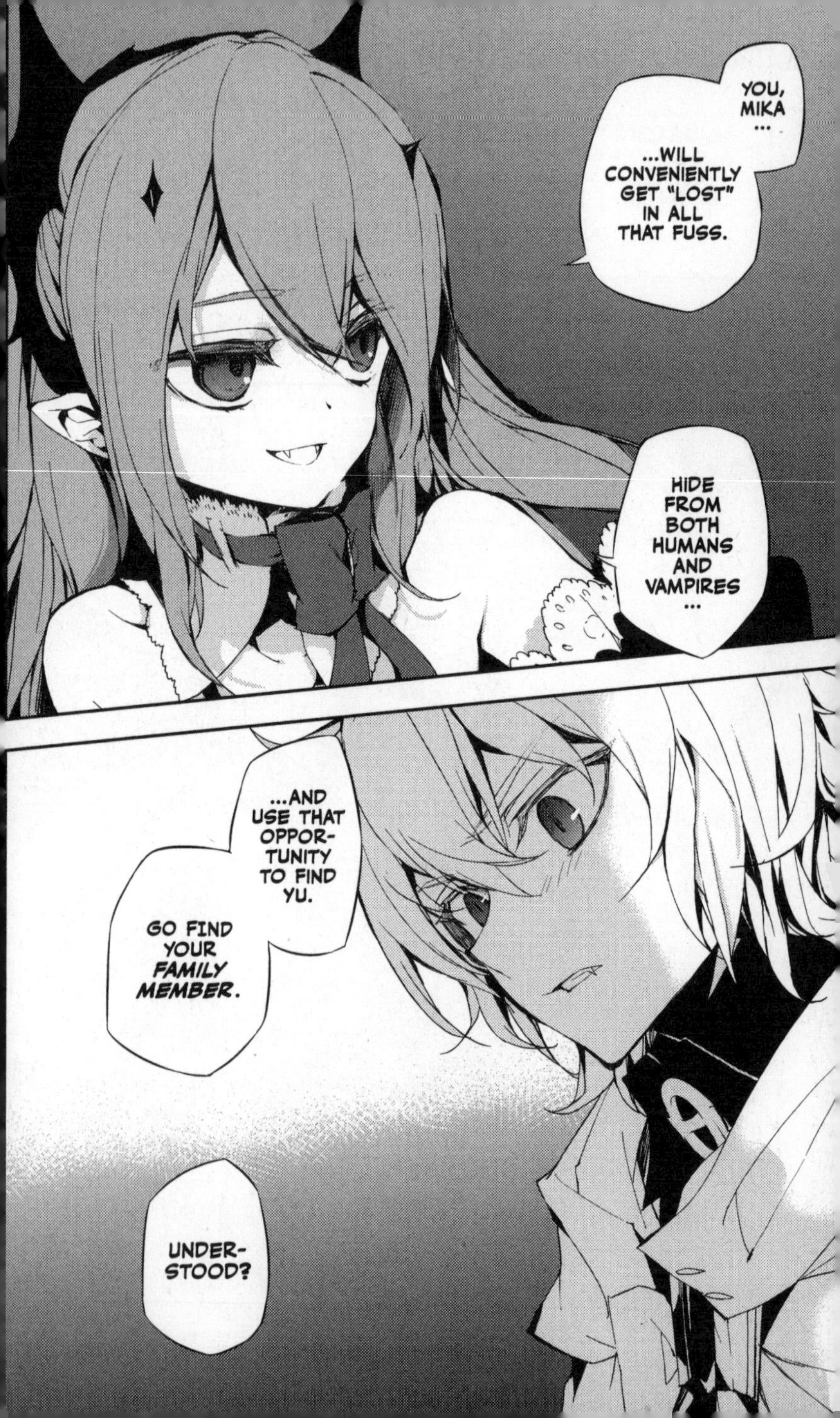
YOU, MIKA...
...WILL CONVENIENTLY GET "LOST" IN ALL THAT FUSS.
HIDE FROM BOTH HUMANS AND VAMPIRES...
...AND USE THAT OPPOR-TUNITY TO FIND YU.
GO FIND YOUR *FAMILY MEMBER*.
UNDER-STOOD?

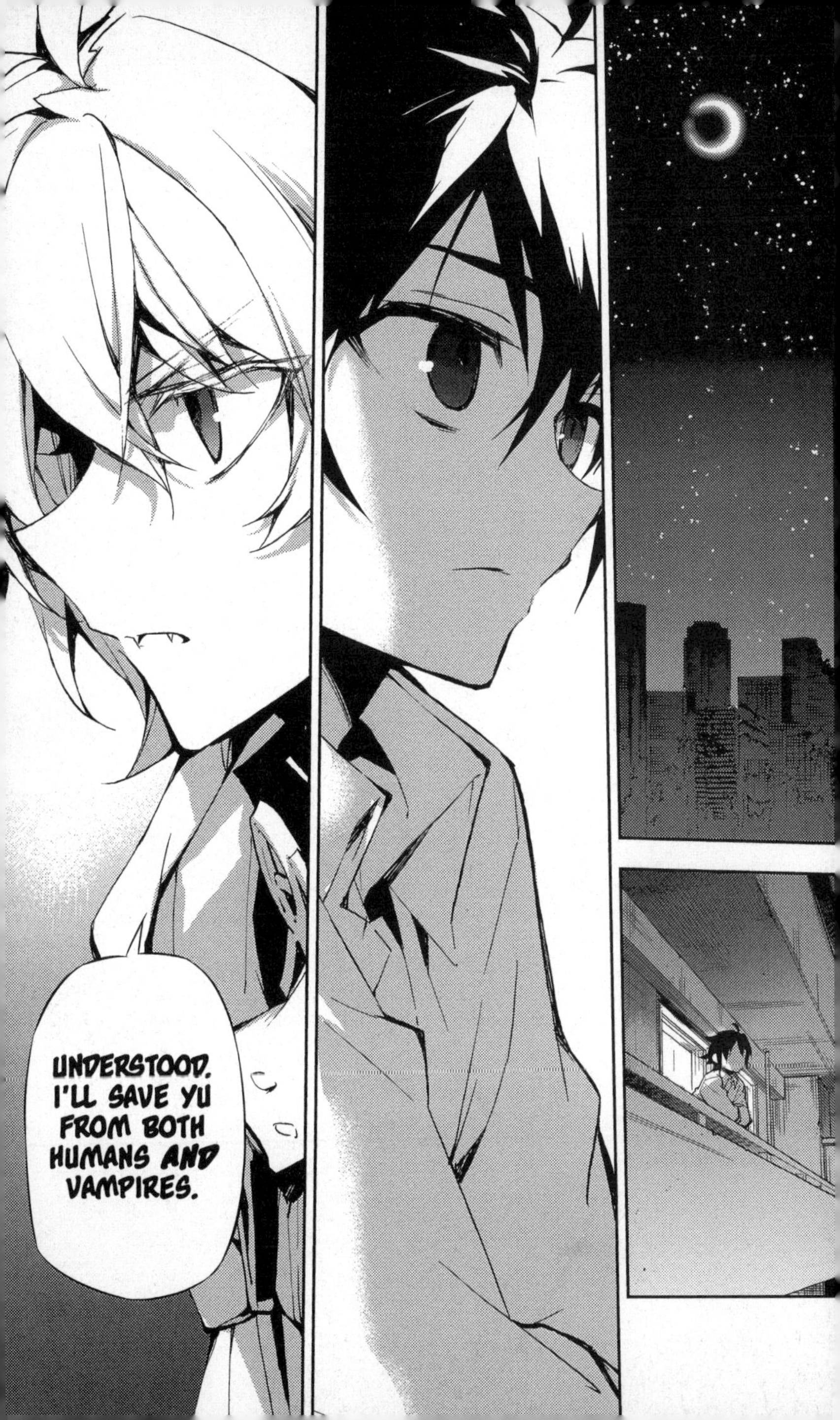
UNDERSTOOD. I'LL SAVE YU FROM BOTH HUMANS AND VAMPIRES.

Seraph of the End

—VAMPIRE REIGN—

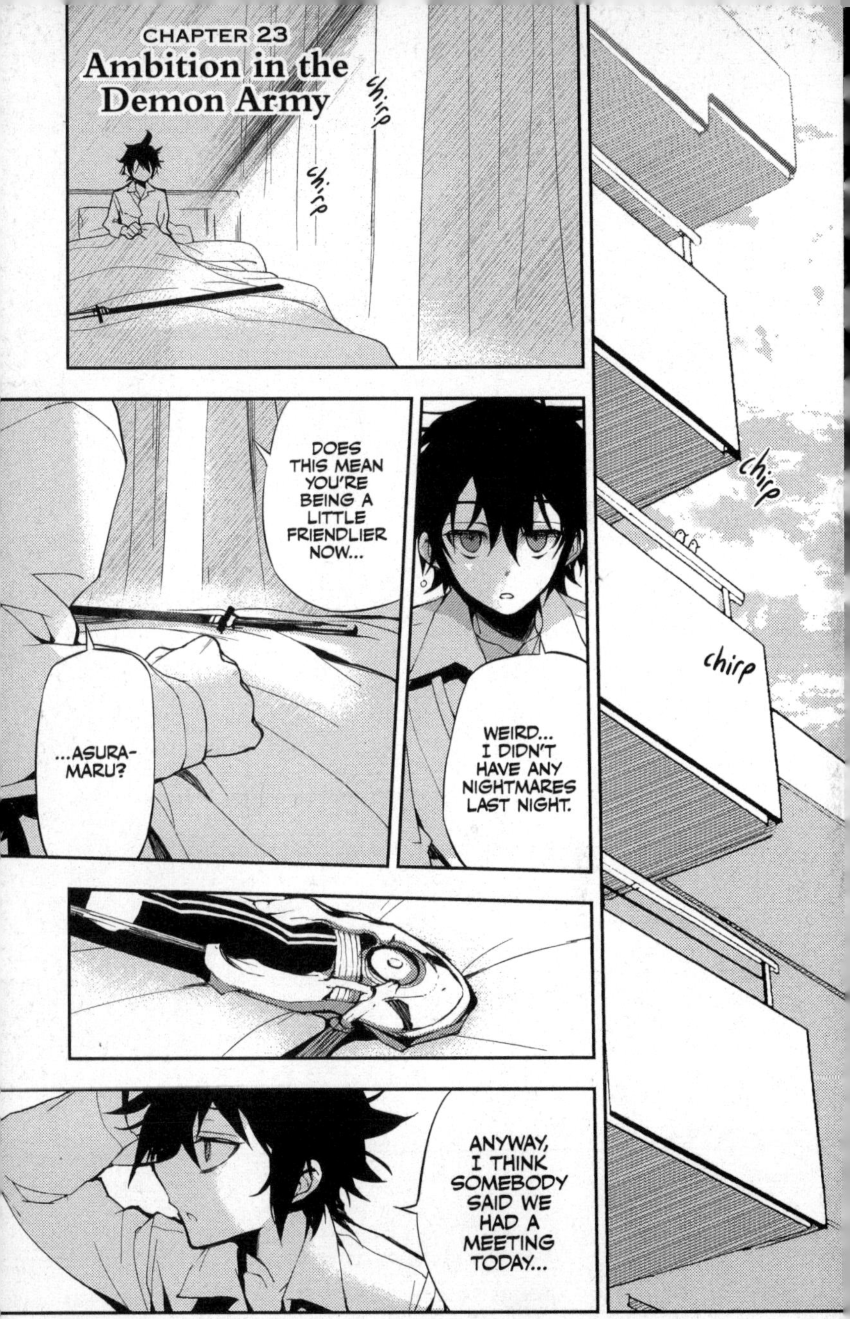
chirp
chirp
CHAPTER 23
Ambition in the Demon Army
chirp
chirp
WEIRD... I DIDN'T HAVE ANY NIGHTMARES LAST NIGHT.
DOES THIS MEAN YOU'RE BEING A LITTLE FRIENDLIER NOW...
...ASURA-MARU?
ANYWAY, I THINK SOMEBODY SAID WE HAD A MEETING TODAY...

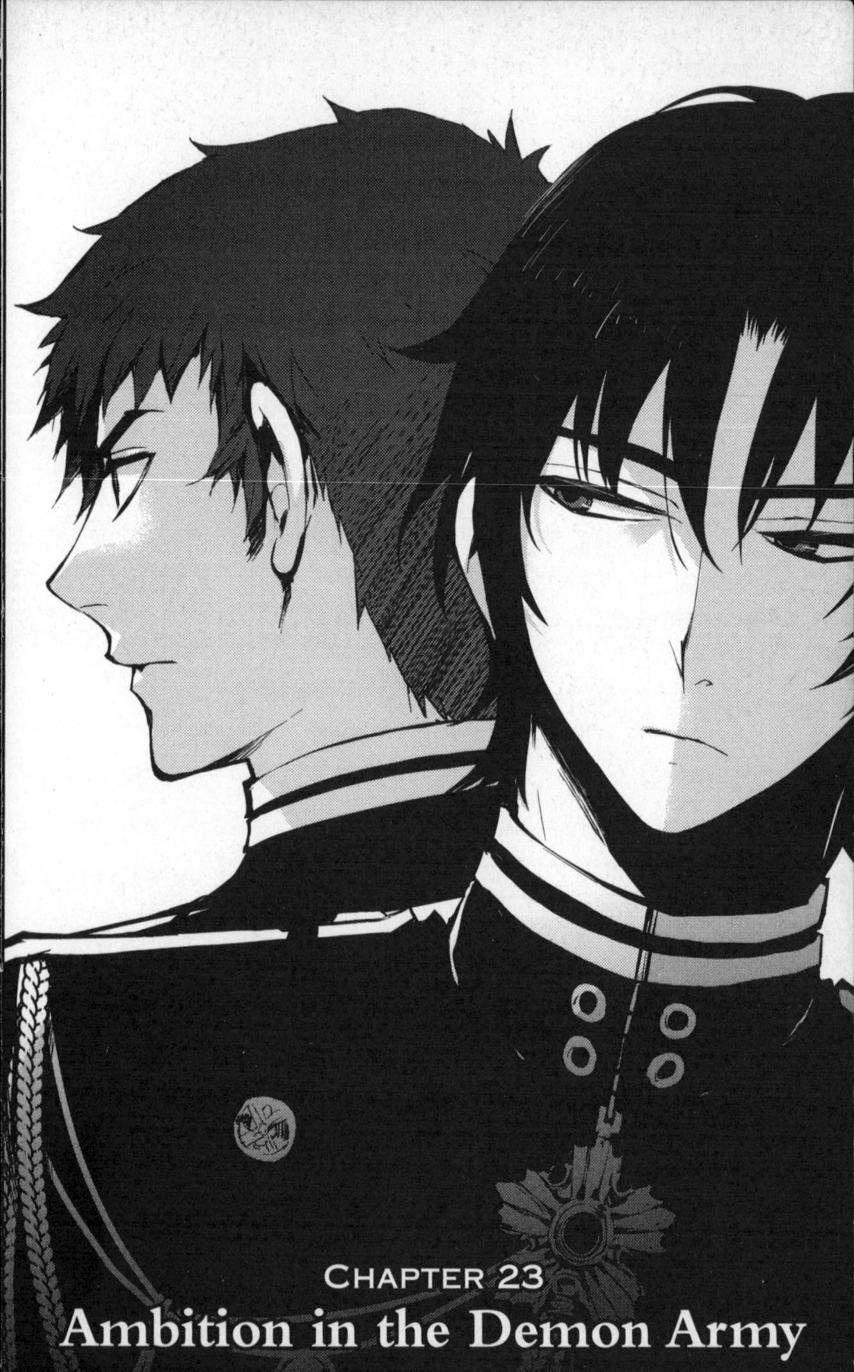

Chapter 23
Ambition in the Demon Army

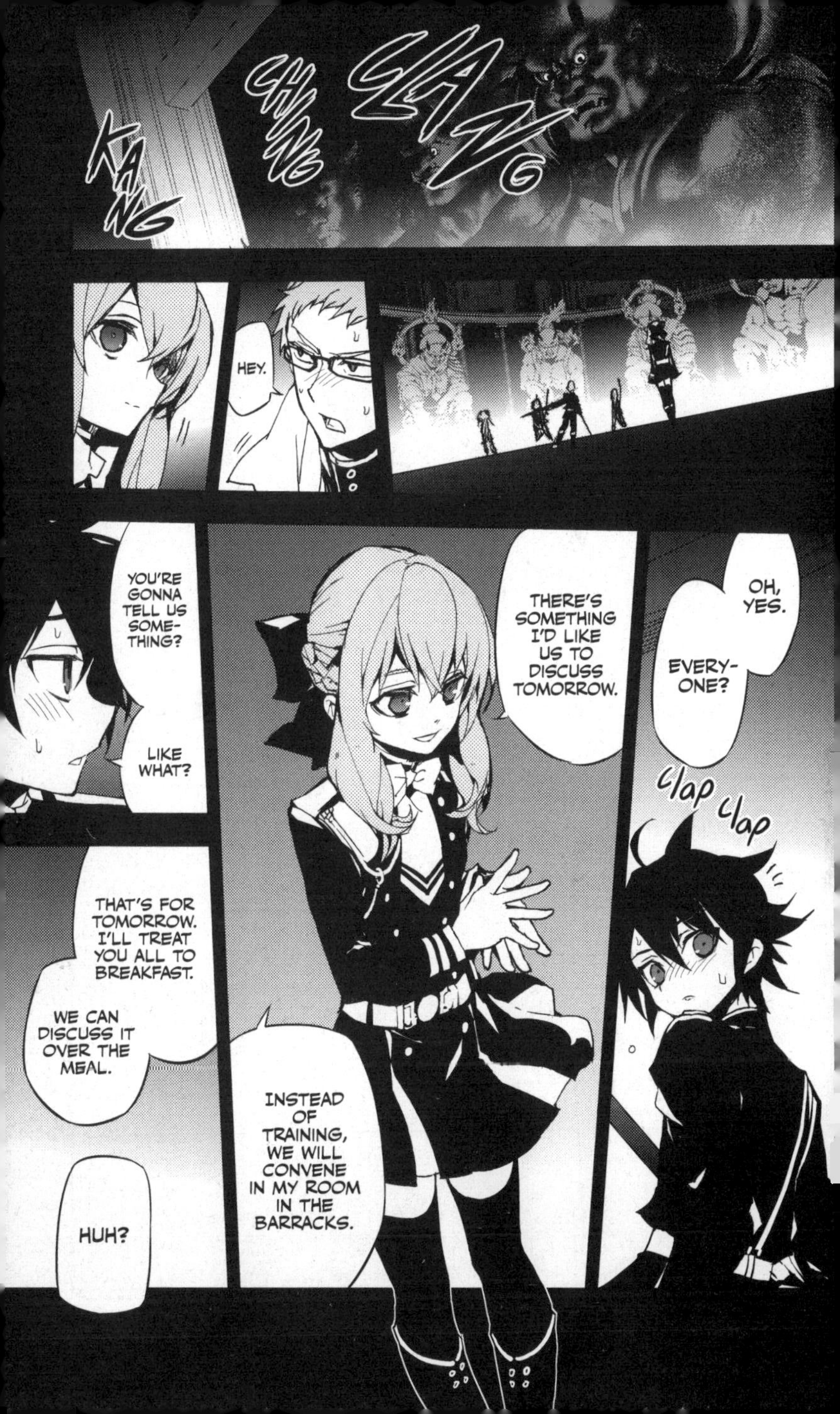
CLANG
CHING
KANG
HEY.
OH, YES.
EVERY-ONE?
clap clap
THERE'S SOMETHING I'D LIKE US TO DISCUSS TOMORROW.
INSTEAD OF TRAINING, WE WILL CONVENE IN MY ROOM IN THE BARRACKS.
YOU'RE GONNA TELL US SOME-THING?
LIKE WHAT?
THAT'S FOR TOMORROW. I'LL TREAT YOU ALL TO BREAKFAST.
WE CAN DISCUSS IT OVER THE MEAL.
HUH?

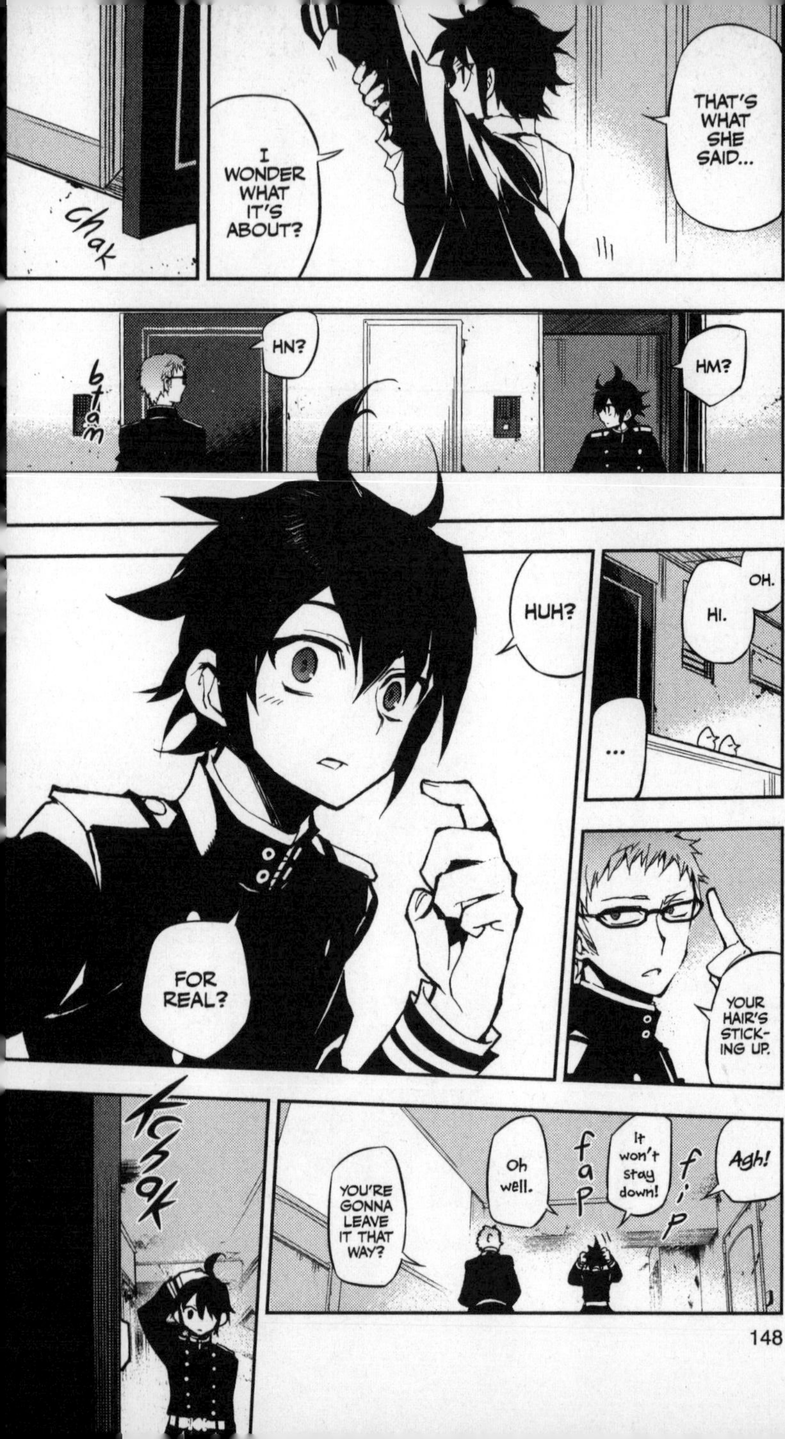
THAT'S WHAT SHE SAID...
I WONDER WHAT IT'S ABOUT?
chak
HM?
HN?
btam
OH.
HI.
...
YOUR HAIR'S STICK-ING UP.
HUH?
FOR REAL?
Agh!
flip
It won't stay down!
fap
Oh well.
YOU'RE GONNA LEAVE IT THAT WAY?
kchak

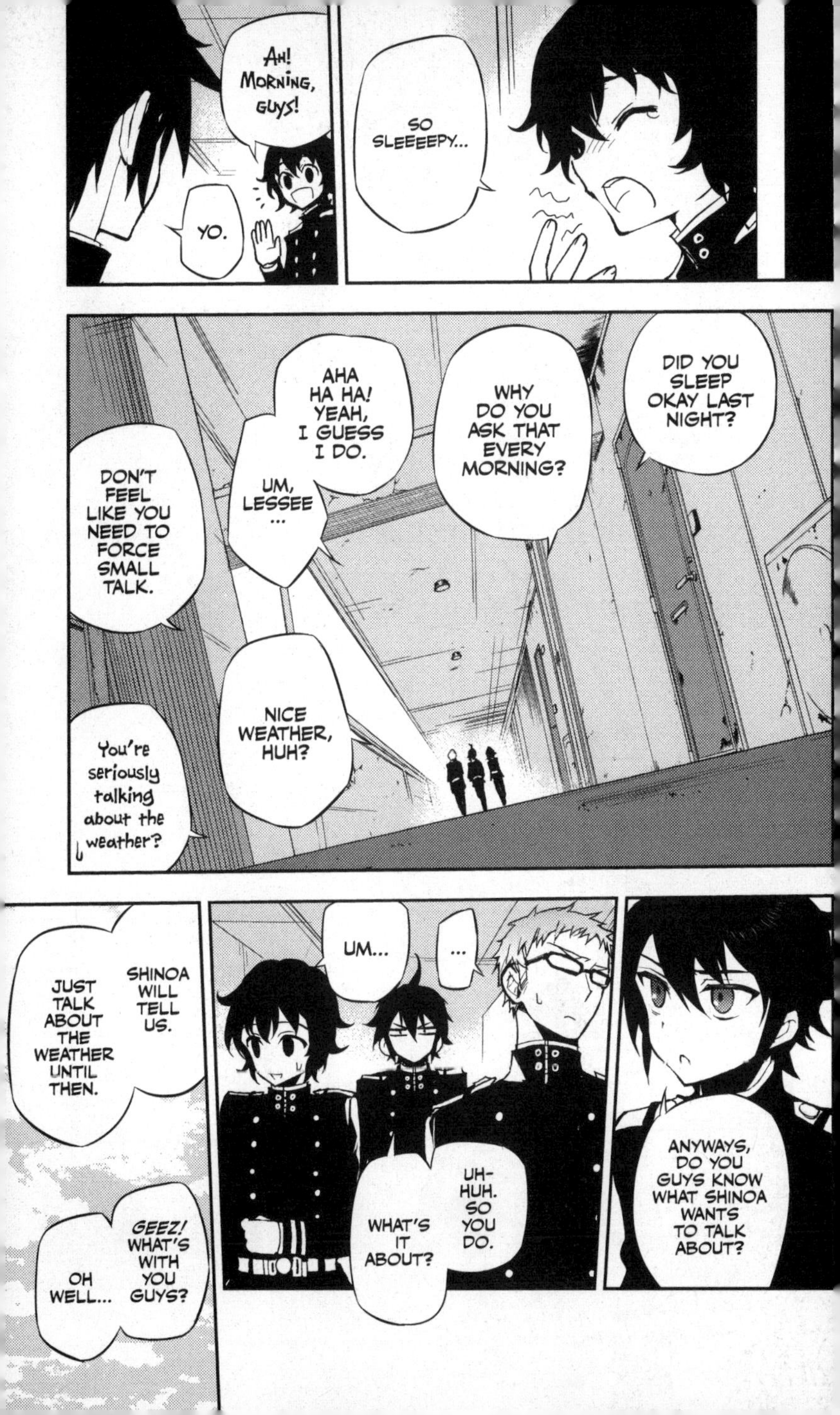
SO SLEEEEPY...
AH! MORNING, GUYS!
YO.
DID YOU SLEEP OKAY LAST NIGHT?
WHY DO YOU ASK THAT EVERY MORNING?
AHA HA HA! YEAH, I GUESS I DO.
UM, LESSEE...
DON'T FEEL LIKE YOU NEED TO FORCE SMALL TALK.
NICE WEATHER, HUH?
You're seriously talking about the weather?
ANYWAYS, DO YOU GUYS KNOW WHAT SHINOA WANTS TO TALK ABOUT?
...
UM...
UH-HUH. SO YOU DO.
WHAT'S IT ABOUT?
SHINOA WILL TELL US.
JUST TALK ABOUT THE WEATHER UNTIL THEN.
GEEZ! WHAT'S WITH YOU GUYS?
OH WELL...

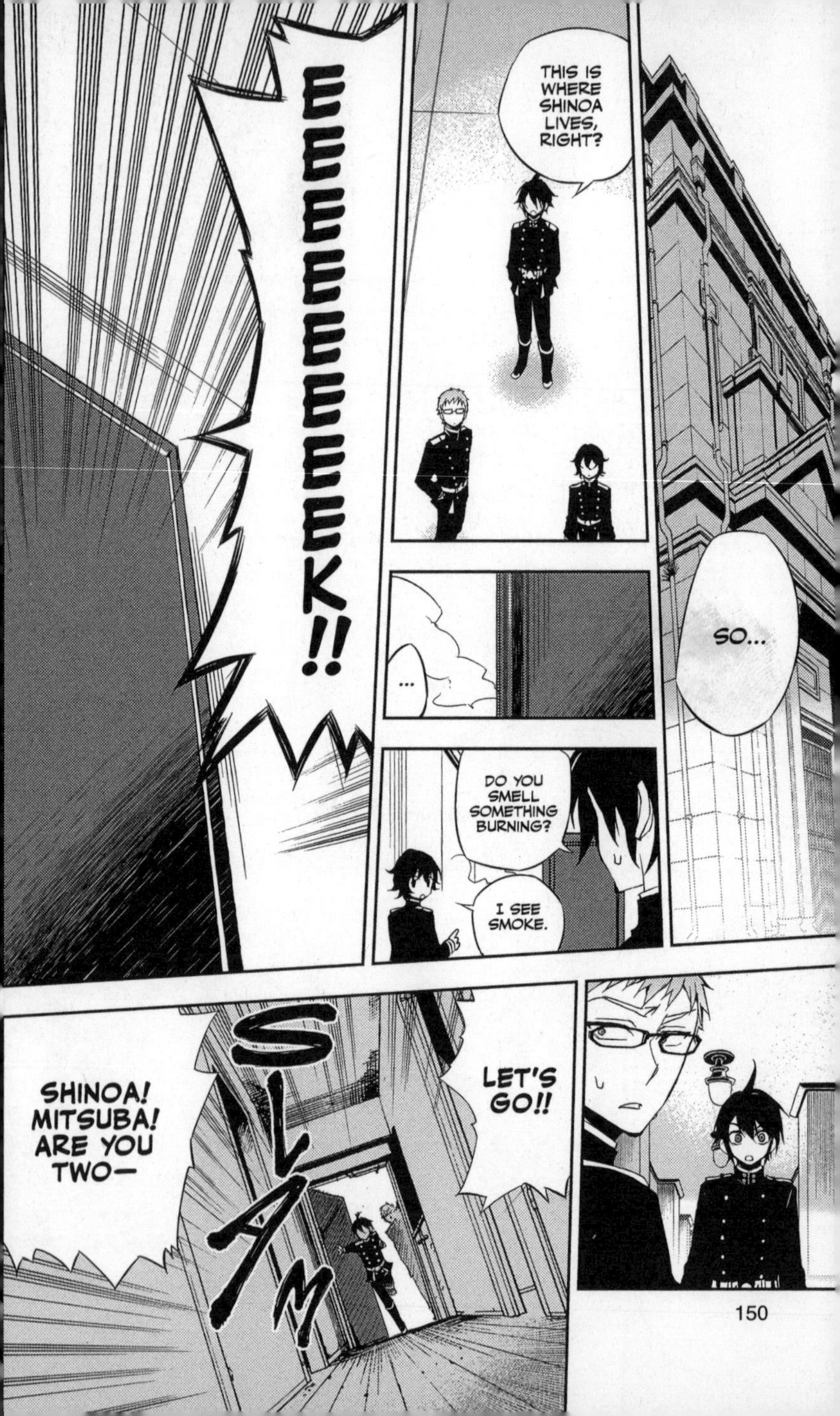
SO...
THIS IS WHERE SHINOA LIVES, RIGHT?
...
DO YOU SMELL SOMETHING BURNING?
I SEE SMOKE.
EEEEEEEEEK!!
LET'S GO!!
SLAM
SHINOA! MITSUBA! ARE YOU TWO—

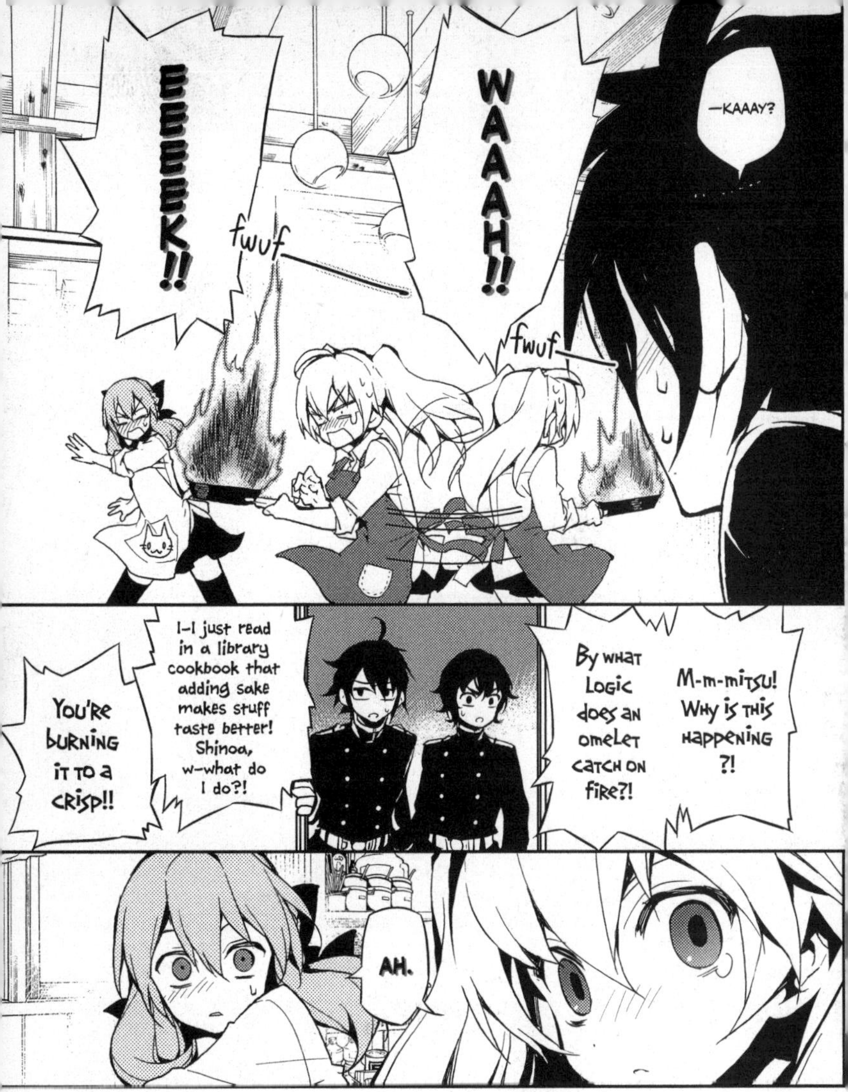
—KAAAY?
WAAAAH!!
EEEEEK!!
fwuf
fwuf
M-m-mitsu! Why is this happening?!
By what logic does an omelet catch on fire?!
I-I just read in a library cookbook that adding sake makes stuff taste better! Shinoa, w-what do I do?!
You're burning it to a crisp!!
AH.

Several minutes later...

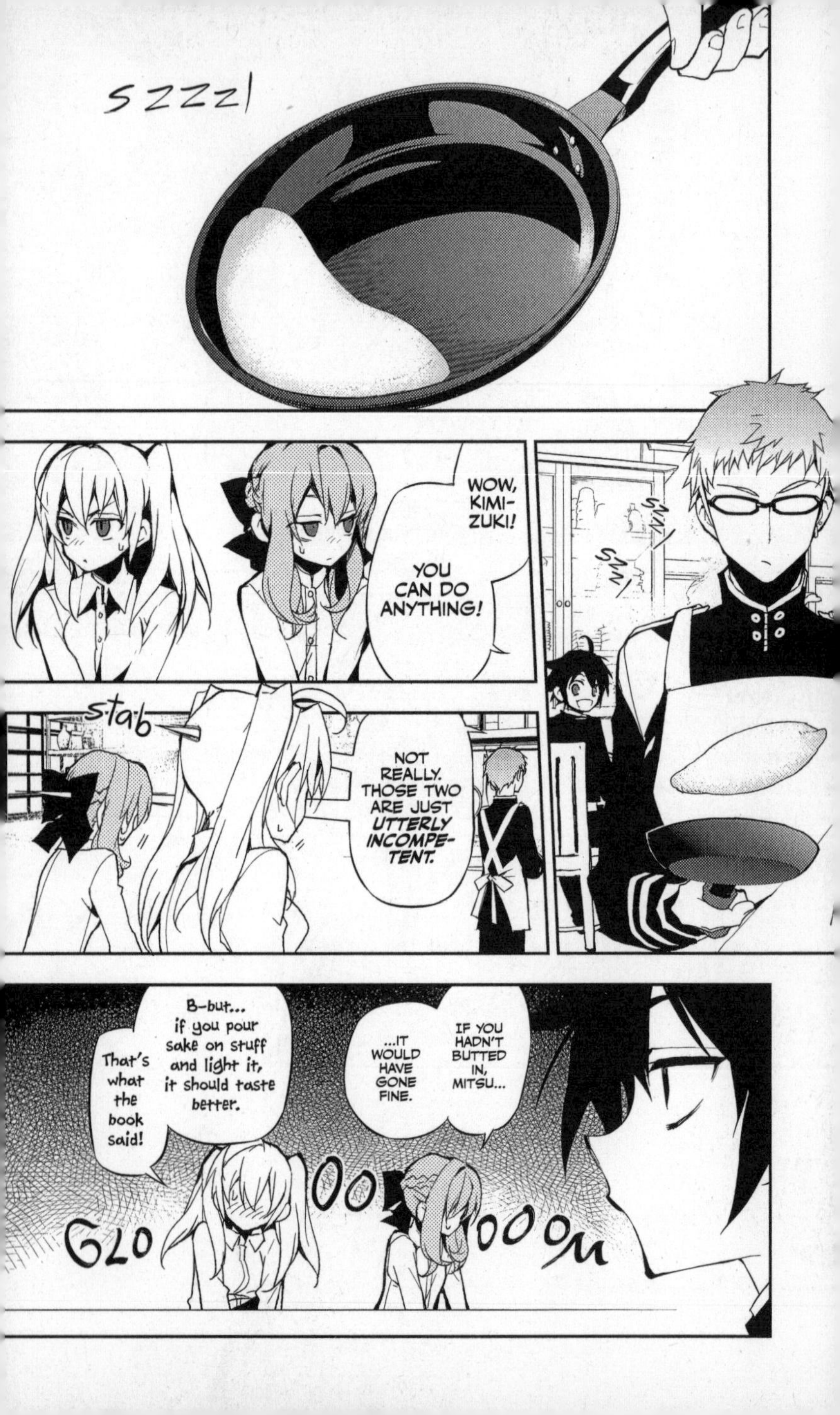
SZZZL
SZZ
SZZ
WOW, KIMIZUKI!
YOU CAN DO ANYTHING!
stab
NOT REALLY. THOSE TWO ARE JUST *UTTERLY INCOMPETENT.*
IF YOU HADN'T BUTTED IN, MITSU...
...IT WOULD HAVE GONE FINE.
B-but... if you pour sake on stuff and light it, it should taste better.
That's what the book said!
GLOOOOOOOM

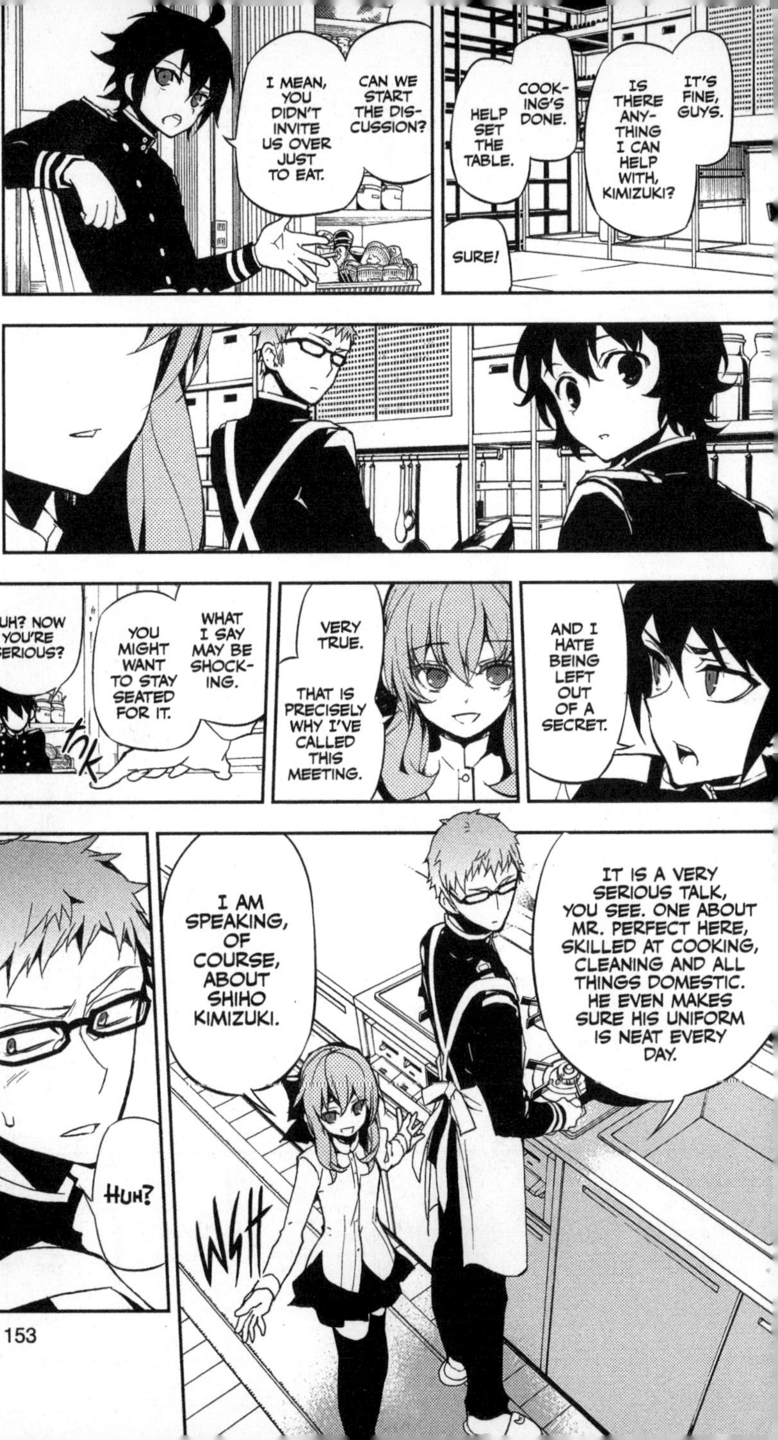
IT'S FINE, GUYS.
IS THERE ANYTHING I CAN HELP WITH, KIMIZUKI?
COOKING'S DONE.
HELP SET THE TABLE.
SURE!
CAN WE START THE DISCUSSION?
I MEAN, YOU DIDN'T INVITE US OVER JUST TO EAT.
AND I HATE BEING LEFT OUT OF A SECRET.
VERY TRUE.
THAT IS PRECISELY WHY I'VE CALLED THIS MEETING.
WHAT I SAY MAY BE SHOCKING.
YOU MIGHT WANT TO STAY SEATED FOR IT.
HUH? NOW YOU'RE SERIOUS?
TCK
IT IS A VERY SERIOUS TALK, YOU SEE. ONE ABOUT MR. PERFECT HERE, SKILLED AT COOKING, CLEANING AND ALL THINGS DOMESTIC. HE EVEN MAKES SURE HIS UNIFORM IS NEAT EVERY DAY.
I AM SPEAKING, OF COURSE, ABOUT SHIHO KIMIZUKI.
WSH
HUH?

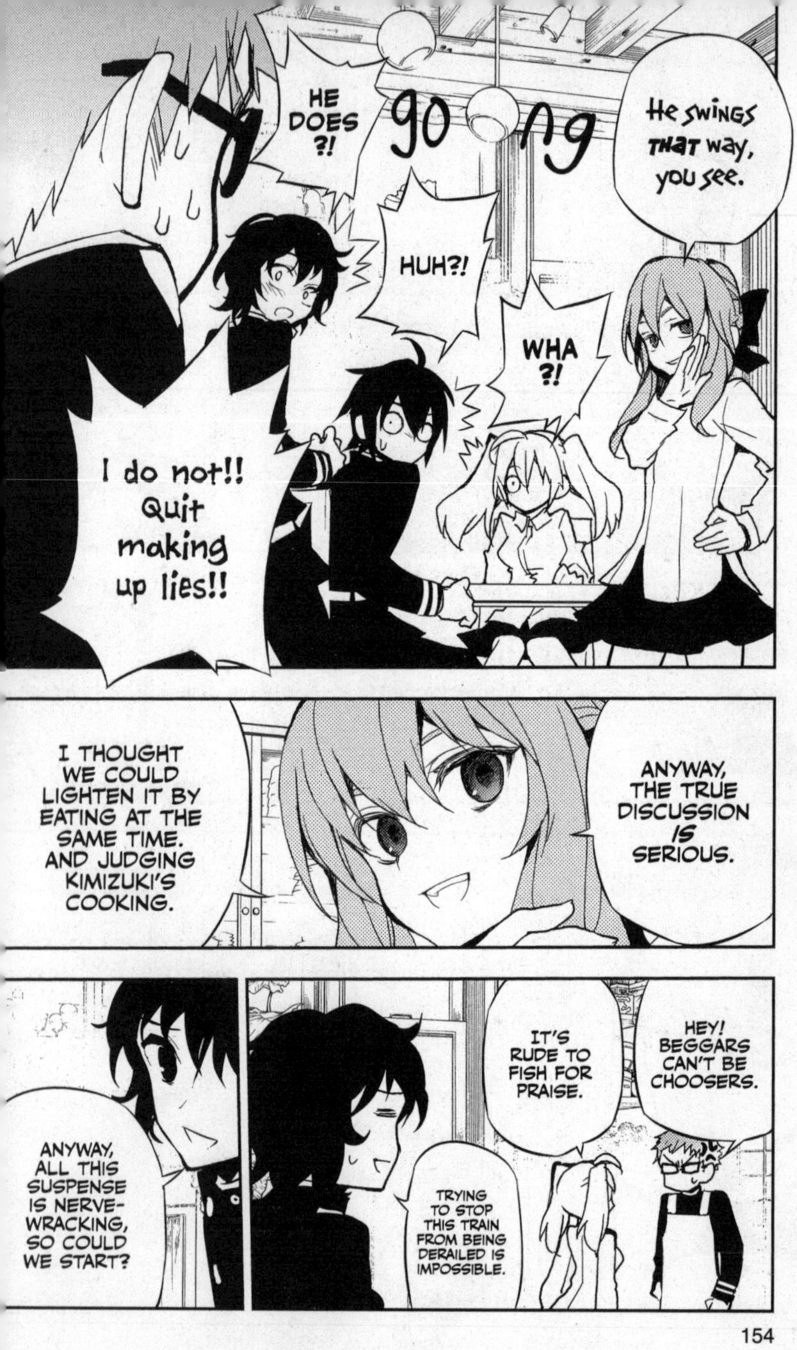
He swings THAT way, you see.
go ng
HE DOES?!
HUH?!
WHA?!
I do not!! Quit making up lies!!
ANYWAY, THE TRUE DISCUSSION IS SERIOUS.
I THOUGHT WE COULD LIGHTEN IT BY EATING AT THE SAME TIME. AND JUDGING KIMIZUKI'S COOKING.
HEY! BEGGARS CAN'T BE CHOOSERS.
IT'S RUDE TO FISH FOR PRAISE.
TRYING TO STOP THIS TRAIN FROM BEING DERAILED IS IMPOSSIBLE.
ANYWAY, ALL THIS SUSPENSE IS NERVE-WRACKING, SO COULD WE START?

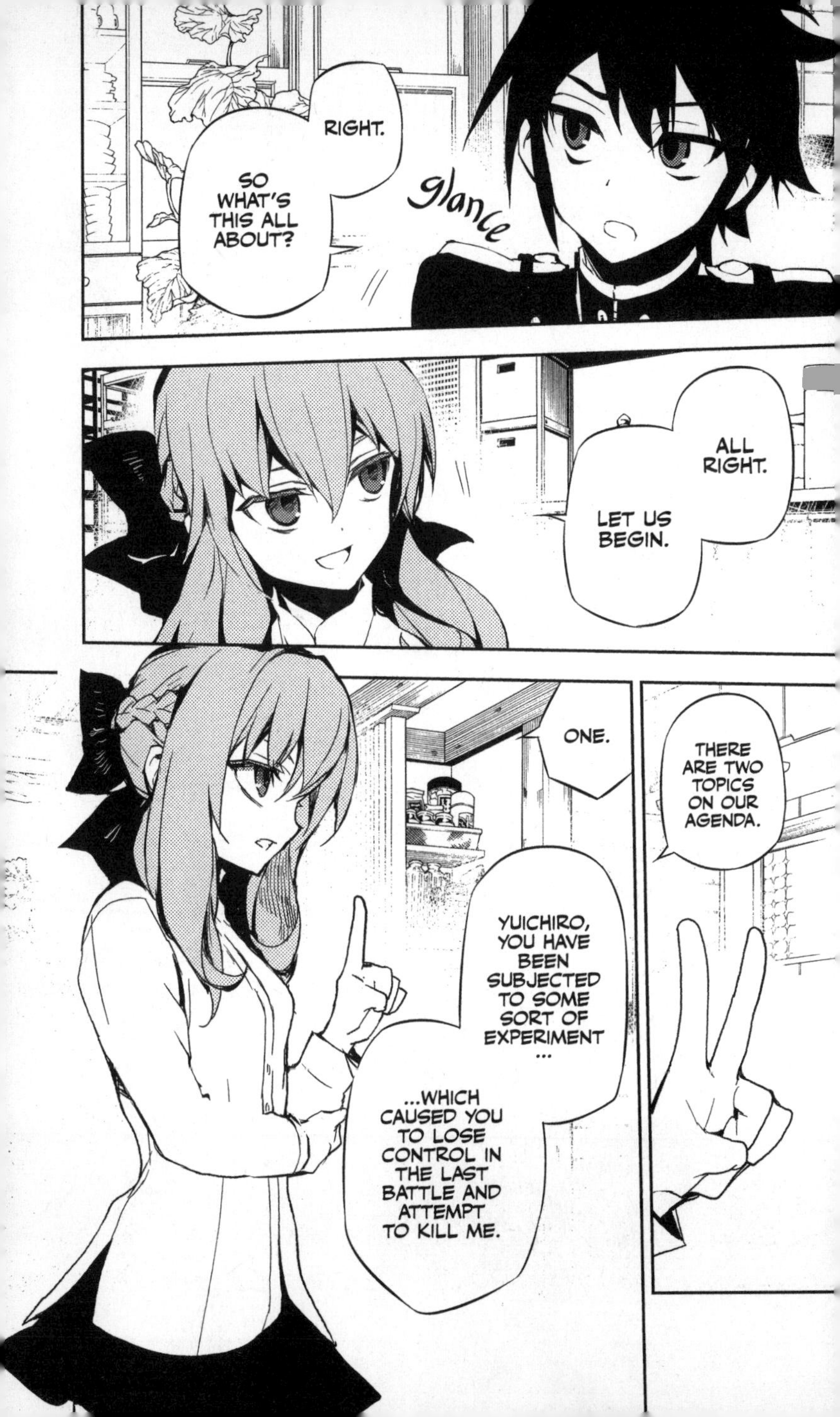
RIGHT.
SO WHAT'S THIS ALL ABOUT?
glance
ALL RIGHT.
LET US BEGIN.
THERE ARE TWO TOPICS ON OUR AGENDA.
ONE.
YUICHIRO, YOU HAVE BEEN SUBJECTED TO SOME SORT OF EXPERIMENT...
...WHICH CAUSED YOU TO LOSE CONTROL IN THE LAST BATTLE AND ATTEMPT TO KILL ME.

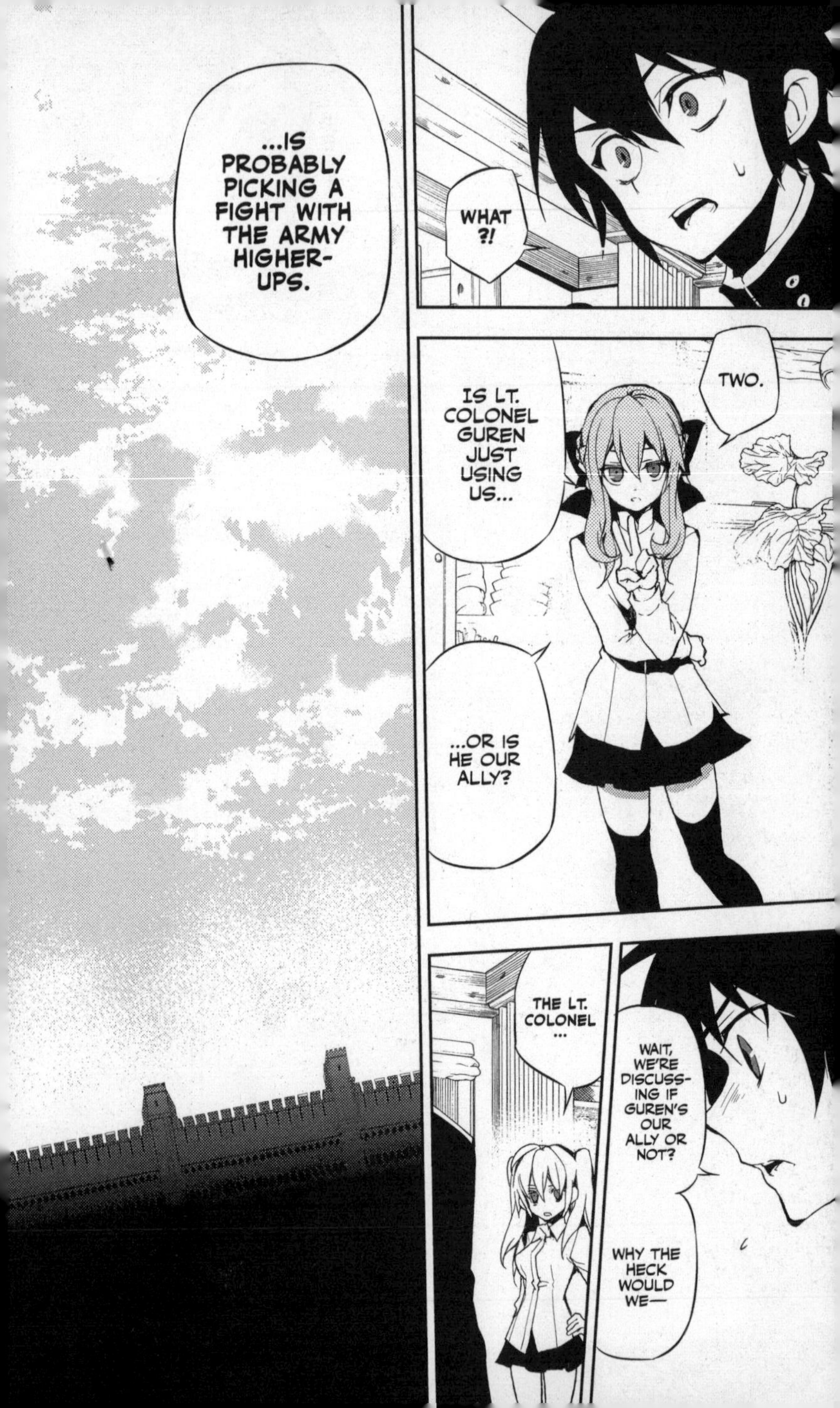
WHAT?!
TWO.
IS LT. COLONEL GUREN JUST USING US...
...OR IS HE OUR ALLY?
THE LT. COLONEL...
WAIT, WE'RE DISCUSS-ING IF GUREN'S OUR ALLY OR NOT?
WHY THE HECK WOULD WE—
...IS PROBABLY PICKING A FIGHT WITH THE ARMY HIGHER-UPS.

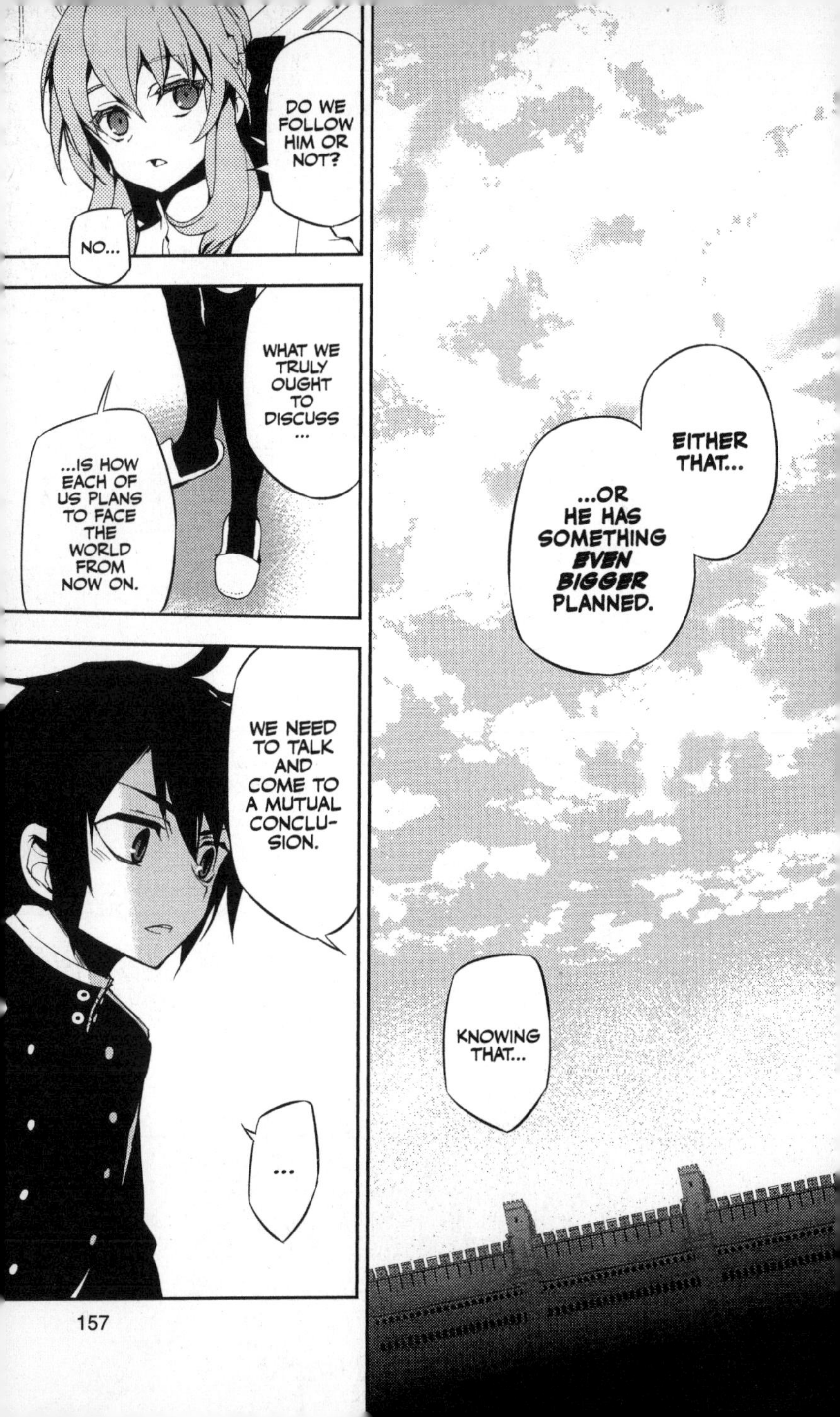
EITHER THAT...
...OR HE HAS SOMETHING EVEN BIGGER PLANNED.
KNOWING THAT...
DO WE FOLLOW HIM OR NOT?
NO...
WHAT WE TRULY OUGHT TO DISCUSS...
...IS HOW EACH OF US PLANS TO FACE THE WORLD FROM NOW ON.
WE NEED TO TALK AND COME TO A MUTUAL CONCLUSION.
...

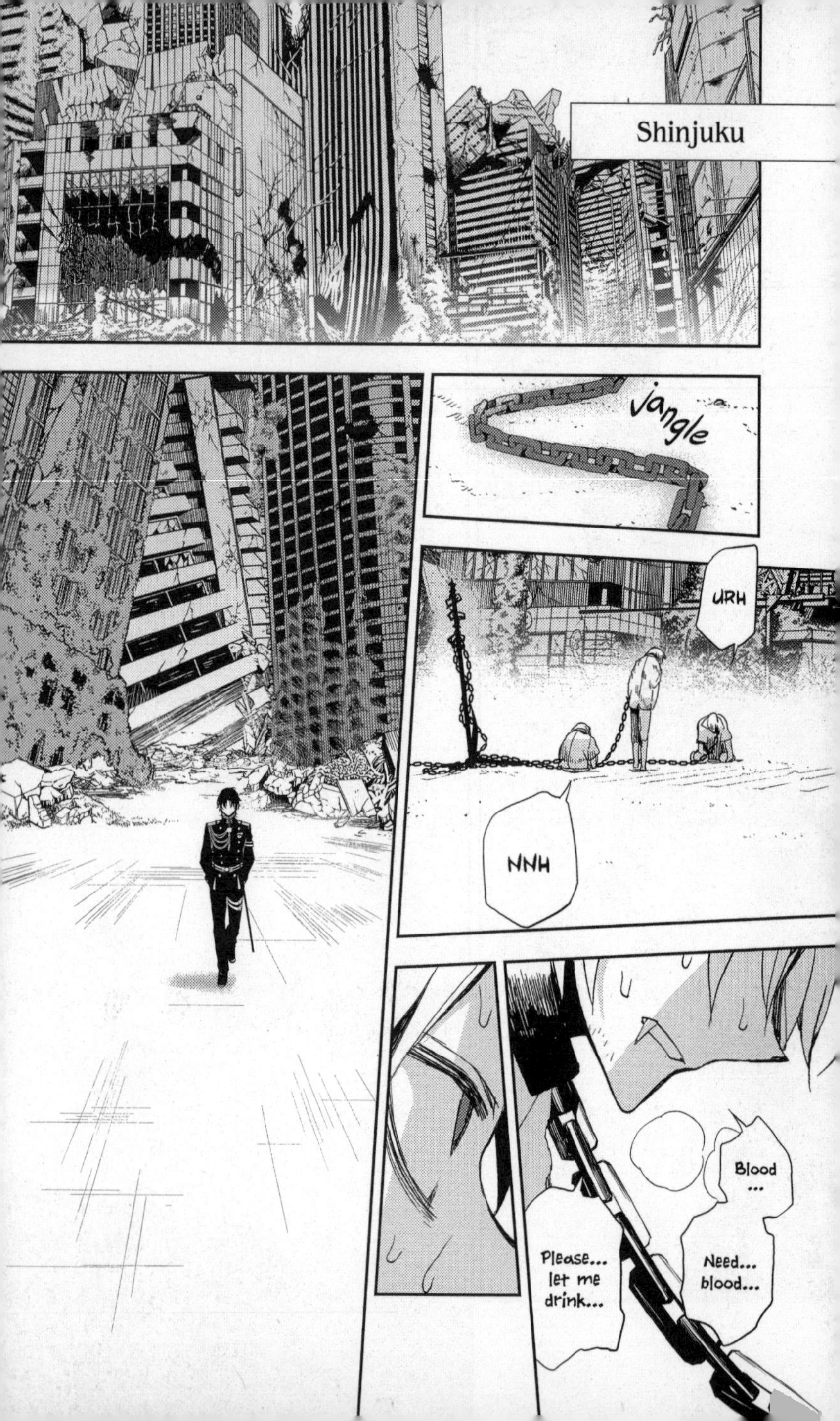
Shinjuku
jangle
URH
NNH
Blood...
Need... blood...
Please... let me drink...

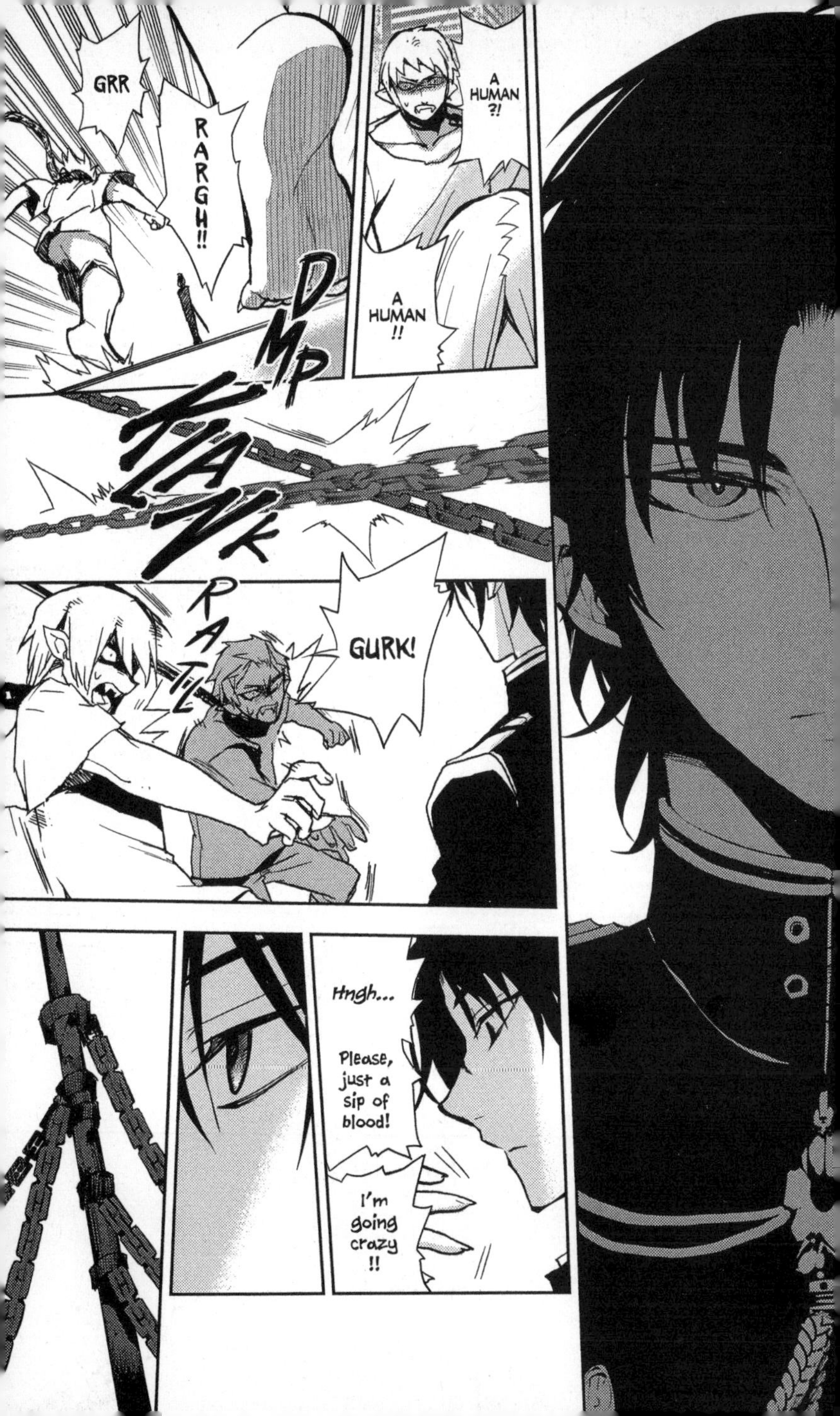

A HUMAN ?!
A HUMAN !!
GRR
RARGH!!
DMP
KLANK
GURK!
RATTL
Hngh...
Please, just a sip of blood!
I'm going crazy !!

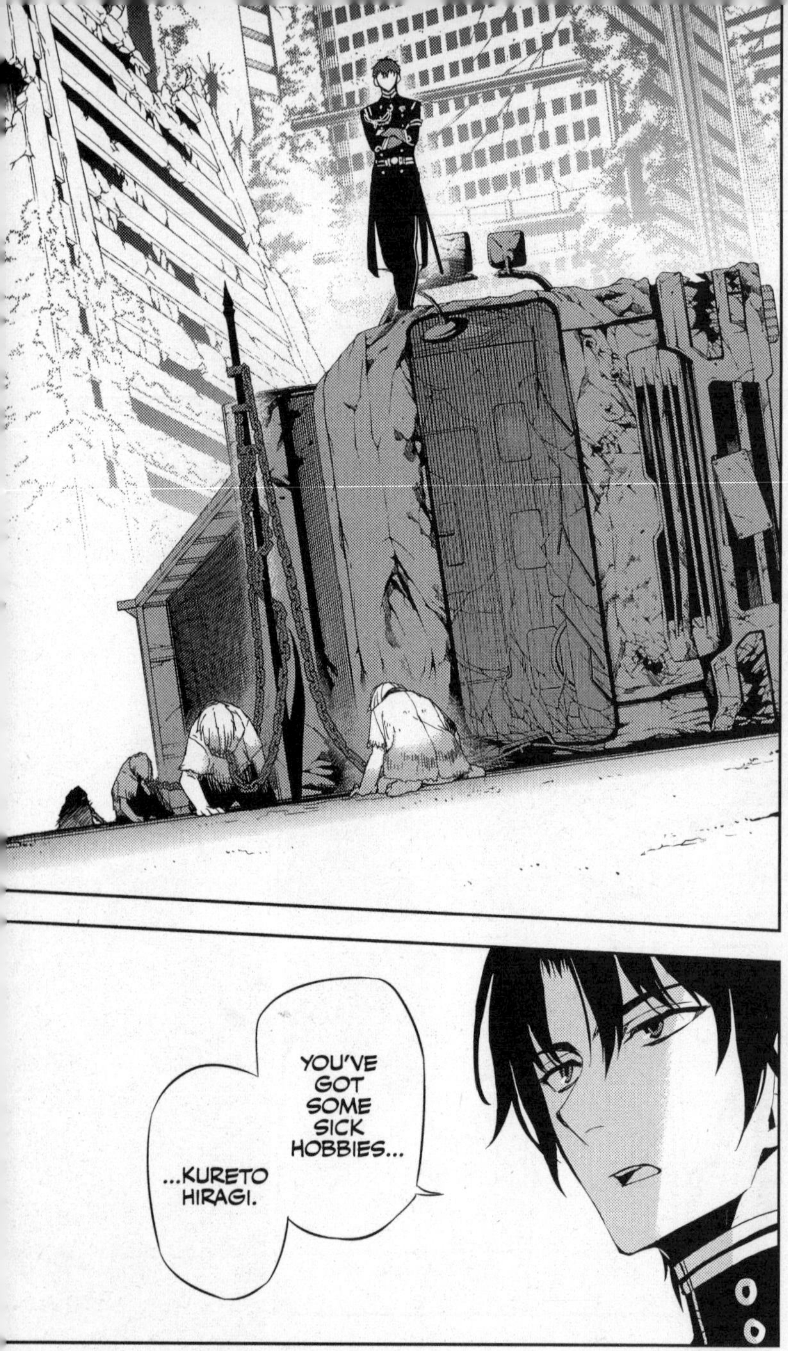
YOU'VE GOT SOME SICK HOBBIES...
...KURETO HIRAGI.

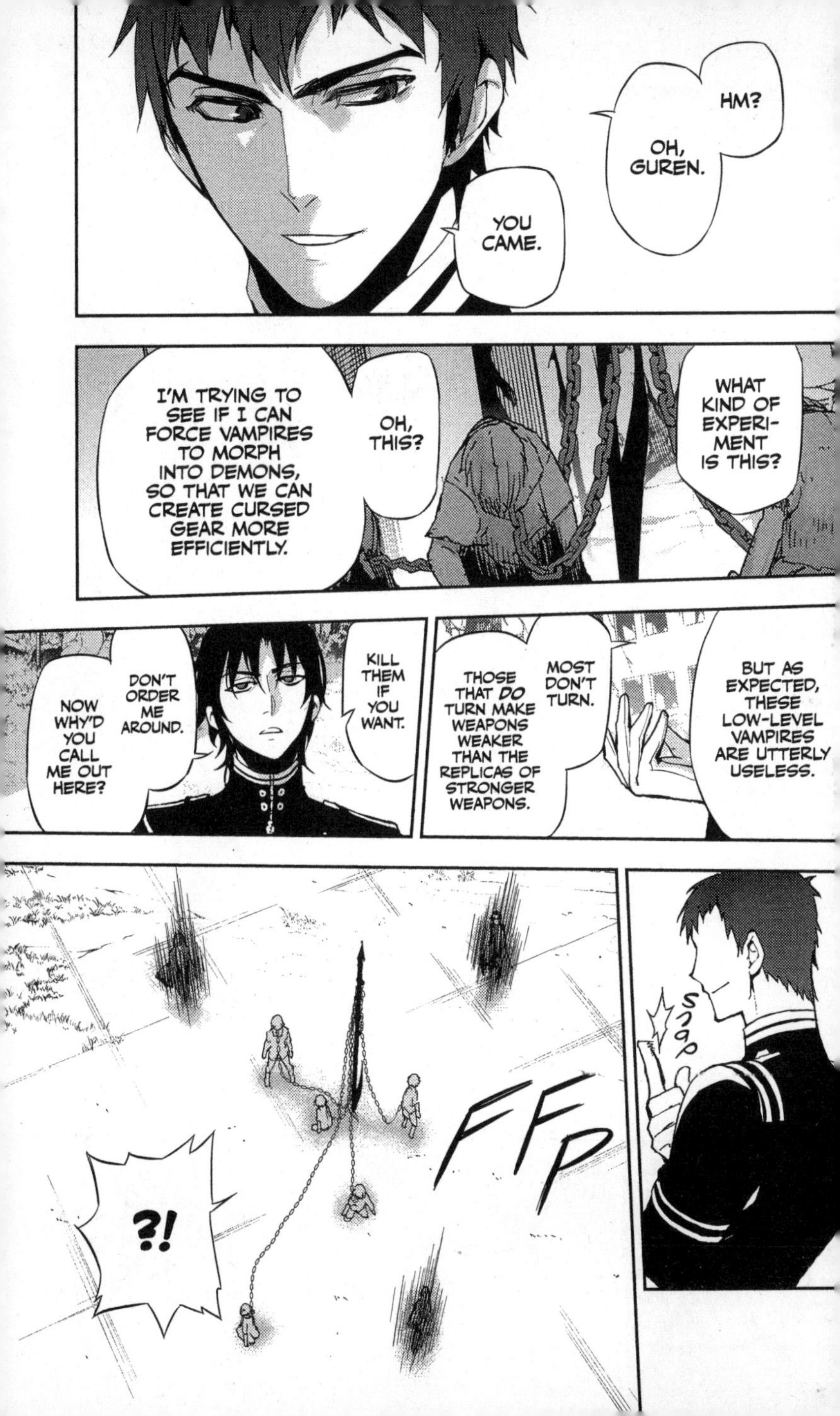
HM?
OH, GUREN.
YOU CAME.
WHAT KIND OF EXPERIMENT IS THIS?
OH, THIS?
I'M TRYING TO SEE IF I CAN FORCE VAMPIRES TO MORPH INTO DEMONS, SO THAT WE CAN CREATE CURSED GEAR MORE EFFICIENTLY.
BUT AS EXPECTED, THESE LOW-LEVEL VAMPIRES ARE UTTERLY USELESS.
MOST DON'T TURN.
THOSE THAT *DO* TURN MAKE WEAPONS WEAKER THAN THE REPLICAS OF STRONGER WEAPONS.
KILL THEM IF YOU WANT.
DON'T ORDER ME AROUND.
NOW WHY'D YOU CALL ME OUT HERE?
SNAP
FFP
?!

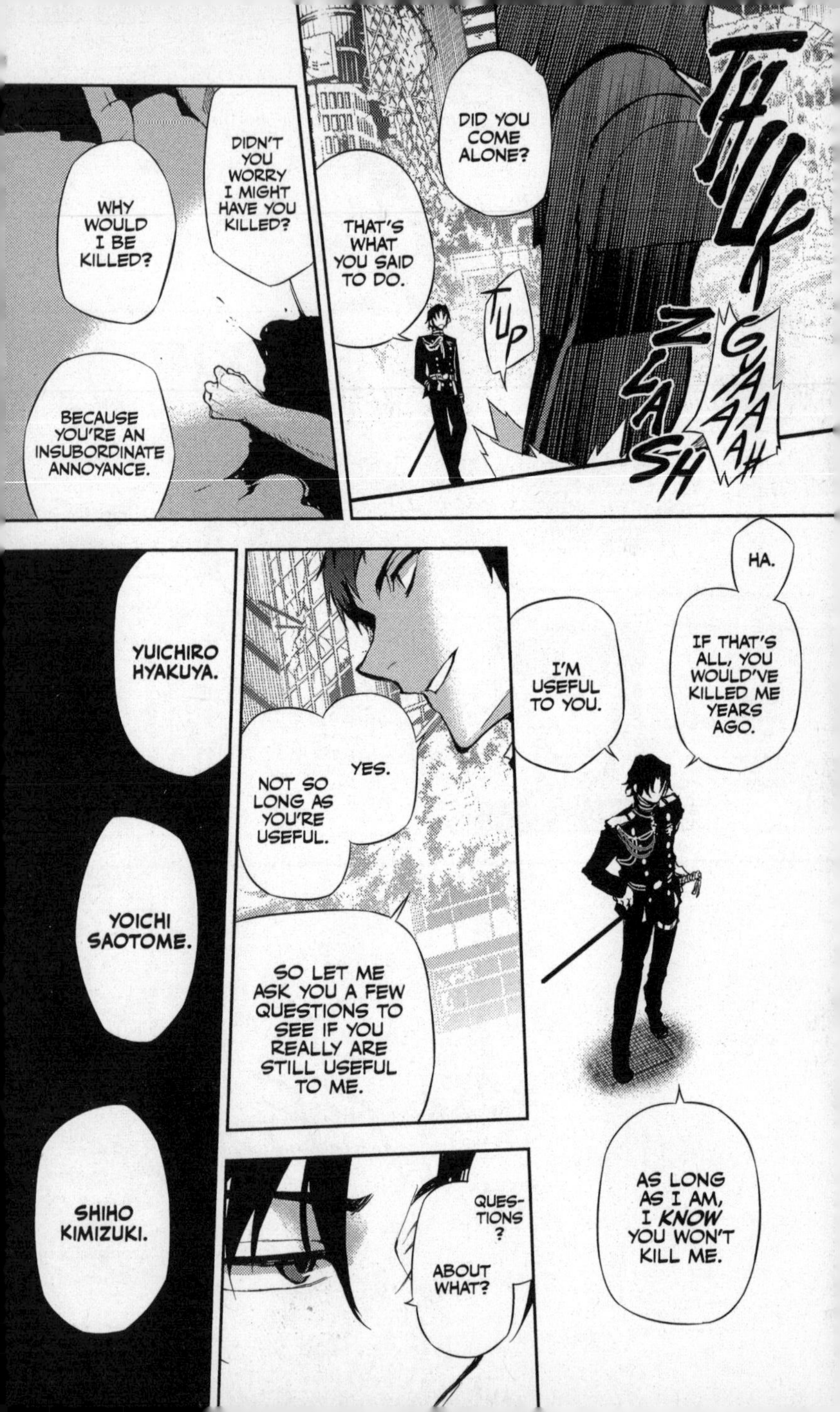
THUNK
ZLASH
GYAAAAH
DID YOU COME ALONE?
TUP
THAT'S WHAT YOU SAID TO DO.
DIDN'T YOU WORRY I MIGHT HAVE YOU KILLED?
WHY WOULD I BE KILLED?
BECAUSE YOU'RE AN INSUBORDINATE ANNOYANCE.
HA.
IF THAT'S ALL, YOU WOULD'VE KILLED ME YEARS AGO.
I'M USEFUL TO YOU.
AS LONG AS I AM, I *KNOW* YOU WON'T KILL ME.
YES.
NOT SO LONG AS YOU'RE USEFUL.
SO LET ME ASK YOU A FEW QUESTIONS TO SEE IF YOU REALLY ARE STILL USEFUL TO ME.
QUESTIONS?
ABOUT WHAT?
YUICHIRO HYAKUYA.
YOICHI SAOTOME.
SHIHO KIMIZUKI.

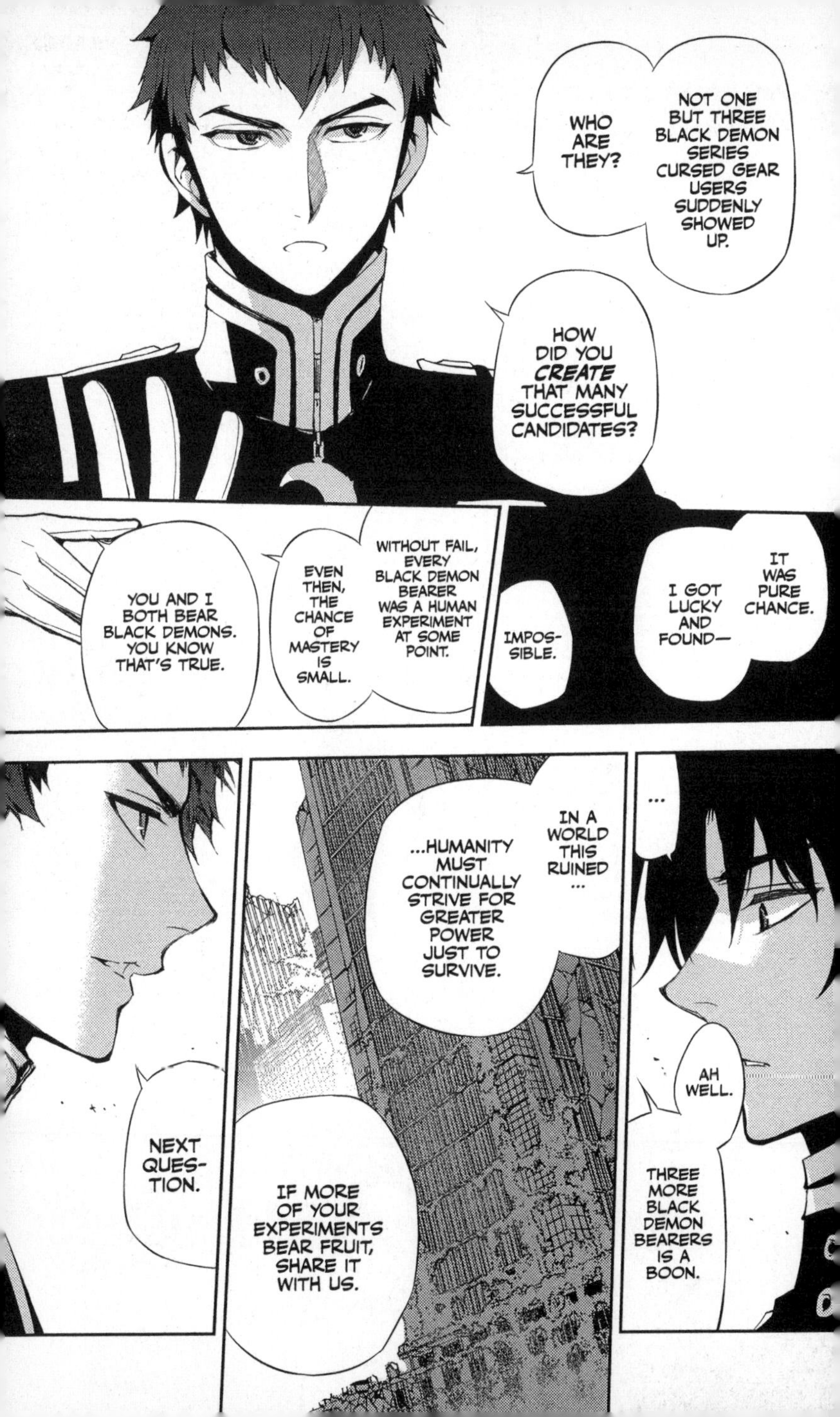
NOT ONE BUT THREE BLACK DEMON SERIES CURSED GEAR USERS SUDDENLY SHOWED UP.
WHO ARE THEY?
HOW DID YOU ***CREATE*** THAT MANY SUCCESSFUL CANDIDATES?
IT WAS PURE CHANCE.
I GOT LUCKY AND FOUND—
IMPOSSIBLE.
WITHOUT FAIL, EVERY BLACK DEMON BEARER WAS A HUMAN EXPERIMENT AT SOME POINT.
EVEN THEN, THE CHANCE OF MASTERY IS SMALL.
YOU AND I BOTH BEAR BLACK DEMONS. YOU KNOW THAT'S TRUE.
...
AH WELL.
THREE MORE BLACK DEMON BEARERS IS A BOON.
IN A WORLD THIS RUINED...
...HUMANITY MUST CONTINUALLY STRIVE FOR GREATER POWER JUST TO SURVIVE.
IF MORE OF YOUR EXPERIMENTS BEAR FRUIT, SHARE IT WITH US.
NEXT QUESTION.

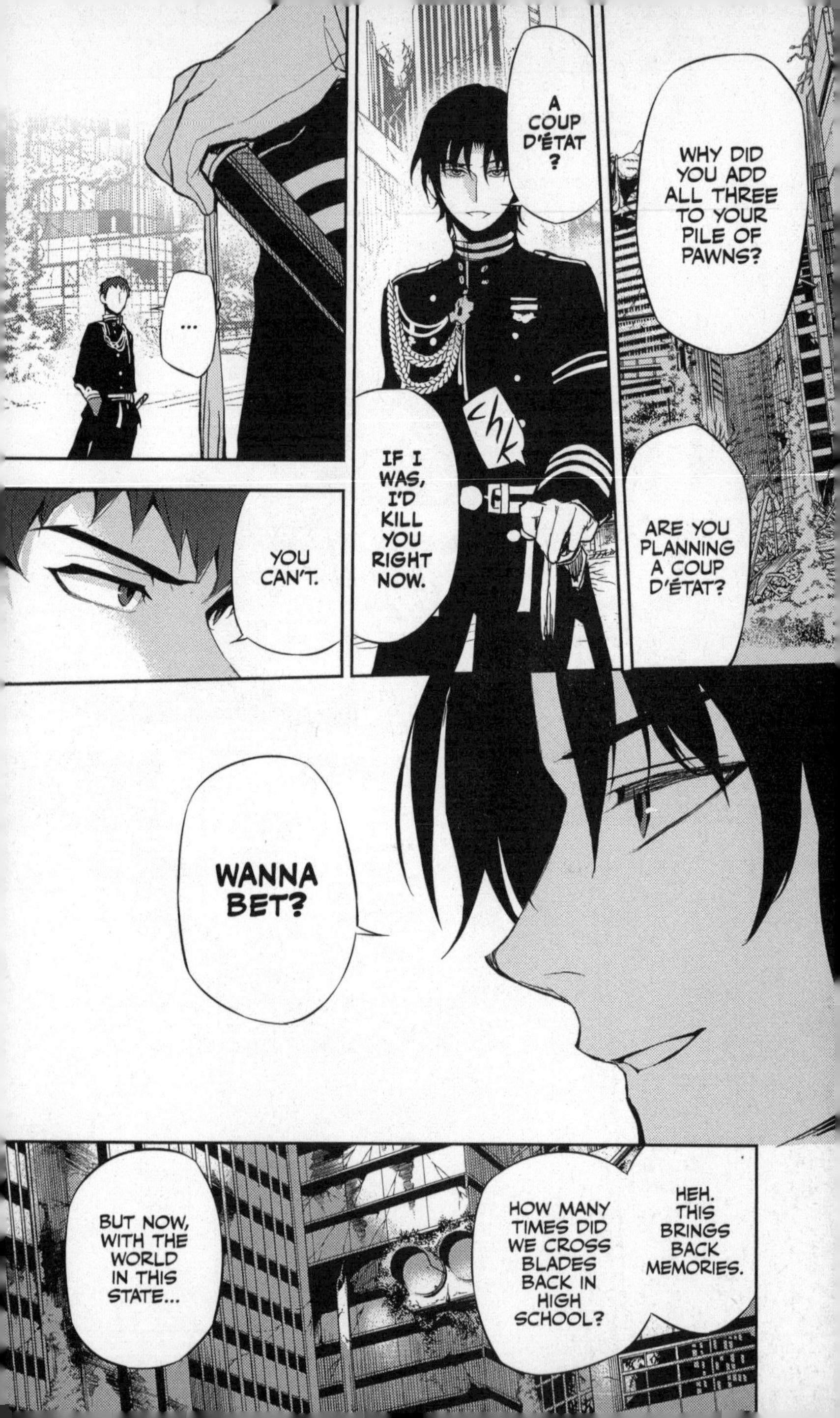
WHY DID YOU ADD ALL THREE TO YOUR PILE OF PAWNS?
ARE YOU PLANNING A COUP D'ÉTAT?
A COUP D'ÉTAT?
CHK
IF I WAS, I'D KILL YOU RIGHT NOW.
...
YOU CAN'T.
WANNA BET?
HEH. THIS BRINGS BACK MEMORIES.
HOW MANY TIMES DID WE CROSS BLADES BACK IN HIGH SCHOOL?
BUT NOW, WITH THE WORLD IN THIS STATE...

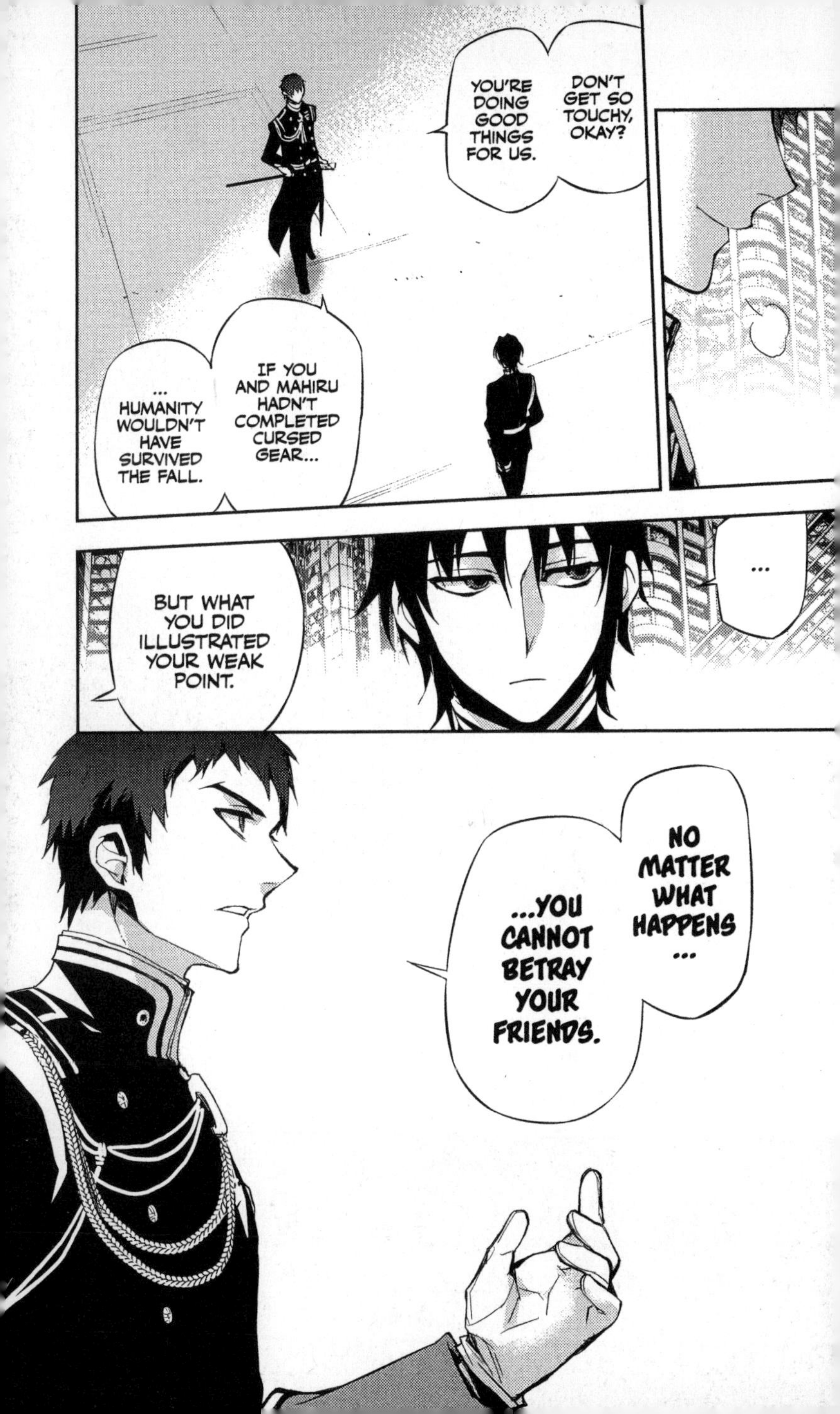
DON'T GET SO TOUCHY, OKAY?
YOU'RE DOING GOOD THINGS FOR US.
IF YOU AND MAHIRU HADN'T COMPLETED CURSED GEAR...
... HUMANITY WOULDN'T HAVE SURVIVED THE FALL.
...
BUT WHAT YOU DID ILLUSTRATED YOUR WEAK POINT.
NO MATTER WHAT HAPPENS...
...YOU CANNOT BETRAY YOUR FRIENDS.

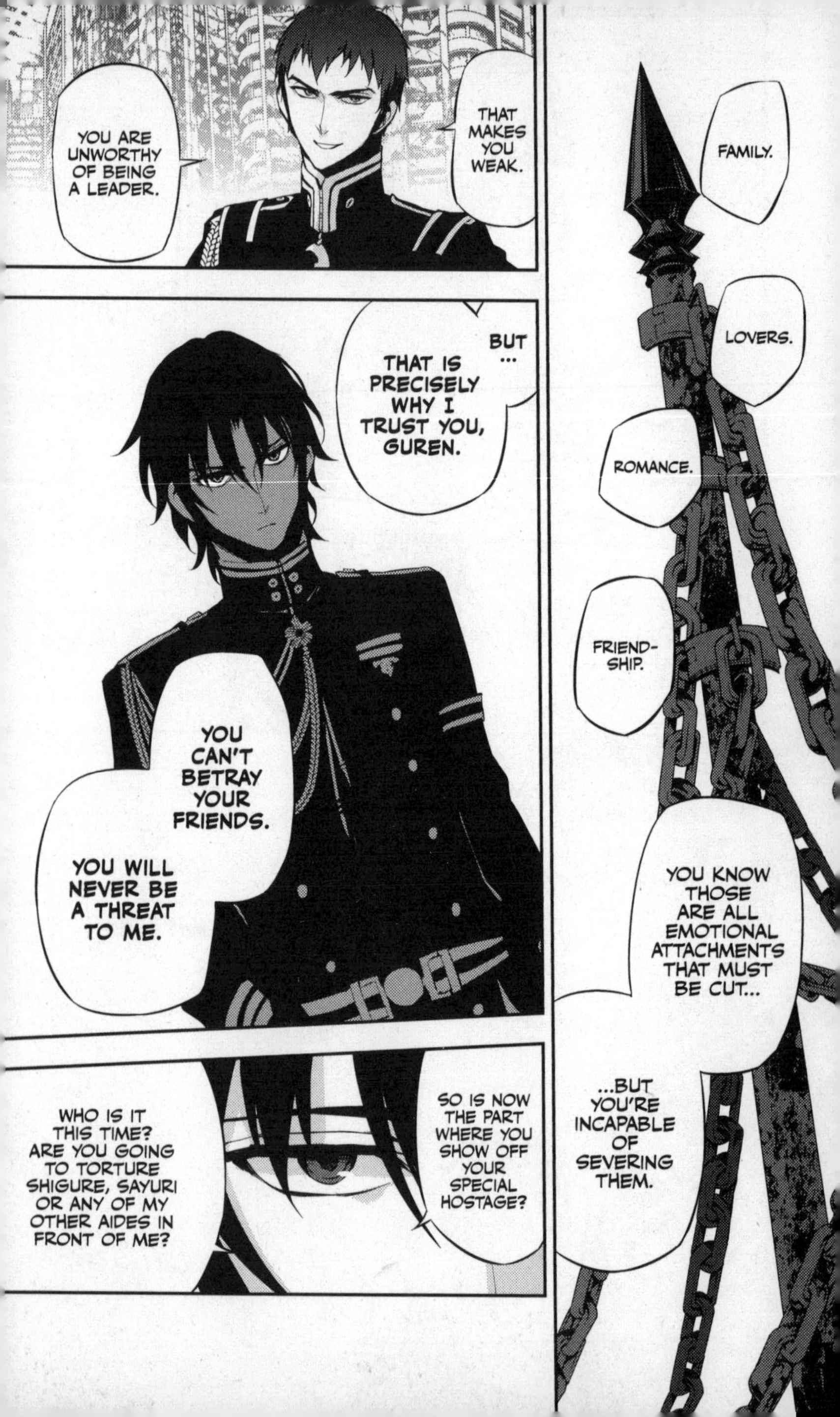
FAMILY.
LOVERS.
ROMANCE.
FRIEND-SHIP.
YOU KNOW THOSE ARE ALL EMOTIONAL ATTACHMENTS THAT MUST BE CUT...
...BUT YOU'RE INCAPABLE OF SEVERING THEM.
THAT MAKES YOU WEAK.
YOU ARE UNWORTHY OF BEING A LEADER.
BUT...
THAT IS PRECISELY WHY I TRUST YOU, GUREN.
YOU CAN'T BETRAY YOUR FRIENDS.
YOU WILL NEVER BE A THREAT TO ME.
SO IS NOW THE PART WHERE YOU SHOW OFF YOUR SPECIAL HOSTAGE?
WHO IS IT THIS TIME? ARE YOU GOING TO TORTURE SHIGURE, SAYURI OR ANY OF MY OTHER AIDES IN FRONT OF ME?

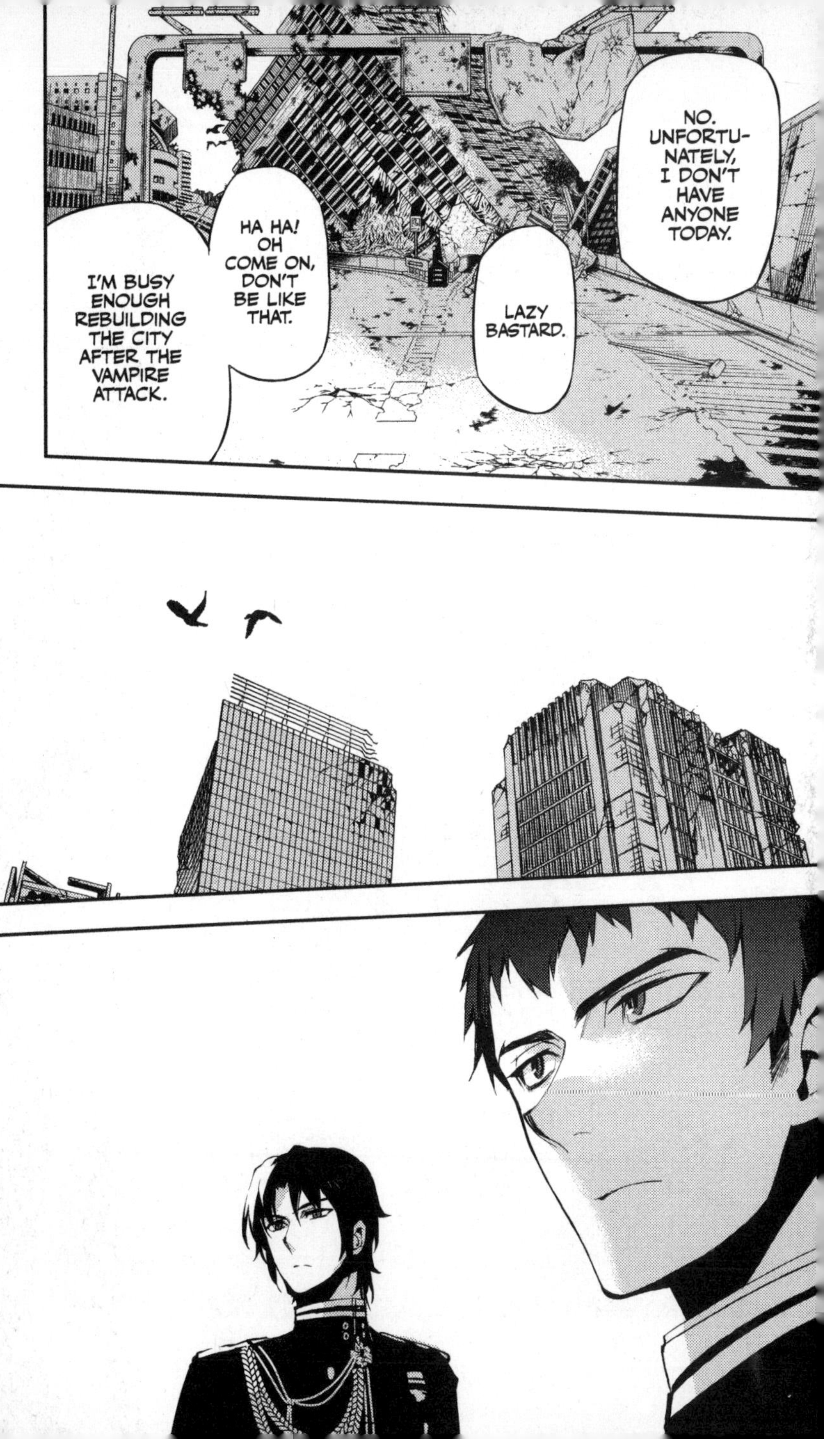
NO. UNFORTU-NATELY, I DON'T HAVE ANYONE TODAY.
LAZY BASTARD.
HA HA! OH COME ON, DON'T BE LIKE THAT.
I'M BUSY ENOUGH REBUILDING THE CITY AFTER THE VAMPIRE ATTACK.

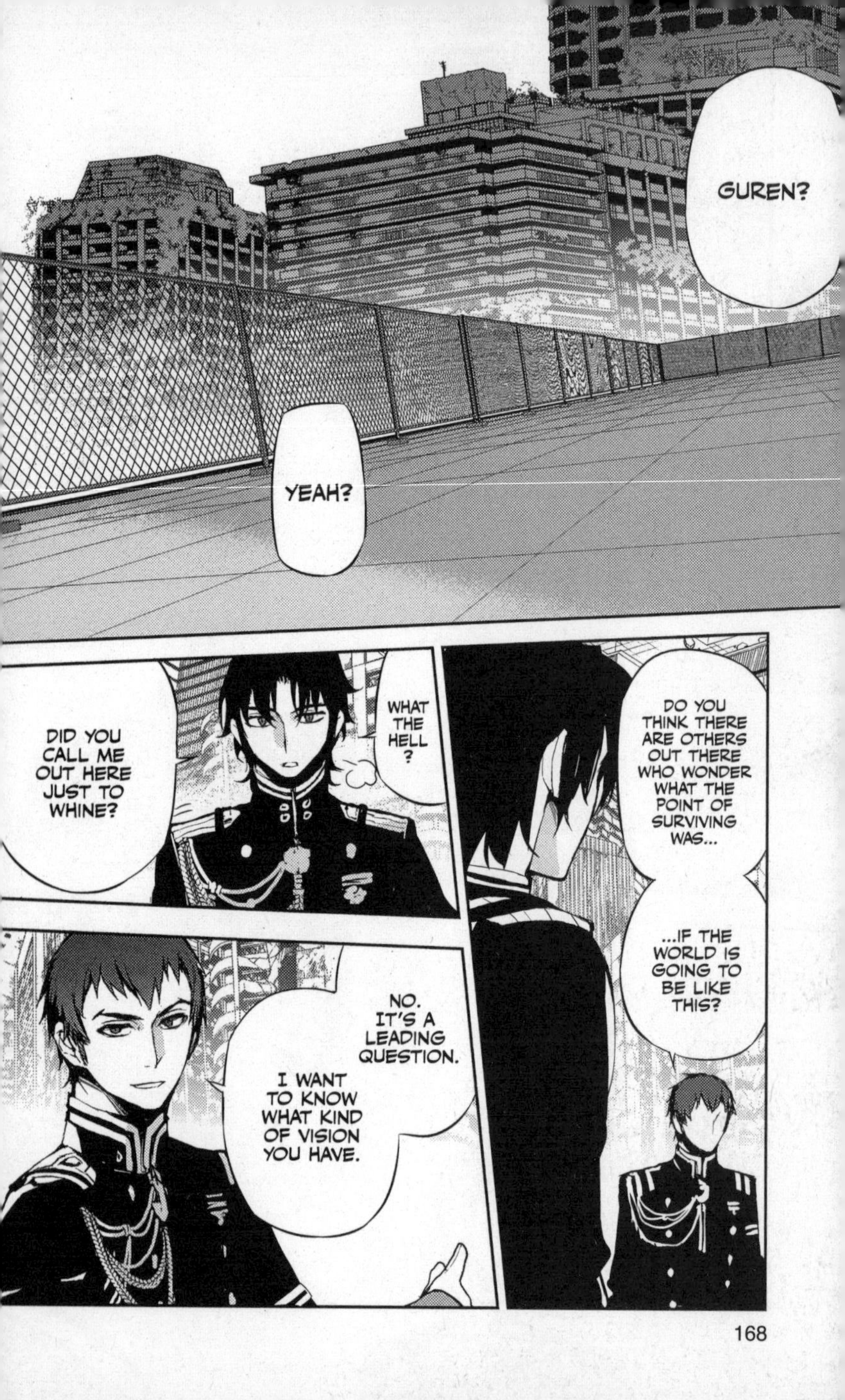
GUREN?
YEAH?
DO YOU THINK THERE ARE OTHERS OUT THERE WHO WONDER WHAT THE POINT OF SURVIVING WAS...
...IF THE WORLD IS GOING TO BE LIKE THIS?
WHAT THE HELL?
DID YOU CALL ME OUT HERE JUST TO WHINE?
NO. IT'S A LEADING QUESTION.
I WANT TO KNOW WHAT KIND OF VISION YOU HAVE.

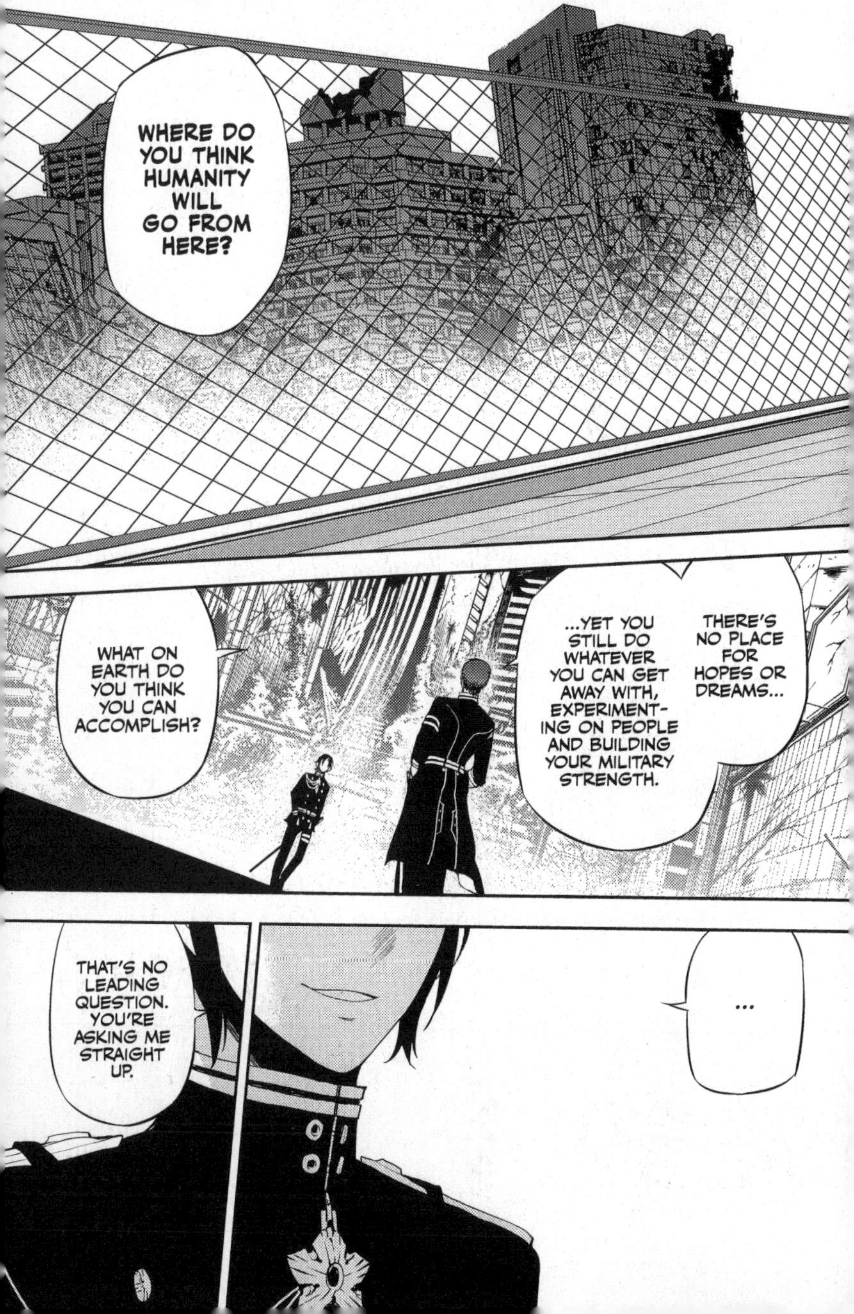
WHERE DO YOU THINK HUMANITY WILL GO FROM HERE?
THERE'S NO PLACE FOR HOPES OR DREAMS...
...YET YOU STILL DO WHATEVER YOU CAN GET AWAY WITH, EXPERIMENTING ON PEOPLE AND BUILDING YOUR MILITARY STRENGTH.
WHAT ON EARTH DO YOU THINK YOU CAN ACCOMPLISH?
...
THAT'S NO LEADING QUESTION. YOU'RE ASKING ME STRAIGHT UP.

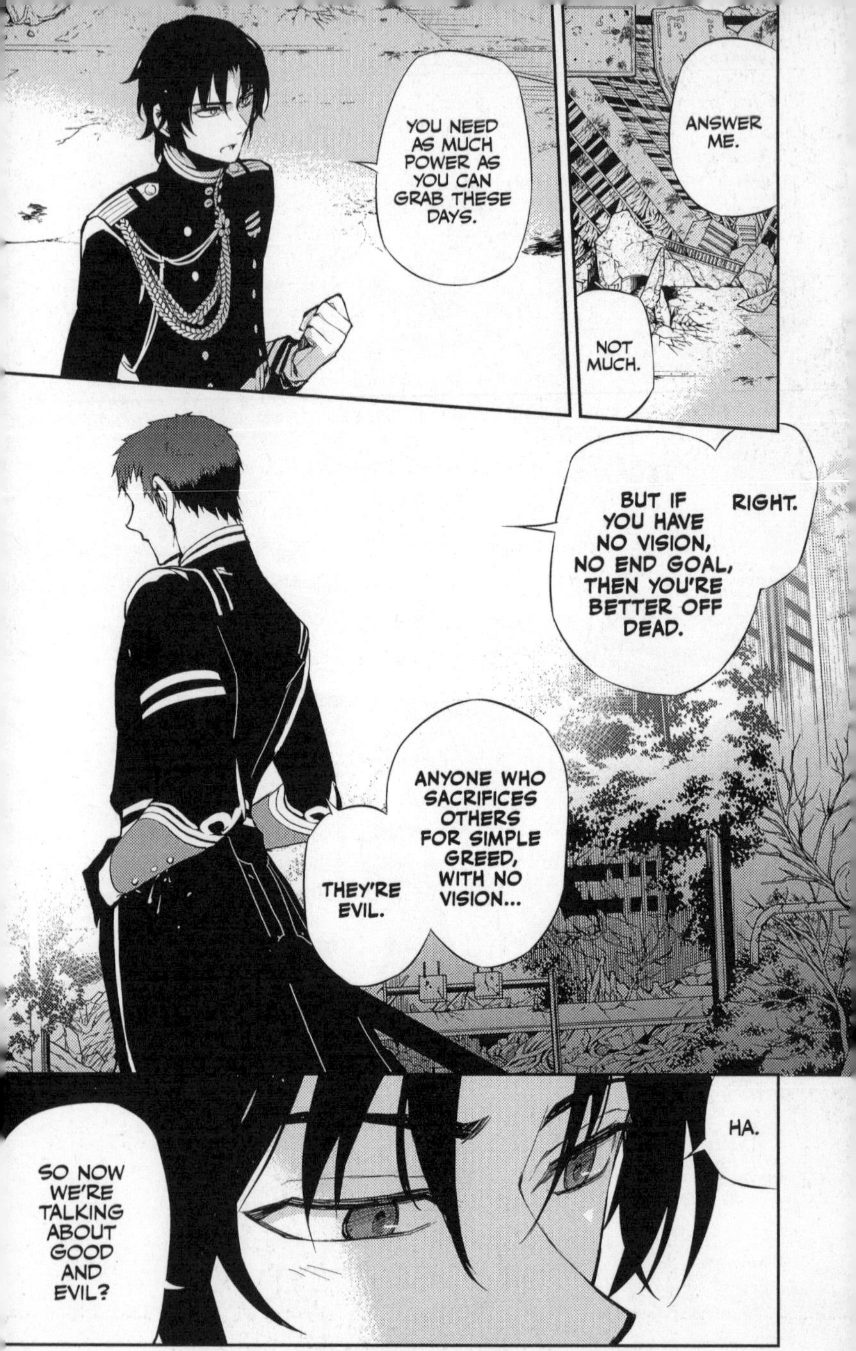
ANSWER ME.
NOT MUCH.
YOU NEED AS MUCH POWER AS YOU CAN GRAB THESE DAYS.
RIGHT.
BUT IF YOU HAVE NO VISION, NO END GOAL, THEN YOU'RE BETTER OFF DEAD.
ANYONE WHO SACRIFICES OTHERS FOR SIMPLE GREED, WITH NO VISION...
THEY'RE EVIL.
HA.
SO NOW WE'RE TALKING ABOUT GOOD AND EVIL?

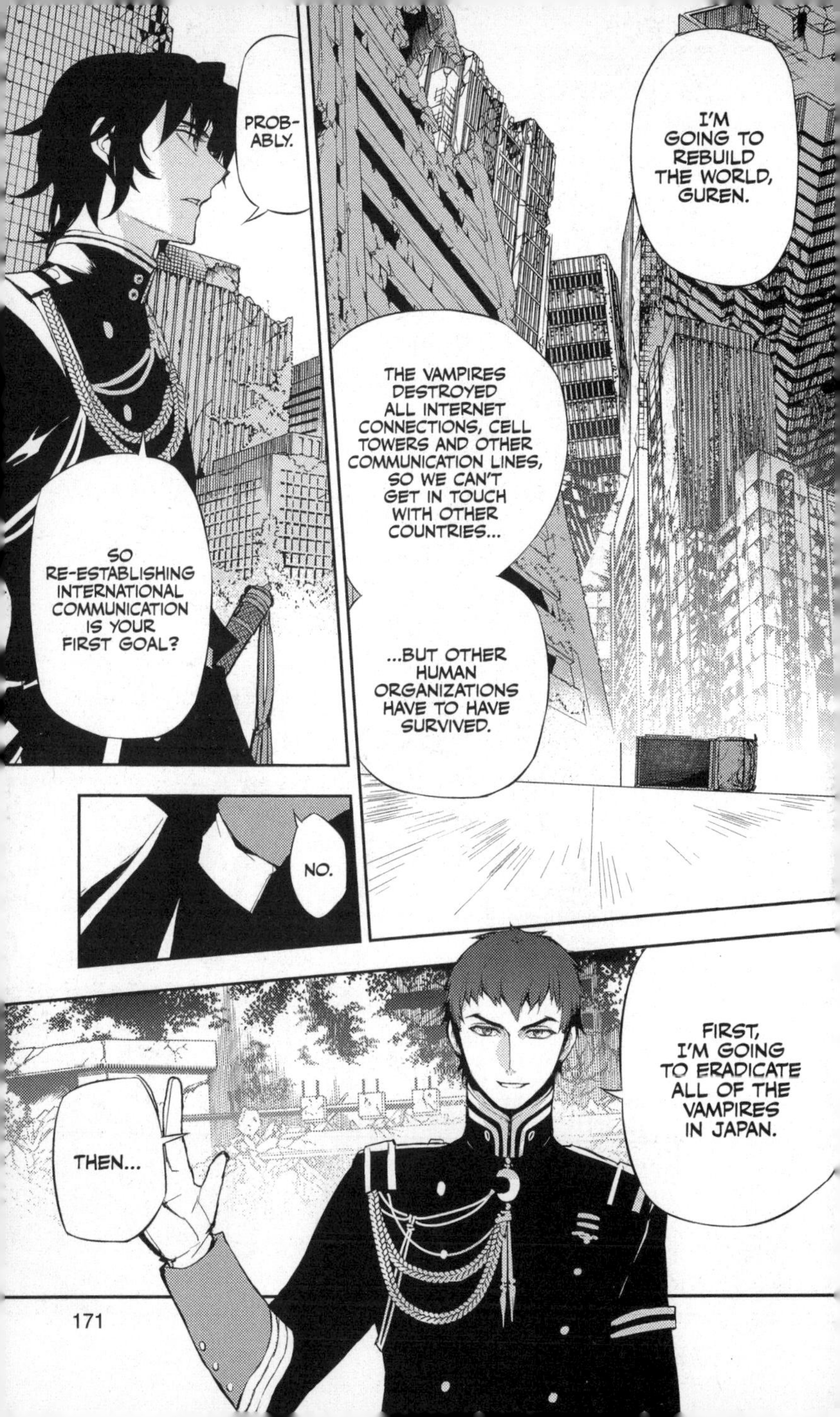
I'M GOING TO REBUILD THE WORLD, GUREN.
THE VAMPIRES DESTROYED ALL INTERNET CONNECTIONS, CELL TOWERS AND OTHER COMMUNICATION LINES, SO WE CAN'T GET IN TOUCH WITH OTHER COUNTRIES...
...BUT OTHER HUMAN ORGANIZATIONS HAVE TO HAVE SURVIVED.
PROB-ABLY.
SO RE-ESTABLISHING INTERNATIONAL COMMUNICATION IS YOUR FIRST GOAL?
NO.
FIRST, I'M GOING TO ERADICATE ALL OF THE VAMPIRES IN JAPAN.
THEN...

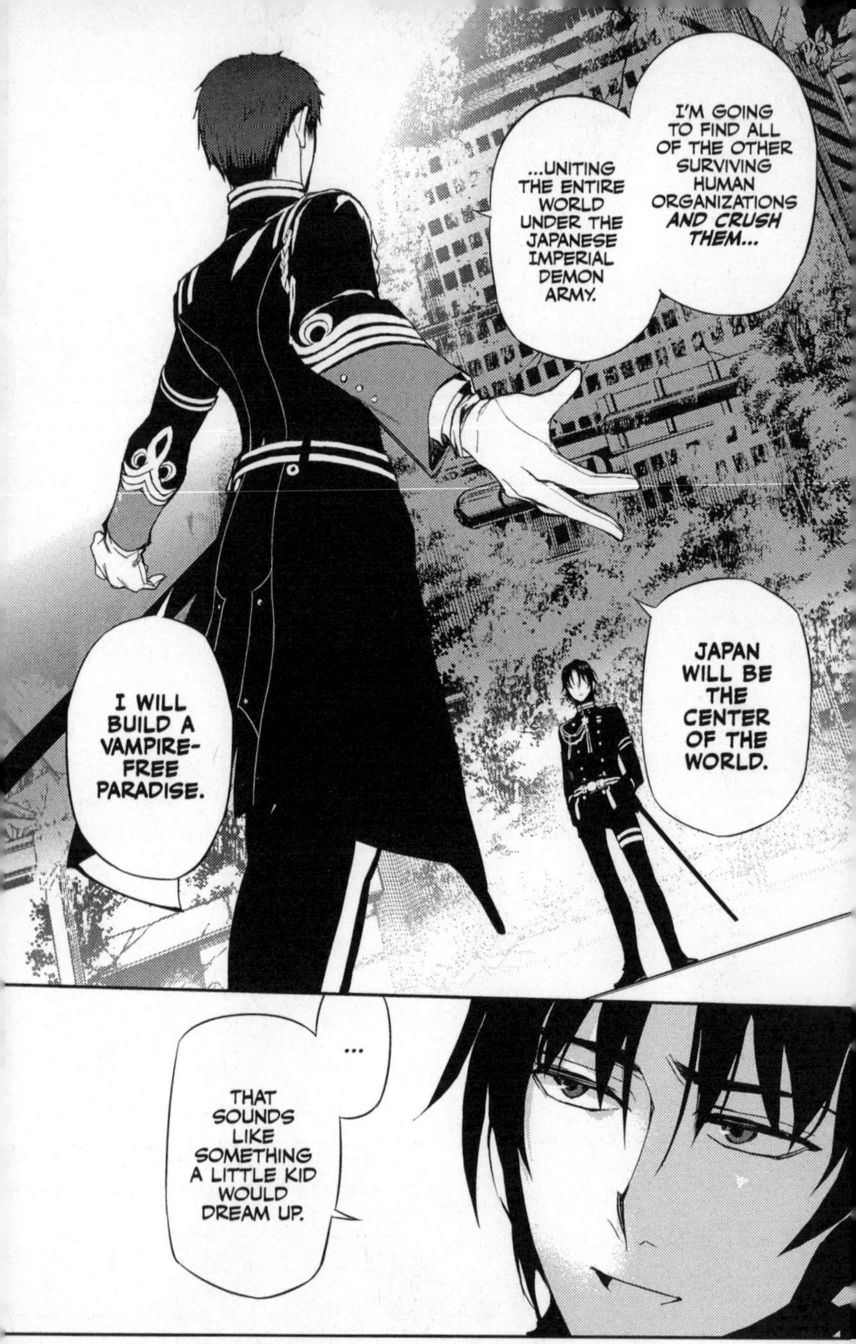
I'M GOING TO FIND ALL OF THE OTHER SURVIVING HUMAN ORGANIZATIONS *AND CRUSH THEM...*
...UNITING THE ENTIRE WORLD UNDER THE JAPANESE IMPERIAL DEMON ARMY.
JAPAN WILL BE THE CENTER OF THE WORLD.
I WILL BUILD A VAMPIRE-FREE PARADISE.
...
THAT SOUNDS LIKE SOMETHING A LITTLE KID WOULD DREAM UP.

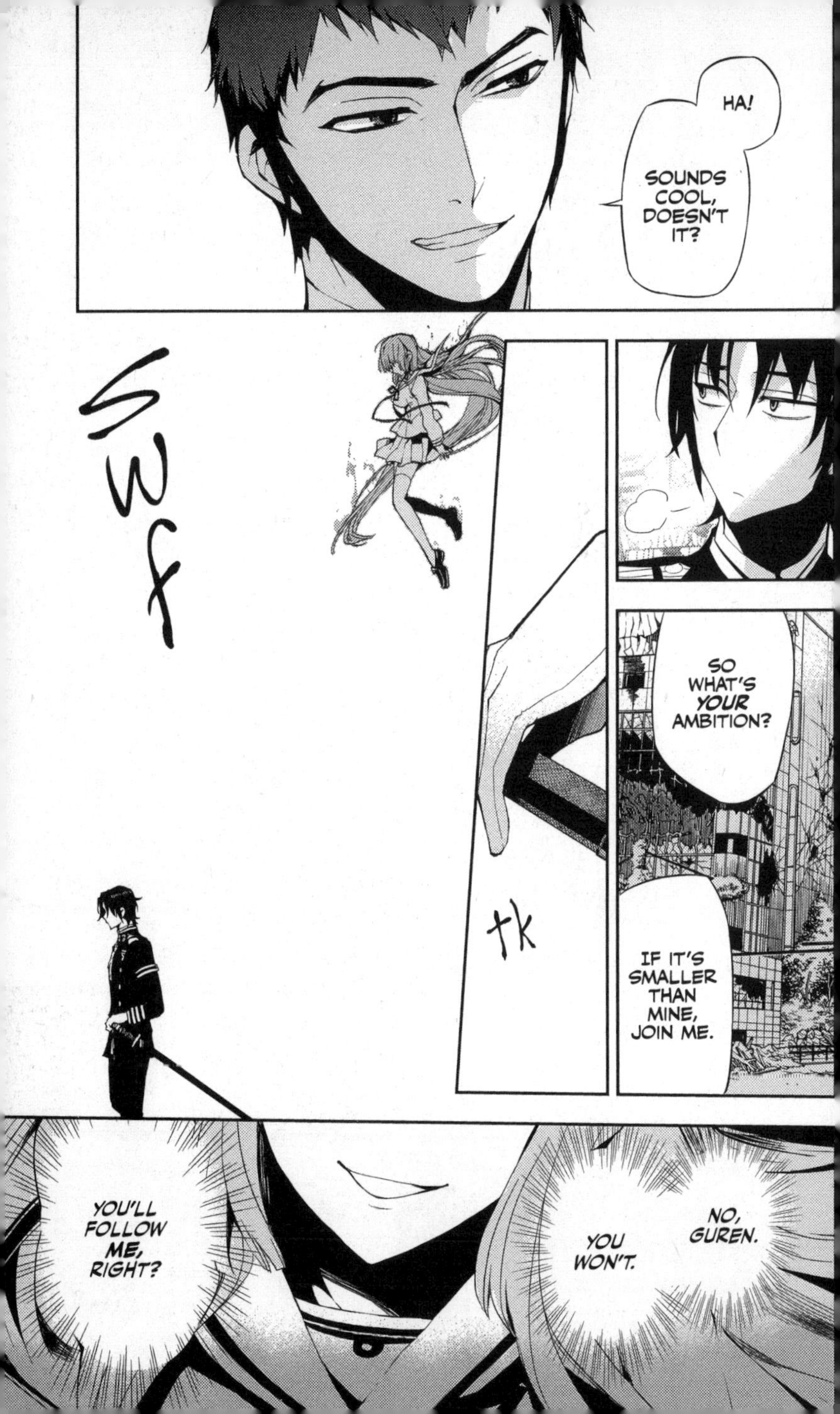
HA!
SOUNDS COOL, DOESN'T IT?
SO WHAT'S YOUR AMBITION?
IF IT'S SMALLER THAN MINE, JOIN ME.
tk
SWF
NO, GUREN.
YOU WON'T.
YOU'LL FOLLOW ME, RIGHT?

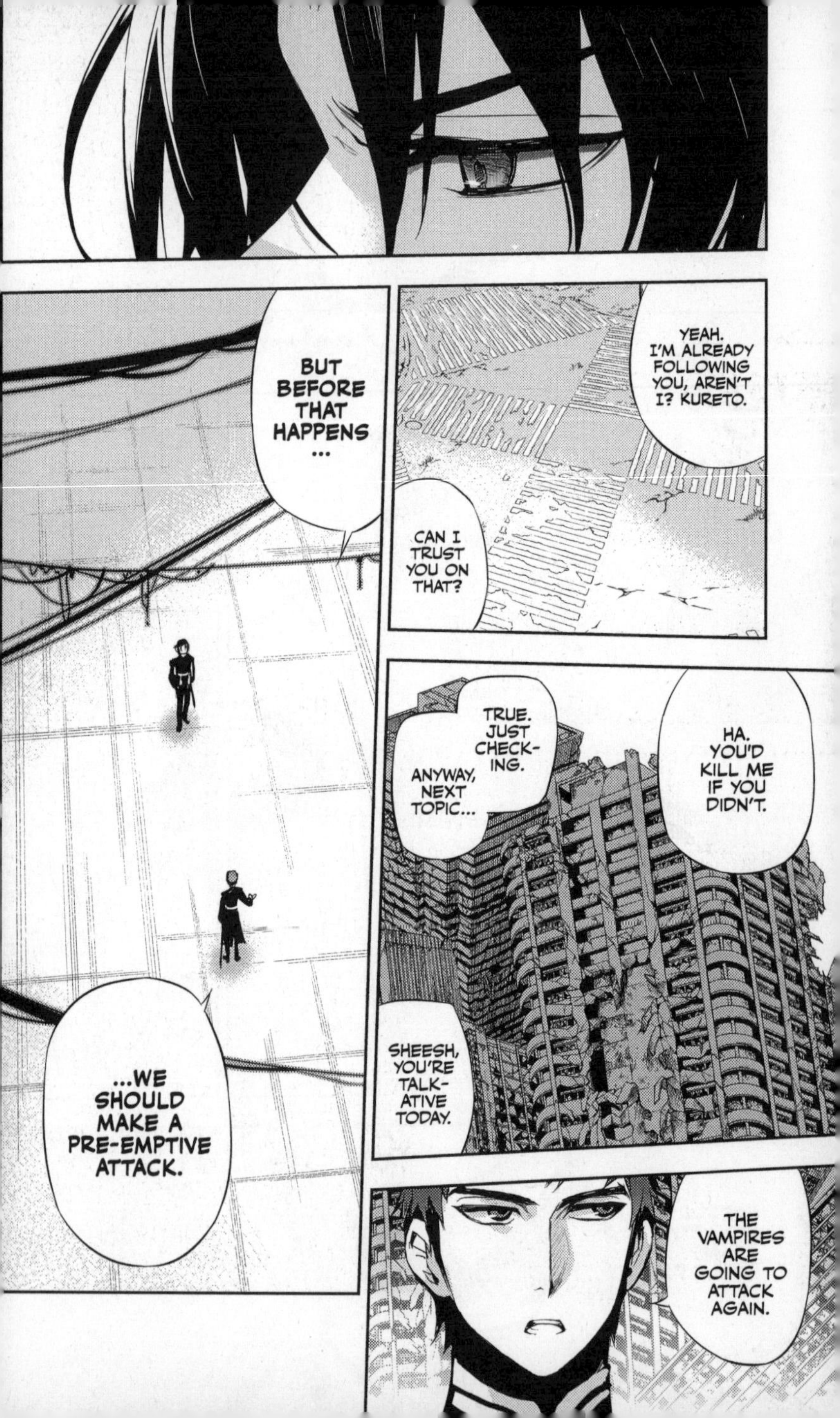
YEAH. I'M ALREADY FOLLOWING YOU, AREN'T I? KURETO.
CAN I TRUST YOU ON THAT?
HA. YOU'D KILL ME IF YOU DIDN'T.
TRUE. JUST CHECK-ING.
ANYWAY, NEXT TOPIC...
SHEESH, YOU'RE TALK-ATIVE TODAY.
THE VAMPIRES ARE GOING TO ATTACK AGAIN.
BUT BEFORE THAT HAPPENS ...
...WE SHOULD MAKE A PRE-EMPTIVE ATTACK.

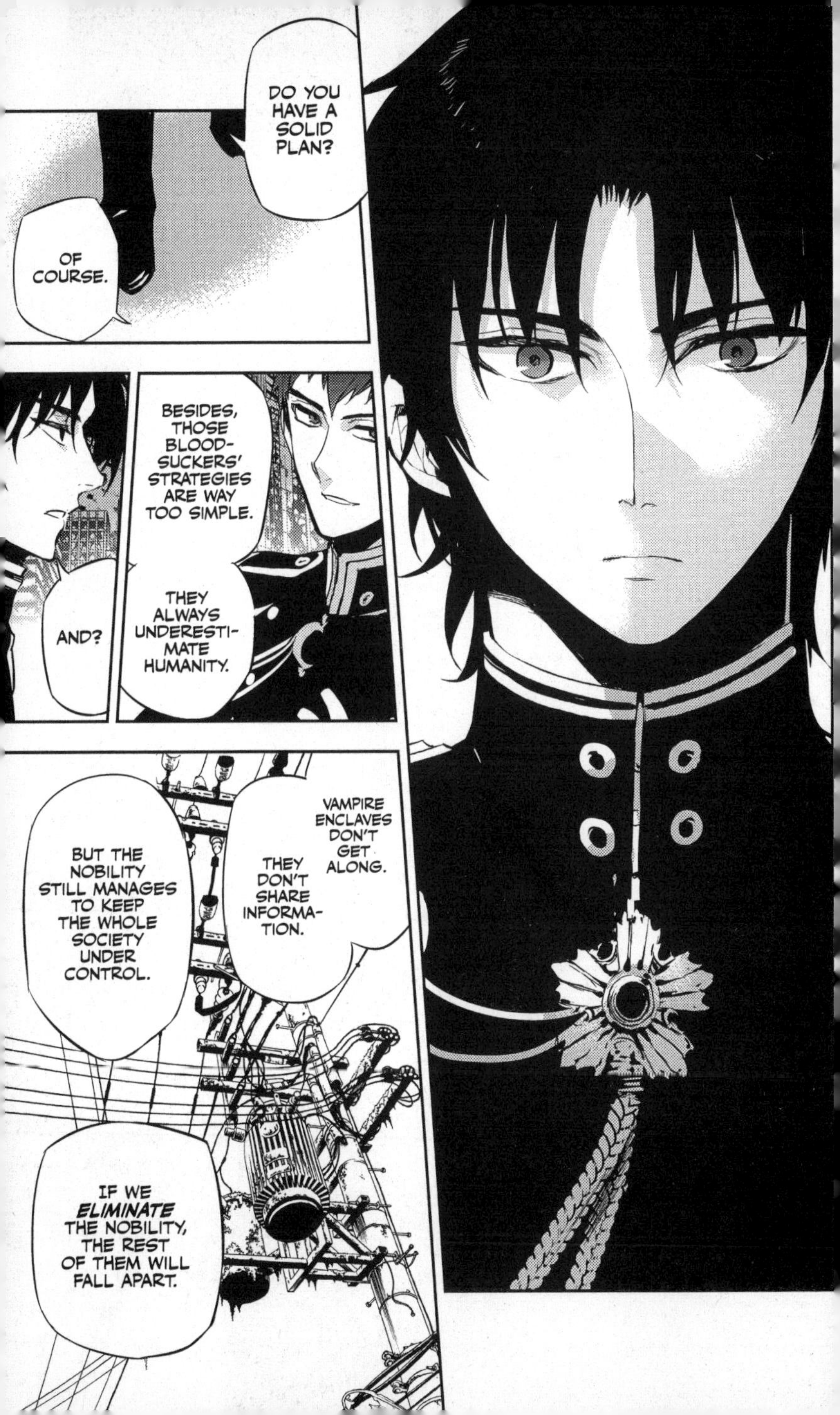
DO YOU HAVE A SOLID PLAN?
OF COURSE.
BESIDES, THOSE BLOOD-SUCKERS' STRATEGIES ARE WAY TOO SIMPLE.
AND?
THEY ALWAYS UNDERESTI-MATE HUMANITY.
VAMPIRE ENCLAVES DON'T GET ALONG.
THEY DON'T SHARE INFORMA-TION.
BUT THE NOBILITY STILL MANAGES TO KEEP THE WHOLE SOCIETY UNDER CONTROL.
IF WE *ELIMINATE* THE NOBILITY, THE REST OF THEM WILL FALL APART.

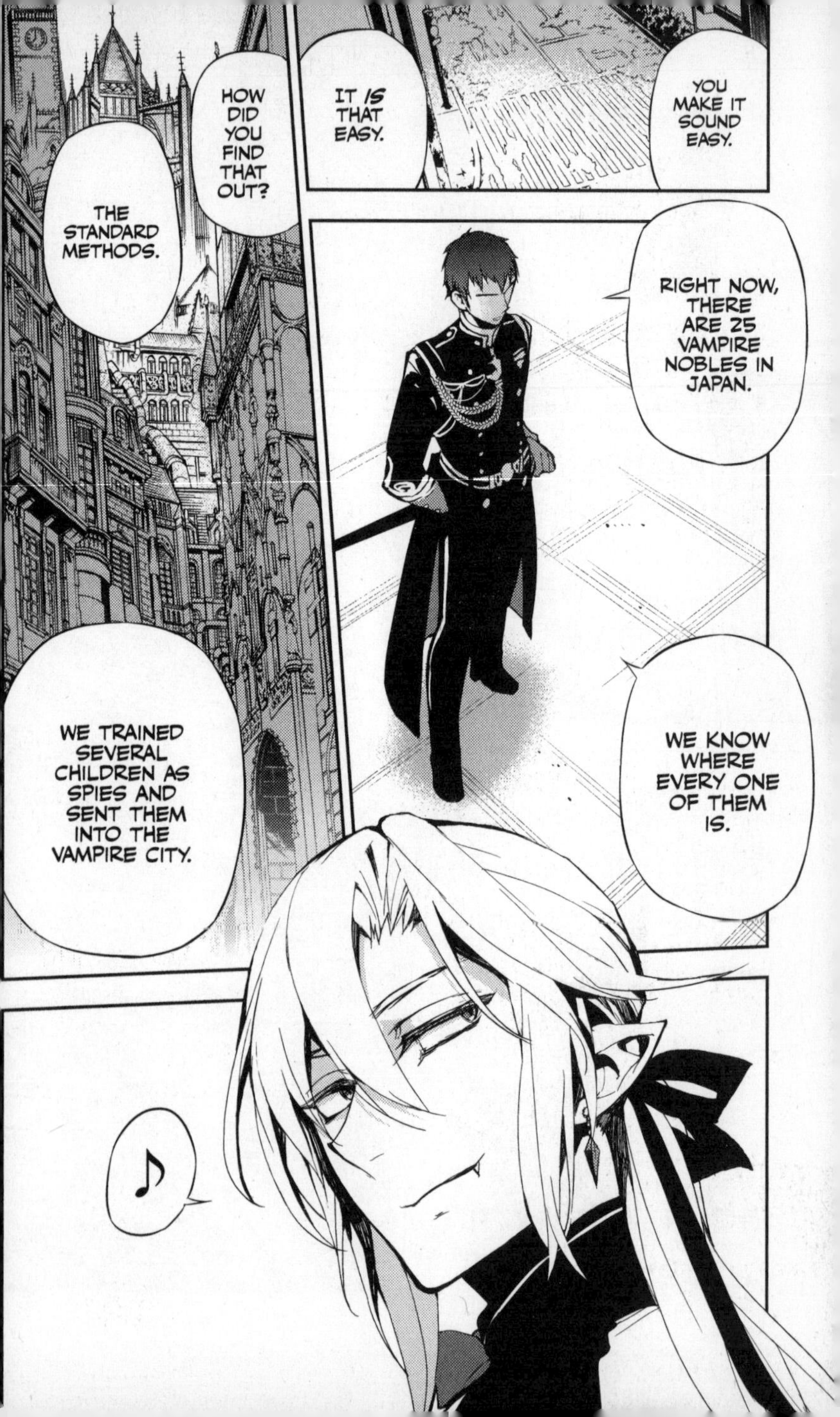
YOU MAKE IT SOUND EASY.
IT *IS* THAT EASY.
RIGHT NOW, THERE ARE 25 VAMPIRE NOBLES IN JAPAN.
WE KNOW WHERE EVERY ONE OF THEM IS.
HOW DID YOU FIND THAT OUT?
THE STANDARD METHODS.
WE TRAINED SEVERAL CHILDREN AS SPIES AND SENT THEM INTO THE VAMPIRE CITY.
♪

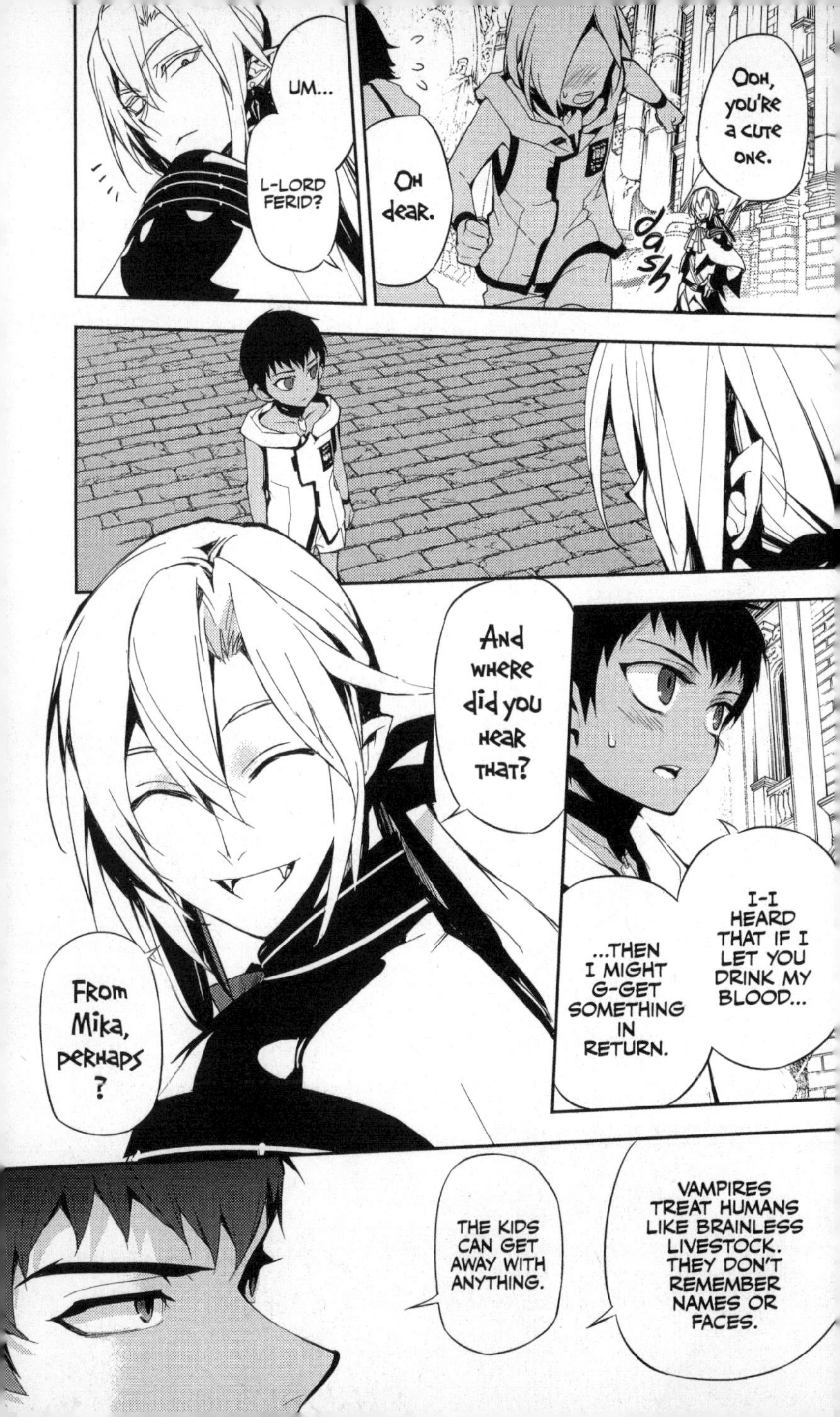
Ooh, you're a cute one.
dash
Oh dear.
Um...
L-Lord Ferid?
I-I heard that if I let you drink my blood...
...then I might g-get something in return.
And where did you hear that?
From Mika, perhaps?
Vampires treat humans like brainless livestock. They don't remember names or faces.
The kids can get away with anything.

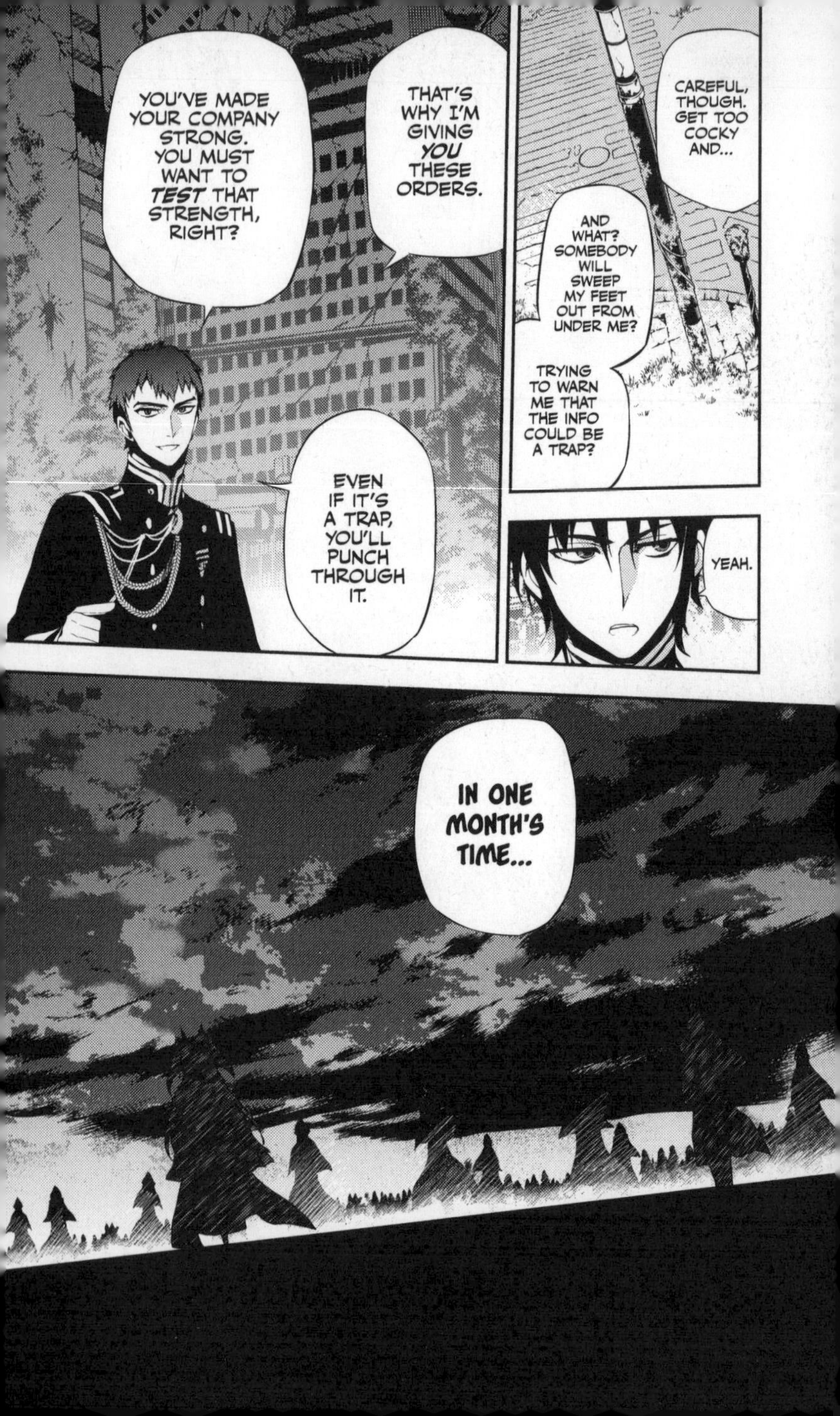
CAREFUL, THOUGH. GET TOO COCKY AND...
AND WHAT? SOMEBODY WILL SWEEP MY FEET OUT FROM UNDER ME?
TRYING TO WARN ME THAT THE INFO COULD BE A TRAP?
YEAH.
THAT'S WHY I'M GIVING *YOU* THESE ORDERS.
YOU'VE MADE YOUR COMPANY STRONG. YOU MUST WANT TO *TEST* THAT STRENGTH, RIGHT?
EVEN IF IT'S A TRAP, YOU'LL PUNCH THROUGH IT.
IN ONE MONTH'S TIME...

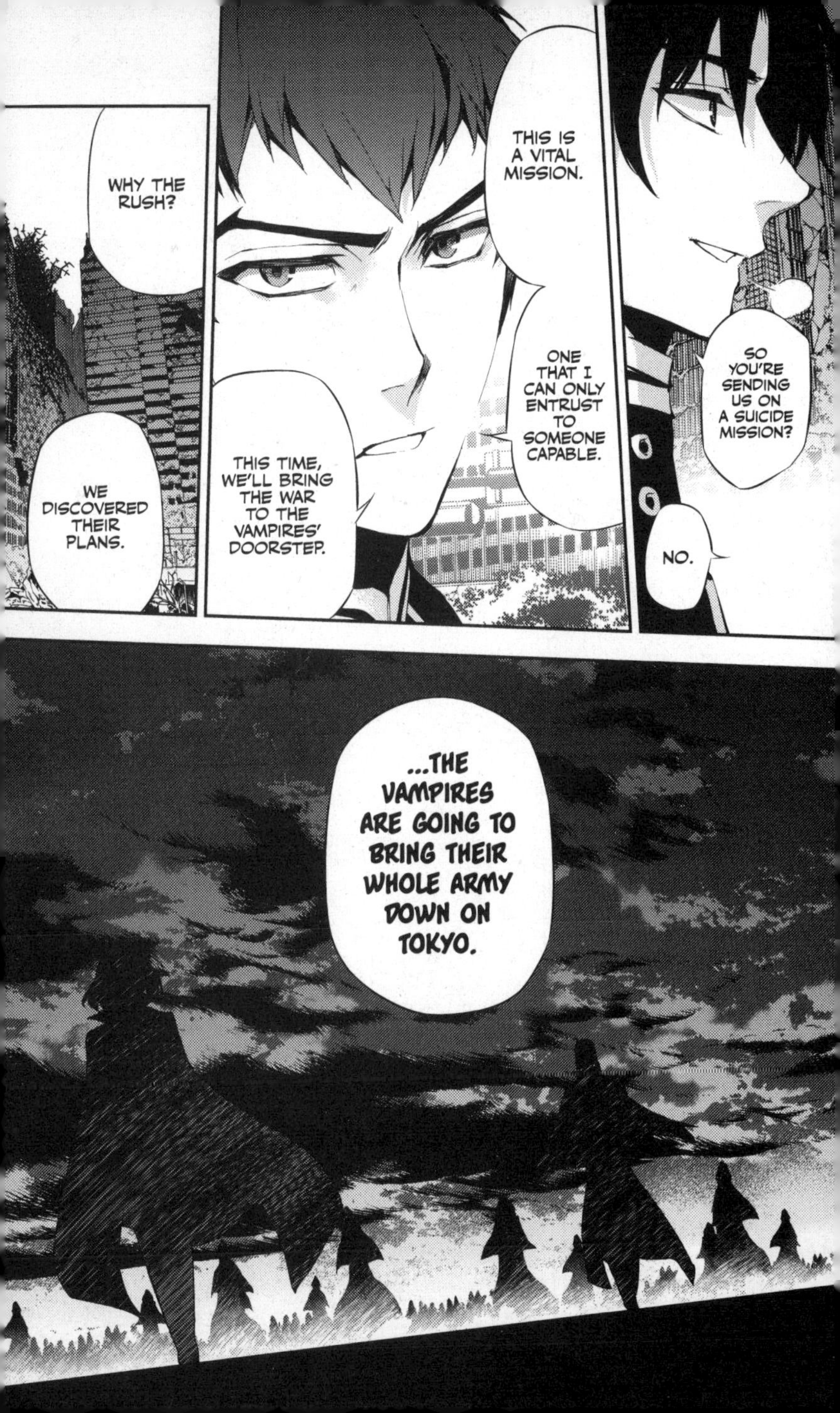
SO YOU'RE SENDING US ON A SUICIDE MISSION?
NO.
THIS IS A VITAL MISSION.
ONE THAT I CAN ONLY ENTRUST TO SOMEONE CAPABLE.
THIS TIME, WE'LL BRING THE WAR TO THE VAMPIRES' DOORSTEP.
WHY THE RUSH?
WE DISCOVERED THEIR PLANS.
...THE VAMPIRES ARE GOING TO BRING THEIR WHOLE ARMY DOWN ON TOKYO.

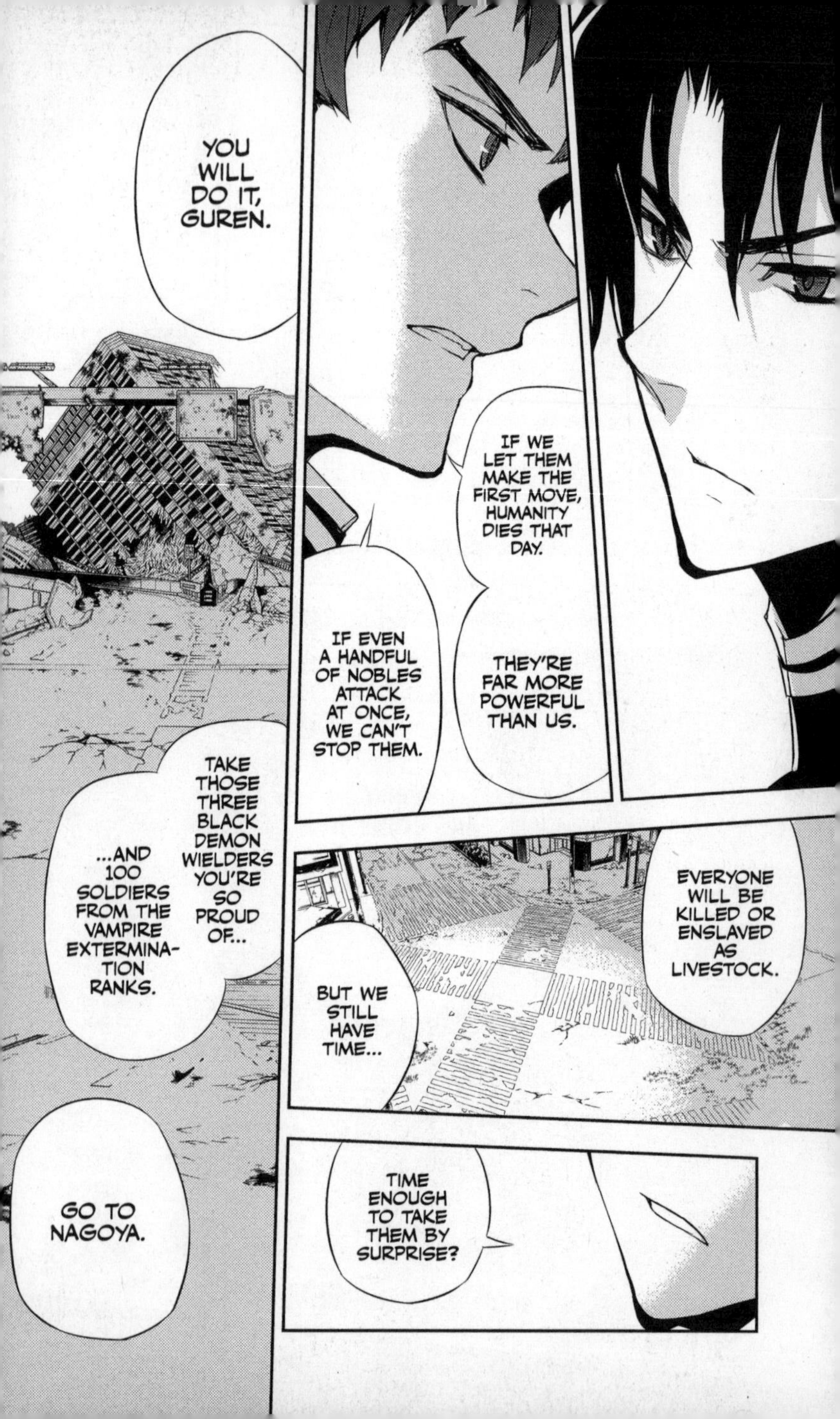
IF WE LET THEM MAKE THE FIRST MOVE, HUMANITY DIES THAT DAY.
THEY'RE FAR MORE POWERFUL THAN US.
IF EVEN A HANDFUL OF NOBLES ATTACK AT ONCE, WE CAN'T STOP THEM.
EVERYONE WILL BE KILLED OR ENSLAVED AS LIVESTOCK.
BUT WE STILL HAVE TIME...
TIME ENOUGH TO TAKE THEM BY SURPRISE?
YOU WILL DO IT, GUREN.
TAKE THOSE THREE BLACK DEMON WIELDERS YOU'RE SO PROUD OF...
...AND 100 SOLDIERS FROM THE VAMPIRE EXTERMINA-TION RANKS.
GO TO NAGOYA.

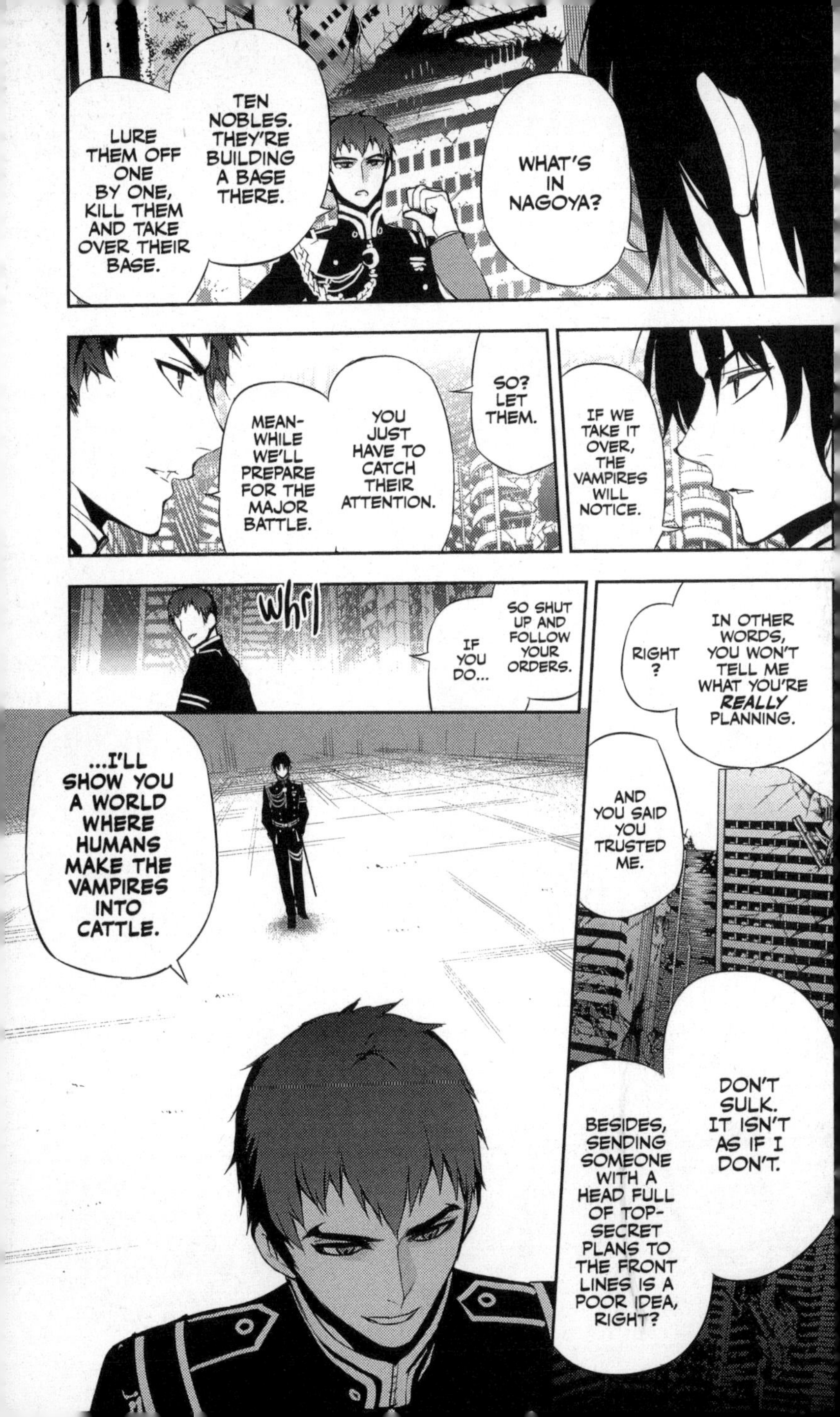
WHAT'S IN NAGOYA?
TEN NOBLES. THEY'RE BUILDING A BASE THERE.
LURE THEM OFF ONE BY ONE, KILL THEM AND TAKE OVER THEIR BASE.
IF WE TAKE IT OVER, THE VAMPIRES WILL NOTICE.
SO? LET THEM.
YOU JUST HAVE TO CATCH THEIR ATTENTION.
MEAN-WHILE WE'LL PREPARE FOR THE MAJOR BATTLE.
IN OTHER WORDS, YOU WON'T TELL ME WHAT YOU'RE *REALLY* PLANNING.
RIGHT?
AND YOU SAID YOU TRUSTED ME.
DON'T SULK. IT ISN'T AS IF I DON'T.
BESIDES, SENDING SOMEONE WITH A HEAD FULL OF TOP-SECRET PLANS TO THE FRONT LINES IS A POOR IDEA, RIGHT?
whrl
SO SHUT UP AND FOLLOW YOUR ORDERS.
IF YOU DO...
...I'LL SHOW YOU A WORLD WHERE HUMANS MAKE THE VAMPIRES INTO CATTLE.

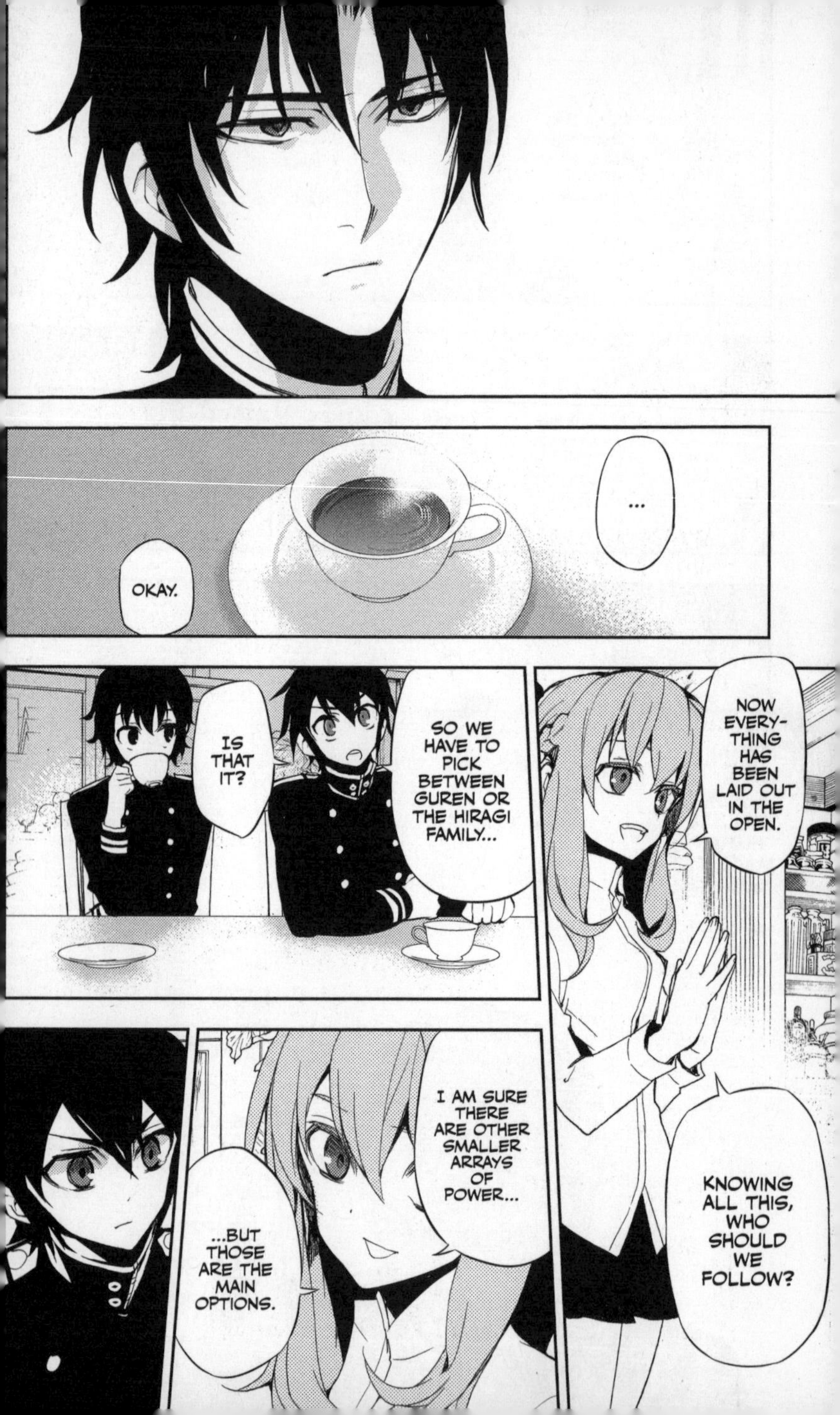
...
OKAY.
NOW EVERYTHING HAS BEEN LAID OUT IN THE OPEN.
KNOWING ALL THIS, WHO SHOULD WE FOLLOW?
SO WE HAVE TO PICK BETWEEN GUREN OR THE HIRAGI FAMILY...
IS THAT IT?
I AM SURE THERE ARE OTHER SMALLER ARRAYS OF POWER...
...BUT THOSE ARE THE MAIN OPTIONS.

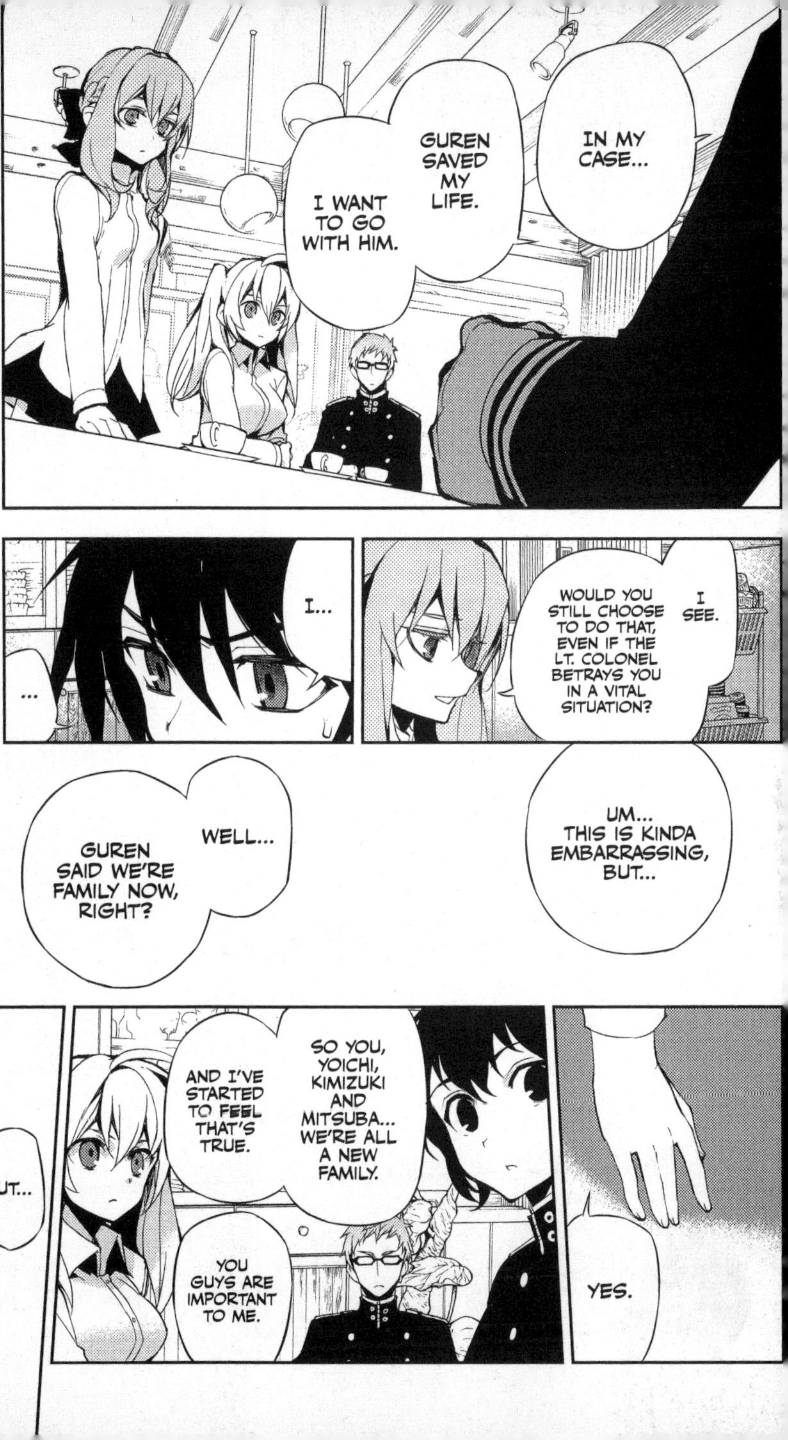
IN MY CASE...
GUREN SAVED MY LIFE.
I WANT TO GO WITH HIM.
I SEE.
WOULD YOU STILL CHOOSE TO DO THAT, EVEN IF THE LT. COLONEL BETRAYS YOU IN A VITAL SITUATION?
I...
...
UM... THIS IS KINDA EMBARRASSING, BUT...
WELL...
GUREN SAID WE'RE FAMILY NOW, RIGHT?
YES.
SO YOU, YOICHI, KIMIZUKI AND MITSUBA... WE'RE ALL A NEW FAMILY.
AND I'VE STARTED TO FEEL THAT'S TRUE.
YOU GUYS ARE IMPORTANT TO ME.
BUT...

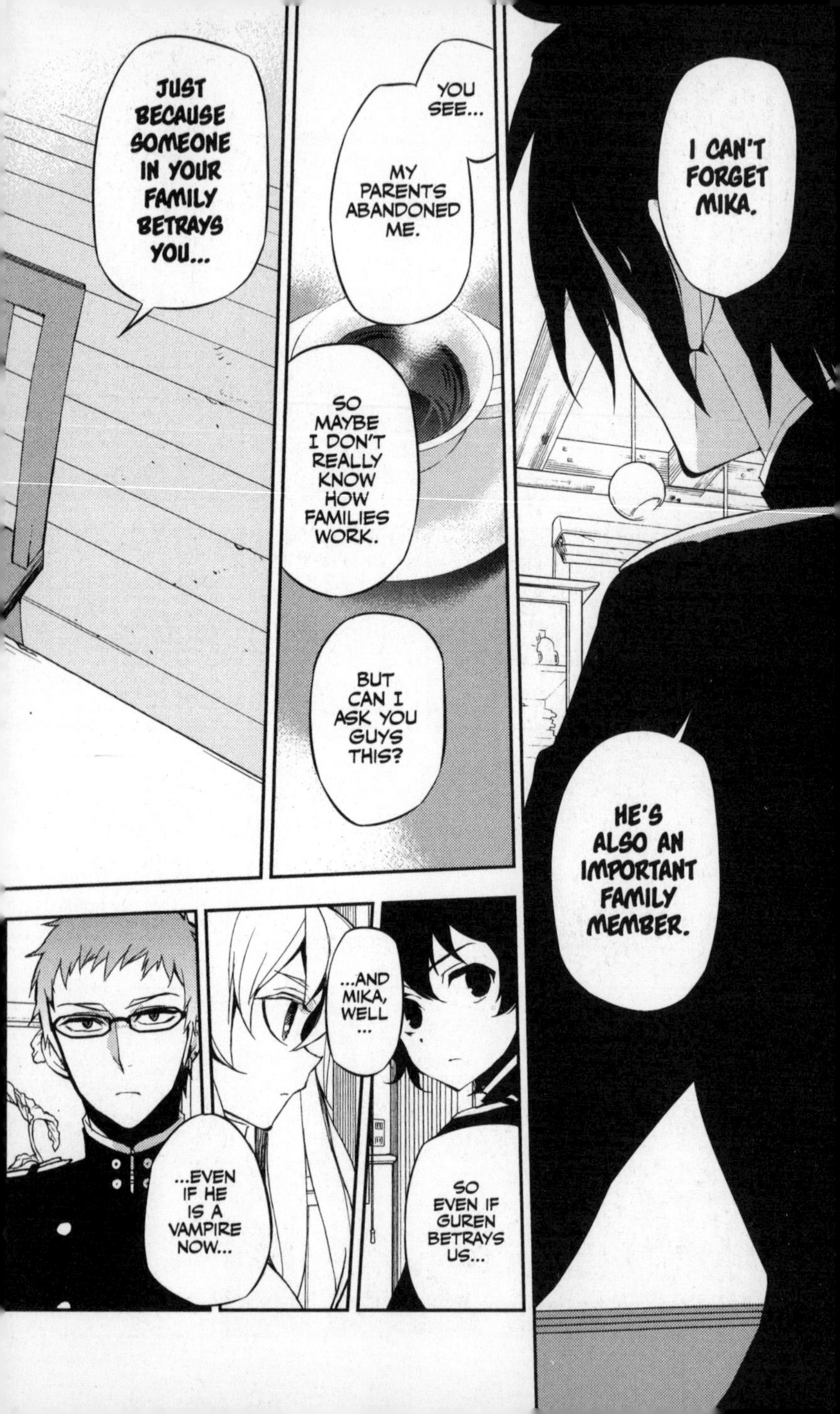
I CAN'T FORGET MIKA.
HE'S ALSO AN IMPORTANT FAMILY MEMBER.
YOU SEE...
MY PARENTS ABANDONED ME.
SO MAYBE I DON'T REALLY KNOW HOW FAMILIES WORK.
BUT CAN I ASK YOU GUYS THIS?
JUST BECAUSE SOMEONE IN YOUR FAMILY BETRAYS YOU...
SO EVEN IF GUREN BETRAYS US...
...AND MIKA, WELL ...
...EVEN IF HE IS A VAMPIRE NOW...

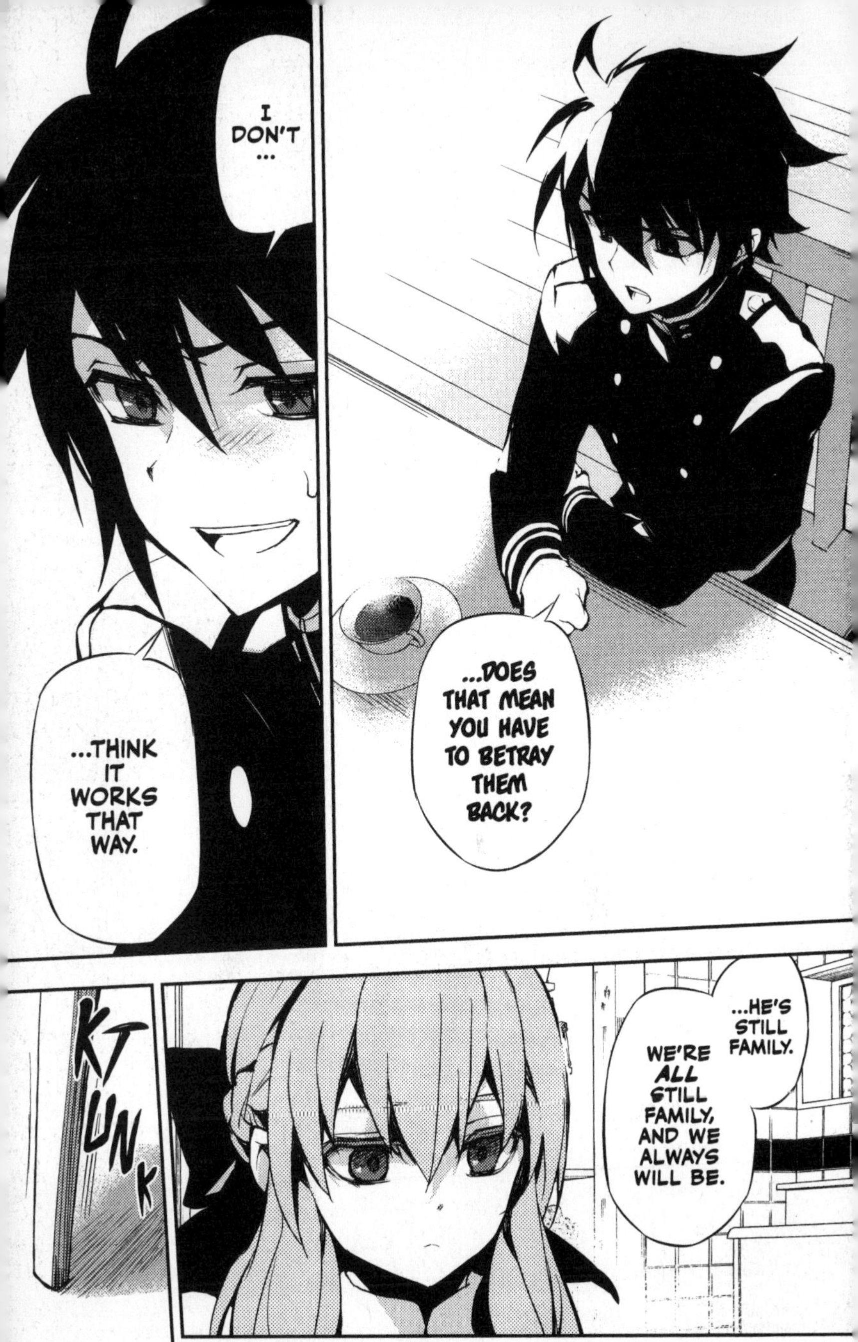
...DOES THAT MEAN YOU HAVE TO BETRAY THEM BACK?
I DON'T ...
...THINK IT WORKS THAT WAY.
...HE'S STILL FAMILY.
WE'RE ALL STILL FAMILY, AND WE ALWAYS WILL BE.
KTUNK

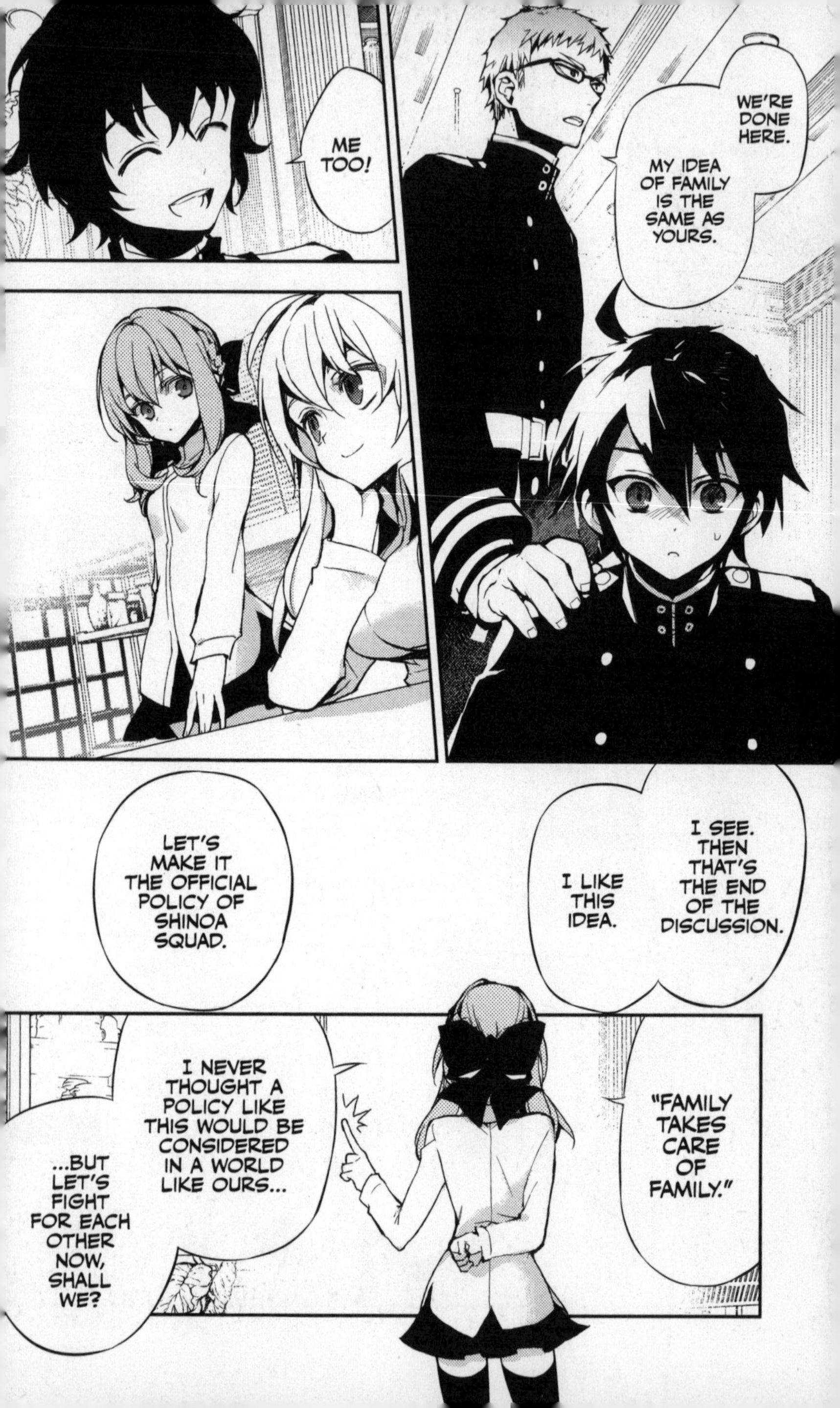
WE'RE DONE HERE.
MY IDEA OF FAMILY IS THE SAME AS YOURS.
ME TOO!
I SEE. THEN THAT'S THE END OF THE DISCUSSION.
I LIKE THIS IDEA.
LET'S MAKE IT THE OFFICIAL POLICY OF SHINOA SQUAD.
"FAMILY TAKES CARE OF FAMILY."
I NEVER THOUGHT A POLICY LIKE THIS WOULD BE CONSIDERED IN A WORLD LIKE OURS...
...BUT LET'S FIGHT FOR EACH OTHER NOW, SHALL WE?

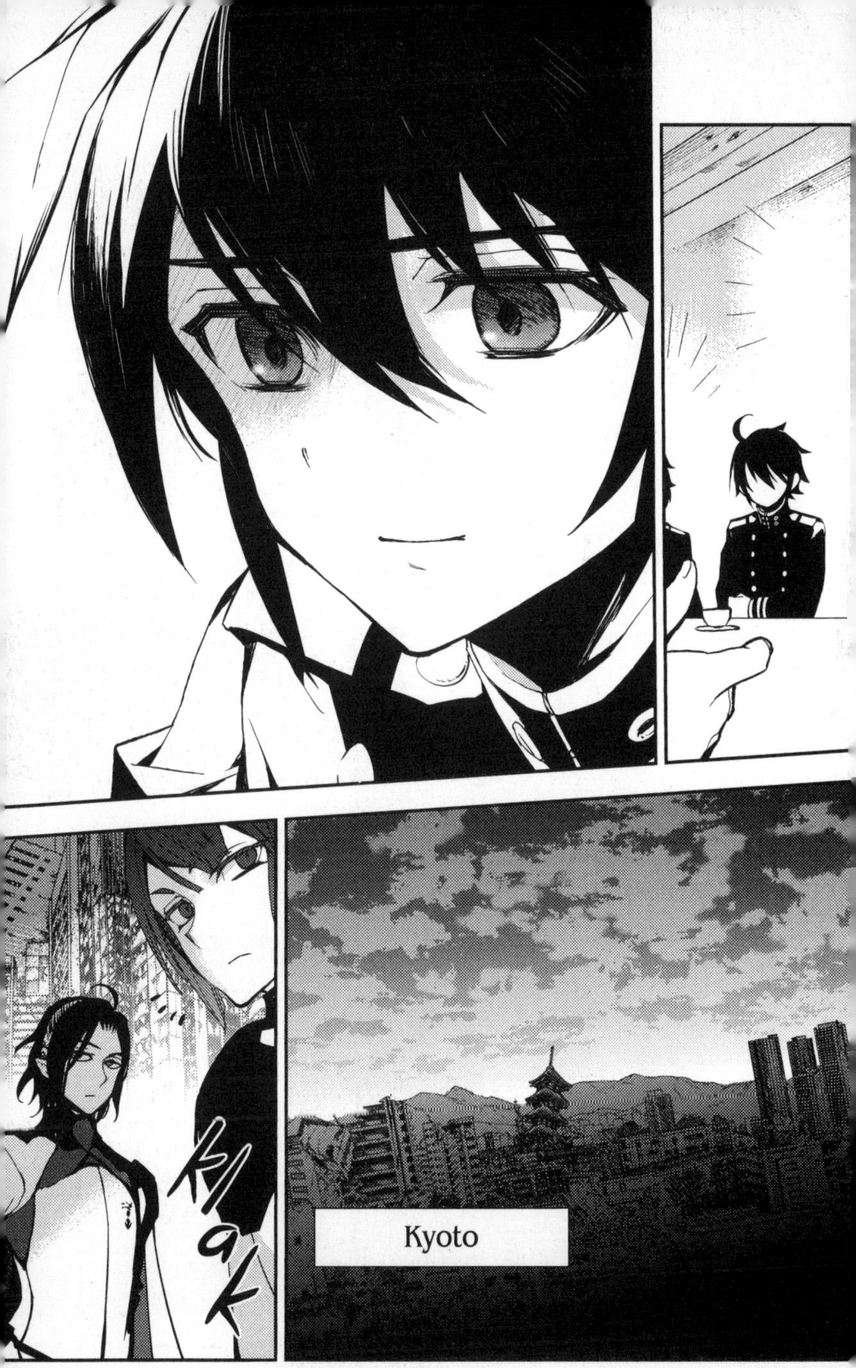
Kyoto
klak

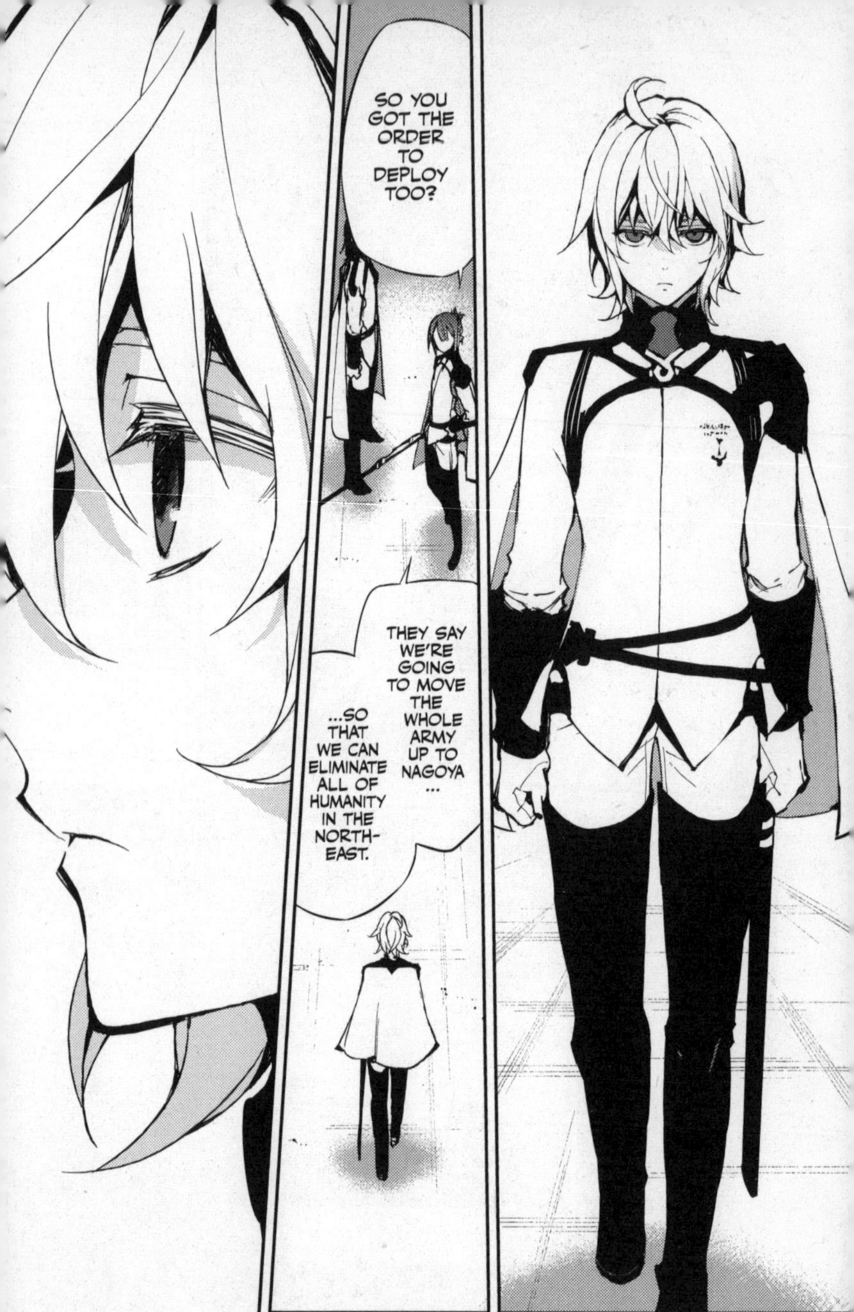
SO YOU GOT THE ORDER TO DEPLOY TOO?
THEY SAY WE'RE GOING TO MOVE THE WHOLE ARMY UP TO NAGOYA ...
...SO THAT WE CAN ELIMINATE ALL OF HUMANITY IN THE NORTH-EAST.

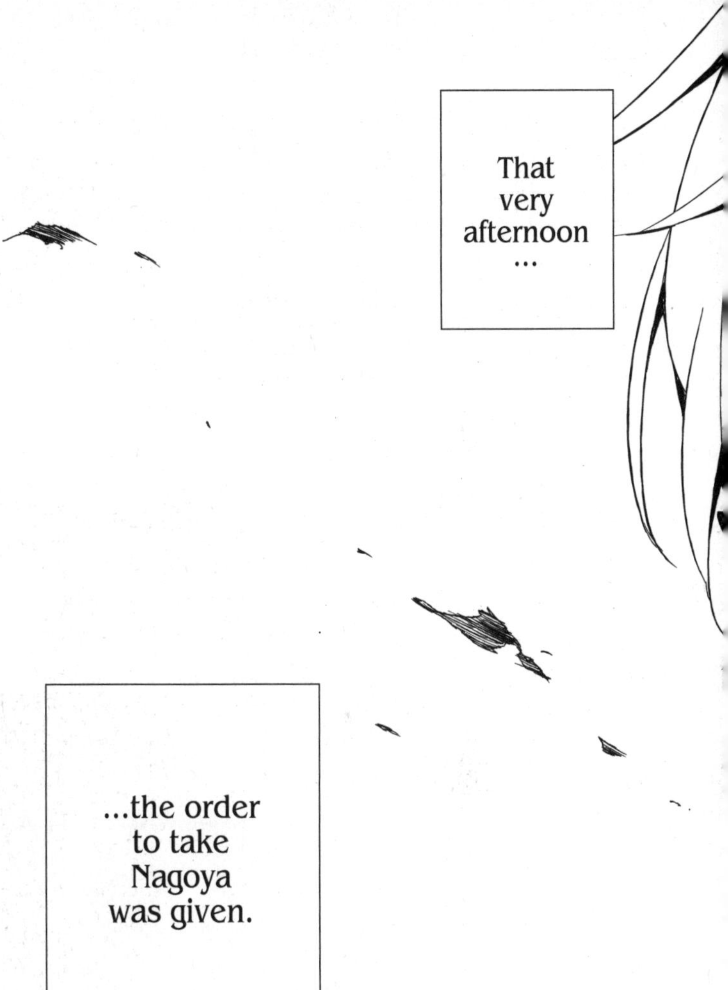
That very afternoon...
...the order to take Nagoya was given.

Seraph of the End: Vampire Reign 6 / END

CROWLEY EUSFORD

He's a vampire noble. A Thirteenth Progenitor, even. He's really powerful. He mostly considers himself part of Ferid Bathory's faction.

FERID: "HM? WAIT, YOU'RE PART OF MY FACTION, CROWLEY?"

CROWLEY: "APPARENTLY. YOU WERE THE ONE WHO RECRUITED ME, Y'KNOW. DID YOU FORGET THAT ALREADY?"

FERID: "YES. I PROMPTLY FORGET EVERYTHING UNINTERESTING AFTER IT'S HAPPENED."

CROWLEY: "AH. I CAN UNDERSTAND THAT, I GUESS."

FERID: "BESIDES, I WASN'T PARTICULARLY INTERESTED IN YOU IN THE FIRST PLACE."

CROWLEY: "FERID, I DOUBT IT'S JUST ME. YOU AREN'T PARTICULARLY INTERESTED IN MUCH OF ANYTHING, RIGHT?"

FERID: "TRUE... OH! OH WAIT! RECENTLY I'VE GOTTEN INTERESTED IN *THAT!* YOU KNOW...THAT THING. FISHING. I THINK I MAY MAKE IT MY HOBBY."

CROWLEY: "REALLY?!"

FERID: "I LIED."

CROWLEY: "SHEESH. WHY DO YOU ALWAYS HAVE TO DO THAT?"

FERID: "HA HA! DO *YOU* HAVE ANY HOBBIES, CROWLEY?"

CROWLEY: "ME? HMM... WOULD IT BE TOO MUCH OF A STRETCH FOR ME TO SAY FISHING? I'VE NEVER DONE IT, TO BE HONEST."

FERID: "AH, I SEE. HIKING IN THE MOUNTAINS, IS IT? YES, YOU DO LOOK THE SORT TO LIKE HIKING."

CROWLEY: "I DON'T REMEMBER SAYING THAT. BUT WHO KNOWS, IT MIGHT BE FUN. COULD STAVE OFF BOREDOM FOR ANOTHER FEW HOURS."

CHESS BELL
HORN SKULD

Both are vampire nobles. The one with pale hair is Horn. The one with the short, dark hair is Chess. Both are Seventeenth Progenitors. They're quite powerful. Due to certain circumstances, both are employed as Crowley's maids. Someday I might write about how that happened.

CHESS: "LORD CROWLEY! WHAT'S WITH THE SUDDEN PACKING? GOING SOMEWHERE?"

CROWLEY: "OH, FERID AND I ARE JUST GOING FOR A LITTLE STROLL IN THE MOUNTAINS IS ALL."

CHESS: "WAIT, YOU'RE GOING SOMEWHERE WITH LORD FERID? I NEVER HEARD ANYTHING ABOUT THAT! DID YOU, HORN?"

HORN: "LORD CROWLEY MENTIONED IT YESTERDAY EVENING. DIDN'T YOU HEAR?"

CHESS: "NOPE! I WASN'T PAYING ATTENTION."

HORN: "*SIGH.* MUST YOU ALWAYS BE LIKE THAT, CHESS?"

CROWLEY: "ANYWAY, IS EVERYTHING TOGETHER YET?"

HORN: "YES, MY LORD. EVERYTHING HAS BEEN PREPARED. WHEN WILL YOU BE DEPARTING?"

CHESS: "ANY TIME NOW, ACTUALLY. FERID SAID HE WOULD BE HERE RIGHT ABOUT THIS TIME."

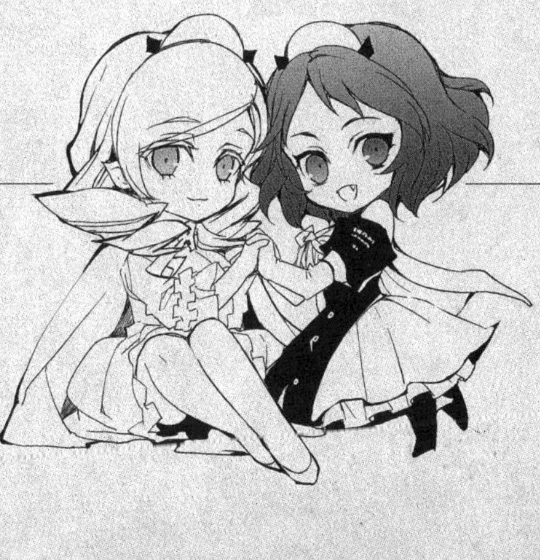

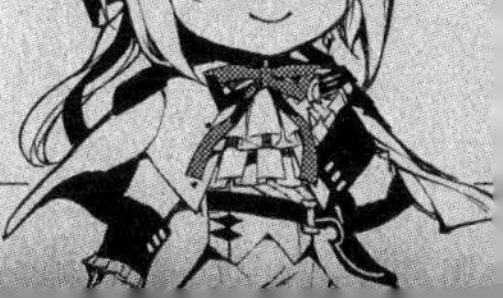

10 hours later, and still no sign of Ferid...

CROWLEY: *"NNN... I KNOW THIS HAPPENS EVERY TIME BUT, WELL... THIS DOES HAPPEN EVERY TIME. MAYBE I'LL TAKE THE HIKE ALONE."*

HORN: *"BUT IT IS ALREADY DUSK, MY LORD."*

CROWLEY: *"SO? WHAT DOES DAY OR NIGHT MATTER TO VAMPIRES?"*

FERID: *"AH, THERE YOU ARE CROWLEY! HELLO, HELLO! WHAT, AREN'T YOU READY TO GO YET? GOODNESS, YOU'RE SO SLOW!"*

CROWLEY: *"NOW HE SHOWS UP."*

CHESS: *"AH! HE'S HERE!"*

HORN: *"YES, HERE HE IS."*

FERID: *"COME, COME! LET US GET THE BARBEQUE STARTED. EVERYONE HAS BEEN WAITING ALL DAY FOR IT!"*

CROWLEY: *"HUH? WHAT ABOUT HIKING IN THE MOUNTAINS?"*

FERID: *"WHAT ABOUT THE WHAT, NOW?"*

CROWLEY: *"ER... SO WHY ARE WE HAVING A BARBEQUE AGAIN? VAMPIRES DON'T EAT MEAT."*

FERID: *"THAT'S TRUE, YES. OH WELL! I'LL BE GOING HOME, THEN. TA-TA!"*

CROWLEY: *"HMMM... Y'KNOW, I THINK I MIGHT WITHDRAW FROM FERID'S FACTION."*

AFTERWORD

HELLO. I'M TAKAYA KAGAMI. HOW DID YOU LIKE *SERAPH OF THE END: VAMPIRE REIGN* VOLUME 6? I THINK, MAYBE, BY THIS TIME, YOU MIGHT HAVE HEARD THAT THERE IS GOING TO BE A *SERAPH* ANIME.

CONGRATULATIONS, TEAM!

WE DID IT!

MR. YAMAMOTO! MR. FURUYA! WE DID IT!

WE DID IT, EVERYONE!! YAY!

THE ANIME STAFF IS EXCELLENT, SO I CAN TELL YOU RIGHT NOW IT'S GOING TO BE AMAZING!

WITH THE UNDOUBTEDLY AWESOME ANIME COMING, I HOPE YOU READERS KEEP UP WITH THE MANGA.

SO! MOVING ON. RECENTLY, I'VE BEEN WRITING AHEAD ON THE MANGA AND NOVEL PLOTS. NOW I KNOW WHAT'S GOING TO HAPPEN WAY IN THE FUTURE. IF THIS IS VOLUME 6, WHAT I'M WRITING RIGHT NOW WILL BE IN VOLUME 8. THE RAMP-UP TO WHAT WILL BE THE CLIMAX OF *SERAPH'S* SECOND ACT BEGINS IN VOLUME 6, SO EXPECT GREAT THINGS TO COME!

IN THE NOVEL *SERAPH OF THE END: GUREN ICHINOSE'S CATASTROPHE AT 16*, WHICH IS SET IN THE PAST, KURETO AND SHINYA HIRAGI ARE STARTING TO GET INVOLVED IN THE EVENTS WHICH LEAD DIRECTLY TO THE PRESENT DAY. IF YOU'RE INTERESTED, I REALLY HOPE YOU'LL CHECK OUT THE NOVELS SOMEDAY. YOU CAN ENJOY THEM AS STAND-ALONES, BUT READING THEM ALONGSIDE THE MANGA MAKES THEM FIVE TIMES MORE INTERESTING! WAIT, WHO DECIDED IT WAS EXACTLY FIVE TIMES? MAYBE I COULD SAY IT'S ONE HUNDRED TIMES MORE INTERESTING! WELL, IF I'M GOING DOWN THAT ROUTE ALREADY, HOW ABOUT I JUST SAY IT'S EIGHT TRILLION TIMES BETTER.

ANYWAY! RECENT STUFF. THE OTHER NIGHT, RIGHT WHEN I'D WRITTEN SO MUCH THAT IT WOULD BE PHYSICALLY IMPOSSIBLE TO WRITE MORE, I GOT A CALL FROM AN AUTHOR FRIEND OF MINE.

"HEY, TAKA! WANNA GO OUT DRINKING WITH US?" HE SAID.

NOW, I CAN'T DRINK A DROP OF ALCOHOL, BUT I WAS SICK OF WORKING FOR THE DAY (THAT'S NO EXCUSE), SO I DECIDED I'D JUST GO AND SAY HI. BUT, WHEN I GOT THERE, SITTING A LITTLE AWAY FROM THE BAR, I NOTICED A KNOT OF PEOPLE— EDITORS AND MANGA ARTISTS FROM SHUEISHA! AND THEY WERE EMBROILED IN A PASSIONATE DISCUSSION ABOUT MANGA!

"UH-OH!" I THOUGHT, "THOSE HAVE TO BE EDITORS FROM *JUMP SQUARE* (WHERE THE *SERAPH* MANGA IS PUBLISHED)! I JUST KNOW IT! BUT I'VE BEEN WORKING ON THE MANGA SINCE FIVE IN THE MORNING! I DON'T WANT TO THINK ABOUT IT ANYMORE!!"

SO I SNUCK IN AND TRIED REALLY HARD NOT TO BE NOTICED. I COULD STILL HEAR THEIR CONVERSATIONS, THOUGH. IN THE END, I WENT HOME WITHOUT FEELING LIKE I HAD THE EVENING COMPLETELY "OFF." ^_^ I GUESS GOD—OR MAYBE ~~THE DRACONIC SQ EDITORS~~ THE DEVIL—WAS TELLING ME I NEEDED TO GET BACK TO WORK.

I TOLD MY EDITOR ABOUT IT THE NEXT MORNING AND WE SHARED A GOOD LAUGH. THEN HE TOLD ME THAT KODANSHA EDITORS HANG OUT AT THAT BAR TOO. SERIOUSLY! IT'S LIKE EDITORS ARE EVERYWHERE, WATCHING OUR EVERY MOVE! ^-^

BUT ANYWAY, I'M RUNNING OUT OF PAGE SPACE. CONGRATULATIONS TEAM, WE'RE GETTING AN ANIME.

THANK YOU, EVERYONE!

TAKAYA KAGAMI

A brilliant sketch of Yuichiro by the author!

TAKAYA KAGAMI is a prolific light novelist whose works include the action and fantasy series *The Legend of the Legendary Heroes*, which has been adapted into manga, anime and a video game. His previous series, *A Dark Rabbit Has Seven Lives*, also spawned a manga and anime series.

66 I write this blurb right after I finish the afterword. Because I write it so soon after, I always feel like I don't have anything left to say. But I think of something. Right now, I'm eating chilled tofu at a family restaurant. I hope you enjoy *Seraph of the End* volume 6! 99

YAMATO YAMAMOTO, born 1983, is an artist and illustrator whose works include the *Kure-nai* manga and the light novels *Kure-nai*, *9S -Nine S-* and *Denpa Teki na Kanojo*. Both *Denpa Teki na Kanojo* and *Kure-nai* have been adapted into anime.

66 Yuichiro begins training with his Cursed Gear. Will he survive? The writing and the drawing of this series is one trial after another. Your comments are a great morale booster! 99

DAISUKE FURUYA previously assisted Yamato Yamamoto with storyboards for *Kure-nai*.

Seraph of the End
—VAMPIRE REIGN—

VOLUME 6
SHONEN JUMP ADVANCED MANGA EDITION

STORY BY **TAKAYA KAGAMI**
ART BY **YAMATO YAMAMOTO**
STORYBOARDS BY **DAISUKE FURUYA**

TRANSLATION **Adrienne Beck**
TOUCH-UP ART & LETTERING **Sabrina Heep**
DESIGN **Shawn Carrico**
WEEKLY SHONEN JUMP EDITOR **Hope Donovan**
GRAPHIC NOVEL EDITOR **Marlene First**

OWARI NO SERAPH © 2012 by Takaya Kagami,
Yamato Yamamoto, Daisuke Furuya
All rights reserved. First published in Japan in 2012 by SHUEISHA Inc., Tokyo.
English translation rights arranged by SHUEISHA Inc.

The stories, characters and incidents mentioned in this
publication are entirely fictional.

Printed in the U.S.A.

Published by VIZ Media, LLC
P.O. Box 77010
San Francisco, CA 94107

10 9 8 7 6 5 4 3 2 1
First printing, September 2015

www.viz.com **www.shonenjump.com**

Claymore

Story and Art by
NORIHIRO YAGI

O SAVE HUMANITY,
UST CLARE SACRIFICE HER OWN?

a world where monsters called Yoma prey on humans
d live among them in disguise, humanity's only hope
a new breed of warrior known as Claymores. Half
man, half monster, these silver-eyed slayers possess
pernatural strength, but are condemned to fight their
vage impulses or lose their humanity completely.

YOU'RE READING THE WRONG WAY!

SERAPH OF THE END reads from right to left, starting in the upper-right corner. Japanese is read from right to left, meaning that action, sound effects, and word-balloon order are completely reversed from English order.

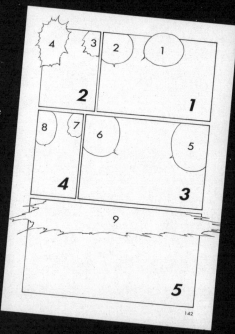